# BOOKS BY P.S. MERONEK

**A Lifetime to Die**

**The Joshua Effect**

Purchase these titles at:

www.ponytalepress.com

Ponytale Press

# P. S. MERONEK

# STAY ANOTHER NIGHT

Copyright © 2013 by P.S. Meronek

All rights reserved. In accordance with the U.S. Copyright Act of 1976, the scanning, uploading, and electronic sharing of any part of this book without the written permission of the author is unlawful.

The story contained in this book is a work of fiction. Names, characters, places, and incidents within the story are the product of the author's imagination or are used fictitiously.

www.ponytalepress.com

**Ponytale Press**

ISBN 978-0-9857096-6-2
ISBN 978-0-9857096-8-6 (ebook)

Printed in India

## Author's Note

It is important to me to acknowledge two very important people in my life. This one's for Alison and Ashley, who taught me more about myself in a single moment than just about everyone else was able to accomplish in a lifetime. Remember those times when you thought the lights were on but no one was home? Well I was still and always thinking about you.

Special thanks to contributors Ken Hunt, Nicole Pucci, and Dr. Duke Mojib. Thank you for your valuable contributions in helping to make this manuscript a reality.

## Chapter 1

Once in a blue moon life throws you a curveball you never see coming. It rises up at you, does a funny little twist at the very last moment, and takes you on a fast detour from the place you expected to go. Such detours can be powerful, like a deuce trump card when no one else around the table has one. Billy Cunningham was my curve ball, and I never saw him coming until it was too late to do anything about it.

I braked hard and pulled off the highway. I barely made it onto the off ramp. My tires squealed in protest, skidding along the surface of the roasting asphalt. The '57 Chevy Bel Air seemed to want to keep going down the highway. I should have listened to it and skipped the dusty turn toward the tiny city of Brittle, Nevada, and kept on going. *Shoulda, coulda, woulda.*

The town of Brittle was fourteen miles down the empty road ahead of me. I figured if I kept to the posted fifty-five mile an hour speed limit I just might make it to town on the fumes cradled in the bottom of the tank. Worst case scenario, no place would be open. It was three o'clock on a Sunday afternoon in the steepest part of July. If need be, I could spend the night in the back seat of the four-door Chevy in a gas station parking lot until morning. It was a lot better than running out of gas in the middle of the Mojave.

The stark landscape blurred by on both sides, parted in the middle by the narrow two lane blacktop. In the distance ahead of me the road shivered and melted into the desert in the afternoon's oppressive heat. I stifled a yawn and kept going, careful not to let go of the speed limit. A dust devil came into view off the road to my left, a whirling dervish dancing in the midst of a small stand of Joshua Trees. I had lost the radio station ten miles ago and just now noticed it. I became aware of a low hum and reached over and dialed the knob on the radio, looking for any kind of life. There was nothing but static, so I shrugged and turned it off. The odometer told me it was still a good ten miles to Brittle. I cursed under my breath, thinking I should have filled up back in Bakersfield when I had the chance.

The steering wheel pulled hard to the right. I pulled back, this time swearing aloud at Murphy's Law. It was hotter than Hades and – bang – just like that I was going to have to switch out what was left of a torn up G60-15 on the front passenger side. I eased the limping Chevy as far onto the gravel and sand shoulder as I could in the unlikely event I'd have company. I was tempted to change the tire right there on the highway, but that might be asking for trouble. On top of that, I knew I would have to somehow block the jack's base with something flat to stop it from slipping on the sandy apron away from the road.

I left the car, a blast of desert air wrapping around me like a smothering hand. The contrast in temperature from the air conditioner I had been running full blast made my head spin. I walked around the front of the Bel Air to assess the damage. It was a flat all right. I kneeled down to get a better look. I couldn't see much, but as I felt around the tread I came across the unmistakable head of the culprit. It had to be at least a ten-d, probably three inches long, buried deep into the rubber.

I stood up and looked in the direction I'd come. There wasn't a soul in sight. There was no one coming the other way, either. The only sound I heard was a static ticking under the hood of the Chevy. The 327 engine was taking a coffee break, cooling a bit even in the ambient, hundred and fifteen degree heat.

I was sweating like a pig when I finally tightened the last lug nut about twenty minutes later. I jacked her down, rolled the spent tire to the back and muscled it into the trunk, glad to be finished. Perspiration had soaked my t-shirt through to my skin. I retrieved the jack and tire iron from next to the spare on the front and threw them beside the shredded tire. I wasn't worried about bolting them down; I would get to that when I replaced the tire. I wiped my brow on my forearm and threw the sweat into the dust, slamming down the trunk lid and peeled off the soaking t-shirt. I smiled in disgust. I could wring the damn thing out and still use it to wipe down the car, I thought ruefully, as a distant drone became more recognizable.

The sound of a strange engine was coming from the direction of Brittle. I peered across the top of the car. I could tell by the sound it was hauling ass, still a couple miles down the road, but closing real fast. "What the hell…?"

An odd wave of anxiety hit me, harder than the heat. I slid up against the passenger side of the car and slowly opened the back door, not taking my eyes off the road to Brittle. The low, throbbing drone grew louder and a shape began to materialize out of the shimmering heat a mile and a half in the distance. I reached into the back seat long enough to retrieve a fresh t-shirt from my overnight bag. I slipped it on, and then locked onto what was coming. Whoever it was had the hammer down. I figured they were coming down the blacktop doing well over a hundred.

As it came nearer, I could make out the telltale rack of lights sitting atop the car. It was the Highway Patrol. I should have felt relieved but that odd, anxious unease which had enveloped me didn't go away. It got worse when the cop begun slowing down. There was no doubt in my mind he wasn't here to help. What didn't make sense was how he had known I was out here in the first place. I sauntered around to the front of the car and sat down on its chrome bumper. I figured I would wait for whomever it was rather than having him turn around to stop me. About a minute later the cruiser slowed to a crawl, crossed the highway and came to a stop not more than ten feet in front of me. The driver grabbed something from the passenger side, looked out at me, and then got out. He had the tanned, wide-brimmed hat of a trooper in his hands, and was sporting the mirrored sunglasses that seemed to be a perennial part of the shtick. He whisked his hat on and side-stepped his open door, closing it as he did so.

"Afternoon," he finally greeted me.

I glanced up at the broiling sun and agreed, "Yep, sure is." I smiled at him then, my reflection clear in his lenses. I still looked pretty good, in spite of a couple of grease smudges on my cheeks. I wasn't wearing any makeup; I didn't have to. I was twenty-five, unconcerned about the lines and crow's feet which were inevitably right around the corner of life's visages. I looked closer at my reflection then, ignoring the thirty-something Trooper. I straightened a few blonde locks dangling in front of my eyes. I was five foot eight inches of drop dead gorgeous, a devil in blue jeans with a tight fitting t-shirt. I knew it, and so did he. He reached up with both hands, smiling along with me, and eased off the shades.

"Thanks for stopping," I said matter-of-factly, still wondering what the Trooper really wanted and how he had known I was here.

"Happy to oblige," he responded. He was self-assured; I could see that right off.

"Looks like you had a little trouble," he nodded at the left tire.

I followed his nod then looked back into his eyes, sighing, "A woman's work is never done."

"I would have been out here sooner," he replied as he reached around to his back pocket, retrieving a white-as-snow handkerchief. His self-assurance bordered on a somewhat attractive arrogance as he stepped across the gravel between us. He licked the hanky and dabbed lightly at a smudge on my cheek.

I grabbed his hand in mine. It was smooth and strong, but gentle at the same time.

"I got it," I assured him, not wanting to sound unfriendly, but setting some boundaries just the same. Chivalry was one thing, but this was something else.

"Thanks," I said, a little more self-consciously than I'd intended. He let me have the hanky and stepped back. He eyes were seasoned with wisdom beyond his years and peppered with a kindness uncommon to someone in law-enforcement.

"How–"

"A buddy spotted you on the highway about five miles back," he interrupted. "He was catching up when he saw you slide sideways onto the off ramp."

I laughed at that. "I almost missed the turn," I admitted. "I'm running on fumes." I shrugged innocently.

He chuckled, "About the only reason anyone comes to Brittle who's not from here these days. Anyway, he called ahead you were on your way. When you didn't show I figured something happened and you might need a hand. You change that tire all by yourself?" I could see he was at the crossroads of surprise and impressed.

"Are you kidding?" I said. "Triple A left just before you got here."

He grinned and held out his hand. "I deserved that. Mark Zarillo, Miss Stevens. A pleasure," he introduced himself.

"It's Coco," I shook his hand, liking its feel even more than the last time. "Who called you?" I decided to cut through the bullshit.

"More like what", he confided.

"A transmitter on my baby," I said as I patted the Chevy's hood. He nodded.

"And you're not really a sheriff from Hicksville," I stated the obvious.

He shook his head apologetically, "No, I'm not."

"Secret Service?" I proffered.

He quickly shook his head, protesting, "No-no, I'm definitely not that."

I folded my arms over my chest, conscious my nipples were showing through the thin cotton as it breathed perspiration.

"Boyfriend," he finally confessed.

"Which one?" I replied. We both laughed at that. "Can't a girl go out by herself anymore?"

"It could have been worse," he replied.

"How so?"

"If I was working for your employer I'd probably be bald and fifty," he answered.

"Sam doesn't own me, you know." I was suddenly serious. I felt that familiar smothering sensation. It wasn't just the heat.

Mark Zarillo didn't say anything, but I caught the unmistakable flash across his face, like a cold blade had just grazed the small of his back. He was afraid, like the rest of them. Suddenly I felt a wave of disgust.

"So what now, Cock Robin?" I suppressed the clammy feeling. I'd realized long ago that none of them had a choice. Fear was the elixir that kept everyone in line. It was Sam's personal recipe. Without it, there would be no order in their world of affairs.

He shrugged, looking away. He probably felt a little disgusted as well.

"You know the drill, Miss Stevens."

"For chrissakes – it's Coco! I'm sorry," I immediately apologized. "It's just…" I trailed off, uncertain how to finish. He was a stranger. I suddenly longed for the intimacy which once held me to higher standards.

"It's okay," he said softly, "I understand, Coco." Zarillo the for-the-moment reluctant soldier smiled at me again, only this time it was more the smile a father gives his daughter on her first date, one that said whatever it was she wanted to hear. "Thirsty?" he changed the subject. The moment was gone. "It's Sunday," I stated the obvious.

"Sam owns a bar in town. I've got the keys."

"To the bar, or the town?"

He didn't reply, but I knew the answer anyway. The penny had dropped as far as the Halloween costume was concerned. Sam did that. He owned more than one small dirt water town in the middle of nowhere. While everyone else in the organization was sticking to the big cities, he had reasoned the feds wouldn't bother to look in places like Brittle, Nevada. He was right and wrong at the same time. They wouldn't give two hoots about the real estate until it was too late, but the electronic banking left footprints wherever he went. He couldn't hide that part of the equation. Sam was ingenuous. Worthless land licensed for gambling, under the right circumstances and in the right place, could be transformed into an oasis seeded on a bedrock foundation of washed green – laundered vice profits under RICO. Sam was a Picasso, the desert his canvas. The big valley of Vegas itself had proven it could be done. More recently it had been Laughlin. Lansky had been the pioneer who'd gone where none had treaded before. If Sam had learned anything from Meyer, it was that there were no rules to learn. You made it up as you went, and Sam was like that. It was one of the big reasons he was always out in front of the pack. Just when the competition figured they had the answers, Sam changed the questions.

"I could use an ice cold Michelob Light. Can you do that, Mark Zarillo?"

"I can do that."

"And one ham and three egg omelet, diced green onions on the side."

"Done," he grinned.

"It would appear you are a man of many talents," I flirted with him.

He considered my offer while that coldness in the small of his back returned. "Not that one," he assured me, not wishing to sign his own death warrant.

"I was jerking your chain, Zarillo."

"Uh-huh. That's something I would just as soon keep my distance from, Miss Stevens."

I shrugged. "Perhaps a different time, a different place," I said.

"Perhaps," he said flatly. "Lock your car. I'll take us into town and will send someone back here to retrieve it. If you're tired, I can recommend a decent hotel."

"No, no, and no," I spoke with indifference. "I'll follow you, and we will have a drink. I'll eat and then I will leave. No offense, but I think I'd prefer Vegas."

"As you wish, but I'll follow you just the same," he insisted, not anticipating a response. He was speaking for Sam now. It wasn't like I could argue with him. Besides, where could I go? I was out of gas, and Mark Zarillo, or more to the point, Sam, had the keys to the pumps.

But still I wondered: why here? As the blacktop arched over a rise and slid down about a mile to the edge of the first unassuming buildings of the small town of Brittle, I suddenly understood. Then I wondered some more, about how I would get my hands on the money I was going to need. Because I knew Sam Spielman was nothing if he wasn't as sly as ten foxes hiding in the shadows of one very big hen house.

Halfway through my second beer and into a nice buzz I decided to spend the night in Brittle. Vegas would still be there tomorrow. No one was waiting up for me, and the parties were all too predictable. Sam knew where I was, so any subterfuge that would involve sneaking into town had been blown out of the water. I shook my head from side to side. The bastard had a lot of balls to bug my car; that was something I hadn't expected. But more than anything, I just felt like relaxing for a few hours. Zarillo wasn't hard to look at and, oddly enough, I felt I could let my guard down a little around him.

I shivered in the cool and dark interior of Spades Bar and Restaurant, one of Brittle's Main Street marquees.

"Are you cold?" Mark noticed.

I shook my head. "Rabbit ran over my grave," I smiled demurely across the table at him. "Chivalry becomes you." I examined him more closely.

"You don't want a sweater?"

I shook my head again. I'd put on a jean jacket on the way in, with the word Bebe stenciled across the back in fake diamonds. "I'm fine. Thanks, though." I played with the lip of my bottle of Michelob. An awkward silence settled across the table.

"So, what is it you exactly do for Sam?" I finally said.

He sucked on his Bud, considering his answer carefully before speaking. "A little bit of this, a little bit of that. If I was corporate, I might go as far as to call it general counsel. I'm a lawyer."

"I'm impressed." I was. "I'm also confused."

"What's a guy like me doing working for a guy like Sam?"

"Something like that. What *is* a guy like you doing working for Sam? From where I'm sitting it doesn't quite fit."

"You don't know me." I liked his smile.

"I'm a good judge of character," I confided, tipping my bottle before continuing. "I can gauge you well enough to know you could have done better."

"I don't know about better. Perhaps different, but thanks just the same." Mark was being genuine. There was a secret behind his dark brown eyes. But then again, I had learned a long time ago everyone had secrets. I was at the front of that line. An old saying came to mind, something about being as sick as your darkest one. It was odd, but I even remembered who had said it to me, now that I thought about it. It was a guy named Jack Holliday.

## Chapter 2

At the time, it had seemed like Jack was the only guy in the whole world who cared. I think he also probably saved my life. I remember I was seventeen, still a virgin. It might as well have been yesterday. Jack had looked across the table at me then too, but in a different way than Mark was now. "How old are you, babe?" Holliday had asked me from behind tired, middle-aged, I've-seen-it-all-twice-and-then-some eyes. I remember looking out over dark tables and chairs. A catwalk jutted out from the stage area separating the main room into what looked like two viper pits. The walk was bordered with bright, pinpoint Christmas lights. It was early morning and the place was empty. I'd started to say something when he stopped me short with his eyes.

I began again. "I've been dancing here three months, Jack. Why ask now? What does it matter how old I am, what's changed?"

He sighed, his chest heaving like a bellows feeding a fire deep inside him. "What's changed, my dear sweet Coco, if that's your name…"

"It is," I defended myself, pouting slightly.

He put his hand out to say he believed me. "Coco," he conceded. He'd accepted the fact I'd been naïve enough to use my real name when I first started at Dante's Gentleman's Club.

"Seventeen, Jack. Shoot me." I stared him down, but gave up after a few seconds. No one stared down Jack Holliday and lived long enough to brag about it.

He sighed again.

"Are you going to fire me?" Then I begged him, "I need this gig, Jack. It's all I've got. I'm on a bus route, damn it. I've been saving every dime. Another month and I'll have enough for a car. I'm getting a driver's license – I'm taking the test next week. Chanel is going with me. Will you please stop *doing* that?" He had sighed again. I was getting pissed off.

Abruptly he laughed. It wasn't much, just a sudden puff of air through his flattened nostrils. But for Jack, it was a lot. In the whole time I'd been at Dante's I had never seen him even crack a smile. "What's so funny?" I asked, my job at stake.

"Nothing," he said. Then, "You're a headliner, Coco. That's what's changed. I should have known better when you first walked in here," he chastised himself. "You're too damn gorgeous for your own good."

"So now it's my fault."

"It's your blessing and your curse rolled into one."

"I don't need a lecture, Jack. I need to keep working."

"I've got orders" Jack said. "You're starting to draw attention. Spielman doesn't like attention."

"Fuck Spielman!" I wasn't thinking straight. What I was thinking about was the shiny new red Mustang on the showroom floor that I'd put a deposit on. My proclivity for fast cars showed up early in life. Losing this job would lose me the ride, not to mention my deposit. And there was that sigh again.

"Look Jack, can't you just keep me off the stage?" I pleaded. Normally every girl worked the stage. No one liked to, but it was advertising. The general rule was everyone had to, to earn the private rooms. But I had gotten to know the other girls. I could throw something their way if I had to. I was sure they wouldn't mind. They would even get more tips off the catwalk without me there. Not everyone could afford the private dances. The plebs leered from the edge of the stage, plugging bills into our garters like addicted gamblers plugged the slots.

"I can talk to the other girls. I'm sure none of them will mind. I can troll the bar area and stick to the private dancing in the back rooms." I was leaning across the table, looking straight into those killer's eyes. I saw in them that I'd gotten through to him, however unfortunate for that hulk of a human. Holliday, I knew, had developed a soft spot for me. He'd probably known all along I was a minor. He had overlooked it at first, along with my fake I.D., but he couldn't do it any longer. Without trying, I had developed a high profile. Lately some pretty upscale regulars were asking for me. I didn't need to advertise anymore. That's when it hit me, like a brilliant flash of lightning on a hot August night. I no longer needed Dante's. At least, not after I scored the Mustang.

Jack looked past me as a couple of the girls laughed their way through the turnstiles near the front door. They were early; we would open for the lunch crowd in a half hour, at eleven. Pretty soon a trickle would turn into an avalanche. An hour from now we would be packed to the gills with the regular crowd of bankers, doctors, boozers, and the usual assortment of other lonesome losers who'd sneak out of the office for their customary four martini, hundred-dollar lunch. Dante's was high class and we had a great downtown location; the sidewalks were capped in gold.

"I'm begging you, Jack."

He stared hard at me.

"I'm not gonna blow you, if that's what you're thinking."

That did it. The final chunk of ice melted, and Jack actually laughed out loud.

"One of my first regulars once told me there were three ways to a man's heart," I chuckled with him. "A good home cooked meal and making him laugh are the other two." There was mirth in my eyes, and he laughed again. Then, as quickly as he had begun to laugh, he regained his composure and leaned his big bulk across the table. He pointed his big tree limb finger inches from my face and I felt a sudden icy chill.

"You stay away from the main bar. You stick to the lounge area and you don't approach anybody. Understood?"

I was nodding. "Agreed," I said quickly, knowing that wouldn't be a problem. I'd sit in the corner with my eyes blindfolded if I had to.

"You let them come to you."

"Agreed. I won't say a word until they speak to me."

Jack relaxed, leaning back. "I need my head examined. If the Liquor Inspector finds you he'll close me down for a week," he muttered to himself.

"Thank you, Jack," I was bubbling over like a schoolgirl on a first date. "I won't let you down, either. I'll stay in the shadows. I'll be nothing but low profile." I was beaming from ear to ear, the cherry red Mustang peeling out in my mind.

"Low profile," Jack just muttered to himself. "Uh-huh."

Jack kept an eye on me. Like I said, he had a soft spot for me. I think I became his pet project. He took the role of a kind but stern adoptive uncle. The stern part was partly him, mostly the shadow cast over all by Sam Spielman, whom I had yet to meet. Sam owned Dante's, and he also owned several other places. This kept him busy. I hadn't seen him in the three months since I'd become his employee. I learned quickly he had long tentacles. He got his power by ruthlessly backing up his decrees. Not unlike a Roman Emperor, he had a cadre of enforcers to execute his own singular brand of justice in the event anyone crossed him. From what I understood, this didn't happen too often. It seemed the rumors about how his enemies were dealt with were, in most instances, more than adequate to cause the insurgents in the General's camp to think twice about any kind of duplicity. There was a saying in that camp: You only stole from Sam Spielman once. Everyone knew what this meant, and it was enough.

Jack coolly appraised the room from his vantage point near the DJ's booth, directly across the room from the edge of the VIP lounge where I was hanging out. It was midnight, the witching hour approaching. His gaze finally cruised around to where I was standing. I blew him a kiss. He summoned me with a twitch of his finger. I held up my hand with my fingers splayed out, signaling I would see him in five minutes. I pointed to the door leading to the private booths at the back of the large main room, below the plush, carpeted stairs which led to the balcony, and more private booths. He barely nodded, and then continued to circle the club's main floor with his eyes, like a hawk cruising high overhead for unfortunate mice below. It took me a few minutes to blow off a couple of small fish – insurance adjusters – in a nice way. I never burned my bridges. Then I moved across the crowded main floor to the hypnotic sounds of Pink Floyd, toward the meeting place we agreed on.

"You look good tonight, little girl," his deep baritone resonated in a big brotherly tone, as I leaned up and kissed him on the cheek. "Any luck?"

"Maybe," I said coyly. I was hedging my bets, waiting on the whales, throwing small fry back into churning waters. Dante's, as was usually the case on a Saturday, was packed. The darkened interior, multi-colored spotlights trained onto its stage, seemed to writhe and vibrate like a hypnotized boa. In the shadows, here and there, no fewer than thirty women moved seductively in the twilight in front of their clients, teasing and taunting, telling them the lies they wanted to hear. We were practically picking their pockets and they all loved it, at least until the hangover of regret set in when they sobered up the day after.

"I may have something for you," Jack said casually. "Something in your league," he assured me. "Might help get that Mustang you're looking at paid for a little quicker."

After last Friday's little talk, I'd learned our new arrangement had strings. Almost immediately Jack had begun to send over the high rollers. It cost me ten percent for his kickback. Jack called it an agent fee, but it was well worth it. The benefits, I soon found out, far outweighed the costs. I'd been amazed as I'd watched my take home pay quadruple the past week, even after I paid Jack his fee. It was a marriage made in heaven. It was our little secret. The other girls would have hissy fits if they ever found out one of their own was getting preferential treatment. They still saw me as their little sister – someone to watch over. I guess you could say I was running a balancing act, playing both ends against the middle.

Anyone of them, I knew, would do exactly the same thing if they found themselves in my high heels.

"It's already paid for, thanks to you, Jack," I confided, smiling my thanks. In my own way I loved Jack. And I knew he loved me, too. Of course, neither one of us were *in* love. That was completely different, but we had gotten close. We cared about each other. I felt safe around Jack Holliday and he knew this. He enjoyed playing the protector role. I think in some way, it made him feel the human part of him hadn't slipped away, shriveled up, and died somewhere. The fact that he still had the capacity to feel gave Jack a great sense of relief, albeit on a shaded, subliminal level which I doubted he could really understand. He just felt good that he could feel good whenever he could look after me.

"Congratulations," he grunted loudly enough to be heard above the jazzy intro of Joe Cocker's, 'You Can Leave Your Hat On', which blasted off the main stage. "You're the only person I've ever known who got into a ride like that, and you don't even have a driver's license. Do you?" he raised his eyebrows. "Kind of put the cart before the horse a bit there, wouldn't you say, Coco?"

I slapped him across his chest-sized bicep in a feigned display of consternation. By this time next week I would be driving to work. He knew this. Jack was playing with me. I liked it.

"What's going on Jack?" Like that, we were back at work.

He looked down at me. "Senior executives, five of them including the CEO. They're into software. They made reservations from their jet – their private jet – on the way in from San Diego." He checked his watch, not missing a beat. "These guys are billionaires, Coco. They'll be here anytime now. They want the best. Money is irrelevant."

"Not for me and you."

"I'll come get you about two hours after they get here. That will give them a chance to get liquored up, among other things. In the meantime just relax."

"I'm hungry," I suddenly realized.

"Perfect. Grab a little something before you go on. Treat them good, Coco. There's no telling what these guys will throw our way." He was thinking about his ten percent cut. I didn't mind. "There isn't a word for how much green they got."

"Sure there is, Jack." I smiled and said, "It's called horny."

I told him I'd be back in an hour. There was an all night diner across from Dante's. I ordered a BLT on rye, mustard and no mayonnaise, and washed it down with a Coke. I rarely thought about my weight; I was seventeen with a runaway metabolism. The excesses of youth were mine to indulge with impunity. I leaned back in the booth. I didn't feel like going back to Dante's just yet. I ordered a cup of coffee, enjoying the relative quiet of the sandwich shop and the company of about a dozen other early morning diners. An hour from now, after some of the bars began to close the eatery would fill up fast. Away from the hustle of the club, I began to strategize.

The money I was making was heady. I was pulling down more than the bragging junior brokers I danced for who worked down the street in the financial district of the city. I knew a few from the hedge funds and capital investment pools who worked in the Transamerica building a few blocks away. They were pulling in low six figures, greedy to move up. Granted, their ceiling was probably a lot higher than mine, but I didn't work a third as hard or a third as long. They had to snort lines halfway through the afternoon just to keep going. Not to mention the fact they got going at four in the morning to be in their cubes when the markets opened in New York, three hours earlier than the clocks in the Bay area.

The Mustang was paid for and then some and I would have my driver's license next week. I knew it would always be a headache to find good parking near where I lived: a modest, older, one bedroom apartment on Pine Street near Larkin. My monthly sublet was situated in a densely populated netherworld, a kind of twilight zone which buffered San Francisco's swanky conservative Nob Hill from the infamous, drug infested Tenderloin District. I was insulated from both by what I called a narrow band of sanity, four blocks wide, bordered by Van Ness to the west, and Hyde to the east.

About once a week I had taken to ambling up California Street, past the majestic Grace Cathedral and eventually through the small park not far from the Fairmont Hotel's front entrance. I would finally stop at the top of Nob Hill, often taking Sunday brunch at the Fairmont. I had gotten to know Eddy, the sixty-something piano player. After that, I never had to pay for a thing. It seemed Eddy had been there forever, his fingers welded to the ivory keys. He had clout.

The Fairmont became my own private lounge. Occasionally someone recognized me from Dante's, but almost always they ignored me. Wives: you couldn't live without them, but you sure as hell wouldn't want to if they ever found out you were spending one of the four or five annual vacations on the likes of me.

San Francisco fit me like an old baseball glove. Still, now that I had the car I was seriously considering a move south, to Burlingame. I fought with the idea as the car got closer. What would be worse: the parking problem, or the commute up and down 101 on the Bay?

Jack Holliday had been a godsend. He was my own private, hulking angel. He'd help put me in this position where I suddenly now found myself, with the luxury of choice. I think for the first time since I had stormed out of my mother's home, I was actually thinking past today. Suddenly I was becoming aware there was a future.

I had to grow up fast after my father's murder. He was shot to death in our living room by a drug addicted intruder when I was six. They never caught the guy who did it, but I don't think they looked too hard. They said my father sold drugs for a living.

Not long after, with a substantially reduced income, we moved out and onto welfare. I grew up unhappy, feeling abandoned and ignored. My mother worked at something close to a Waffle House until her feet got sore. Then she lay on her back. It was easier and paid better.

At thirteen, I was cornered in the kitchen of our run down two bedroom apartment off Haight Street by Arnie, one of her drunk, erstwhile musician boyfriends. It was dumb luck the six inch steak knife was on the counter behind me. I used it, burying it into a spot just an inch below his heart. The only remorse I showed on the way to the juvenile detention center was that fact I had missed and dear old Arnie was still around to try to bury me at the hearing. But his lies found him out, and they didn't put me away.

I stuck it out for as long as I could, my mother and I barely tolerating each other in a weird kind of truce. Word had gotten out. None of her boyfriends tried anything with me again.

Sometime later I took a bus ride that changed everything. I kept on riding until I was pushed out the door, right in front of Dante's. I went inside and met Mr. Jack Holliday.

# Chapter 3

By the time I got back, Dante's was rocking. That day was one of the hottest on record. The temperature had risen into the mid-nineties in downtown San Francisco. People were thirsty and restless. They wanted to party.

The five software gurus from San Diego had picked up a posse on the way over from the airport across the Bay. Jack figured there were fifteen of them. They had been drinking Cristal since the moment they arrived. It was going to be a long, raucous night. I was looking forward to it.

"How are you doing?" Jack asked an hour later without counting the wad I stuffed into his outstretched hands.

"That's a hundred and fifty," I said, pleased with myself. "Consider it a down payment."

"Damn," his mouth came open. "All this in an hour?"

"Hang onto the rest for me, ok?" I handed him a smaller roll of larger denominations. "It's just over thirteen hundred. I have a private session with the boss in five minutes."

He grabbed me by the arm. His grip was firm, but tender at the same time. "Little girl, you ain't"?

Before he could finish I scolded him, "You know me better, Jack."

We stared at each other. He nodded slowly. "The club has rules."

"I know all about the rules." I also knew Jack's concern was more for me. I pecked him on the cheek. I didn't care who saw, even if Jack did.

"Go make some more green, Coco," he said, almost reluctantly.

"Don't lose your edge, Jack," I warned him, thinking way beyond my years. After all, business was business.

The CEO was Asian. He was also tipsy. I was on autopilot myself. The money had become a vaguery brought into focus only by Jack's reaction to the amount. I was aware it was piling up but I was detached, much the same way a teller is who handles it all day in a busy bank. After a while it doesn't mean anything. It becomes a commodity.

The CEO wasn't drinking excessively, but he had a low tolerance for alcohol. We got along. He and I got playful in a private room upstairs, with a crimson plush velvet curtain pulled closed across the front of it, for over an hour. I poured him another glass of champagne every time I felt he needed a primer. I complimented him, though not gratuitously. I listened and understood, but did not stroke his ego. He had billions. Other people did that to him every day. I surmised correctly that he, Philip Wang, age thirty-two and married, just wanted to relax and enjoy one of the few nights he would have off this year.

When he grew tired of watching me, I put my g-string back on but stayed topless, sitting down beside him on the comfortable love seat. My hands draped across the lapels of his thousand dollar suit jacket. I listened as he regaled me with the stories of his very fascinating life. I wondered what kind of woman he had married. The whole time he never brought her up, aside from the fact his marriage had been recent. I found out later she was the daughter of the Governor of Hong Kong.

We spent about two hours together, probably the best two hours I'd spent with anyone the whole time I'd been at Dante's. In the end, we parted and I went away with an odd kind of emptiness I couldn't quite understand. I had everything I should want, but for the first time I felt something had been left out.

"What's wrong, little girl?" Jack had been looking for me. He found me upstairs. I was deep in thought, nursing a diet soda in the corner at the end of the VIP bar. I felt all alone in a packed house of strangers pretending to be best friends, at least for tonight.

"Nothing," he snapped me out of my self-indulgent reverie. "Not a thing," I smiled to emphasize my point. I felt like talking to Jack. I could see he knew I was lying to him. But now wasn't the time and this wasn't the place. He winked as if he had read my mind.

"Did you see your chit?"

I shook my head, "I trust you, Jack. You know that."

"For a billionaire, he tips pretty good."

"How good is good?" He had my full attention now.

"The two of you must have had fun."

"Don't jerk me around, Jack," I feigned indignation.

"How does five big ones an hour sound?"

I did a quick mental calculation. We'd been in the private room for around two hours. That made it a thousand bucks. It wasn't what I thought it would be, but I couldn't complain. A grand for a few nude dances and some very pleasant conversation was something I could more than live with. Tonight had been good to me. I was walking home with twenty-three hundred dollars.

"Sorry, Jack," I said, apologizing.

"For what?" he replied as his brow furrowed into a neat series of lines as he waited for me to answer.

I looked at him quizzically. "Your cut," I said, as if it was obvious. "With the other bill and a half that gives you only two-fifty for the night if I include the hundred off this thousand."

"This thousand?" he seemed confused. Then he began to laugh. It seemed he was doing more and more of that lately. It was contagious, too.

"What?" I asked, unable not to smile.

"I said five *big* ones," he thought it had been obvious. Now my brow furrowed. "As in five thousand an hour. Mr. Big Shot tipped you ten grand, Coco. He left you ten thousand."

I stared dumbly at him. When what Jack said sunk in I jumped into his arms, squealing like a little pig caught by its tail.

When I finally let go, I looked up at him excitedly. "Let's do something. Let's celebrate, Jack!"

Stuart was the bartender in the VIP lounge. He had been watching us, smiling at my childlike exuberance. I waved him over. A couple of patrons in tailored suits sidled up next to us. They had probably just finished a private dance. Along with three or four other people, there was now a small crowd gathered around the little bar.

"Let the party begin," I whooped. They all seemed amused. "Champagne, Stuart," I said as my eyes twinkled. "A glass for everyone," I demanded.

Jack was working, but he acquiesced without a fight. He wasn't going to rain on our parade. He hadn't lifted a finger, and he was leaving the table with fifteen hundred, since I decided to give him a tip. I also had decided I was done for the night as far as dancing was concerned. The

Mustang was paid for, I was getting my driver's license, and I had just earned enough to pay my bills for the next three months.

Stuart filled nine glasses in total. The suits waited until my second sip of the champagne, I suppose to make absolutely certain I'd taken a drink, and then came down on us hard and fast, like a diesel locomotive hitting a tanker at a railway crossing.

I laughed at first, confused when the one nearest me snatched the glass from my hand. Jack took a quick step forward, instant menace in his dark eyes. He was stopped dead in his tracks by the shiny badge that was shoved into his face.

"ATF, Mr. Holliday," the suit nearest him barked over Van Halen's song 'Panama'. "Don't do anything stupid."

Jack hesitated. The laughter permeating the bar a moment before was gone now.

I could feel my pulse pounding in the back of my skull like a hammer as I watched the events unfold around me. I noticed the four gentlemen who had all too eagerly joined our celebration, absent of chivalry, fleeing as fast as they could in the direction of the stairway to the main floor. They parted suddenly to allow what I would soon learn were three more ATF agents scrambling up those same stairs past them. I was scared. I glanced at Jack. I saw that he was worried. It was quickly dawning on everyone we were in the midst of a full scale undercover operation – a raid on Dante's.

"Who's in charge?" Jack demanded. His momentary anxiety had vanished. Now he was angry. The lights suddenly came on, and the music stopped. I saw another suit clamor across the stairway's threshold and head directly across the carpet toward us. He was confident. He strode deliberately, his lips were pursed. He was powerfully built and appeared to be slightly over six feet tall. He was about thirty-five and strikingly handsome, like a movie star. His tanned complexion stood out, even in the suspect lighting. His hair was pitch black and longer than it should have been.

"Relax, Jack," the suit tapped a reassuring hand across the huge man's shoulder. Jack turned toward him, and instant recognition flashed across his countenance.

"Mr. Spielman, I —"

"Don't worry Jack," he assured his club manager. "I'll take it from here." He smiled, revealing a perfect row of ivory teeth. For a moment, as he quickly assessed those around him with a seemingly casual appraisal, his eyes found mine. I thought they stayed a second too long, but I couldn't be sure. He moved his gaze to the guy who'd flashed his badge to Jack.

"Roger," he acknowledged the ATF agent.

"Hello, Sam," Roger replied cordially. The agent showed only a hint of what might have been mild frustration. This raid was supposed to be a surprise, and yet Sam Spielman had somehow learned of it. This was obvious by his very presence. As Sam stood there, an older bespeckled man in his fifties wearing a blue, pin-striped banker's suit edged up to him. His cherubic face indicated a life of luxurious debauchery liberally sprinkled with a lot of late nights, women, and alcohol. He seemed bored. Sam introduced him.

"Roger Carlton, this is Nathaniel Katz, my attorney."

The lawyer looked down his nose at the agent. Getting right to business, but still appearing bored, he demanded, "Warrant." Roger Carlton dug into that finely tailored suit jacket and produced paperwork signed the day before by a judge located in San Francisco County, coincidentally the only county in America whose geographical boundaries exactly matched those of its encompassed namesake municipality. He extended his arm and offered the warrant for the lawyer's inspection.

Nathaniel Katz ignored it. He smiled a patronizing smile, as if humoring a lesser man – a mere bureaucrat – and said sardonically, "Just keeping you honest, Carlton. I'm sure it's legal."

The senior ATF agent flushed angrily, realizing again the agency's move had been compromised, no doubt, within hours of the judge's signing the warrant. He wondered whom Spielman knew.

"What are you looking for?" queried the arrogant attorney.

"Read the warrant." Score one for the feds.

Nathaniel Katz shrugged unconcernedly. The clash of egos was like watching water being thrown on a grease fire. "We will," he assured him with that same bored tone. "Don't overreach your scope," he warned Carlton. "You wouldn't want to have the fruits of your efforts squashed in the gutter by a sorry Jew like me. That would be downright embarrassing for you," he taunted the federal agent.

If Roger Carlton was rattled, he did a better job of hiding it than me. I was confused, and frightened. I wasn't sure what was going on, and I wondered if I was even a part of it. I just wanted to get out of there, maybe go back to the diner while they sorted out whatever it was that needed sorting out. I shivered. I wasn't wearing much in the way of clothes. This drew a little more scrutiny from the suit that had first snatched the wine glass from my hand. He kept looking from me to his boss and back again. Something was brewing in his mind. Jack stood beside Sam Spielman, stewing in helpless frustration.

"I'll be careful not to trip and skin myself, Mr. Katz," said Carlton.

"Do your fishing," Katz dared him. He had been through this before. "Within your scope, of course," he reiterated. "When you're done and you don't find anything I'll have a chat with a few judges I know. We'll talk about a little thing called harassment and how it relates to the Fourth Amendment," he threatened.

"Talk is cheap, Mr. Katz."

"And it takes money to buy whiskey, Mr. Carlton. You ought to remember that," the sparring continued unabated.

The whole time all I could think about was my age. I began to understand its implications. What had I pressured Jack into? What did it mean if they discovered I was seventeen? I tried to remain calm. Surely they weren't looking for that. But if not, then what?

Jack had always run a tight ship. But the girls, myself included, were always pushing the envelope. Part of what Holliday did was buffer the constant barrage of that pushing just enough so we never crossed the line. It was, I realized, the height of hypocrisy. We could strip all our clothes off, polish the clients' faces with our breasts, grind into their hard-ons and they had to sit there, had to lap it up. During a lap dance, the customers could never touch back. That was the rule, but it was not always strictly enforced.

It had been obvious from day one that some of the girls, for the money, went a lot further. Some of them took their work home with them. I never did. I had promised myself I never would. It probably helped that I didn't have to. But all that didn't matter now because I was a minor. And if they found out, what had Jack said?

They would shut down Dante's. And then what would happen to me? I wondered.

"Why don't we start with everyone's ID?" Roger Carlton was talking now.

"Let me see that warrant once more," Katz was taking him more seriously now. This time Katz took the warrant, produced a pair of eyeglasses, and began to read. He knew where to look, and thirty seconds later he shoved it back at Carlton.

He nodded to Spielman, who said to Carlton, "As unobtrusive as possible, please." Sam was smoother than the silk suit he wore. "I'm a respectable businessman. I run my show with integrity."

"I'm sure you did, Mr. Spielman," Carlton replied, no small hint of sarcasm in his tone. The past tense of his comment was ominous.

"Why don't we start with her?" the suit who couldn't keep his eyes off me volunteered, nodding in my direction. The blood in my veins seemed to instantly freeze as everyone followed his gaze and stared at me.

I looked helplessly at Jack. He met my gaze and then looked away.

They shut down Dante's for three days. I wasn't so lucky. I lost my job, of course. But that, as it turned out, was only the beginning. I was turned over to the juvenile authorities; charges of prostitution, they claimed, were pending. They were good at parking the hearse.

The good news, if any, was I could keep all the money I'd earned. Nathaniel Katz clarified that one for me. I had only been working three and a half months. I hadn't evaded any taxes – yet. The money was mine to keep. I spent the next two days in the god awful detention facility. Somehow, they finally found my mother. She showed up to claim me on the morning of the third day. It was my only way out.

She ran to me when I entered the front lobby, putting on quite a show.

"My baby," she cried, hugging me. I thought some of her tears might even be real. It had been over three months since we last spoke.

"Hi Mom," I said, managing a short smile.

"Where have you been? I came as soon as I heard. Is that your bag? Oh, baby you look different," her voice rose slightly, as if she were asking a question instead of making an observation. She hugged me again. "I was worried sick. Why didn't you call? I'm so glad you're all right." She was babbling.

"I'm fine, Mom," I assured her. "Can we get out of here?" We were causing a scene. A couple of the staff and a number of visitors had stopped to watch.

"Yeah, sure honey. Carl is waiting in the parking lot." I grabbed the only possession I had brought with me, my overnight bag from work. It contained a couple of costumes, some makeup, and the pair of stiletto pumps I'd been wearing when they'd busted me. I was dressed in what I had worn to work: my jeans, t-shirt, jean jacket, and a comfortable pair of Nikes. I followed her out the door, wondering if she had changed and who Carl was.

Mom headed across the parking lot, swaying seductively under a cloudless San Francisco sky. For the first time it occurred to me that at least as far as looks went, she could easily be mistaken for my older sister, and certainly not my mother. She looked good in a comfortable cotton print dress, with red and yellow flowers, a wide black leather belt cinched around her narrow waist. She wore matching black high heels that exaggerated her gait. Her blonde hair was the same as mine, thick with a slight curl. It framed perfect features: high cheekbones, a narrow chin, a straight nose, and pouting lips. She had applied makeup like a master artist. Like I said, we could have been sisters. I noticed she wasn't wearing a bra. It was hard not to notice. When I caught up to her, I was surprised when she put her arms around me and pulled me close.

"I'm sorry baby." She was nervous. It could tell she fought to hide the beginning of tears, which threatened to spill out from behind her dark sunglasses. "I love you, sweetheart. I love you with all my heart." We walked slowly together. They had parked at the far end of the lot. I wondered now if that had been intentional. "When your father died, I lost touch with reality for a while. I hope you can forgive me for that, and for the way I acted. I'd like to start over, if you would." She sounded sincere. "We're all we've got, Coco. It's you and me against the world," it poured out.

Suddenly I started to cry. I wrapped my arms around my mother's waist and hung on for dear life. "Yes," I finally managed to say, sniffling like a baby with a runny nose. "I think I would like that, Mom. I think I'd like to start over. At least we can try." I searched my mother's eyes. She kissed me on the forehead, sniffling back her own tears.

"Oh, baby, you will never know how much I've prayed to hear you say that."

"I'm sorry, too, Mom. I love you," I said meekly. I wanted with every fiber of my being for it to be true.

# Chapter 4

That was eight years ago, the first time I laid eyes on Sam Spielman. The time had passed in a heartbeat.

"You *are* cold," Mark Zarillo had noticed me shivering. I sniffed, pushing away the memories of those days. Life was moving far too quickly.

"Are you crying?" Mark was suddenly concerned.

I shook my head. "Hay fever," I laughed it off, reaching into my purse for a clean handkerchief. "It happens every year about this time," I lied, forgetting we were in the desert. The nearest pollen was seventy miles away, in Las Vegas Valley. Mark wasn't stupid, but he let it go.

"You want another beer?"

I shook my head again, more to smother the last painful remnants of days gone by. I focused all my attention on Zarillo.

"So tell me Mark," I began cautiously. "What's a lawyer doing impersonating a cop in Brittle, Nevada? And a good lawyer nonetheless, because Sam only hired the best. What's Sam got you doing out here in the middle of the desert?"

He raised his eyebrows. I waited while he finished his beer. He set the empty bottle down soundlessly. "I guess I could ask you the same question. You're Sam's girlfriend. I don't buy the coincidence you just happened to run out of gas at the Brittle exit. I think you know a whole lot more than you're telling."

"You don't believe in coincidences," I retorted.

"Uh-uh," he said quickly. "I've been around a little too long to be fooled by that one."

"All right, let's say it wasn't a coincidence. This is the Mojave Desert. Anyone who travels through it without an extra can of gas in the trunk is either an idiot or just plain crazy."

"Or both," Mark agreed.

"I know Sam has been busy out here. Look at you," I pointed out the obvious. "Maybe I came out here to have a look for myself. So far I can't say I'm disappointed. I did get an armed escort into town. That gun shoots real bullets, doesn't it? I'm not blind, Mark. I saw what I saw on the way into town. Brittle might as well be an occupied territory. There were thugs on every street corner. Did Sam buy this whole town? What's so valuable about a small patch in the desert that Sam would go to this much trouble? Do you shoot tourists?"

"No tourists out here," Mark replied sardonically. "There's no reason to come here."

"Not yet."

"What do you mean by that?" he plumbed for knowledge.

"You tell me, Mark. You're one of Sam's lawyers," I countered, fencing him off.

"What are you doing tonight?" he did a one-eighty.

"Are you asking me out?" I flirted with him.

"Easier to keep an eye on you," he smiled innocently.

"Did Sam tell you to do that?"

"Nope, that was my idea."

"In that case I accept." I suddenly felt tired. "I need a power nap first, though, and a shower afterwards." I glanced at my Rolex. It was already five-thirty. "I suppose I should find a motel."

Zarillo leaned back and reached into a pocket. He held out a plastic card. It was a programmable key. "Two blocks down, on your left. It's not the Bellagio, but it's the best one this town's got."

"Sam thinks of everything." I saw the quick flash in his eyes as I grabbed the plastic key. "Or is this another one of your ideas?" I quickly corrected myself.

"Yup," he sighed.

"Why, Mr. Zarillo," I tried my best southern belle accent out on him. "I do believe you care about little ole' me." We both laughed.

"Here's my card. Call me when you're ready. We'll tour the town. Dinner and drinks after the sun goes down."

"Sounds like a plan." I wasn't smiling when I added, "We'll start the tour down by the river."

He looked puzzled. "There's no river in this place, unless you're referring to that dried out creek bed on the north side of town."

I still wasn't smiling when I said, "That's exactly why I'm referring to. See you in a couple of hours." I didn't wait for his reply. I got up and left him sitting at the table, staring after me. I was sure he wasn't thinking about my ass, even as I sashayed through the bar's front door and exited into the bright desert sunlight beyond.

It was a Days Inn, a notch up from what I expected. I found the remote and clicked on the satellite TV. I found the music stations, clicked around a bit and got lucky. I fell back onto a comfortable queen sized bed to Toby Keith's 'Whiskey for My Men, and Beer for My Horses', a duet he had recorded with his good buddy Willie Nelson. It was a song about gunslingers, like the ones who now roamed this town, I thought ruefully. They were led by the worst rogue of them all, my boyfriend Sam Spielman.

I first learned about real estate options at Cal State University in Sacramento. I got a degree in Business with a minor in Geology. Sam wanted to pick up the tab, but I refused. I never wanted him to tell me I owed him. It was my way or no way. He respected that, especially since no one else ever had the guts to dictate terms to him.

Nevertheless, on my birthdays as well as Christmas and Easter, he was always incredibly generous. He laid a heavy guilt trip on me the first time. I realized my checking account had jumped an exponent, and I returned the money to him. He acted hurt and said friends accepted gifts from each other if they really were friends. He said he thought that's what we were, before and after anything else. Sam did a job on me, and I ended up taking it all back and even telling him I was sorry. I was young then, still gullible. The cash came in handy. Still, I stayed in a dorm on campus and banked the difference for rainy days. I was always a practical girl, even back then.

I got myself a decent education. The concept of land options was fairly simple when you broke it down to its barest elements. It was all about leveraging. The trick was to find a motivated seller who didn't need the money. Then, you talk him into selling his real estate two or three years down the road, maybe even ten years, for an agreed upon price. This deal cost the buyer an option fee, a small percentage of the total price for entitlement to the land. This option blocked anyone else from buying the land for as long as the option remained in effect, sometimes for as long as ten or fifteen years. The deadline to buy the land for the agreed upon price was the same day the option to purchase the land expired. If you wanted the land, you exercised your option to purchase and paid the agreed on sum, becoming the new owner. If you decided not to purchase the land, the option to do so would finally lapse. This was good for the original owner, because all along the way if the options were renewable, he would receive fees. In return, you would keep the sole right of purchase until the option lapsed – good for you.

Sam had optioned every square inch of Brittle, Nevada he could get his fingers on, for as many years as possible. Sam knew something about Brittle that no one else did. I wanted in, and I didn't want him to know it.

I called Mark Zarillo at seven-thirty on my cell phone. He picked me up in the motel's front lobby ten minutes later. "This is new," I said as he held the baltic blue Range Rover's door open for me. The porte-cochère shaded it from the dying sun. His ride was spotless. Either it had been recently washed, or it hadn't been off-road in a while. That was about to change. I threw my bag onto the console between the front seats and got in. He climbed into the driver's seat.

"No more Mr. Highway Patrol?" Zarillo had changed his apparel. He was dressed in a pair of stone washed jeans and a breathable, long-sleeved shirt of blue cotton. He had on well-worn cowboy boots kind of like the Marlboro man wore; only Mark looked better.

"It wasn't me," he replied, dry wit showing through.

"You're a looker, Mark."

He causally gazed sideways at me as he pulled out from under the portico. He saw I wasn't flirting; I had just made an observation. I winked at him. He nodded and made a right turn out of the Days Inn parking lot onto Main Street.

"Where are we going?" he asked conversationally, tipping his hand. So, Mark knew something too. He wouldn't have asked me if he didn't.

I bent my head down as if I wore reading glasses and wanted to see him over the top of the frames. It was a look that said: 'Are you kidding?'

"Right," said Mark, accelerating northward. "The lady wants to see the creek bed." He steered deftly around two five-ton trucks and a trailer loaded with thirty foot lengths of steel pipe, all parked in the right lane near the motel. We headed north.

The Range Rover stood out; a pagan anomaly plopped in the middle of at one time in ancient history had been a raging whitewater tributary of the Colorado River basin. The river was now extinct and its secrets long buried beneath a sun-baked mix of stones and sand melded with red clay.

We walked about a hundred yards from the vehicle. I kicked nonchalantly at loose piles of stones here and there, negotiating the shrubs and low lying vegetation that had taken hold, prickly sentinels to the human intruders moving among them. A spotted lizard which had remained motionless and perfectly camouflaged showed itself, darting away from me as I tread across its home. Its tiny legs were a blur, moving at light speed in the hopes they wouldn't become a meal for the source of the vibrations and changes of light it had sensed. Flight: a mechanism of survival honed by millennia of ancestry. The tiny creature had survived. It just might live another day.

I caught a direct glimpse of the setting sun and swiftly turned away. Tiny black spots danced across my retinas. The desert could fool you. The sun was still bright, even though it didn't seem to be because of the contrast of only a few hours earlier, when it hung higher and brighter.

As its magnificent rays travelled further through the earth's paper thin, polluted atmosphere the sun changed colors, dimming. But it was still strong enough to blind if stared at.

"Just what is it you're looking for out here?" Mark's voice cut across the still air between us.

I sighed, sorry to look away from the beautiful hues of blended oranges still threatening strength as the sun sank closer to the horizon. I shrugged, turning to meet his gaze. The Marlboro man, I thought again. "I'm not sure," I said.

Mark stared past me. He was enjoying the sunset. He focused on me again, doubt in his expression. "You have any theories?"

"Oh, I don't know," I hedged. I kicked at another loose pile of rocks. Another lizard flew from under some foliage and high-tailed it for cover across the sandy river bed. "Haven't you wondered?" I turned his question around.

"About this?" he gestured to the stark beauty around us, his tone reverential. "All the time. About what Sam is up to? Why bother? That's saying if he's even up to anything."

"We both know he is."

"I wouldn't be able to do anything about it even if that was true. I wouldn't want to. He pays me well enough for sticking to my job."

"Yeah, sure," I was not convinced.

"What do you want from me?" For the first time since I had known him, Mark seemed angry.

"Take it easy," I scolded him. "I'm not the enemy." I wrested my oversized canvas purse from my shoulder and squatted down between two large shrubs to inspect its contents. This way I was hidden from view should any prying eyes be observing us from a distance through high powered binoculars. I rummaged through it and found what I was looking for, but stayed in a crouch between the bushes.

Zarillo frowned. "What're you looking for?"

"I saw some trucks – mobile drilling rigs – on the way out here. They were parked near the motel. You know anything about them, Mark?"

He looked out across the desert, toward town. If I didn't know better I could swear he was suddenly nervous. Lawyers were just like cockroaches: you couldn't live with them, and you couldn't kill them fast enough.

"There's talk Sam is thinking of developing the land out here into a casino and resort hotel. The rigs are with some engineers. They're sampling soil densities for a location."

"Those rigs are designed to go deep," I called him on his bullshit, "down at least several hundred feet or more. I saw the lengths of pipe extensions," I spoke to the ground in front of me. "Far below any excavations required for putting in the structural foundations of a major hotel." I looked up at him, seeing his shocked expression. "I'm more than just a pretty face, Mark." I smiled, for a second, and then continued filling the three glass quart sized jars with soil samples of the river bed. I screwed on their tin tops, and then shoved the filled jars back into my knapsack. I stood up and slung the canvas bag back over my shoulder.

"That's it. I'm done for now," I announced. I looked back over my shoulder at the setting sun. I was in awe of its beauty. The pale orange and yellow of the western sky had brightened. It seemed to flicker now, as if on fire, playing a game of celestial tag with the rich blue heavens above it. "Let's blow this popsicle stand. Hungry?" I asked Mark innocently, walking past him.

Zarillo didn't say much as he drove us out of the creek bed and onto the dirt road. A mile later, the road hooked back up to the blacktop where it veered left, becoming Main Street as it snaked into Brittle. I'd trashed his ego with my knowledge. I guess he was still massaging the bruises.

By the time we turned into the parking lot of the restaurant the cloud over his head had lifted and he had returned to his usual charming self. There was an empty spot up front, next to a faded handicapped parking sign. Mark pulled it, braking hard to somehow drive home a point I had completely missed. The male ego was simple, silly, and as old as the dried out creek bed we'd just come from. A sign above the door announced we had arrived at the Dab Haus, the only original Bavarian Restaurant this side of Vegas, German tap beer included. The parking lot, I noticed, had few empty spaces.

"You're going to love this place," Mark promised, slipping the vehicle into park. I got out, not waiting for him to come around for me. He followed me inside.

"So you took some soil samples."

"Yup."

And that was it. For the rest of a mouthwatering, traditional German-style dinner and on into drinks afterward, he never brought it up again.

Halfway through my second pint of Haaker-Shor I looked more closely at Mark. The place was quieter now, the cacophony surrounding the onslaught of late afternoon diners having dissipated. The beer aficionados had filtered in and were taking over. They weren't yet drunk enough to be boisterous, but they'd get there. With strong beer like this it wouldn't take very long. 'Edelweiss' was wafting through the air, coming at us through two large speakers mounted over the bar. I soaked up the pleasant ambience. We could have been in the Swiss Alps. No Brittle, no Sam, no worries…*You look happy to meet me*…I listened to the words as they melted into the subdued conversation, the sudden bursts of laughter, and the musical clinking of happy glasses. For a little while – a few minutes or an hour – I could forget. I could slow down and live. I could feel what others took for granted. I could taste a peacefully easy freedom. I felt like that when my mother tucked me into bed that first night, the first I'd spent in my own bed in close to four months back in the San Francisco days. Had I gained some independence through escape, riding that bus until it stopped in front of Dante's? Or had I ran away?

## Chapter 5

My mother kissed me softly on the forehead. The clean, lilac scented pink down comforter tucked warmly around my neck. "Sleep with the angels, baby," she whispered that first night home. "I'm here if you need anything."

I reached up over my guilt, wrapping my arms around her. "I love you, Mom," I repeated, tears pattering on my sheets.

"I know baby, I know," she massaged the small of my back. "You're home, now. Everything is fine." She unwrapped my arms from around her neck and smiled at me. "Sleep now, we'll talk in the morning." She kissed me again, and turned back to look at me for a few seconds before she finally shut the light off and eased my bedroom door closed.

I woke the next morning to the tantalizing aroma of hickory smoked bacon and fried eggs wafting through the crack under my door. I was back in the Haight.

My mother had cleaned the flat since I'd left. I thought there might be a fresh coat of paint on the walls as well. Maybe she had changed. I knew I had, of course.

Mom was thirty-seven years old. She'd had it rough, I realized. She'd been only twenty-eight when Dad died, saddled with a precocious six year old kid. It hadn't been easy for either one of us, but I figured we both deserved a new beginning.

Carl turned out to be a pretty decent guy. He wasn't anything like Mom's usual bevy of suitors. Apparently, sometime after I'd left, she'd had a change of habit and switched from quantity to quality. Carl wrote romance novels for Harlequin. He worked six months of the year, banging out three of them, one every two months. He was well paid, smart, and best of all I could tell he was in love with my mom. From what I could see she was ready to settle down with him, too. He was five years her senior, and handsome in his own unique way. It looked like it might work. I was happy for them both.

I'd slept in late, so the bathroom in the hallway was empty. I tiptoed into it, feeling oddly self-conscious, a bit like a guest in a seldom seen friend's home. I knew this would pass quickly. I guess I still felt a certain amount of guilt at having left her. I eased the door closed. I could hear Mom and Carl talking softly in the next room, she cooking breakfast, he was listening and responding. Their words were muffled; I couldn't hear what they were saying but I guessed it was about me.

I stripped out of my pajamas and stared at myself in the full length mirror hung on the wall opposite the vanity. Somehow I looked a lot older than I remembered when I had last looked at my reflection in this same mirror, only a few months earlier. I remembered Philip Wang, the billionaire CEO, and his ten thousand dollars. Was that really only three days ago? It seemed like it had been a lot longer than that. What had he seen when he looked at me, what had the rest of them seen? What in the mirror in front of me was worth all that cash? I frowned at myself, jumped into the shower, and turned the water on as hot as I could stand without scalding myself.

"Good morning," my mother greeted me, rising quickly from where she sat at the breakfast table. Carl rose halfway out of his chair, hesitated, smiled self-consciously, and then sat back down again. This was not a business meeting.

Mom kissed me on the cheek and headed towards the stove to fetch me breakfast, which was still warm in the frying pan. I sat next to Carl, probably feeling as awkward around him as he did around me.

"Good morning, Coco," his smile was genuine.

"Good morning, Carl," I smiled back at him. Mom set a full plate of bacon and eggs in front of me. My stomach growled its approval and I dug in. Next, she set a large glass of orange juice next to my plate and seated herself across the table from me. That left only one empty chair tucked under the small but comfortable table, which was recessed into the apartment's only bay window overlooking Haight Street. The morning was gray and cloudy. A fine mist had collected outside the windows, further obscuring the limited light which filtered through a heavily overcast sky. Werewolf weather, as some San Franciscans called it.

"So," Mom began tentatively. "I called the school this morning." I looked across the table, curious now. I'd almost forgotten. I had made it through the eleventh grade. I had finished the year at the top of my class with straight A's. It had been a walk in the park. I had taken that bus ride soon after, about a week into the summer break. By my calculations, school had started back up about six weeks ago. Now that Mom had brought it up, I realized I missed school. I missed being around the innocence of people my age, whom I had considered my peers not so long ago.

Mom saw I wasn't going to say anything, so she went on. "You're six weeks behind. But," she paused, glancing at Carl for support. "In light of your scholastic achievements they said you could go back. You'd have to work in study groups during the week for a few hours after class, and on the weekends, you know, until you caught up."

I liked what I was hearing.

"They all like you, Coco," Carl chimed in. "They all agreed you were an outstanding student. They felt it entirely unnecessary that you be held back a year. They feel with a serious effort on your part you could easily catch up –"

Mom interrupted, "You can still graduate in the spring, I know you could do it." She faltered. "If that's what you want, that is."

I put my fork down, a piece of stringy yellowy-white egg stuck in its tines. I swallowed a delicious piece of bacon. I drank from my glass of orange juice, sizing them up from behind its edge. The juice was cold, fresh, and sweet. I set it back down on the kitchen table, licking my lips.

"You had me right after they said I could come back." I smiled. "I think we should all take a deep breath and relax. We're putting ourselves under way too much weird, unnecessary pressure. It's me, Mom," I assured her. I reached for her hand and she took mine in both of hers. "I haven't changed that much. I'm ok. And Carl," I turned to him and his smile, "I haven't seen my mom this happy in a very long time. Whatever you two are eating, keep it up." We all laughed then. The ice was broken.

"What's it like writing romance novels?" I asked Carl. I scrunched up my face. "Where do you come up with all those juicy lines?"

Carl chuckled with humility. The more we spoke, the more I found myself liking him. He had a gentle spirit. Carl had dirty blonde hair that fell a half inch below his collar and his ears, like he was three weeks past a much needed haircut. He looked almost scruffy, but not quite. He looked at me with kind blue eyes, devoid of judgment. He was tanned, a complexion often times absent in people from the Bay area. There was never enough sun here, and when there was everyone was usually indoors making far too much money, or sleeping like I did. "It's as natural to me as breathing," he explained. "It's my God given talent. Most people have a talent singular to their own unique personality. Earlier in life we call them our dreams. But the coat of dreams, they say, is foolish when worn by older men," he waxed philosophical. "Everybody grows up, so they say."

"And everyone, so it would seem, gives up on their dreams."

"For someone so young, you have insight," he conceded with a compliment.

"But you didn't give up, Carl."

"I was lucky. Success came early."

"Carl was first published at twenty-six," Mom informed me proudly.

"Would you have given up on your dream, I mean? Let's say you got real old, and you never got there, and your heart was broken. Would you have kept going?"

Carl leaned back in his chair, a breath of air escaping from his soul like a giant ball deflating itself. His fingers rested on either side of the table. I could see he had wondered about this himself, probably more than once.

As if reading my mind he said, "It's an interesting question, Coco. One I've thought about every time I've come across someone still trying. As your mother said, I got my first break early. I was lucky. Sometimes I think about that and ask myself, 'why me?' Let's say someone gets in a horrible car crash and loses both legs. It's different of course, quite the opposite for me. But it's the same lottery. Both of us still ponder the 'why me' scenario."

"I guess that's what life ends up being," I said with resignation.

"A lottery? Accidents of happenstance?" Carl considered this for a moment, rolling it around in the cage of his brain as he had done all those times before.

"I don't know the answer to that," he admitted for the umpteenth time. "I *can* tell you what it took for me to do what I did: dedication, education, discipline, hard work. It didn't just happen on its own. Having said this, I know it's different in every case. Life is a minefield, Coco. The battlefield of the human condition is littered with the corpses of broken dreams."

"Aren't those from the people who give up and sell out?"

He was shaking his head even before I had finished. "It would be entirely unfair to say that."

"Why?"

"Because," he leaned onto the table to emphasize what he wanted to say, "They are the courageous ones. Think about it. We don't all get through. We win a fantastic race up the canal just to get here; millions of sperm swimming like mad to make it to the egg first. The winner gets the biggest reward imaginable: life itself. I've always been convinced that what happens after is a bonus. Yeah, admittedly a lot of folks squander their lives. They waste away in prisons of drug and alcohol addiction, by working way too hard and way too long, and by toiling through a myriad of all kinds of other meaningless excesses. That is, of course, our entitlement as human beings. We have free will. We're the captains of our own ships. So a wasted life goes along with the privilege of choosing it. The good news is we can choose differently."

"We can dream," I said.

"We do dream," he nodded. "Each and every one of us does. It's what we do with our dreams — how we end up living our lives — that counts the most. Our choices, made freely and with good conscience, determine what happens while we're here."

"It must pay to make the right choices," I said.

"Huge dividends," he pointed out, with kindness.

"It helps to have guidance." He knew what I meant. A dead parent at six years old surely didn't help the cause.

Carl sighed. "Coco —"

I interrupted him, "It was a cheap shot, Carl." I looked at my mother. She was concerned. I could see the pain behind her eyes. I'd struck a raw nerve. "I'm sorry," I said to them both.

"We've all got issues," Carl freely admitted. "You're right, though. Guidance does help. Without it — or with bad guidance — we can certainly stray," he sermonized.

"What about people whose dreams don't come true?" I asked naively. "What happens to them?"

"Broken dreams," Carl sighed. "They continue their lives. They move on, like people always do when someone they love dies. They marry, have kids, get mortgages, they press forward."

"And have regrets," Mom spoke softly. Carl looked at her, and slowly nodded.

"That, too," he admitted, understanding. He was silent then for a few moments. Suddenly I became aware of the sounds of the traffic and people outside on Haight Street two floors below us. The big bay window, divided into its sixteen single glass panes, didn't afford much resistance to the assault. Apart from the hush of traffic, it became so quiet in the small breakfast nook you could hear a clock tick.

I finally broke the pregnant silence. "I'll start back on Wednesday, Mom. Can you tell them that?"

"I'll tell them Coco. Not any sooner?"

"I've got a couple of things I have to do. Tomorrow, especially," I was thinking about my driver's test. I'd have to call Chanel. Virginia Slotkis was here real name, her Czech name, and have her pick me up. There was no reason to think she wouldn't, in spite of what happened on Friday night.

Mom and Carl exchanged quick, 'we'll-talk-about-this-later-in-private' glances, but said nothing more. If this was going to work, and the three of us were going to get along, then there had to be trust. No one, it seemed, wanted to risk a replay of this past summer.

"I'm sure they'll be fine with that," Mom promised.

"Don't worry," I'd heard the slight trepidation in her voice. After all, she was my mother. "I'll report to the gulag bright and early on Wednesday morning ready for the slave mill," I joked. Reassured, both of them chuckled.

"I'm looking forward to going back. I've missed my friends. I won't have a problem catching up, either. It's a promise," I added seriously.

Mom came around the table and kissed me on the forehead this time. She began to clear the table, truly a sign she was comfortable with the way things were going my first day home in a long time. She had missed me. My heart felt light and airy. It was a strange feeling, new to me. It wouldn't be difficult to get used to, I thought to myself. Warm embers burned in my soul, and for the first time in a long time I felt like I belonged.

## Chapter 6

"You're drunk," said Zarillo, unsteady himself. I'd been right; the beer aficionados were now out in full force. And if there's one thing that is surely contagious, it's drinking good European brews with a rollicking, rowdy bunch of Germans. The Dab Haus had drifted through the dinner crowd and cruised into the turbulent waters of the night, now rudderless in a choppy, frothing sea of suds. The party was in full swing and I, not alone by any stretch, was having fun.

"You've got a penchant for the obvious, Mark Zarillo," I spoke loudly enough to be heard above the Beer Barrel Polka. The speakers above the bar had been cranked up, as was customary when the drinking crowd took over. The boxes boomed loudly, the bass pushing powerful vibrations into the main hall to the delight of the boisterous crowd of fifty or more. It was a mix of all ages and backgrounds. They sang along in unison with the polka song, a giant karaoke choir of drunks; Mark and I included.

It was good fun. We left around midnight, Mark dropping me off safe and sound right under the portico of the Days Inn. He promised to call me in the morning around nine for breakfast.

I didn't bother to shower. Exhausted, I lay down on the comfortable bed in my clothes and was asleep in fifteen seconds flat. I awoke to the sound of the clock radio, vaguely recalling that I had set the alarm previously, before Mark had picked me up to go out to the river bed. I had a bad headache to remind me of last night's indiscretions. I fumbled around the nightstand and somehow found the snooze button. It was eight o'clock. I buried my head under a pillow, praying for relief. I got up ten minutes later when it went off the second time. I switched off the radio and was able to find a couple of Tylenols in my purse. I washed them down with a cold glass of water and took a look at my reflection in the mirror – scary. Bloodshot eyes stared back at me as I mouthed the words, "You deserve this." The inside of my mouth felt like wet sandpaper.

There was a coffee maker in the bathroom, with the requisite accoutrements, enough for two cups of coffee. I managed to rig it up, fill it up with water, and pressed the red start button. An orange light signaled success.

I kicked off my clothes and dragged myself into the shower, wondering how in the hell so many people put themselves through this so regularly. Why did so many people drink so much booze if this is how it made them feel?

The shower helped. The coffee helped more. By five to nine, when my phone rang, I was almost feeling like a human being again.

"Hi, Mark."

"You up?"

"Barely," I came clean with him.

"How does fifteen minutes sound?"

"I'll be waiting downstairs in the lobby. I'll watch for you."

"See you then. Oh, by the way," he hesitated, changing his mind in mid sentence.

"What?"

"I'll fill you in over breakfast. See you in fifteen." The line went dead.

This should be interesting, I thought with a shrug. Almost immediately my cell phone rang again. I answered again and said to Mark, "Forget something?"

Only this time it wasn't Zarillo.

"I heard you were doing some sightseeing."

"Hi, Sam." I recognized his voice. "I've been expecting your call."

"I know where you are. I just don't know what you're doing there."

"You know me, Sam. I'm naturally curious."

"Yeah, well just remember curiosity killed the cat. I'm coming out there."

"When?"

"Tonight."

"I won't be here."

"Wait for me, please. I want to see you."

I breathed a sigh into the mouthpiece.

"If you wait you won't have to analyze the soil samples you took from the creek bed yesterday."

"You've got to stop doing this, Sam. First you bug my Chevy, and now this?" I had no idea how he had done it, but he had. It may have been Mark, but I truly doubted it. I wasn't that bad at judging character. I was convinced Mark had integrity. Sam probably had one of his thugs break into Mark's SUV while we were inside the Dab Haus. No doubt we'd been followed there from the creek. I couldn't take those mason jars into the restaurant with me, so I'd left them in the vehicle. Motive and opportunity.

Sam sighed. "I love you, baby. I don't want to see anything happen to you."

"I'm going to need a bigger shovel, Sam. The only way anything would ever happen to me would be if you let it, so don't bullshit me. You never have. Don't start now."

"Guilty," he confessed. "And I'm sorry for bugging your car."

"And the mason jars?"

"The hired help was just doing their jobs," he pleaded. "They got a little carried away."

"I said don't bullshit me, Sam! Not now. Not after all we have been through together." There was too much water under that bridge.

"I'll call off the dogs," he offered.

"I have to go, Sam." Mark would arrive at any moment.

"I heard you got drunk with one my lawyers."

"Yeah, and after we got back to the motel we made mad passionate love until the sun came up. It's why I'm so tired right now."

"You're hung over and you're grouchy. Stay in Brittle at least until I get there. We'll talk. If you want to leave afterward, I won't stop you."

I thought about it. "Promise?"

"You've got my word on it." I knew, as everyone who ever came into contact with Sam Spielman found out, he was old school – a man of honor. The only problem was, that swung both ways. If Sam decided you were an enemy, you had better find a real good place to hide – and quick. But if he gave you his word on something, you could take it to the bank. And I never, in all my years of knowing Sam, ever saw him change his mind once he'd decided on something, one way or the other.

"Sam, I hate this. I don't want to fight with you anymore. What happened to us? It never used to be like this. We used to be so happy. Look at us now. You're spying on me. We're spying on each other," I corrected myself.

"I love you," he interrupted me. "I always have."

There was a silence then, too long, although it lasted only a few seconds. "I know," I said. And then, more quietly, as if someone else was listening and I didn't want them to hear, "I love you too Sam, but this has to stop."

There was the silence again.

"You'll stay then? At least until we can talk?"

"Yes, Sam. I'll stay another night," I capitulated.

"I'll see you tonight."

"Goodbye, Sam," I hung up, wondering if I had made the right decision. I felt helpless as a caged canary at the bottom of a cold, dark mine. It was a bitch to be in love with someone you hated.

I took a last glance at myself in the vanity mirror. I didn't look too bad for having felt as poorly as I had only an hour ago. Age may go before beauty, but I'd take the resilience of youth for a hangover any day of the week.

Mark Zarillo pulled up outside as I crossed the lobby. He was shaking his head at me as I got in, again before he'd had a chance to get out and open my door. He looked a little like I'd felt an hour ago. I laughed, in spite of myself. I apologized immediately by retrieving two Tylenols from my purse.

"Thanks," he said gratefully as he popped the pills.

"Sorry I didn't bring water."

"I'll live," he said dourly. "You're another story."

I laughed again. "You didn't see me an hour ago. There's nothing like a bad hangover to remind me why I don't do the Dab Haus thing too often. What's your excuse?" I needled him good naturedly.

"Believe me," said Mark. "I do it less than most."

I smiled at him. "It shows."

"Uh-huh." He accelerated past the Citgo station on the corner of Main and Second. Mark turned right onto Third Street. Half a block down, he slid into a spot on the right side of the street. On the other side of the street was a bakery and coffee shop. A sign with a yellow happy face next to it hung in the window. It read: *The Best Bagels in Town – Guaranteed.*

A tiny bell above the door jingled as we entered. It reminded me of Christmas. The girl behind the counter greeted us warmly with a toothy smile. We found a table near the back. It was square, covered by a recently laundered linen tablecloth. The same young lady, still smiling, came around the counter and handed us two menus. She'd be back in a jiffy to take our order, but she poured us coffee before she left. Its pungent aroma was as good as it gets.

"Sam called me this morning, right after you hung up," I watched him closely.

"I'm not surprised," said Mark. He stirred cream into his coffee.

"He knew about me taking the soil samples from the creek bed."

Mark didn't stop stirring his coffee. He poured a tiny waterfall of sugar into it from the standard, tin-topped glass dispenser, one of which occupied the center of each of the ten tables in the small restaurant. He replaced the sugar container, his movements almost mechanical. He was still hurting from last night. He lifted the full cup to his lips, spilling a small amount before carefully sipping some. He put the cup back onto the table and finally looked up at me.

"Are you accusing me?" he failed to hide his defensiveness.

"You *are* hung over. If this is how it's going to be, I would just as soon pass on breakfast." I started to get up to leave.

He grabbed my arm. "I'm sorry, Coco. I was out of line. How about you give me another chance?"

I slowly eased back into my seat.

"Thank you." He seemed relieved. "I deserved that. You're right, I'm afraid alcohol and I don't do so well together."

"You'll do better in twenty minutes," I said, thinking of the Tylenol and realizing for the first time that he felt a lot worse than he was letting on. I dug back into my purse. Without asking his permission, I dropped a couple of small blue tablets into his coffee. "Xanax," I answered his unasked question. "You'll be right as rain in no time flat."

"Thanks. Do you have any idea how your boyfriend found out about your samples?" He wanted to put some distance between his earlier faux pas by moving on.

I shrugged. "What's done is done. You work for him, not me. You'd probably know more about that kind of thing than me." I sipped my coffee. "Anyway, Sam said he was coming out here."

Mark was nodding. "It makes sense. He's due. I heard he was in Vegas, and it's a short drive." He stirred his coffee again, further dissolving the medication. "So you're spending another night, then?"

"Don't fall in love with me, Zarillo. That would break all the rules."

He shook his head, smiling. "You'd be easy to love, Coco – but *in* love? No such luck. No offense, but I prefer redheads."

"None taken," I said, relieved. I didn't need to add such complications to the ones I already had.

"Enlighten me. What did you hope to learn from a few jars of sandy dirt anyway? Not that it's any of my business, but if you're so curious about this place then why don't you just ask Sam about it?"

"I'm an actress, Mark."

"I'm a fan," he admitted. "You're good, Coco. I saw 'A Day in Philly'. The film grossed eighty million, if I remember correctly. And that wasn't counting sales and rentals, which probably doubled that amount. Why this?" he gestured to the front of the little shop, meaning the enigmatic town of Brittle. "Why bother? I have a mortgage, I have to be here. I assume you don't."

"You don't get it," I said. "How could you?" I explained, "Sam doesn't tell me anything. He absolutely never discusses his business – ever. That's how it's been from day one. There are rules, Zarillo. If you're smart, you don't break them.

"I'm bored with the movies I make, with Sam parading me around town like a piece of choice sirloin, the parties, the premiers, and then more parties. I've got a brain. Sam's moving on something big. I'm pretty sure it involves Brittle, and I want in. Nothing in the rulebook says I can't compete. If I come in sideways, on my own steam, Sam and his partners can't complain."

"You won't break any rules."

"Exactly," I said. I'd been watching Mark carefully, examining the subtle changes in his expression. I believed he was ignorant of Sam's master plan, whatever that was. He was simply a lawyer, one of many. Sam made a meticulous habit of holding all his cards close to his chest. He never gave anyone in his organization anymore information than was absolutely necessary. His minions operated within small, individual cubes, isolated parts of a much larger matrix. I'd bet my last dime Sam confided in only one person. The only person aside from Sam himself who would know everything would be Nathaniel Katz. He'd been with Sam from the beginning, two Jews in a pod. They'd always worked brilliantly together. Probably the only thing which Nate Katz intentionally distanced himself from, for obvious and legal reasons, was the enforcement end of Sam's illegal enterprises. That was so Katz, as Sam's lawyer, would always be available to defend his client's interests in a court of law, in the unlikely event Sam ever came under indictment. As far as I knew, Sam had only been arrested once, for conspiracy to commit murder. That had been twenty years ago, long before he and I had ever met. The authorities had been forced to drop all charges when the only witness, who had stubbornly refused government protection, paid for his stupidity with his life. I liked to convince myself that, in those two decades, Sam Spielman had mellowed into a less violent man. After all, he certainly didn't need blood money. His various other criminal endeavors had left him a wealthy man in and of themselves. He had continually segued his riches into legitimate enterprises. Sam had donated heavily to the prevailing political winds and given to all the right charities until he had attained a venerable and respected position equal in stature to that of his peers. Even though most of Sam's peers preferred the more tried and true legal schemes of stealing their wealth. All this meant was that the political and financial elite he'd surrounded himself with didn't have the stomach for strong arm tactics and murder. Sam did. It worked for him. It gave him an element of danger, a subtle yet dangerous mantle which seemed attracted more than it repelled. People, it seemed, couldn't get enough of gangsters.

Mark Zarillo seemed different than most of the reptiles Sam used as mouthpieces. So I decided to trust him a little.

"Do you know what a REIT is?" I probed.

His brow furrowed in three perfectly even rows. "Where have I heard that acronym before?" he fought to pull the memory from his clouded mind. Before he could speak, he was interrupted by the toothy smile girl. Two plates in her hands, she shuffled sideways up to the table with breakfast.

"One onion and cheese omelet, two eggs," she announced as she placed one of the plates in front of me, "and one omelet with ham, onion, and cheese, three eggs," when she put the other one in front of Mark. "Will there be anything else?" that smile refused to leave her face. The amazing thing was it appeared to be genuine. Anna, as her name tag read, was probably Brittle born and bred, liked her job and liked the people who frequented her small restaurant. As I told her we were fine, it occurred to me she probably enjoyed her life immensely.

"If you change your mind, just wave at me. I'll be over there behind the counter. I hope you like the food." Her eyes sparkled with life, like fairies' silver wings fluttering through rain drops. We watched her retreat with appreciation.

"The simple life," I muttered to no one in particular, digging into what the fairies had brought.

## Chapter 7

"A REIT is a Real Estate Investment Trust, and I will never drink like that again," Mark promised. The omelets had vanished. We were on our respective third cups of coffee.

"I see your head has cleared. As for the beer we drank last night, it was stronger than your standard American brews. More in the category of what the brewmeisters would call a Barley Wine. It hits like a three hundred pound linebacker. Just be aware and take it easy next time," I advised him.

He looked embarrassed. It was that male ego thing again. "Why'd you ask? About the REIT, I mean," he quickly changed back the topic.

"I saw something in Sam's office in Vegas," I was trusting Mark at this point. "I guess he forgot to put away the offering. Sam was downstairs in the casino and I was waiting for him. He'd left it on his desk."

"You were snooping."

"I was bored. I couldn't help it."

"I know a little about REITs, but not the finer points," Mark admitted. "Why don't you fill in the blanks?"

If it wasn't so early, and he wasn't just coming off a bad hangover, I would have made a clever joke. Instead I said, "A REIT is a limited public offering, usually parceled out to select brokerage houses, to raise money – a lot of money – to be used in the purchase of developable real estate."

"So the whole thing is closely monitored by the Securities Exchange Commission?"

"You got that right," I gave him.

"How much cash was my boss thinking of raising?" In asking this question, I realized that Mark Zarillo was trusting me, reciprocating what I offered him a few moments earlier when I first brought this whole thing up. He'd just crossed a line by asking into the personal affairs of his boss, something he had no business doing. If Sam got wind of this, Zarillo would probably lose his job. If that was all Zarillo lost, he would be lucky. I was thinking of his mortgage. I wasn't certain, but as far as I knew Mark did not have any kids. Thank heaven for small blessings.

"A quiet six billion," I said softly, speaking into my hand, making certain none of the other diners could hear.

Mark let a soft whistle escape his pursed lips. Self-consciously, his eyes searched the diner. Nothing but locals, he was sure. That was the reason he'd picked this small, off-the-main drag place, I realized. "That's a lot of dinero, even for Sam," he spoke barely above a whisper.

"Yeah, I thought so too. At first I thought he must be going ahead with another hotel on the Strip. That would make sense. But then, just as I heard him outside in the reception area talking to his assistant, Jill, I caught the name of the location."

"Brittle."

I nodded, "One and the same."

We didn't speak for a while, both of us lost in our own private thoughts. I'm sure his were now the same as mine had been then. How in hell could you spend six billion in a place like this? On What? Or, better yet, under what ruse?

Mark postulated, "Couldn't it be that Sam is just doing what Sam does? Maybe he's going to develop some kind of mega-resort – a destination spot – like Laughlin."

"He probably will," I said. "Sam's got experience, the money, and the political clout. Most importantly, he has the will. He's a driven man."

"But…"

"There are a lot of buts. One big and so obvious it's driving me crazy," I admitted. "No one should go along with this, *but* it's obvious they are."

"What do you mean?" Zarillo wasn't following me.

"Sam has the rights to Brittle. He optioned the entire town for a song and a dance. Some of the six billion will be used to buy land Sam doesn't own. He's got it tied up with the options, but he doesn't hold title. It's a classic flip. If he's putting in a hotel, I'm sure he didn't pay more than chump change to tie up the footprint. He'll turn fifty grand into thirty million overnight, because it isn't just the hotel. He'll need land for parking, a couple of golf courses, shopping and who knows what else. Never mind the collateral tenants who swoop in on the periphery of the development."

"Is all that legal?"

"Hell yeah it's legal, but when it's so obvious it gets a lot of scrutiny. It becomes a lot more difficult to raise capital. Often the deal gets passed over. Investors don't mind a developer making a reasonable profit off them, but they certainly don't appreciate being screwed over. Don't get me wrong, SEC approval helps but it's no guarantee, especially if you're trying to start up something in the middle of the desert."

"Then it won't get done," Mark concluded.

"No such thing in Sam's vocabulary. He doesn't know the meaning of the word 'won't'. In all the time I've known him he's always successfully finished anything he's started. It isn't just the Midas touch, either. He and that slimy lawyer of his, Nathaniel Katz, *fix* things. They do it quietly, long before they move forward with anything."

"I've heard about Mr. Spielman's connections," Mark admitted. "Ninety-nine percent of people go along because of the money. The rare few who don't cooperate end up dead."

An involuntary chill coursed through me even though I knew of this part of Sam's world, a part he took great pains never to expose to me. I was, ironically, the beneficiary of his gentle side, the side he never exposed to his business associates or subordinates. In Sam's mind, they would equate any hint of compassion with weakness. Sam could move from the one world into the other with the deftness of a Swiss watchmaker, never allowing the two to collide, or be seen in one place at one time. I often wondered what would be the results, what cataclysm would ensue if that were ever to happen. If Sam was with me at the time, which world would he choose?

I had read the report on Sam's desk for as long as I dared. It got a lot more interesting as I kept going. I was prepared to discuss most of what I had read with Mark, but not all of it, especially not the line scrawled in ink near the bottom of the last page. Couched vaguely, it was penned under the air rights that had been granted surrounding a five by five mile square area just past the north edge of town, the center of which looked to be the dried out creek bed. For now, this information was for me alone.

"Were you able to read anything else about the offering before Sam came in?" fished Mark.

"That was all I had time for," I lied. "I could tell he was done talking with Jill. I had just enough time to replace the offer in exactly the same spot I'd found it. I barely made it to the other side of his desk before he entered his office. When he saw it lying there on his desk I saw a flicker of something in his eyes, surprise he'd left it there maybe. The first thing he did was put it in his wall safe."

"So you didn't see anything else?" Was Mark cross-examining me?

"I didn't have time."

"Well, what do you make of the whole thing?"

"I've got a theory, that's all. There's no proof, only shadows. I think the core of it is a classic land flip. There's no doubt in my mind all the proper people have been paid."

"You mean bribed."

"Maybe. There are ways to do it legally, don't forget that," I pointed out. "Huge amounts of money can be transferred in the form of broker's percentages, commissions, legal and accounting fees, and the like."

"Yeah," Mark nodded almost reluctantly, as if a little ashamed. "Smart guys steal legally, using lawyers." It was a rare admission.

"You're not going soft on me, are you Mark?" I pointed out his confession. After all, he was one of them.

"I'm an in-house minion. My ambitions just aren't that lofty," he spoke candidly. Most of me believed him. All of me wanted to.

"Then what about the mobile drilling rigs?" he continued. No matter what else I thought of him, Zarillo was intelligent. He may not have been the most motivated man I'd ever met, but that didn't do anything to quell a bright, inquisitive mind. "And what about the soil samples you took? What could they possibly reveal about a crooked, albeit legal, land flip? And there's one other thing that's occurred to me, as well." He was on a roll now. "What about water? Where is Sam getting the water for this little megalopolis? We're miles from the only source, the Colorado River."

"That's where it gets murky," I admitted. "I had problems with that one, too. I came up with two possibilities. Initially, for grading and construction, they won't need much water. They could truck it in from Vegas or wherever, but then what? I'll admit I was stumped. That's one of the reasons I came out here to reconnoiter the place. But yesterday…"

"The drilling rigs." The penny dropped for Mark. "They've found water."

"That's the way I figure it. A pipeline would be cost prohibitive." Of course, I knew different. "Sam may have his pocket full of Nevada politicians bought and paid for, but not the feds – no way. Common sense tells me the Southern Nevada Water Authority would never permit him to tap into the ground water basin. The Colorado River basin is drying up. We're in the worst drought in Nevada's history. All you have to do is take a trip out through Boulder City and have a gander across the Hoover Dam. You can see it on the canyon walls on the reservoir side. Lake Mead has dropped thirty feet in the last ten years alone, with no end in sight. Global warming is a bitch, and Nevada is no Dubai. So I concluded the same thing you did. It has to be an underground reservoir of some kind. Sam found his own supply of water, a subterranean lake, his own private oasis in the middle of a worthless desert. And everyone knows that water in a thirsty, dried up desert is better than gold."

"That son-of-a-bitch," Mark muttered, absorbing the implications.

"That *smart* son-of-a bitch," I corrected him, smiling. Mark Zarillo had taken my bait. My smile grew broader as I thought about Sam. He would be thinking the exact same thoughts about me when Zarillo reported his findings. You may be sly, Sam, I thought to myself with satisfaction and a growing sense of excitement, but so am I.

## Chapter 8

The shiny new Mustang purred like a big female cat in heat, prowling the savannah in search of her ideal Alpha male. It was quite a machine. True to her word, Virginia had picked me up early Tuesday morning for my driving test. By lunchtime I had my California driver's license. She had dropped me off at the showroom where I'd taken final delivery.

I had loved cars from my earliest memories of them. I adored the sparkling, multi-colored miniature replicas of sports cars made by Mattel. The ones called Hot Wheels were my favorite. My love affair had never waned, and now I finally had one of my own.

Mom heard me revving the engine as I rolled up to our flat on Haight Street, right below the bay window next to the breakfast nook. The Mustang was a convertible and I caught her staring out of the window. She had an expression of concern across her face, but for all her trying she couldn't hide the lustful twinkle in her eyes. Smiling mischievously, I waved her to come down.

"Whose car is this, Coco?" she asked guardedly. I was still sitting in the driver's seat.

"Wanna go for a ride?" Not waiting for an answer, I said, "Hop in." She hesitated and frowned. "Come on, Mom. You're not *that* old."

"Who is the owner?" she asked again, getting in.

"You're looking at her." I took off, snapping Mom's head back, telling her to buckle up. Off we went, for a ride on the wild side through the roller coaster streets of San Francisco. Mom held on for dear life, but she was into it. At one red light, a carload of frat boys pulled up hooting and hollering their 'hey-babies'. Mom and I played it cool. We both laughed when the light changed and I peeled out, leaving the college boys in our dust.

Mom had the afternoon off from the mall, where she was the manager of a Brookstone. We drove across the Golden Gate Bridge and slowed as we took an off ramp and finally cruised onto the conservative streets of Sausalito.

Sausalito was a weekend town. This was Tuesday. Parking wasn't a problem, so I picked a spot directly in front of a quaint wine shop. We two girls were going to have one, maybe two, and talk. No one had asked me for an ID. Not lately, at any rate.

"So you and Carl are getting pretty close."

Mom wore a smile of contentment. "It's going well. I want it to work. I think he does, too."

"Duh-uh," I emphasized the second syllable of what I'd made into two, rolling my eyes at the same time.

"Rarely has anything in my life turned out the way I expected it to, sweetheart," she confided in me. "You know how it was. Now..." she thought about it and began again, "Now, I have a hard time trusting it."

"Do you mean Carl?"

"No, no," Mom immediately protested. "Carl's an angel from heaven."

"Then stop doubting things, Mom," I admonished her with kindness, sipping my wine. It was a sunny day for a change. We had chosen a small round wrought iron table set up on the sidewalk in from of the bistro. A diamond danced in my white wine as I held it up to the sun. It was a perfect day; one I wished would last forever. The air was still and crisp. Soon, the weather would change. The Marin Headlands were as predictable as the tides. By late afternoon, the low hanging clouds would roll in off the Pacific Ocean and head up the hills, groping ape-like for each purchase over the rocky cliffs in an unrelenting duty. For now though, we had a ringside seat in utopia.

She looked at me from behind a stylish pair of Ray-Ban knockoffs. "I know you're right, Coco. I'm trying, but I can never seem to shake the sense that disaster is right around the next turn. It's like some kind of horrible boogie man has been stalking us, ready to pounce and deny us any happiness we should come across. I guess our luck has been so bad for so long I've accepted the notion we weren't meant to be happy."

I became concerned. If Mom was depressed, there was no reason for it. Worst of all, I had heard all I needed to know about self-fulfilling prophecies.

"Stop it, Mom! We deserve to be happy more than anyone else I know." I was suddenly pissed off. Yes, we'd had it rough, but we didn't own the franchise on it. Bad things were always happening to good people. The six o'clock news had a field day with those stories. It was how you handled life's adversities that made the difference, though. Like dice on a craps table, sooner or later, luck changed. Ours had. And I was determined it was going to stay this way.

"We have to believe in ourselves, Mom. We've got to believe in the love we have for each other." I was leaning into the small table. Without realizing it, I was pleading with her. "You have to fight those feelings of despair. We deserve this!" I repeated almost angrily, not at her, but at all both of us had been through. "All that crap is in the past. We have to bury it and be done with it. We have to look to the future. Carl is a good man: he has a good heart and he loves you deeply, Mom. He wants to be with you. He wants to marry you."

She grabbed my hand, "Oh, honey, do you really think so?" I sensed tears behind her glasses.

"I do," softening my voice. "I do believe it, and you have to as well. Because it's true."

Mom sighed heavily and let go of my hand. She picked up her half filled glass of wine, twirling it in her dainty, vulnerable fingers, examining it in the sunlight, much as I had done.

"Maybe you're right," she spoke softly, but it broke my heart to see she didn't believe it; she believed instead in the boogie man.

We drove back across the Golden Gate Bridge with the top down, cool moist air whipping in our faces with the big estuary beneath us. Alcatraz was off to our left, a lonely sentinel of past sins, a stark reminder that such deeds never quite disappeared, they just faded into folklore. I only remembered later that Mom never did ask me how I got the car.

School was predictable as the seasons. As my teachers suspected would happen, I caught up quickly, and then passed most everyone. My Ford was a big hit. I enjoyed the camaraderie of my last year in high school immensely. Before I knew it, I was two weeks away from graduating. I was thinking very seriously about which college I would attend the following autumn. It was Saturday morning and I was lying in bed, daydreaming, not tired enough to go back to sleep and too tired to get up, when there was a rap on the bedroom door. It was Mom. She looked worried.

"Coco, there's a limousine out front in the street. A very large black man with no hair is looking at your car."

"Jack!" I squealed with delight, instantly awake. I grabbed for my jeans just as the doorbell rang.

"You know him?" Mom sounded bewildered.

"It's ok, Mom. It's Jack Holliday, my old boss," I could barely contain my excitement. Soon after the bust, I'd received a very official looking letter from Dante's legal counsel warning me not to go near the club. Litigation was pending: blah, blah, blah. I took it seriously, especially after my nights in juvenile hall. I had wanted to see everyone again, especially Jack. I'd sent a big warm hug back with Virginia when we had said our goodbyes after she'd helped me with my license. We agreed to stay in touch, but like many such agreements made with the best of intentions, it had proved a singular emotional moment. I went back to school and Virginia went back to being Chanel. The two didn't have much in common. A week turned into a month, Christmas came and went, and then I was suddenly a couple of weeks away from graduating, never having seen or spoken with my old friends since.

Mom had the apartment's door open when I ran across the living room. I flung my arms around Jack, that monster of a man, doing my best to hold back a tide of tears. I barely got my arms around his huge shoulders but I hung onto him like there was no tomorrow, burying my head into his massive, tuxedo covered chest. Jack, always a man slow to emote, gave in and lifted me off the ground in his own warm brotherly embrace. It must have seemed to Mom like King Kong reuniting with Fay Ray.

"I missed you Jack," My voice was muzzled into his chest in our mutual bear hug. "I'm sorry. I should have called you."

We finally released each other. He was grinning from ear to ear. He looked me up and down, like he was seeing me for the first time.

"I missed you, too, little girl." His eyes squinted then.

"What?" I asked him.

"You've changed a bit, Coco. You look great as always, but much healthier and happier now."

I slapped him on the lapel, just like I used to do at Dante's in the good old days.

"Come on in, you've got time, don't you?"

"A little, yeah. I have to pick up the boss in a little while." He stepped inside, almost brushing both shoulders on opposite door jambs as he moved across the threshold.

"This is my mother, Louise Stevens," I introduced them. "Mom, this is Jack Holliday, one of my best long lost friends who has come by for a visit and a cup of java." My eyes sparked with tiny bolts of electricity. Memories rushed into my mind like a runaway train. I steered Jack into the living room and onto the largest piece of furniture, the sofa. Carl, now a regular and repetitive overnight fixture, had left early for something or other, so it was only the three of us. Mom took my cue and immediately made for the kitchen to work on the coffee. I sat opposite Jack in the room's only La-Z-Boy.

"It's me who should apologize. What's it been? Nine months? I meant to call," he was shaking his head. "You know how it is. There's really no excuse. I always thought about you, little girl, wondering how things went for you." He glanced around the apartment and then back at me. "I'm glad you're ok."

"It's been good, Jack. It's actually been a lot better than I could have hoped for. Mom's in love. I'm happy.

I'll graduate from high school in two weeks." Oddly, I saw he wasn't surprised.

"I'm happy for you, Coco. I hear you got straight A's."

I stared at him, not comprehending. How would *he* know? I guessed he'd just assumed it. I guessed wrong.

Jack leaned into me, speaking more quietly, obviously, so Mom couldn't hear. "The boss would like to see you, Coco. He remembered you from your last night at Dante's," he called it; I guess not wanting to open old wounds by referring to it as 'the bust'.

An image flashed through my mind and my heart galloped ahead of itself, only to run faster when it finally recovered. The face I remembered was that of a handsome movie star, powerful in a strong and quiet way. Sam Spielman was full of mystery. He was looking at me, his eyes fixed on mine. So I hadn't been imagining things. He *had* noticed me. And now, after all this time, he was asking to see me. It was of no consequence he was probably a good fifteen years my senior. Sam had that peculiar countenance that defied aging. He was a very handsome man by anyone's standards.

Mom returned from the kitchen before I had time to reply. Jack accepted the mug of steaming java with gratitude. "Thank you, Ms. Stevens."

"Louise," she smiled. "Please."

"Louise," Jack repeated, smiling warmly.

Mom retrieved our mugs from the kitchen and set them in the center of the coffee table. Lastly she placed a small pewter decanter of cream and a ceramic jar of sugar beside them. Jack, I noticed, drank his coffee black.

There was an awkward silence I used to add cream and sugar to Mom's coffee and then mine.

"So, Mr. Holliday –"

"Jack." He smiled.

"Jack. Coco tells me you were her old employer."

"I was the general manager of Dante's, not the owner."

"My daughter has always spoken highly of you, Jack."

"Flattery," he chided me. I stuck out my tongue at him from behind Mom.

"Are you still employed by him? I'm assuming it *is* a he, of course." Mom seemed to be enjoying our unannounced visitor. Jack had that effect on people, if he cared to. He was a walking dichotomy: at once menacing and massive, yet disarming at the same time. He used his size only when absolutely necessary and that, fortunately, was practically never.

"Yes ma'am, but I'm no longer at the Gentleman's club," he called it. "I'm the owner's chauffeur now," which was a catch-all job meaning Jack was now Sam's personal bodyguard, among other things. Chauffeur? I guessed so. This new position allowed at least the appearance of a more respectable legitimacy to Sam Spielman's public persona. Plus, it made communication between the two of them a whole lot more practical. They probably couldn't risk talking on an open line, given the content of some of their more private conversations.

"Jack's invited me for a ride in the limo," I interjected. Timing was everything. "Mom knows me and cars, Jack."

"Jack is probably busy, Coco."

Jack was waving his hand in protest. "Nothing is going on for probably an hour, Louise. I'd be happy to take her. We'll swing by Fisherman's Wharf and stop for some ice cream." The image of Jack Holliday licking an ice cream cone made me pinch myself so I wouldn't start laughing.

Jack put his almost empty coffee mug on the table and lifted himself out of the sofa. "Thank you for the coffee, Louise. It was a pleasure finally meeting this young lady's mother. She spoke highly of you, too. It would seem the acorn truly doesn't fall far from the tree."

Mom flushed. "It was nice meeting you, Mr. Holliday – Jack. I hope you can come again and stay longer next time."

"That would be nice." Jack's deep sonorous voice seemed to resonate throughout the entire suite, music more than language.

"I'll see you in a while, Mom."

"Remember we are going to Chinatown with Carl this afternoon," she called behind us.

"I won't forget," I said. Mom stared after us as we made for the stairwell adjacent the second floor's mezzanine. I heard the latch click as she finally closed the heavy door, only when we'd disappeared from sight. I could almost be certain she was watching from the bay window in our little breakfast nook as Jack held open the front passenger door for me. We eased out into the flow of traffic and took off down Haight. I didn't look back.

## Chapter 9

"How'd you know I got straight A's?"

"Oh, that. Must have been a slip of the tongue, I guess." I could tell Jack was lying.

"It's me, Jack. Remember?" I said flatly, ticked but not entirely disappointed. I intuited he was following orders. He'd slipped up earlier when he spoke out of turn, a rare blunder but understandable. He'd been happy to see me, though. He'd let his guard down and spoken a little too freely. Now, I was making him pay for it.

Jack looked across the wide bench front seat at me. He laughed, releasing a gust of air through his nostrils.

"I like it when you laugh like that, Jack. It's very becoming. Now fess up or I'll smack you one," I pretended indignation.

"Spielman likes you," he began.

"How can he like me? He doesn't even know me."

Jack examined me from the driver's side, debating how much he should disclose.

"We're friends, Jack. We always will be. What happens in this limo stays in this limo." We stared at each other in silence. He sighed deeply.

"You got the power, little girl. My Mama in Orleans called it the *stupifyan dust*. You've got more than your fair share of it." Jack was shaking his head, probably recalling what happened the last time he'd let me talk him into doing something he wasn't supposed to do. But this time it was different. This wasn't about business; this was personal.

I remained silent, waiting him out, sprinkling my *stupifyan dust* his way fast and hard.

"If you breathe a word of this –"

"I won't Jack," I said with incredible sincerity. "I promise, no matter what."

He nodded. "I believe you, Coco." A car horn blasted from somewhere beside us and Jack made a minor correction back into our lane of traffic.

"Sam's taken a shine to you."

"You mean from that night in Dante's?"

"That's right." He looked at me, his expression grave. "Sam's been…," Jack searched for the right way to put it, "Let's just say he's been keeping an eye on you."

"Is that sort of like he's keeping a file on me?" I was, more than anything, confused.

"Yeah, that's a good way of putting it."

I was quiet for a moment, letting it sink in.

"Are you ok?"

"I think so. That's not stalking, is it?" I asked, not at all concerned if that's what it was.

Jack laughed again. "Sam Spielman doesn't do stalking. He doesn't have to. For some reason known only to him, he likes you. He waited until now to meet you because he wanted you to finish high school first."

"He may not like me once he meets me, Jack," that flutter in my heart had returned with a vengeance. I wanted nothing more right now than to meet him. I was nervous as hell, though. I sat on my hands to hide my trembling fingers.

"Don't sell yourself short, Coco. You're a fine woman, inside and out."

"Thanks. So are you telling me that Mr. Spielman spied on me?" I didn't know whether to feel somehow violated or flattered. What I did feel was flushed. I think, on some level, I must have adored the attention.

"I wouldn't exactly call it spying," Jack quickly jumped to Sam's defense. "He wouldn't do that. Not on you, anyway. It's more like, from time to time, he made some discrete inquiries."

"What do you mean, from time to time?"

"You know. He was interested." We hit a pothole. Jack applied the brakes and we eased to a stop at a red light. I looked out the window on my side. I noticed we were closing in on City Hall. The majestic building looked cold and aloof. Its giant facade towered above its surroundings. We moved northward, across the city.

"Is Mr. Spielman in the Wharf area?"

"He's close, just west of there. Can I give you a piece of advice? I wouldn't call him Mr. Spielman. I don't think he would like it. It might give the boss a complex, you know, the age thing."

"What should I call him?"

"Try Sam," he smiled. "I think he'd like that."

"Are you sure?"

Jack looked at me with a knowing smile. "I guarantee it, Coco."

Sam Spielman's office was nestled in the midst of some pricey real estate between Fisherman's Wharf and the Golden Gate Bridge. It was close enough to San Francisco Bay, yet high enough up the hill to afford a panoramic view that included Alcatraz and Treasure Island. It was rumored the only men to ever escape Alcatraz swam to in a makeshift raft made from rubber raincoats fastened together with glue from the woodshop. I remembered the movie. Clint Eastwood played the main character. In spite of themselves, people seemed to have an insatiable compulsion to root for the underdog, even if he was a rogue. Eastwood, of course, had made it easy to do just that.

"Mr. Spielman will see you now," said Sam's executive assistant, a woman named Yvonne. She was professional and courteous. When Jack first ushered me into the spacious outer office, she acted like my new best friend. This wasn't at all what I expected. It was a world removed from the darkened hustle of Dante's Gentlemen's Club. I didn't realize what Sam used the club for: washing a ton of cash and, of probably equal importance, as his private game park. He was smart that way. It had worked and I was here. I hoped I wasn't part of a harem; I had no ambition to become a wannabe Hefner bunny. If that was going to be the case, I was prepared to take a pass no matter how good the employee benefits plan was.

Jack left the outer office after guiding me into the waiting area. He said he had some business to take care of, and that he would meet me later. Yvonne took over. I followed her through a solid, recessed oak panel door behind her desk and into what I assumed was Sam Spielman's San Francisco office.

Sam sat behind a large, organized desk with his back to us, talking on the phone. The wall Sam faced, as well as the wall to our right, was made entirely of tinted plate glass windows. In the distance, it seemed like I could see all of San Francisco. Sailboats and large container ships dotted the brackish green-gray water, arriving with stories from distant lands, the bigger ships setting out brimming with exports from all across America. From where I stood, the ships seemed like toy boats in a huge bath tub. The sailboats might have been the gleaming colored dorsal fins of large fish swimming to and fro among the strong and unpredictable tides of San Francisco Bay. I remembered reading how a piece of the Bay Bridge, dislodged by an earthquake, had plummeted into the murky Bay waters below. It had finally been found several years later, floating near the surface in Half Moon Bay, many miles down the California coast.

Yvonne offered me a comfortable mahogany colored chair in front of the room's centerpiece, Sam's desk. She glided silently across the deep golden carpet, closing the door on her way out. I gazed around Spielman's office in wonderment. Where the glass left off, recessed oak paneling took over. Lush green ferns and other plants probed the high ceiling, giving the room a living, breathing quality. I felt relaxed and unrestrained at once, as if I was lost on a deserted Caribbean island. There was a wet bar, which I noticed in a large alcove near the door I had entered. Paintings hung strategically about the room, filling the empty spaces between the many plants. My chair swiveled around the room like a slow moving fantastic ride, in a circus from another world. I had never seen anything like this except in magazines. I turned back to face Sam's desk as he began ending his call. He turned to face me. He pointed at the phone and shrugged apologetically.

"That's right, that's what I want. You do that, ok. No. No more. That's right. I gotta go, Teddy. Someone just came in. Yes, she's important. I'd say she's a hell of a lot more important than you are right now," he winked at me. I was suddenly aware I'd come to his office in an old pair of Levi's. They were tight and faded in all the right places. I'd run out of the flat in a pair of sneakers, Adidas, by the three stripes on their sides, and had thrown on a sensible denim shirt over my lacy bra. Self-consciously, I reached up and buttoned the third button. Now only two of the buttons remained open.

"I'll see you at the hotel in Vegas on Wednesday. Good. Tell that gorgeous wife of yours I said hi. All right, Teddy, I'll see you then." He clicked off, sighing, appraising me with eyes that missed nothing. Suddenly I felt like the center of the universe.

"Sorry about that. Politicians," he shrugged. "They always want something." He got up and came around his desk. I got up to greet him. He extended his hand, saying, "I'm Sam Spielman."

"I know," I said, cursing to myself when the words broke in my dry throat. I coughed it away. "I'm Coco Stevens." I felt myself blush.

"I know, too," Sam smiled warmly, wanting to put me at ease. His hand felt warm, and it was softer than I would have guessed. It was smooth, not at all like that of a rough and tumble Oakland dockworker's hands, as I had stupidly imagined. Sam Spielman was the antithesis of the cliché gangster.

He was shorter than I remembered from my last night at Dante's. I guessed he was a shade under six feet. His manner was genteel and warmly gracious. His eyes were as dark as the black onyx pieces of a chess board, emoting a clarity rarely evident in a world of gambling, money grubbing zombies. He was lithe, his expensive dark suit jacket draped across his shoulders like a cape. He dressed impeccably in pricy, chic clothes, but conservatively enough to blend in rather than stand out. The subtle cologne he wore was barely discernible; it was musty, like a forest's floor after a downpour which never quite made it through its canopy to the semi-dried leaves below. His hair matched his eyes. It was combed backwards, the only overt, old school hint of the possibilities which lay hidden behind a cleverly polished veneer of respectability. Sam reminded me of a sleek, shiny King Cobra. He was the master of his domain. He slithered smoothly through the underbrush of his world, fearing nothing and no man, a natural force to be reckoned with and respected.

"I like your office," I offered lamely, imagining I must have sounded trite.

Sam cast a glance around the room, and then back at me. "Thanks. I like it. It's a little small, but it works for me."

"Small?" It was larger than our apartment.

"It's a satellite." He saw I didn't understand. "Our main headquarters is in Vegas. Now *that's* an office. I need a road map just to find the john." I laughed with him. Sam was charisma personified. His essence was mesmerizing. "I've got offices in Los Angeles, New York, London, Frankfurt, and let's see," he was looking at the ceiling, pretending to concentrate, "and we just opened one in Beijing." He smiled triumphantly.

I didn't know what to say, so I muttered, "I'm impressed."

"You should be," he raised his voice suddenly. His eyes bore into mine. They were dark round crystals, blazing brightly from within. "I'm joking," he admitted. "I do that sometimes."

"About your offices?"

"No, I meant you shouldn't be impressed. I do a job. The offices are tools I use to perform my duties."

"Oh, I see," was all I could think to say. And then, "I once lived in Vegas with my parents. We moved after…" I caught myself, and then began again. "My mother and I moved to San Francisco when I was six."

"That was a long time ago," Sam spoke gently. He must have noticed I didn't mention anything about my father, but was polite enough not to say anything. I was glad he didn't.

Sam got up from where he had sat on the edge of his desk after greeting me, a respectable distance from my chair. He walked over to the bar, speaking with his back to me.

"I grew up in Las Vegas. Our family was originally from Sicily. My father immigrated to New York. He came out here in the sixties. He was still a kid back then. He dug in, worked hard, met my mother, and she gave birth to a healthy boy – me."

"How old are you, Sam?"

He turned his head and looked directly at me. Sam had taken the heavy crystal stopper from the top of a decanter of what I thought was probably whiskey. He held the half-filled decanter in his other hand, poised to pour its contents into a glass cup in front of him. He relaxed, turning back to the bar. "I was born in nineteen seventy-three, Coco. I'm thirty-five years old. Does that bother you? You're not afraid of older men, are you?"

"Old is relative, Sam. For what it's worth you look my age."

He turned, two glasses in his hand, and sat back down on the edge of his desk, closer to me this time, and offered me a crystal glass filled with something dark. I took it from his outstretched hand, trusting him more with each passing moment. He noticed me hesitate, albeit ever so slightly.

"Go ahead," he prodded me. "It's straight cola. You're too young to drink alcohol." His eyes sparkled like those long stemmed fireworks you hold in your hand and write with in the sky on the fourth of July. "If I gave you booze they might arrest me for contributing to the delinquency of a minor. Then what? All my friends might accuse me of robbing the cradle."

"I don't see any cradle," I faked like I was looking for one, glancing on either side of my chair. Sam nodded, one of those classic touché gestures.

"You're all right, Coco," he smiled.

"You're not half bad yourself, Sam Spielman," I said, taking a long sip of cola. Ice tinkled musically as it struck the sides of my glass. Sam reached onto the desk behind him and grabbed something. He placed a coaster on the desk directly in front of me, and I set my glass down with a thank you.

There wasn't much of the amber liquid left in Sam's glass. If he'd poured himself a whole ounce of whatever it was over top of his three or four ice cubes, I would have been surprised. He touched the amber to his lips, barely tasting it, and placed the glass on top of another coaster beside mine. Sam preferred quality over quantity.

"Let's go somewhere," he suddenly said, startling me.

I was a little taken back, thinking I already *was* somewhere.

"Let's go down to the Wharf and watch the seals. We'll pretend to ignore the smell." We both chuckled. "After that maybe we can cruise out to Ocean Beach, through Golden Gate Park. We'll stop at the windmill and look at the flower gardens on the way back."

It sounded wonderful, and I almost found myself saying yes. That was until I remembered Mom. I frowned.

"What's wrong?"

"I can't although I'd love to," I quickly added. "But I promised by mother I'd go with her to the market," I whined, scrunching up my face, hoping this absolutely wonderful man would understand.

"You and your mother are close." It was a statement.

"Yeah, we're pretty tight. It wasn't always this way, though. After my father died Mom kind of lost it for a few years. We fought a lot. Mine wasn't a happy childhood."

"I'm sorry." I could see he was.

"Shit happens," I shrugged, showing my age. "We both came around, eventually. I guess now we make it a point to spend quality time together. I guess neither one us wants to backslide."

"I understand. It must have been rough. Losing your father, I mean."

I sighed. "It was, but we're fine now. A lot of things seemed to take a one-eighty right after I got busted."

Sam laughed. "You mean after *we* got busted. They closed down Dante's for three days because of you. It cost the club two hundred thousand dollars that weekend."

I was stunned. Sam's eyes caught the light as the sun finally poked a hole through a persistent patch of cloud cover and the office brightened. His gaze bored into mine. I was hypnotized. "Don't worry. You were worth every penny."

## Chapter 10

Mark Zarillo dropped me off back at the Days Inn. It was another scorcher. At noon it was already a hundred and twelve in the shade. I went straight up to my room. I switched on the television and instantly muted the volume, more from habit than anything else. It was company on my terms: Drew Carey hosting the 'Price is Right', an American pop icon, hawking bauble to what little remained of the fat, ignorant, middle class. I lay across the big double bed and massaged my closed eyelids, thinking.

I liked Mark. But I also knew that in a pinch he would vote with whomever stuffed his wallet. He had said as much when he'd mentioned his mortgage. This didn't necessarily mean he would tell all, but I couldn't take that chance. I'd fed him neutral information. Mine were theories anyone with half a brain could put together. Everything I had told Mark, including my take on the mobile drilling contractors parked down the street, was public knowledge. Even the rights for the air above the land, which included the area above the dried out tributary on the north side of town, could be gleaned from the State's permitting office back in Vegas. Mark would go to Sam. He'd spill his guts because, after thinking it through, he wouldn't see it as a betrayal. But I'd drawn the line before full disclosure about the rest of what I knew. I felt a twinge of guilt, but not enough to bother me. If he ended up being the kind of man I thought he was he would understand later, when it all came down, *if* it all came down. That, I knew, was a mighty big *if*.

Sam called me again in the middle of the afternoon. I was in the motel cafeteria grabbing a late lunch, still thinking about Mark. We didn't talk long. He let me know he'd be flying in on his Gulf Stream. He'd get here around six. There was a small landing strip Sam had ordered cleared not too far from the creek bed. I saw the lone hangar when Mark and I went out there. I told Sam I'd pick him up and that he should call me from the jet if he was going to be late.

The soil samples were a red herring that had accomplished more than I'd intended. Not only had I been able to point Sam the wrong way down the proverbial garden path, but I was now also able to gauge the quality of security which surrounded what, by all outwards appearances, amounted to one more grandiose scheme in the desert by yet another snake oil salesman, in this case Sam. But bugging my car, spying on me at the creek bed, and then breaking into my room showed me the extent to which Sam was willing to go in order to protect his investment. His zeal was a red flag in itself. Spying on me meant Sam was taking great pains to micro-manage and control every aspect of this scenario. The unintended consequence of this was me sharpening my own blade. I was going to have to be a lot more careful from now on if I was to stand even a remote chance of consummating my mad scheme. The more I thought about it, the more outrageous its brevity became. I realized there was a good chance I might end up getting myself killed if I actually went ahead with my plan.

Sam never relaxed. That would be too much to hope for. But as long as he didn't know how much I knew, he would tolerate my meddling. I would amuse him, like a fox trying to get inside a battened down henhouse would an egg farmer.

If I were to believe my intuition, Sam's drilling project was an elaborate and sophisticated ruse designed with one purpose in mind: to raise the necessary capital to implement his real plan. Sam was mounting the diabolical initiative because he was tapped out. He desperately needed money. When I really thought about it, everything made perfectly good sense. Sam had always been heavily mortgaged. In a healthy economy, the acquisition of debt and its corresponding leveraging power to acquire even further debt was actually seen as a sound business practice. That was before.

The United States had recently changed. Even worse, it was still changing. Its present trajectory carried ominous overtones. The poor were still poor, the middle class was decimated, and the rich, as always, were doing just fine.

It had started at the pumps. Gasoline, a relatively stable commodity for all of the twentieth century, had quadrupled in price within the first five years of the twenty-first century. For an oil dependent populace, this spelled trouble with a capital T.

America was designed around interstate highways. In the beginning, as the country pushed ever westward, the huge concrete thoroughfares began as no more than rutted tracks in the mud, sometimes barely discernible as they wound their way over plains and desert alike, interrupted by seemingly impassable rivers and mountain ranges. Over time these sparsely travelled, muddy trails of yesterday became the congested freeways of today. Thanks to the internal combustion engine, the ability to move goods and services across the country became something all too quickly accepted as not only necessary, but absolutely essential in the development of the aspiring brave new world. America prospered and became the most powerful culture to ever visit the planet, both economically and militarily. All of this was accomplished within the paradigm of the apparently limitless supply of fossil fuel. Things began to change quickly as other nations such as China, Japan, and India developed their own unquenchable thirst for oil. Others too drank and became addicted.

Sam hadn't just discovered water in Brittle. He'd found oil. And he had absolutely no desire to share it with anyone else.

His good fortune was a double edged sword. With the price of oil skyrocketing Sam's overhead had gone up as well. Everything he needed to ply his wares moved to market along those same interstates; food that ended up on the buffet tables of his casinos, for instance. The cement and concrete to build with had to be trucked in. It was the same for lumber. Everything was moved to warehouses, and then trucked across the roads to the construction sites by diesel engines thirsty for that costly fuel. And finally, there were taxes to contend with. All things necessary to operate a profitable, multi-national corporation like the one Sam was running had risen in price.

To counter the upwardly spiraling cost overruns, Sam had increased prices. Most of what he was involved in was consumer based. And horror of horrors, the little old ladies who plugged his machines with the corners and edges of their retirement incomes – the very foundation of his empire – had stopped coming to the buffets. They had quite simply run out of money. Of course, not long afterwards, Sam had begun to feel the pinch.

So Sam Spielman had gone out and done what he did best. He had responded to the new threat to his empire by looking for new opportunities. He'd begun buying land through options. He had finally found what he'd been looking for, but not before he'd severely compromised his cash flow position. No one knew it, but Sam was flat broke. At least, he had no cash to speak of.

It was a twisted irony. Sam had become a wildcatter and succeeded beyond his wildest dreams. He'd purchased to what the rest of the world looked like worthless patches of hard baked sand. Then he'd hit pay dirt in Brittle. I couldn't even begin to estimate the potential yield. The big problem was he had no money to extract it.

He couldn't sell the options on all the other little back wood desert communities he'd ended up owning because they were essentially worthless patches of dirt. He would actually have to eat those losses as the non-refundable land options expired.

With Brittle, however, he'd hit the jackpot.

I first learned of this a year ago in Sam's office. It was there, buried in the very last page of the report he'd left on his desk. Not surprisingly, it was right below the section on the air rights over the creek bed. As I glanced quickly through those air rights and wondered why on earth anyone in their right mind would bother to secure them for a resort, the answer was penned in ink in the margin right beneath it. Scrawled by excited, nervous, trembling fingers, barely legible, had been the words: *Estimated five hundred million barrels plus / Seventy-five billion plus.* Sam's ship had come in.

I reread the line because at first it didn't make any sense to me. That was when I heard Sam talking with Yvonne in the waiting area. I scrambled to put everything back in the precise spot I'd found it and barely managed to kiss Sam and pretend that everything was exactly as it had been.

In the months following my discovery, I went on a surreptitious hunt for more details. I learned as much as I could through filings in the Land Titles and Courthouses of the State and County offices. Separately, the bits of information I gleaned meant little and pointed nowhere. Put together and sprinkled with a liberally suspicious mind, they added up to perhaps the cleverest, most well-concealed shell game imaginable. Sam, cash broke and desperate due to circumstances entirely beyond his control, had dreamed up a Mega-Resort in Brittle.

I knew what no one else did, and I had learned it by good old fashioned detective work. I searched the county tax rolls which applied to Brittle and came up with the names of most of the people who had optioned their land to Sam's development company. I paid particular attention to those who owned most of the five by five mile area where I suspected that most of the wells would be drilled. Of course, the field Sam held options on fanned out from the creek bed's epicenter for miles in all directions, just in case the find proved to cover a larger area than initially expected.

Surprisingly few landowners proved to be involved. I had their names and addresses. Most of them lived in Brittle, a town of about thirty-five thousand residents, equivalent to about half the population of Miami Beach, Florida.

Brittle was a small town where everybody knew just about everyone else. Rumors ran rampant about what was coming. Brittle had already become the newest target for land speculators. Most of them came from Vegas, but some from as far away as Oregon and New Mexico had begun to descend upon the small town, hoping to cash in.

The medium price of the quaint, middle class homes had already begun to show signs of the impending mega-development's influence. It had spiked twenty percent since a leaked article hinting at plans for a major development had appeared in the local weekly newspaper, *The Brittle Gazette*.

But Sam had most of the larger tracts sewn up with his options. I'd only needed to place four or five calls to find out the options were expiring before Christmas, and that Sam would have to renew them by then. The holdings were extensive. In order for his plan to work, Sam needed all of the land. He didn't want someone tapping into his find by, say, drilling at an angle from outside his perimeter.

Any real estate owned by the government was administrated by the Nevada Bureau of Land Management. With Sam's connections and political influence, these tracts had been the easiest for him to nail down. They had been secured with long term leases. After all, it was desert. If someone wanted to risk billions on a road to nowhere, there wouldn't be much opposition. The leases had been quietly reviewed, stamped, and approved.

The privately held land in and around Brittle had been more problematic. In Sam's vernacular, this meant more expensive. I'd heard rumors he'd even borrowed from some of his associates back East. I knew these rumors couldn't possibly be true. The boys in New York would want in to stay in if there was even a hint of a windfall. Sam was far too greedy to open that Pandora's Box. He would have raised the funds himself.

He was in a bind now, though. In order to satisfy his looming financial obligations, and continue to move forward with the scheme before anyone found out about what he was *really* up to, he needed access to the money soon.

I was actually surprised he'd been able to keep it a secret along the way. Only for as long as it took me to fully appreciate how cunning he was.

All Sam had to do was to maintain the facade. He'd convinced his investors, and Wall Street, that he'd found water. In and of itself, this was more than enough to set them drooling. It was so huge that no one would ever think to look under it, literally. Because that's where the black gold was – under the aquifer – kept there by geological forces I barely grasped.

The hydrology reports would have been accurate and more than adequate to withstand the scrutiny of independent analysis. The seismographic readings, all certified by geologists and scientists hand-picked by Sam, would have shown what Sam wanted them to show. If any of those scientists saw something that piqued their interest, aside from what they were supposed to be looking at – the water – well, they all had families. And Sam's tentacles reached everywhere. So, at least for the time being, his secret was safe.

The inquiries I'd made to the private landowners had been more than discreet. I'd insulated myself with a half dozen lawyers who didn't know each other. The lot of them had been instructed to use local realtors. There had been three landowners, and by the time they were asked about their land and the options on it held by Sam, even close scrutiny would barely reveal that yet another interested party from somewhere out of California was looking for some quick bucks with an even quicker flip. My secret was also safe, at least for the time being.

The only thing I had yet to figure out was, not surprisingly, the hard part. How was I going to squeeze Sam so that I could steal the land options he so desperately needed out from under him? If he found out it was me, well, I just didn't want to go there anytime soon.

# Chapter 11

I squinted to spot the sleek private jet as it made its almost soundless approach from the west, sinking smoothly as its white body and art deco blue markings suddenly materialized out of the pale azure sky behind it. Selling it would buy Sam some time, I mused, but the transaction would take time he didn't have. Besides, it wouldn't bring nearly the amount of cash he now so desperately needed.

Sam's pilot brought the thirty million dollar aircraft in for a pinpoint landing. The jet taxied in the direction of where I was standing, in front of my Chevy which was parked close to the hangar. The fifty-seven Bel Air looked as if it had burst into flames, its metallic green blazing in the reflecting sun. To Sam, this must have looked from his window in the air like a million glass crystals on fire. I knew he thought the Chevy was tacky and I knew it was cliché, but I loved it anyway.

The jet pulled up to within twenty feet of where I was standing. I heard several dull thudding sounds as the stair latch disengaged. The stairway lowered away from the body of the Gulf Stream. Sam appeared in the doorway shielding his eyes, momentarily blinded by the sun's brilliance. He smiled when he saw me, and climbed down from the jet to greet me.

Our eyes melted into each other's, and for an instant I could almost forget. We kissed, long and deep, before coming up for air.

"I missed you, baby," Sam's throat was dry. I picked up a hint of scotch on his breath. He'd been drinking more than usual lately, but I'd still never seen him drunk. His eyes were the same clear, dark crystals. His loose white cotton shirt caught in a sudden gust of breeze and billowed like a sail in the wind. He wore jeans and a pair of comfortable hiking shoes. This wasn't the office, after all.

"I missed you too," I told him.

He raised his eyebrows, motioning to my car. "I see you've still got the Chevy."

"It beats the hell out of a yellow taxi cab."

"As long as the AC works, I'm not complaining. Let's get out of this heat."

The car's wide rubber tires barked like an injured dog on the tarmac surface. I peeled away from the lonely terminal and headed towards town. Sam didn't say anything as we drove down the service road and passed the spot where Zarillo and I had gone off-road and had entered the dry creek bed. If he noticed at all he ignored it, looking ahead.

We were both hungry so we stopped at an Italian restaurant on the Main Street named Napoli's. It was the best Brittle had. Sam ordered wine and an appetizer; we stared at each other in awkward silence across the red cotton tablecloth, and through a tall flute of long stemmed roses the owner had wrangled from who knew where. Placida Domingo sounded his usual amazing self in the background. Two murals depicting a Venetian canal, resplendent with gondoliers and their lovelorn passengers splayed out in the hulls of the boats that had been painted across the entire two sidewalls of the restaurant. The room was perhaps one third full. The mostly elderly couples spoke in muted, reserved conversations which could not be understood above the renowned opera singer's voice drifting from somewhere above the murals.

"I don't like it that you don't trust me." I brought my gaze back around to Sam. His expression didn't change.

"Have I given you a reason?" I attacked him, suddenly spoiling for a fight.

Sam looked sideways, toward the back of the restaurant, sighed, and returned his gaze to me. He looked tired.

"I didn't come here to fight with you, Coco."

"My question stands." He wasn't getting off the hook that easily. He sighed again, glancing once more at the kitchen and the bar area beside it. He looked relieved when he spotted our waiter on his way with the wine.

We remained silent while the waiter popped the cork, and poured a sample. Sam waved for him to fill the rest of the glass, and mine as well. If the wine had turned Sam would have sent it back, but the Cabernet Sauvignon was excellent. The waiter bowed subserviently and left quickly.

"All right," Sam said, resigning himself to the inevitable. "Where shall I begin?"

"So you've got a list, then," I said, petulance staining my tone.

"What were you doing out in the middle of that creek bed yesterday? Taking what, soil samples of all things?"

"What were you doing spying on me? Why did you bug my car?"

"I was only concerned for your safety."

"That's bullshit and you know it," I raised my voice.

"Calm down, all right? We can at least be civilized about this."

"I don't like it when I'm spied on, Sam. It's a no class move."

Sam leaned forward, resting his palms on the table. "I've got a lot on my plate right now, Coco. I can't keep an eye on everyone. For what they do, my security is the best in the world. They were following orders. You shouldn't take it so personally because it isn't about you. You came onto the radar screen. They were just following protocol, sweetheart. I didn't tell them to go after you and no one singled you out."

"You're telling me you had nothing to do with it?" I accused him.

"I hired them, but no one singled you out. They're extremely thorough. Sometimes, baby," he reached for my hand across the table and I let him hold it in his, "they can be a little overzealous. It was an innocent mistake. They see numbers, not people. You know how that is."

I didn't believe him. "Nathaniel Katz had nothing to do with this?"

"Nate? No – of course not. He's a lawyer, not security."

"He's a card carrying member of the Nazi Party as far as I'm concerned." I pouted.

Sam chuckled at the inadvertent irony. He brightened as he saw I was beginning to thaw. Some of the heavier lines that had recently appeared around his eyes and across his forehead receded with his smile.

"We go back a long way, don't we?" he spoke softly.

"Yeah, we do, Sam."

"What's happening to us, Coco? We never fought like this before."

I shrugged, still uncertain of Sam's motives. "You're working too hard, Sam: Russia last week, Hong Kong on Tuesday, New York on Wednesday, two days in Los Angeles, the weekend in Vegas, and now here. Why? It's going to kill you. It's going to kill *us*, Sam."

He let go of my hand as the waiter returned with the appetizers, this time accompanied by a man who appeared to be the chef. The waiter left and the chef, wearing a stained white apron, introduced himself as the owner.

"It is an absolute honor to meet you, Mr. Spielman," he gushed in a thick Italian accent. "I make a special dinner for you; my secret sauce. It has been in my family for five generations – since back in Sicilia."

"You honor me, sir," Sam spoke with no accent. "Grazie," he politely dismissed the man. The chef bowed, all smiles, assuring us if we wanted anything at all, we need only to ask.

"I've always gone away. I always come back. You used to not mind."

"I'm older now, Sam. We both are. A person's priorities can shift."

"You're not pregnant?" suddenly Sam was concerned.

"Maybe I should be," I answered him. He instantly looked relieved. "Would that be such a bad thing?"

"Your agent would have a hemorrhage. Pregnant sex symbols don't do so well at the box office."

"What about you, Sam?" I ignored his humor. "How would it make you feel if I had one in the oven?"

"I've never really given it much thought. Why? Do you want a baby?"

"No, that's not why I asked." I could see in his eyes, he was thinking that women made no sense at all. Maybe we didn't to men, but that was our prerogative. *We* knew what we were talking about.

"Look," he continued, "I'm sorry I haven't been around a whole lot lately. I've been really busy putting this deal together. It's very…" He searched for the right word, "It's very involved. There's a lot that can go wrong if I don't stay on top of things. It's not forever. Hump time is coming up in a few months." I knew he was referring to the renewal options. "When I nail it down how about if we go somewhere together? It'll be the two of us, just like before."

"Just like the old days," I said. My tone was as flat as my tire had been on the road into town yesterday.

"No problem, we'll take a cruise or something. Remember when we went to Africa?"

"Yes, I remember," I brightened somewhat. And then I smiled.

"I took you on that safari right after your second year at Sacramento State."

"It was my third year."

"Your third year, that's right!" he stabbed at the air in front of us. "You were like a kid in a candy shop when we first stepped off that plane in Kenya."

"It was the time I rode the elephant." I had to admit, the memories were good ones. They took me back to a time of innocence, a time when I believed in the things I saw and what people said. Like Sam, who told me things that warmed me inside, like hot chocolate in front of the fireplace on a freezing winter's night, the wind kicking and scratching at the front door. Sam had made me feel safe. That was before. This, I reminded myself, was now. And that made all the difference in the world.

## Chapter 12

Jack Holliday drove me back to Haight through San Francisco. We had a conversation, me up front with him in the long black limo, but all I could think about was the hour I'd spent with Sam Spielman. That was like a dream.

Even though he was older than me by eighteen years, he had never seemed that way. The conversation never dragged. By the time I had to leave both of us were sorry to see it end. We'd gotten to know each other better, it seemed, than most people did in a much longer time. Yes, I had to admit, it probably had been love at first sight. I found myself tingling all over; already looking forward to our next meeting which I secretly hoped would turn into our first official date. Sam said he would call me during the week. I didn't know how I could last that long.

Seeing Jack again had been great, and I knew we would now see a lot more of each other. I gave him another giant bear hug when we got back to the apartment, kissed him on the cheek, and bounded up the front walkway to the door. I turned, just in time to see him look back before he climbed into the limo. I blew him one more kiss. He smiled and waved, shaking his head in wonderment, reminded one more time at what young love looked like.

Mom was waiting for me upstairs. I splashed some water on my face in the bathroom and met her at the front door. We took my car. I didn't mention I'd been with Sam for some reason, I didn't think she would understand. I was her little girl. I didn't think she would ever see me as my own woman. I may have only been seventeen, but I'd felt a whole lot older than my age for several years.

The next afternoon when I arrived home from school, Mom met me at the front door. She had a slightly bewildered look on her face. I could see why when I looked over her shoulder. They were hard to miss. I walked into what could have passed for a small flower shop. The entire front hall was ablaze with a magnificent rainbow of colors, every combination of flowers available in San Francisco. The musky, sweet odors almost picked me off the floor. My mouth dropped open as I staggered inside. I looked all around me – flowers were everywhere – from ceiling to floor, like multi-colored magical waterfalls. I looked back at my mother and I couldn't speak.

"There's a note," she said, handing me a small, white, envelope, gold letters spelling my name embossed across the front if it.

I gulped, finally managing a hoarse croak that came out more like the high notes on a rusty harmonica. "They're for me?" I couldn't believe my eyes. "Who…?" I looked lamely at the note, then the flowers, and then I broke into a wide grin that stretched forever as tiny electrical pulses exploded inside my stomach. "Sam", I whispered in awe. My hands were shaking as I fumbled to open the envelope.

"Who's Sam?" Mom managed to say, rhetorically.

The paper inside the envelope was shaking like a broken filament in a spent light bulb as I hungrily read the hand written note:

*Looking forward to a long and prosperous relationship.*
*Sam-*

"Who is Sam?" Mom was definitely talking to me now. This was, after all, more the kind of attention she'd wanted but never received. She wasn't jealous or envious in any way, but she was curious.

I handed her the note. She read it, a couple of times, seeming even more bewildered. "Who's Sam?" she asked for the third time, a hint of a conspiratorial smile beginning to form at the corners of her mouth. "He's surely not someone from your school."

"He's definitely not someone from school." I told her everything about Sam, there among the flowers. I was surprised at her reaction. Of course she played the concerned parent, but I could see she was genuinely happy for me, too.

It was right about then that Carl walked in. His reaction to the flowers was about the same as mine had been. There were a few more 'Who's Sam?' queries and then Mom finally suggested we get some water for the flowers.

Sam and I started seeing a lot of each other after that. I think we became 'an item' soon after my eighteenth birthday, about two months after I graduated high school. A polite way of saying we started sleeping together. And just like the song says, 'mother what a lover' Sam was. The only difference being *I* wore *him* out, not *Maggie May*.

I picked Sacramento State because it was close to San Francisco. Sacramento was a fast hour and a half east on I-80, more like two if I took the roads through Napa

Valley. I could visit Mom on the weekends and Sam too, when he was in town.

Someone once said life is what happens while you're making plans. I was too busy living to make any. I just let things unfold, like flower petals in spring.

I stayed busy, burying myself in the books. I soaked up knowledge in a wide array of subjects. I majored in Business, but was oddly fascinated with geology: the aging of the earth, rock formations, erosion, subterranean caverns and eventually oil and gas formations. Unwittingly, I was laying the groundwork for the twists and turns the road map of my life would end up taking years later. I had no idea where these studies would lead me to, and didn't really have any time to think about it. I was on a busy, wild roller coaster, and there was no getting off.

The years passed too quickly. Summers were mostly spent with Sam, whenever he wasn't travelling on business trips. We fell deeper and deeper in love.

Mom and Carl stayed together. They married halfway through my third year, on a crisp January morning. It was a lovely ceremony attended by twenty-three of their closest friends. Unfortunately Sam was out of town and couldn't be there. Somehow I found it in me to throw off my melancholy. It was Mom's day. I wished for nothing more than her and Carl's happiness, but I couldn't stop thinking about Sam. When Mom finally said 'I do', I couldn't help imagining that I was her and Carl was Sam, looking deep into my eyes, losing himself inside of *my* soul.

Sam did make my graduation ceremony at the end of those three years. He said Jack made quite a stir as they sat in one of the back rows next to Mom and Carl. Probably close to a thousand people kept stealing sidelong glances in their direction. Jack and Sam, if they noticed, ignored them and concentrated on me. All four of them stood and cheered, applauding wildly with the rest of the graduating class when my name was called. I hadn't planned it that way, but my Mustang and I had become very popular among the rest of the students. Earlier, they had elected me class Valedictorian. I'd spent hours of work on a lengthy speech, only to chuck it when I reached the podium. I spoke from my heart, unrehearsed and genuine. They appreciated it and gave me – and themselves a standing ovation. The cheers were deafening. I looked to the back of the room and fought back my own tears when I saw Mom blow her nose into a handkerchief. Jack was all a toothy grin. I could almost hear him saying, "Way to go, little girl." Sam winked, applauding with the rest of them. My heart melted in the abundance of love aimed in my direction.

When the final speech and the ceremonies ended, I waded through the hugs, kisses and 'we'll-stay-in-touches' until I found myself among my family and Jack and Sam. Mom began crying again as we hugged. She was happy I had accomplished something she'd never had the opportunity to do. I hugged Carl and Jack warmly, saving Sam for last. We embraced and he kissed me a little longer than etiquette would call for, a hint of the private celebrations to come later that night.

"You did well, sweetheart. I'm proud of you," Carl said.

"All of us are," Mom chimed in.

"You guys gotta cut this out," I said, feeling all warm and fuzzy inside. I hung onto Sam's shoulder, his arm around my waist. "You're going to make *me* cry."

Later that night, Sam and I flew to Vegas. We stayed in the penthouse of his big casino, dining on steak and lobster. We stripped down to nestle into the outdoor hot tub afterwards. Sam reached over his shoulder and poured us another glass of Dom. The lights of the city cast a romantic glow over the balcony. The stereo played softly in the background. We were thirty-nine floors above the Strip. We might as well have been in heaven. Sam handed me one of the glasses. I sipped and leaned my head back onto the side of the hot tub. I stared up at the stars. The distant sound of a jet either taking off or coming into McCarran could be heard just above Dean Martin's rendition of 'That's Amore'.

"Penny for your thoughts," Sam brought me back from somewhere between Alpha Centuri and the Big Bear.

I moved over and snuggled my head into the crook of his shoulder, just under his chin. The boiling turbulent water of the hot tub made every movement sluggish and deliberate. I wanted to stay there forever. One of the jets tickled my leg with its roiling bubbles. I inched closer to Sam, and moved my leg over his.

"Happy?"

"Very," I purred. "You?"

"Life is good. Elvis said it best: 'With wine on your lips and money in your pocket, and your sweetheart in your arms, you're rich as you can be.'"

"Who's Elvis?" I grinned.

He splashed water onto my face. "Don't be a smartass."

"Sam?"

"Yeah Coco."

"Where do we go from here?" I said cautiously.

He put his glass down and reached for the ashtray with his dry hand. He lit a perfectly rolled joint, deeply inhaling the rich pungent smoke. It was a one hitter – the best. He held it to my lips and I did the same. Almost instantly I began to feel a different kind of warmth than the hot tub produced. The senses in my body began to explode. Everything began to exaggerate itself. The music, now a haunting acoustic version of 'Somewhere Over the Rainbow' by the late, great, Hawaiian singer IZ, sounded like the saddest most inspiring music in the world.

"Sam?" I said softly.

"Uh-huh?"

"You didn't answer my question."

There was a long silence. Sam finally said, "I got you a present." My heart began to race. "You see those envelopes over there on the table by the bed?"

I looked past the patio's large sliding doors and into the darkened bedroom. I barely made out what appeared to be two letter-sized white envelopes where he'd indicated.

"Yes," I said, my tongue tingling from the taste of marijuana, "On the table next to the bed."

"We're going on a trip to celebrate your graduation."

I scrunched up my nose. It wasn't quite what I had hoped for.

"Where are we going?"

"Africa – Kenya. We're taking a safari, babe."

"As in wild tigers and lions, and those obnoxious little monkeys swinging from the treetops?"

"They're not exactly little."

"The young ones are. The baby ones, I mean."

"They're not all babies, sweetheart."

"Africa," I said, not sure what to think.

"Africa," Sam repeated, finality in his voice.

We took off from McCarran at noon the next day. I didn't know it at the time, but the trip would hurtle us both headlong onto a course which would change our lives forever.

## Chapter 13

We stopped in Miami to refuel and pick up a fresh team of pilots, then again in London to refuel once more. The flight itself didn't seem long at all. Of course the bar was well stocked, the weed was excellent, and Sam must have had over two hundred movies in his collection, not to mention the onboard array of music. The back of the jet had been turned into a very comfortable bedroom, and we used it to full advantage on the way to Africa. There was something about making love thirty-five thousand feet in the air, stoned immaculate among the stars, Jimmy Morrison mournfully crooning the lyrics to 'Moonlight Drive' with the jet's twin Rolls Royce engines droning backup on the bed track.

We finally landed in Kenya on April twenty-sixth. The hotel was the best one Sam could find in the capitol city of Nairobi. It certainly wasn't Vegas, but it was nice. A whole lot of bamboo furniture was sprinkled liberally throughout the front lobby. Most everyone was black, everybody seemed to speak English, and all of them seemed to smile a lot. They were really friendly, probably in no small way a function of their tips. A large fan rotated slowly above the lobby's center. The valets did everything. By the time our suitcases were brought to our room, Sam and I were suddenly exhausted. It was two o'clock in the morning; we'd had been up for most of the last twenty-six hours. We didn't even get undressed. We passed out on a very comfortable bed under a large screened in window in less than five minutes.

"Get up sleepy head."

Sam groaned and rolled over. He covered his head with a pillow. I tickled him under his arms.

"All right, I'm up," he protested lamely. His eyes were a little bloodshot, but he was awake. "Is that coffee I smell? What time is it?" he grunted.

"It is coffee. We're in Kenya, and it is eleven-thirty in the morning Kenya time. The animals have been up for five hours."

"Yeah well they didn't just fly halfway around the world, did they?"

"Neither did we."

He looked up at me. His eyes asked me what the hell I was talking about. I was nude. He was disheveled, but coming around fast.

"The pilot did," I smiled mischievously. "C'mon Sam, get up! The day's half over."

"Do you realize this is the first vacation I've taken in over ten years?" he whined.

"That's why we can't waste it. Now come on," I emphasized the last two words. "It's beautiful out on the porch."

"Who made the coffee?"

"Moi. I sent the maid packing an hour ago."

"I'm hungry," he said, sitting up. He rubbed his face, and then tossed his hair. It was a mess. "Did you order breakfast?"

"As a matter of fact, I did. They dropped it off ten minutes ago."

"Now I smell it. The coffee was overpowering it. Did you order eggs?"

"Straight from the ostrich, and the biggest bowl of fruit you can imagine. I've moved them onto the veranda, Sam. It's private. I want to eat breakfast with no clothes on. I'll be the waitress. See?" I held up a small white lace apron. It wasn't going to hide much, in fact nothing at all in the back.

"I'm up, Coco."

"I can see that, baby. I guess breakfast can wait a little while longer. The eggs will get cold, though."

Sam grabbed my arm and pulled me back into bed. "I won't complain. Now get back in here."

The hotel guests were an eclectic, at times eccentric group, of about thirty five people with entirely too much money. We had all come from every corner of the globe to see a part of the world like no other. The sunsets and sunrises across the Kenyan veldt were worth the ticket prices by themselves. The wildlife, though, was the country's jewel. Most of the guests had come for this specific reason. We would hunt the wild game. I was relieved to find out none would be killed though. We were shooting with cameras, not guns.

The next photo opportunity was near sunset. The early risers had gone out before sunrise. Sam and I spent the afternoon lounging by the large screened-in pool area, which was directly adjacent the restaurant adjoining it. Three or four sets of sliding glass doors had been pulled apart to remove the barrier between the two, creating one continuous area. The air conditioning ran constantly. Fans dotted the ceiling of the dining room. The cold air in the dining room waged a constant war with the invading African heat. A fine mist of cold vapor sprayed out from an overhead pipe which delineated the two temperature zones. When it became too hot, as summer came closer, the hotel staff would shut the system down and close the sliding glass doors. For a few months Mother Nature would be victorious. Now, at the end of April, it was sunny and partly cloudy beyond the charcoal colored pool screens. It was eighty-eight degrees in the shaded pool area where Sam and I reclined. We both wore dark sunglasses. For the moment I had on a wide brimmed, cheesy straw hat that looked more like a Mexican sombrero than something that belonged poolside in Kenya. The afternoon was teasing the dinner hour. We noticed the restaurant get busier. The participants of the early morning safari had returned. Some guests ate in their rooms; like we had this morning, but most preferred mixing among others they adjudicated to be part of their own kind. We may have been on a holiday, but status was not.

"Are we going on safari tonight?"

Tiny beads of perspiration, like fine dew on a morning lawn, trickled between the dark hairs on Sam's chest. "I overheard them say it was cancelled. We probably wouldn't have seen much," he guessed. "From what I've been able to pick up, we go out on those caged army vehicles parked out front."

"I saw them."

"Did you see the big spotlights mounted over their windscreens?"

"I bet they light up the savannah like daytime," I said.

"We can go out tomorrow night if you'd like," Sam sensed I wanted to go. "But for sure in the morning."

I knew Sam wouldn't have a problem rising at five the next morning. He was a workaholic. I guessed he slept about five hours a night when he was working. I smiled, thinking I was the reason that he'd recently moved his wake up call to more like seven.

"I'll tell the concierge we're going. I wouldn't want them to leave without us," I volunteered.

We lolled around the rest of the day and into the evening, sticking mostly to ourselves. The other guests, sensing our desire for privacy, left us alone. I recognized a couple of actors and a model or two, and marveled at what a small word it had become. But the rich and famous held membership in a small club. They frequented many of the same spots in isolated, out of the way locations across the globe. Almost all of them lusted after the privileges success and fame garnered – the adoring adulation – but that notoriety, by its very nature, demanded quiet down time. This necessitated exclusive, private safe houses like this one, where they could kick back and relax and not have to worry about autograph seekers or the dreaded paparazzi.

By a quarter to five the following morning, about a dozen stalwarts – no actors – had accumulated in the hotel's main lobby. Sam and I brought up the rear, stifling yawns, still fighting a nagging case of jet lag. All present and accounted for, a much too awake and cheerful guide dressed in green khaki shorts and matching shirt led us out to a vehicle in front of the hotel. We climbed aboard and headed out. The vehicle resembled a cross between a cutaway version of an oversized Hummer and a swamp buggy which I'd once seen used in the Florida Everglades. The row of halogen lights, mounted on top of the roof, were switched on the moment we left the road on the outskirts of town. The lights cut a swath in front us, exposing the well worn ruts of the dirt road.

We ambled our way between low lying brush and shrubs of varying heights. The road winded its way ever farther into a hostile and primitive landscape. We rattled and bounced across the landscape for perhaps an hour or more in a restless silence. The sky was beginning to turn a lighter shade of purple and blue near the eastern horizon. All but the brighter stars were melting into the rising light as the earth rolled relentlessly forward on its axis.

In the seat across the aisle from me, I noticed a man I had first seen in the lobby. He was screwing a large lens onto the front of a Pentax camera in preparation for the sights soon to behold. He caught me looking and smiled. He appeared to be in his late thirties. He wore a gray flecked beard and silver, metal rimmed glasses. His full, bushy hair bounced wildly every time we hit a rut. He stowed the camera in a basketball-sized canvass carry-on bag, and then extended his hand across the aisle.

"Michael King," he introduced himself. His eyes twinkled in the semi-darkness.

"Coca Stevens," I shook hands with him. "And this is Sam Spielman," I introduced Sam, who sat near the barred window on the bench beside me. Sam nodded and said hello.

"Sam Spielman?" Michael concentrated. "Where have I heard that name before?" he fought to remember.

"I don't know," said Sam, confident they'd never met.

"Oh well, I'm sure it'll come to me later."

"Probably when you least expect it," said Sam.

"Are you a photographer?" I asked him.

"I tinker with it."

"Mr. King does more than tinker with it, Coco."

Michael King registered surprise.

"Who doesn't read the swimsuit edition of *Sports Illustrated*?" Sam confessed. "Sweetheart, you're looking at probably the world's premiere photographer of the most gorgeous women in the universe. Isn't that right, Michael?"

"They do all the work," Michael returned with humility. "I just capture on film what nature provides me."

"You're much too modest," Sam retorted. "Without you there wouldn't be the girls."

"I suppose we need each other," he confessed, again with modesty.

I suddenly realized everyone on the tour with a camera was probably world class. It's why they'd come here. Kenya was breathtaking. As if on cue, the sky had moved from the purple hue of a few minutes ago to a rich blood red blanket which now lay across the edge of the horizon.

"Are you scouting a location?" I asked him.

Michael shook his head, "No, at least not in that sense. I'm here more for the pure enjoyment than anything else, I suppose. My cameras and I have been married to each other for over twenty-five years," he joked. "The first one I owned was back in grade school. I've never been without one since. For this trip, I have decided to use good old fashioned film rather than digital imagery. This is the third time I've been to Kenya. I fell in love with Kenya the first time around and I've never tired of the landscape. It's a fantastic location," he admitted, his attention divided between us and the inexorably rising sun. "It's like looking into the eyes of God," he proclaimed. "I can take pictures, and they help me to remember, but this camera can never capture all of it."

"It?" I asked.

"I mean the true essence of the beauty around us. Sadly, it's the beauty most of us take for granted. Most of us walk through this world with blinders on, unappreciative of the magnificence bestowed upon us by our maker. We wage war in the beautiful jungles. We raze those same jungles, destroying everything that gets in the way because pastures are needed to raise cheap beef for the hamburgers we eat that make us fat and sick. We stare into the eyes of experience and see worn out old people instead of our enlightened selves."

"You sound bitter," Sam interjected.

Michael stopped. "I didn't mean to lecture, I'm sorry. I just see so much waste. It hurts me. I wish it was different. I've often wondered why God didn't make all of us a tiny bit smarter. Not geniuses, mind you. We've already got our fair share of those. But I wish everyone was smart enough to understand what we're doing to this tired old world of ours. We don't have another one, you know. This is it. If we ruin it, there's no replacement."

"So you take pictures," I said, "of women."

"In bathing suits, in places like this one to remind people what's at stake."

Sam pointed out, "I don't think they buy the swimsuit issue for the background scenery."

"Maybe not," Michael agreed, "but I can still try, can't I?"

The vehicle slowed, slewed sideways over a mound of dirt, and stopped on the flat bed of soil beyond the hump.

"Looks like we have arrived," Michael said.

"Yeah, but where?" I looked out through the truck's barred windows.

The driver, our guide, got out of the seat behind the steering wheel. Gone was any hint of levity. He was serious now. "For the newcomers among us," he began, "I am Joseph Sangari, your guide and your protector. Momentarily we will be going outside for a few pictures. We are in the middle of a migration area. Please stay close to the vehicle. The animals which use this migration route are food for other animals. We are now in their world. We are also a part of the food chain. In other words, the lions you will see today have been known to eat people. That means, if you give them the opportunity, they will eat one of you." He paused, letting his eyes come to rest on each of us. "I am glad I have your attention. Please be careful. When you are outside the vehicle you are extremely vulnerable. Be alert. If you hear me blow on this," he showed us a large silver whistle which hung on a string from around his neck, "please – for your own safety – return to the vehicle quickly and orderly." He looked at us again, to be certain we were still listening. He needn't have bothered with me. I was bug-eyed and my heart was pounding rapidly in my chest. I was scared. I glanced at some of the others. A couple of other guys with cameras looked bored. They were obviously seasoned and, like the speeches on commercial airliners just before takeoff, they'd heard it all before. Michael King smiled reassuringly. A couple in their early thirties clung to each other near the back bench of the truck.

"Are there any questions? No? Good. Stay Close. Take all the pictures you like and remember, if I blow this whistle, move quickly back inside the vehicle. Don't panic. Just get back in here." He looked at each of us again. "Okay, follow me."

One by one, we stepped out of the truck and onto the wild Kenyan savannah. I silently prayed none of us would be eaten. Michael King, together with four others, began to set up tripods. In the rising red sky of pre-dawn their dark silhouettes possessed a strange, ethereal quality, as if they were more spirit than men. The tripods began to resemble eerie, dormant three legged spiders, cameras mounted in place of their heads. Would the sun wake them? I imagined them beginning to move, coming alive, their spindly pointed appendages digging into the dusty soil beneath us as they clawed their way toward the truck, Joseph blowing shrilly on his whistle the whole while.

The beautiful morning spent itself quickly without incident. A large herd of antelope, followed by lumbering water buffalo, came and went. We saw giraffes snacking from the upper reaches of tall acacia trees in the distance. Michael allowed us a closer view through his powerful telephoto lens. It was amazing to study these animals I'd either only read about, seen on television or, sadly, in zoos. They belonged here, free to roam the African steppes and live out their lives as God intended, not in cages for man's entertainment. In zoos, I began to understand, these beautiful wild creatures were reduced to a pitiful sideshow. They lined the pockets of carnival barkers who, in their selfish arrogance, looked to squeeze every cent they could from the enslavement of these noble beings.

We witnessed, finally, a hunt. We watched in horrible fascination as a skilled pride of lions worked in tandem to bring down a young buffalo. Like a traffic accident we wanted to turn away, but were instead riveted – hypnotized – as the age old life and death struggle unfolded about a mile from where we stood watching. The older male buffalos put up a valiant, losing battle to save their young. Two particular buffalos would charge dangerously with their lethal horns aimed like missiles, and charge the lioness hunters which had cornered the hapless young bull. The female lions would retreat only to regroup and then pounce again. Their attacks were relentless. Back and forth the struggle played itself out. Finally, inevitably, the spent young buffalo succumbed, its elders moving aside, their diminished intelligence only dimly aware it was finished. Death was a very large part of life, and one could not exist were it not for the other. I wondered how long their primitive minds would miss their offspring, or if they did at all.

As riveting as the hunt had been, no one wished to stay and watch the prey being devoured. We were emotionally spent. Wordlessly, the photographers packed up their cameras and stowed their expensive lenses. The tripods were folded away. One by one in silent consensus, as if leaving a funeral, we filed back into the truck. Exhausted, Sam and I said very little to each other during the ride back to the hotel. Our guide, too, lapsed into an introspective silence soon after several unsuccessful attempts to elicit conversation from two of the cameramen nearest him. I'm sure all of us were thinking the same thing: What had the young buffalo felt when the lions had begun to eat it while it was still alive? I shuddered, picturing a human in its place.

## Chapter 14

Sam was on the phone. In all fairness, I couldn't have expected him to completely sever the long umbilical cord that attached him to his business interests. I had changed into one of my thong bikinis. I kissed him on the cheek, he mouthed the words I love you, and I headed out our room's front door in search of a comfortable poolside wicker recliner.

I'd been soaking up some rays for a half hour when a familiar voice asked, "Mind if I join you?"

I opened my eyes beneath the pair of dark sunglasses I had on and stared into the smiling face of Michael King. I gestured to the recliner on the other side of a small table next to mine. Happy to see him, I said, "Of course you can. I'd love the company."

"Sam not up yet?" he asked conversationally as he unfolded onto the wicker furniture. He was too white. He wore a dark blue pair of boxer swimming trunks. Yellow surfers hung ten all over the front and back of them.

"Oh, he's already been up for a couple of hours." A smiling cabana boy appeared out of nowhere. I ordered a Virgin Mary; Michael got himself a gin and tonic. We toasted nothing in particular. I sipped at the Virgin Mary. By now the staff knew exactly how much Tabasco sauce I liked. I smiled with satisfaction.

"He's taking care of business." It was a statement, not to be rebutted.

"I see," Michael's tone was absent of judgment. He changed the subject. "I've been meaning to ask you something. I just never found the time."

"Please do, Michael," I encouraged him, suddenly interested. I peeled off my sunglasses.

"What did you think of the lions?"

I thought back to three days ago. "You mean the hunt." I shivered involuntarily. "I haven't had a good night's sleep since. It was so," I searched for the right words, "savage, almost prehistoric. I don't ever want to see something like that again for as long as I live."

Michael started to say something and I interrupted him. "I *know* it's what they do and it's how they survive. I'm not a hypocrite. I absolutely hated watching it, Michael, but I'm no different than everyone else. I couldn't look away. I tried," I was shaking now, "But I just couldn't turn my eyes away from it." I fell silent, hearing my own breath, raspy and labored, as if I'd just sprinted thirty yards.

"What you felt is normal," Michael spoke softly, trying to reassure me. The easy cadence of his voice relaxed me. I began to breathe easier. "It's a natural reaction to be horrified the first time a person sees something like we saw. It was brutal, primitive and unforgiving. I have a confession to make, Coco. And I hope you'll forgive me."

I stared at him, not sure where he was headed. I could see whatever he was about to tell me was weighing heavily on his mind. We hadn't gone back out since Tuesday, when we'd all seen the hunt. Three days had come and gone. Sam and I went shopping in the city, taking in African culture. We went to a music and dance extravaganza put on at the downtown plaza. We were busy from sunup until sundown. Each of those nights, I fell asleep in Sam's arms and he rose silently from our bed and went out to the private porch. There he made his calls to the States. Each night I woke up several times reaching for him, hearing the soft drone of his voice as he spoke with his associates. I listened in the darkness. Sam's words were indistinguishable, but he spoke with unmistakable authority. Each night I went back to sleep, disappointed but understanding. I saw nothing of Michael King in these last three days, but thought of him often. From the moment we first met, he'd seemed like a brother I never had. I had trusted him instantly.

"I took some pictures out there." It was as if he was confessing a sin.

"Yeah, I saw you taking them," I said, not sure what to make of him.

"No, you don't understand. I took photos while you were watching the lions. Only they weren't pictures of the lions. I was shooting you, Coco. I'm sorry, but you were extraordinary. Really!" he whispered the word loudly, his passion rising. "I saw it when I was photographing you. You captivated the lens, Coco."

"What do you mean?" Michael could've been a nut case, I thought. But he wasn't. He *was* one of the most sought after photographers on the planet.

"I developed the film – just to confirm what I saw out there on the savannah." He saw my confusion. He leaned up in the recliner. His face was flushed with excitement.

"I want to photograph you, Coco. Out there," he waved his arms. "I've been photographing people for most of my life. I've never come close to capturing on film what you showed me in your eyes three mornings ago! I want your permission to show those pictures to some people I know. Have you ever thought about being a model?"

"Are you serious?" I was flabbergasted.

"I think you could be one of the best."

"You're joking."

He stared at me, measuring my reaction. He wasn't kidding about anything.

"Wow," I said, taking his offer more seriously. "You honestly think I measure up to those women you photograph for *Sports Illustrated*?"

"Scout's honor," he held up his right hand.

I smiled, warming to the idea. "Let's say I decide to do this with you. When would we start?"

"Tomorrow morning. Some of us are going into a village not far from here. The locals run a small logging operation. They use elephants to haul out the trees. I was going to do a photo essay, but I've just come up with a better idea. If you're willing, that is."

"What are you thinking, Michael?" I asked suspiciously.

"How would you like to ride an elephant? We'll do that tomorrow. The rest of the week I'd like to go back to some locations I'm familiar with around here and do some shooting with some animals in the backdrop. The days will be long, Coco. I won't sugarcoat it. It's hard work. We'll have to catch the light when it's just right, but I can promise you, you will not be disappointed with the results. Sam can come with us. I think he would enjoy seeing a different side of Kenya. It's off the tour, more primitive and more dangerous. I'll rent a Land Cruiser. We'll be careful, and just in case, I'll pay Joseph Sangari to come with us."

"What can he do?"

"Ride shotgun. He comes with a scoped, high powered rifle, just in case."

An image of the lions tearing apart a still moving buffalo came to my mind. "I'll tell Sam to bring his gun, too."

"Great. It's settled then." Michael slapped his knees.

"Yeah," I nodded, unsure of what I'd just agreed to. "Kenya and I. This might be fun."

"We'll have a blast," said Michael. "I'll send out the ones I took on Tuesday now," he said, rising from the recliner. "I was never one much for lying around a pool." He was anxious to get started. "It's bad for the complexion."

"Shouldn't we sign something? I mean, we don't even have a contract."

"You own everything until you say otherwise."

"Will I need a manager or an agent or something like that?"

Michael chuckled. His laugh put me at ease. "I can refer you to a friend in L.A., if you like. He handles some of the other models I shoot. He's real good, Coco. I think you'll love him."

I frowned.

"What's wrong?" Michael was suddenly concerned.

"Well, it's just, can't *you* be my agent?"

He chuckled again. "I'm a photographer, Coco. I'd be doing you a disservice. I don't know a thing about business. You're going to need someone who knows what he's doing. There are more sharks in L.A. than lions on the savannah. Sebastian is one of the best in the business. He'll look after you. If he doesn't, I'll cut him off."

"Cut him off?" I didn't get it.

"We're partners, Coco," he winked. "Sebastian and I are lovers. You won't have any problems at all. I guarantee it."

I waited for Sam by the pool. I was dying to tell him. He finally sauntered out through the restaurant about an hour after Michael left. He looked relaxed in a pair of white Dockers and a green, loose knit polo shirt. He leaned over and kissed me before sitting in the recliner Michael had occupied.

"You've had company," he noticed the half empty glass of gin and tonic on the small wicker table between the chairs.

"Michael King was here. He's the photographer from the safari Tuesday morning."

"I remember. How is he?"

"He wants to shoot me, Sam."

"That's going to hurt," he smiled.

"He thinks I could become a successful model," I ignored him. "He thinks I look like those women in some of his swimsuit layouts."

"And what do you think?"

"I don't know. I didn't think that I was in their league. I'm asking you."

He looked at me, amused. "Sweetheart, it's they who aren't in your league."

"Do you really believe that?"

"I wouldn't say it if I didn't think it was true." Sam looked deep into my eyes.

"You wouldn't mind if I gave it a shot, then?"

He smiled. "If you want to, go ahead. You can try it here with him, and if you don't like it, at least you'll know. He's one of the best, Coco. Personally, I think you'd make a great model."

"Michael wants to hook me up with an agent he knows in L.A. The agent's his lover. Did you know he was gay?"

Sam thought about it for a moment. "Nope, not that it matters. But come to think of it that might explain a few things. Like why he takes such beautiful pictures, for instance. He's a man with a strong effeminate side. He's able to combine the beauty of both genres: modeling and landscape photography. Maybe that's what it takes to be a great artist, that and an abundance of talent."

"Neither can hurt," I agreed with Sam. "He wants to start in the morning, and he thought you'd like to come along for the ride."

Sam hesitated. He hadn't expected this. I got out of my chair and sat down in his. He moved over to give me room. I curled up beside him, stroking his chest, kneading the fine hairs between my fingers.

"I love you, Sam." I whispered into his ear.

"All right, I'll come," he said quietly.

"Tonight. Of course you will." I kissed him gently on the nipple through the knit shirt. "While I ride the wild elephant."

## Chapter 15

The village was close to an hour's drive from Nairobi, in the opposite direction of the way we'd gone on Tuesday. The road was paved right up to the village. That was when it turned into a dirt road. Either the government had been unable or unwilling to run it any further, but no one seemed to notice. We drove the Land Cruiser through the congested main street. In some places, where the road narrowed, women with baskets balanced on their heads moved aside to let us pass. They stared at us with wide, black eyes, mildly curious but not surprised. Kenya was no stranger to visitors. The women wore sarongs of many different colors. Most trudged along through the dust in bare feet. They avoided the pools of standing water which had collected during the seasonal rains the night before. There was no danger of flooding, though. As May marched into June, the seasons transformed from the monsoonal wet to a drier more stable climate. Where a month earlier Kenya had wished for the rains to stop, a month from now they would pray for their return. One of the benefits of the dry part of the year was the reduction in the number of mosquitoes. The small insects, mere pests in the U.S., carried death here. Malaria was Kenya's biggest killer, driving its infant mortality rate through the stratosphere. Tremendous strides had been made recently to bringing the terrible disease to its knees, most notably through the Bill and Melinda Gates' Foundation's efforts. But this was only a good start, and there was still a long way to the finish line.

Men drove cattle through the village streets. The oxen were slaves. Harnessed to their respective wagons, their drivers atop makeshift wooden seats, the beasts toiled daily to move goods up and down the muddy, dusty trails both within and between the nearby villages.

The village we passed through was a living ant hill, constantly in motion. Yet no one hurried. Movement was deliberate. Villagers stopped constantly along the way, talking animatedly with one another. In a land where most would never read or write, this was their method of communication. This was their newspaper – their daily dose of the six o'clock news. People seemed more content than happy. They weren't resigned to their tasks. Far from it, their daily regimens were the glue that gave their lives substance. They worked, not to attain wealth or status, but as a form of social interaction. Simply put, from what I could see it gave them something to do. Not unlike the artisans and merchants of our own forefathers' time, they too, passed their knowledge and skills on to their own sons and daughters. The cities, of course, fought to westernize. But here in the village, life still remained simple. I wasn't prepared to think either way of life was better than the other.

On the outskirts of town, the logging operation came into view. The Land Cruiser bounced along laboriously in second gear. It was a strong machine, designed for off road trekking through rugged and sometimes flooded terrain. Instead of a standard muffler system which was usually hidden beneath a vehicle, this vehicle's tailpipe was directed upwards, rising above the passenger side of the cab. This way, when it drove through two feet of water, the engine would stay dry.

Joseph Sangari finally pulled the Land Cruiser over into the dirt not fifty feet from where four elephants were being coaxed to work. I watched in amazement as the powerful creatures moved a heavy, twenty foot log stripped of its branches. The animal wrapped its trunk around the base of the recently cut tree and lifted it as if it were a matchstick. A man with a sweat stained cloth wrapped around his waist and down to his thighs touched the elephant on its side with a long, thin bamboo pole. I assumed this was to steer the beast. The elephant moved like a laboring tank. It turned, carrying the log toward the roadway using its giant tusks like a forklift, and dropped it onto a large pile of other similar sized logs. A flatbed truck had been pulled off the shoulder of the dirt road and parked beside the logs. A crane mounted near the front of the truck lifted and positioned the logs lengthwise across the flatbed. The crane resembled a crooked metal arm. Three villagers hopped nimbly across the logs as a new one was lowered onto the pile. They guided it at both ends, trying their best to position the new addition securely. The goal was to add weight to the other logs with the new one to keep them from cascading off one side or the other of the flatbed. I noticed no one ever stood on the ground near either side of the truck.

Sam and I stood off to the side of the vehicle while Joseph took Michael over to the man who owned the logging company. The negotiations took less than five minutes. A hundred U.S. dollars had bought an elephant and its handler for the rest of the morning.

Michael walked back, smiling.

"All right," he clasped his hands together with joy. "We're in business." He looked toward the sky. "The light is perfect, only a few clouds. I suggest we begin immediately. We'll start over there, at the edge of the forest," he pointed beyond the workers to a stand of trees on the perimeter of the logging operation.

We walked through an already cleared area of forest along a meandering path which had been beaten down by the elephants. We stopped short of where the trees began again.

"Where do you want me?" I asked Michael.

"I'll take some test shots first, to set my meters. Why don't you change into the first bathing suit? The tan one might be good to start with."

"I'm wearing the black one under my jeans," I said.

"That'll be fine. We can start with that one. I can adjust the aperture on the camera to accommodate the different light. How many different colors did you bring?" We talked about this last night when Michael dropped by for a few minutes after dinner, going over what I would need today.

"I brought ten to choose from," I referred to my colorful assortment of bikinis. "You name a color and style and I have it."

"Good girl. We'll shoot them all," he didn't hesitate.

I looked at him to see if he was serious.

Michael shrugged, his head slightly bent, already adjusting one of his cameras. "I warned you it would be hard work."

I threw my hands up in a gesture of defeat. "Do with me as you must," I sighed in resignation, wondering again what I had gotten myself into.

Sam said, "I see you're developing the model's attitude."

"She's just jerking my chain, Sam," Michael was focusing his cameras. I was stripping out of my jeans. Joseph Sangari was pretending not to watch me. We could all now see an elephant, handler sitting atop its giant shoulders, moving between the stumps of the cut trees and lumbering forward in our direction.

"It's what models do," the banter continued. "Give me a smile," Michael started shooting, testing everything.

"I'm not even undressed yet," I peeled off my cotton pullover. I had brought a loose button-down shirt for later, when it warmed up. Now I shivered as the last of the early morning coolness licked at my bare skin. A half hour from now I'd probably be perspiring, the African sun having burned the last remnants of the cool morning from the village streets.

Eventually, it became time for me to be hoisted onto the shoulders of the elephant. The handler remained on its back. Two villagers lifted and then pushed me up the animal's side while the handler caught my outstretched arms. I found myself looking down from what seemed like the roof of a small house. I was breathless. It was exhilarating. I was balanced in a spider-like crouch on the animal's back. The handler was all smiles. The other two men laughed, speaking rapidly in their local dialect. The handler, who was closer to the elephant's huge ears, motioned for me to switch places with him. I signaled that I was fine right where I was, splayed out across its huge back. The animal's hide felt hairy and course to my touch, a cross between leather and sandpaper. Everyone watching laughed as the handler somehow climbed over me and began to prod me forward. I squealed in protest. This produced more laughter, even from some villagers who had stopped what they were doing to watch what was fast becoming the most bizarre scene they'd ever witnessed. Here was a white girl playing Sheena, Queen of the

Jungle, in real life. Michael never stopped taking pictures, missing none of it.

Sam wasn't any help. "You're doing great, sweetheart," he grinned. I scowled at him, feeling awkward as hell and anything but sexy as I played Spiderwoman on top of the elephant. I managed to move closer to its massive head. I finally straddled my legs on both sides of what I thought must surely be its neck.

"Oh – oh no!" I screamed as the creature actually began to move. I began to panic as I suddenly became aware the elephant had decided to go for a walk. This, of course, was accompanied by more laughter. By now I thought the entire village was watching us. People applauded, some cheering. Theirs were happy, mirthful eyes, steeped in the ancient traditions of ages and ancestors long since passed but not oblivious to a new world which sped by them at warp drive. Perhaps reluctantly, I thought, they must put up with us. Michael's camera never stopped taking pictures of the strange juxtaposition.

After a while, I began to feel more comfortable onboard the behemoth. I relaxed a little and began to have fun. I marveled at the strength of the elephant. I appreciated its temperament and patience. I wondered what it must think of us. How did the elephant view the world of humans? Did it resent its work? Was it angered by what it would, if it could, surely perceive as the unfettered destruction of its environment? Or was it saddened, knowing it too must go along. Elephants had no fingers. Only man could pull the trigger of a gun. Only we were intelligent enough to kill for greed.

I spent an hour on top of the elephant. Finally, Michael said it was enough. Reluctantly I was helped to the ground. I rubbed the elephant's rough hide, leaning against it and hearing the shutter of Michael's camera click one last time at the exact moment I kissed its noble hide, tears streaming down my cheeks. Five months later, the shot appeared on the cover of *Time Magazine*. The accompanying story was a poignant one about the shrinking of precious habitats of wild animals all over the world.

We broke for lunch. Sam and I ambled around the village for the better part of an hour, soaking up the culture. Michael found us overpaying for some local garments that I'd fallen in love with. It was an intentional act. I found myself falling in love with Africa.

"We're done here. We've got a few more hours of this light, and I know a place. It's a bit of a drive I'm afraid, but we'll get there in time if we leave now." Michael checked his watch. "But we must leave immediately."

I looked at Sam. He shrugged. "We haven't been disappointed yet. In time for what?" he turned back to Michael.

Michael said mysteriously, "If I promised you Heaven, would you ask why? Trust me. It's worth the drive. After all, we've already come halfway around the world. What are a few more miles? We're almost there." We headed out of the village and travelled northward over mostly dirt roads. Two hours later we came upon one of the most unbelievable sights I had ever seen.

The shallow inland waterway, still partly filled from the monsoon rains, stretched out before us. Pink flamingos, numbering in the thousands, waded knee deep in the still waters near the shoreline. The day had raced by. It was past five in the afternoon. The bright sunlight of the daytime was changing. Different colors, still subtle, had begun to bleed out across the landscape. Hints of turquoise melted into pastel bluish oranges. The effect this new light had on the landscape around us as the sun began to sink on the horizon was breathtaking. It was as if the flamingos had started to burn. The birds moved as one, a swaying mass of molten feathers. Their color was a result of the food they ate. Carotenoids in the shrimp and algae they consumed gave them their brilliantly colored plumage that mimicked their sustenance.

"Put on your red bikini, Coco." We had stopped near the lake. The flock had migrated a short distance from us. The nearest outer edge of the brightly colored sea of birds was perhaps a hundred yards away, a safe enough distance from their perspective. Even though we'd strayed from the migration routes of more dangerous animals, we weren't taking chances. Joseph Sangari leaned against the vehicle, scanning the horizon in all directions. The scoped rifle he had brought with him lay in easy reach on top of the truck's hood.

"I've got a better idea," I said.

"I don't know if another color will photograph quite as well in this light, Coco," Michael said patiently. He was being polite, but he was making a point. He was setting up his tripod. "We've got maybe thirty minutes at the most to get these shots. Hey, where are you going?" He suddenly noticed I was walking away. Sam, too, was puzzled. I winked at him and said to Michael, "Just have your camera ready, Michael." He put his hands on his hips, clearly flustered. He tossed a glance in Sam's direction, who shrugged that 'your-guess-is-as-good-as-mine' gesture. I kept walking in the direction of the flock of thousands of the pink flamingos. I got to within about twenty-five yards of them before the first of the birds in front began to become agitated. I stopped in the damp clay just as a few of them spread their wings and started to fly away. As one, the birds moved, now all of them teetering on flight. I began to undress, careful not to agitate them any further. I kicked off my sandals and then unbuttoned my cotton shirt, dropping it at my feet. Next I unzipped my jeans and pulled them off. I left them on top of my shirt. I looked back at the boys, smiling, totally nude against the falling sun. All right, I thought to myself. You want pictures? Take some.

I broke into a sprint. I ran right at the middle of the flock. The scene was dazzling as ten thousand pink flamingos took flight at once, me sprinting onto a tiny peninsula of damp clay which jutted out into the shallow lake. It was as if the air above the lake had suddenly burst into flames and I was running right into the inferno. The cacophony of wings beating against air and the utterances from the birds themselves was like the roar of a freight train as it cascaded across the lake. Michael had been right. It was a heavenly scene which none of us could hope to revisit in ten lifetimes. I laughed and twirled about, my arms raised in the air, as if I were conducting an orchestra of light and sound. It was awesomely beautiful. It was raw. It was me and Kenyan memories that would last forever.

## Chapter 16

In Brittle, Nevada, Napoli's Italian Restaurant was a jewel. That's what I was thinking halfway through the most delicious vegetarian lasagna I'd had in recent memory. The Cabernet Sauvignon was excellent. Not surprisingly, it went well with the entrée. Sam had settled for the same as I had.

We ate mostly in silence, he and I both perhaps trying too hard to second guess the other's thoughts. Sam wiped a spot of sauce from his chin. He leaned back in his chair, satiated. He stared at me. I didn't say a word.

"I suppose we can dance around this all night. Pretend nothing's going on," he finally said.

I remained silent, meeting his stare.

Then Sam said, "Did you read that file I left on my desk?"

"What file?" I said cautiously. I tried to respond with just the right inflection of surprise and curiosity. Too much of either would tip the scales of suspicion against me.

He searched my eyes. His eyes had become cold daggers. The light in them from moments before was absent. They were someone else's eyes now. The man across from me was no longer the Sam I knew.

"A couple of months ago I was in a hurry. I left a file on my desk by accident in the office in Vegas. You were there."

"I live there, Sam."

"Not in my office, you don't. You were meeting me for lunch. You were waiting for me in my office when I got back. There was a file on my desk."

"What the hell would I want with one of your files?" I spat at him. "What was in it? What's so important about one of your many files, anyway? Why give me the third degree, Sam?"

"So you didn't look at the file?" His eyes were black crystals of ice.

I stared at him. The moment hung on a high wire.

"Did you look at the damn file?" he slammed the flat of his hand on the table. It sounded like a gunshot in the quiet restaurant, which instantly was devoid of all conversation. Eerily incongruous with the raw tension, Pavarotti reached a crescendo in the background.

I was scared, but it would be a cold day in hell before I'd show him.

"What would I want with your file, Sam?" He stared. The tension mounted. "Are you going to shoot me Sam, or break all my fingers first?" I fluttered my fingers on the table in from of him.

He suddenly softened, deciding something. "I'm sorry. I had to know." He reached for my hand and I snatched it away from his grasp.

"Fuck you!" I was angry now, for having been threatened by him. The fear was still there, but it was buried beneath my indignation. Would he hurt me? Could he hurt someone he loved so much? I used to think not. Now I wasn't sure.

Still out there, like a naked man in a public fountain, were the three mason jars of soil.

"Yes, I took soil samples from the dry creek bed," I admitted.

"I'm listening," he leaned onto the table, his hands clasped under his chin, holding his head up.

"I thought that's where you might be putting the hotel. It would save time to build on compact rock, rather than drill for piles."

"Six of one, half a dozen of the other."

"Yeah, well I didn't know that."

"Why?"

"I want in. If you haven't sewn up everything, that is. I've got some money saved. I figured if I got a piece of the action I could make a score."

Sam was slowly moving his head from side to side.

"What?" I demanded.

"You're out of your league is what, sweetheart. You don't have the foggiest notion about what's going on out here."

"Tell me."

"Uh-uh. No can do. I've signed non-circumvent agreements, non-disclosure contracts, you name it. If I talk I'll be sued before you can count to three."

"No one would know."

"Oh, they'd find out all right. Sooner or later. These aren't some kind of playground games, Coco. Everyone is playing for keeps out here."

"You've found water, haven't you? Lots of water. I've seen the drilling rigs, Sam. Don't lie to me."

"Those are for core samples. We're doing site surveys and density tests."

And drilling everywhere but the creek bed, I thought to myself. Everywhere except under where you have the air rights. Five miles by five miles and then some is one hell of a field, isn't it Sam? I smiled inwardly. Because I knew I'd convinced him I was his dumb blonde, poking around like a blind bat in business – his business – I knew nothing about. He'd moved on from the subject of the precious file he'd left open on his desk. No doubt he secretly hoped I would too. Put some mileage on it by redirecting the conversation and maybe I'd forget about it altogether.

"You don't need three hundred feet of drilling pipe for soil testing, or for sinking piles. I'm not stupid, Sam. I minored in geology, remember?" I must have sounded like an amateur to him; which is exactly what I'd intended.

"We're not anchoring the deal in land on the creek bed," he gave me, pretending to cave.

I lapped it up. "Why should I believe you?"

"Don't," he shrugged. "It doesn't matter anyway. Land titles and the Nevada Bureau of Land Management will tell you every bit of real estate out there has a noose around it. There isn't anything left. So it's a moot point."

I stared at him, feigning disappointment, an expression of doubt still evident across my face.

"Check with them. Satisfy yourself. You don't have to believe me. I can't understand why you're doing this anyway. You're rich in your own right. Plus I've always given you anything you need. You make no sense, Coco. I can't understand you anymore. This whole thing started not long after you began making those pictures. What happened to make you change? You use to –"

"Do whatever you wanted me to?" I finished his sentence for him. An awkward silence followed. I listened to my own breathing.

Customers, elder ones, uncomfortable with the obviously arguing young couple, had finished their food and left. Others had filtered into the restaurant, oblivious to what was still going on. Fortunately for them, emotionally spent, Sam and I spoke more quietly now.

I reached for his hands. I cradled them in mine, massaging them, feeling their smoothness. The hands of a killer, I thought. I quickly forced the notion from my mind.

"Maybe I just grew up, Sam. Maybe I'm not a little girl anymore, or a porcelain doll to be put on a shelf and admired, taken down every once in a while and played with and then finally replaced when I get old and worn out. Maybe I'm a woman with a heart, a mind, and a soul. I *feel,* Sam, all the time. And lately I haven't been feeling so good about a lot of things. My life isn't turning out the way I thought it would."

"You're the envy of the world! You have everything. Most people can only dream of a life like yours."

I sighed. "I'm bored Sam. And it won't go away."

"It's normal, baby. It happens to everyone at one time or another. I call it life's quicksand. You've got to slug through it. Look at the bright side."

"I'm all ears."

"Have you ever heard of a mid-life crisis?"

"Are you serious?" I couldn't believe what he was saying.

"Hear me out," Sam pleaded. "The last ten years of your life have been like most other people's twenty or thirty. You've lived life in the fast lane. You've probably been around the world twenty or thirty times by now. You've had at least two – three if you count the business side of things – very successful careers. Of course things have lost a bit of their shine. You're running out of new and exciting challenges. It happens to everybody," he repeated himself.

"How does 'everybody' deal with it, then? Or are there just a bunch of bored people walking around after a while?"

"Have you looked in people's eyes lately?" he pointed out. "A lot of them are walking around glassy eyed by the time they reach forty. By fifty they're zombies."

"They're not me, Sam. I'm only twenty-five and besides, I don't see you walking around with glassy eyes."

Sam exhaled through his nose. "You need some hobbies," he declared. "You need something to rekindle the passion in you."

"Maybe I can put a spark plug up my ass. Sam, I don't need this. If I want a lecture I'll go back to school."

"I'm trying to help you, Coco. All this running around behind my back – this skullduggery – it's got to stop, damn it. People are starting to say things."

"So, let them talk. What do you care?"

"You want a piece of the action? All right, I'll give you some. I'll put you on the president's list."

"Thanks for nothing, Sam." I knew what that was. It was a group of preferred investors. They were allowed into a deal early, putting up money virtually risk free. Their return was almost guaranteed. Usually the list was comprised of close friends and relatives. The terms, however, were still dictated by the developer.

"Think about it. You'll double your investment in the first year."

"I'm not interested." I was adamant.

"I don't know what you want." Sam was frustrated.

"I want you to stop spying on me. I want you to leave me alone. I'm not meddling in your affairs, either. I'm an independent businesswoman who incidentally happens to be your lover. If I uncover an opportunity by my own efforts and without any help from you, then I figure I'm entitled to make my own informed investments. I don't need your table scraps, your president's list. Those are *your* rules, Sam, not mine."

I was about to call him a hypocrite, but I thought that would probably be going too far. Sam was smart. Sooner than later, he would come to that conclusion all by his lonesome. He stared at me for a while, trying to figure it all out. Wordlessly, he poured out the rest of the wine, splitting it equally into two half glasses. He caught the waiter's attention, which wasn't difficult; he'd probably been keeping a nervous eye on us the whole time we'd been here, hoping our little tiff wouldn't progress into a full blown train wreck. Sam waved the empty bottle in the air, signaling for another. I didn't mind it a bit.

"I feel like getting drunk," he spoke out of character.

"I'm willing," I admitted.

"Truce?"

I lifted my glass and tapped the one he held outstretched in his hand. It sounded like a tiny church bell. "For now", I capitulated. I drank, emptying most of the wine down my throat before I replaced the glass on the table in front of us. I smacked my lips like one of the guys.

"I'm getting my piece of the action and you'd better get used to it." I pronounced boldly.

Sam smiled. It seemed an almost paternal gesture. "Good luck," he tossed back his half glass just as the waiter pulled up with another bottle.

Sam and I returned to my motel room drunk. Making up was always what they say, only in our case more. In the morning we both woke up with bad hangovers. It hurt like hell, but I figured it was worth it.

"I'm leaving today," he said. "I've got a meeting tonight at the casino. Need a lift?"

"I've got my car."

"Zarillo can drive it back for you," he offered.

"Only if you promise to remove the bug," I demanded.

Sam walked over to me from where he'd been shaving at the sink. A white Days Inn towel was wrapped around his waist. I was still in bed, lying on my stomach, my legs bent in the air behind me. He leaned over and kissed me on the forehead. "I can do that," he said.

"I've got a few things to do in Brittle," he continued. "Leave the keys to your Chevy at the front desk." He glanced at the clock on the desk beside the bed. It was nine o'clock. "Why don't we shoot for just after lunch, say one o'clock? That way we don't have to go to war with the traffic when we get back to Vegas. We can have a late lunch on the jet if we get hungry."

"I can live with that. Are we meeting here, or at the airstrip?"

"I'll have Zarillo pick you up. I might even be with him. As a matter of fact he's probably out front now." As if on cue Sam's cell phone chirped to life. He retrieved it from the night stand. "Mark? Give me fifteen," he said into the mouthpiece. "Yeah, that's right. I'll talk to you out front." He spied his Rolex beside the lamp and slid it onto his wrist.

"Why do you still do it, Sam?"

"Huh?" I could see I'd interrupted his thoughts. His mind was already racing, plotting out his strategy for the next few hours.

"When is enough, enough?"

He looked at me, considering my question carefully. I got the impression no one had ever asked him before. I suddenly saw myself standing in his place, fifteen or twenty years down the road. Maybe that's why I asked him the question. I didn't ever want to be where he was. There had to be another way, a different end and a way out.

Sam shrugged. "I guess I'll know when that time comes," he tried to be insightful.

"What if that doesn't happen? What if it never ends, Sam? What if it's like some cruel merry-go-round on an episode of the old 'Twilight Zone'? One you pay your token and get onto, thinking it's going to be all kinds of fun and then it turns into a terrible nightmare and you can't find a way off?"

"There's always a way off, Coco. You just have to know when."

"Will you know when, Sam, when it's time?"

He'd never stopped looking at me. He seemed oddly vulnerable, and for a moment I almost felt sorry for him. "I hope so. Sometimes you don't get to choose. Sometimes that's part of it. But I really hope I'll be different." He was thinking about all the others who'd thought the same thing, but fallen off nonetheless.

# Chapter 17

Vegas is a town of addiction. If you're not addicted, then you're feeding off addicts. But their addictions find their way to you, one way or another. They consume you slowly at first, as you dance with the devil and his lies and promises which beguile you. By the time you realize he's got you in his clutches, it's too late. You let yourself go, and the slippery thrilling downhill slide is on. You just have to remember, there *is* a bottom. That's where most everyone goes wrong. They either forget that, or if they remember they're at a point where they no longer care. Greed and the devil wage a clever courtship on your soul. The end is inevitable, and always the same. When it finally arrives you have to pay the piper.

Sam fed off of the addicts, providing the fixes they demanded. He was good at it, one of the best. Surrounded by a veneer of respectability, he purveyed poison openly. He was revered for it, because it had made him rich. In America, that's all that counts. No one much cared about how Sam's wealth had been acquired, just that he possessed it.

I saw him coming. He wended his way through the blackjack tables, avoided the roulette wheels and waved to his subjects and the pit bosses, occasionally stopping and huddling with them. When he did, they spoke in low inaudible monotones. Money was the god they worshipped.

The pit bosses lusted after it, would kill to get it, and would kill again to keep it.

Sam broke free of the last of them. He strode swiftly across the remaining twenty feet of durable, softly cushioned carpeting to where I was waiting for him. We agreed to meet at the entrance of Le Crème, a high end restaurant that spilled off the main gambling concourse of the Miorca Casino, his flagship hotel. The casino had somehow jostled and muscled its way into position among the Strip's elite. The majestic building stood proudly, a sentinel of success among its peers: the Venetian, the Bellagio, the Wynn, and others. Monuments all built on the heartache and broken dreams of fools who believed in the improbable myth of money for nothing. People like Sam, I knew, worked very diligently for long hours to take their money, and to punish those who would think of taking his.

"You look busy," I noticed. I kissed him quickly on the lips.

"It's always something," his attention remained divided. "I leave town for a day and the roof falls in."

"I see it's business as usual."

"Pretty much," He forced himself to focus on me. "How's your day been? Are you hungry?"

"That's what I wanted to talk to you about." Someone hit a jackpot on one of the machines on the floor. A siren sounded. Bells sounded and lights flashed. A rotund, middle aged tourist jumped up and down and screamed, a pig caught by one leg at a carnival. No one could have missed her. That was the idea.

The commotion died down quickly, replaced by the constant ping-and-bong tones of the machines as the computers inside spewed out just enough intermittent reward to keep gamblers coming back for more. I shook my head as I watched the gleeful jackpot winner thirty feet away being congratulated. For what, I wondered, knowing she could never really win. The casino would get it back. Sooner or later the tourist would lose it all and then some. Maybe not on this trip, but she'd be back. In the meantime she'd tell everyone back home how she'd made the big score, money for nothing, a walking billboard extolling the virtues of good clean fun in the entertainment capital of the world. She, like all the others, would lose. Because they weren't kidding when they said what happens in Vegas stays in Vegas. People seem to forget that includes their winnings. I looked back at Sam.

"Can I take a rain check on lunch? I've got a one o'clock downtown and a conference call with a director and my agent at three. I've been burning the candle at both ends since we got back."

Sam checked his watch. "I was going to ask you the same thing. Sorry."

"I'm free tomorrow." I was hopeful.

Sam sighed. "I'm with the Governor in the morning, the Gaming Commissioner for lunch, and the Mayor's office in the afternoon."

"Friday?" I asked.

He sighed again, "I meant to tell you. I just found out. I have to go to Beijing again for three or four days. I'll probably be back Wednesday of next week. I'll call you, same as always. I'm sorry, baby. We'll spend some time together next weekend," he hoped.

"I'll be in Bel Air, Sam. We're signing those contracts on the new film I told you about."

"I'd forgotten all about that." He put both hands on my shoulders. We stared into each other's eyes. I wondered if he was thinking about what I was – a merry-go-round with no way off.

"Mr. Spielman?" Two of his security staff wanted to speak with him.

"I'll be with you in a minute, gentlemen." They backed off immediately, reading his mood swing. The men hovered a few feet away. Evidently the message could wait.

"Like ships in the night we are," I said.

"I enjoyed making love with you in Brittle, even if we both *were* drunk."

"So did I, Sam," I smiled at the memory. "You better go. They need you."

He kissed me again. He started to speak.

"Don't," I touched my finger to his lips. "I'll see you when you get back."

He stared at me for a moment longer. Then he turned and walked away with his two maroon-jacketed minions.

I left the hotel right after that. I had my own place, even though Sam and I spent a lot of time together upstairs. He owned a penthouse on the top floor of his own building. I had a key, but I needed the privacy of somewhere away from the prying eyes of the Strip. Sam knew too many people in the industry. They knew me. I had three days, and the more anonymity I could garner the better.

I owned a home in Summerlin, on the way out to Red Rock Canyon. My backyard opened onto the tenth fairway of a private golf course. Sometimes I'd watch duffers and pros alike go for the green on the long par three. It was a quiet, gated community with a guard out front, as they virtually all were. The locals sometimes called Vegas, and especially Summerlin, the City of Walls. Everyone, it seemed, lived behind them. They had developed the Del Webb Retirement Community, a virtual cookie cutter ghost town, adjacent to the sub-division I lived in. Almost nothing happened here. Aside from the sporadic domestic violence 911 calls, and the even rarer drug raid, the neighborhood was generally quiet. People minded their own business and avoided unnecessary contact with their neighbors.

The guard recognized who I was and waved me through with a nod and a smile. I wound my way through the palm lined streets and finally pulled into my own two car garage. There was lots of room for the black 2006 Corvette, since Mark Zarillo hadn't yet delivered my classic Chevy. I punched the remote on the visor to close the garage door and went inside the house. I headed straight to my office. I sat down and flipped open my laptop. A few minutes later I was looking at a satellite image of Nevada. I zoomed in several times to the small town of Brittle and the land that surrounded it. Another couple of clicks and I was looking at the same map, only this time smaller areas of it were marked out like counties on a state road map. These areas around Brittle represented the geographical demarcations of private and public land in and around the town. I clicked again and they were instantly color coded. Blue represented all public lands, red private, and yellow unknown. There was very little unknown. I moved the cursor and clicked a rectangle near town. Instantly, a file popped onto the screen. It was a title history. It began with the identity of the original landlord and listed each subsequent buyer and title holder right up to the last known owner of the plot. The address, lawyer, agent of service, and other pertinent pieces of information were all included. All of this information, although not compiled in the way I had put it together, was available online. All you had to know was how to find it. I moved the mouse around Brittle, clicking as I went. I split the screen. Now each delineated piece of real estate was accompanied by all recorded information about its lineage of ownership. The date purchased, the amount paid, its current status vis-à-vis taxes owing or not. Everything was in front of me. What was not readily available online, some good old-fashioned detective work had accomplished.

Only actual transfers of titles – change in ownership on the private land parcels – had to be registered in the Land Titles Office. The same applied to leases on public lands, particularly pertaining to land held in trust by the Nevada Bureau of Land Management. I clicked the mouse again, typed a password, clicked, and presto. Most of the map around Brittle turned green. I was looking at the most updated information in Nevada on the extent of land Sam Spielman now owned in and near Brittle. Most of the map, not surprisingly, had turned lime green. I had one task left and this was one I couldn't perform with a computer. I hit print and picked up the phone.

# Chapter 18

Billy Cunningham, or B.C. as he was known to his few friends, was ninety if he was a day. The B.C. moniker had evolved recently, because of his age. He'd been generous to a fault his entire life. It was known that B.C. would give you the shirt off his back if you needed his help. His family migrated across America from New York at the turn of the century.

A young man of twenty-two and recently married to his pregnant wife Becky, Billy's grandfather came west with dreams and ambition, but not much in the way of intelligence. What Bobby Cunningham lacked in the smarts department he tended to compensate for through stubborn determination and hard work.

Becky gave birth prematurely, at the side of a creek bed somewhere they thought might be close to the Nevada-California State line. The baby was small and fragile, and they weren't sure the tiny newborn would survive more than a few days. When the child was strong enough, the Cunninghams decided they would pack up the wagon and continue westward to the Promised Land.

They named their son Brittle, after the porcelain teapot they brought with them that broke from the heat of the fire that night. Brittle fooled them, though. He was a tough little runt. He lived through the first couple of weeks and he even began to put on a little weight. By the time he was big enough, and it was safe enough to continue their westward haul, the Cunninghams contemplated staying put beside that little creek. It was into the fall when Brittle's dad finally decided they would stay and not travel further across the Sierra Nevada Mountains. Having heard horror stories about the plight of others attempting to cross the mountains as winter neared, he decided his family would sit tight where they were. In spring they would complete their journey, probably end up in San Francisco, Bobby would say to his wife. They huddled together in front of the fire, under the clear starry nights that passed over that little creek in the middle of nowhere. Baby Brittle lay in the wagon by the two horses bundled up nice and cozy against the desert chill, fast asleep.

Billy Cunningham had long ago forgotten his age, if he ever knew it to begin with. Such things never had much importance to the old prospector. He'd find things, mostly in the desert, and then sell them, making just enough money to keep up with the taxes he owed on some land he owned. He paid little attention to changes in the amount he was required to pay each year, concerned only with having enough to get by. In his mind he still had a notion the government was of the people and for the people, that they were fair and mostly honest. Billy didn't spend much time in town, and never read newspapers. He hadn't watched television since he could remember.

B.C. owned a home on the edge of Brittle, a stone's throw from where his grandmother had given birth to his father, after whom Bobby had named the town. The house had deteriorated since Billy didn't spend more time there than absolutely necessary. Sometimes Billy would sojourn into the desert for months at a time. 'Prospectin', that's what *he* would call it. The truth was Billy didn't cotton much to people. They talked out of both sides of their mouths, he'd say. So he'd pack up some supplies and set out, pots and pans strung over the back of his trusty burro, Pete. They both knew how to survive in the desert.

On two separate occasions back in the sixties, because he'd been careless, both Pete and Billy had been bitten by a diamondback. Lucky for them, they'd been close to Brittle both times, about ten miles north, along the now dry creek bed. Billy had actually cut Pete over top the rattler's bite with his razor sharp bowie knife and sucked out most of the venom. He'd bandaged up the wound nice and tight and stayed with the animal until it could walk again. It was Billy who'd carried the supplies back, Pete in tow, limping the whole way. They'd made it, though, and the burro had made a full recovery.

Sam got lucky. He dropped by and found the old man home, a new donkey tied to an old fashioned hitching post out back of his place. The old man had named it Pete, after the first one. Billy Cunnningham was between trips.

Sam had talked him into signing an option. But the salty old dog was smarter than he appeared. He'd signed an agreement which would last for one year. He smelled rats by nature, and he'd sized up Sam as the king of all rats. Billy wasn't about to give a sweet talking city slicker from over the hill, as he'd taken to calling Las Vegas for the past few decades, anymore rope than was needed to hang himself. When he got time, he'd have a closer look at what was obviously of importance to the young fella from over the hill. Imagine. Who would pay money for *not* buying his land? It smelled bad to him. But Billy had bigger fish to fry. He knew of an area about thirty miles out that looked interesting last time he'd been out there. At least that's what he'd told the guy at the supply store in town. It definitely needed a closer look. Not that lately Billy did anything more than camp out under the pristine starlit skies of his ancestors; he'd stopped looking for gold over thirty years ago. As everyone knows, the desert is a good place to get away from people.

Billy didn't know it when he signed the land option for Sam, but his prospecting days were about to come to an end. Since his grandfather first staked out and filed the claim for the land over one hundred years earlier, the five-by-five mile swath surrounding the now dry creek bed had become more valuable than any of them could have imagined.

For me, it had come down to a footrace. I recalled Mark's Range Rover and the streets of Brittle, liberally sprinkled with other all terrain vehicles. Billy Cunningham was out there, somewhere among the cacti and hard-packed, sun-baked sand and clay, not wanting to be found. He never filed a flight plan when he left town and never told a soul where he was headed.

Sam had been looking for him. This also explained the propeller driven airplanes I saw parked near the hangar on the airstrip. They were looking for him from the air. But so far, they hadn't found the man and his donkey. It was a big desert. B.C. would come back when he was good and ready, and not before. Besides, I knew you couldn't find someone if you weren't looking in the right places.

B.C was one of the discreet inquiries I had made back in Brittle. B.C. always got his supplies from the same place not far from where he lived. It was probably a two mile jaunt from his home to the supply store. He took Pete, preferring the company of the mule to the nineteen sixty-four Ford pickup in his front yard. They would walk from his place into town, load up, and head out.

The owner of the Brittle Farm and Supply had remembered exactly when Billy bought his supplies. How could he forget? It had been his mother-in-law's birthday. That meant B.C. had gone on his own special walkabout a little more than a month ago. More importantly, the store's owner had parted with a couple other precious gems of information. I'd charmed him into digging up the sales records from Billy's purchases. B.C. had been a regular customer, if you could call six or eight times a year regular. I had asked the owner how long he thought the supplies could keep Billy out there. After a cursory examination of the produce items, the owner had guessed somewhere between six to eight weeks. That was, if he didn't decide to stay longer. I had asked him what he meant by that. He'd told me that even at his age, which he wore extremely well, B.C. knew how to survive out there. He knew how to hunt for food, and how to find water. In short, if he wanted to he could stay out there indefinitely, but usually it was his habit to come back when he ran out of supplies. After all, B.C. wasn't a young man anymore. And lately, he'd been showing his age a little more than the old codger cared to admit. He'd be back all right, probably in two or three weeks.

I offered the owner a twenty for his information, but he refused it. Then I thought hard about my last couple of questions, because if I read him wrong, the owner would go back on his word and I'd inherit a busload of damage control. Sam would find out what I had in mind. I asked him if anyone else had asked him about the old man and his supplies. Not that he could recall. I then asked him with a big smile, if anyone *did* come around, could he see his way clear to not telling whomever it was about me, or what he'd told me about B.C.? To which he quickly replied with a smile equal to mine, we never had the conversation. I laid out ten twenties on the counter then, because I knew he'd refuse to take them, too. "For your thirty-fifth," I'd winked.

"How'd you know it was our anniversary?" he'd asked in surprise.

"There's only one bakery and pastry shop in town." I'd picked up some bagels there for the trip back. "Your wife introduced herself to me. She was picking up your cake." I wished him the best, confident if anyone in Sam's employ was clever enough to chase down the supply clue, Arthur Wippet wouldn't tell them a thing. Neither, I suspected, would his wife.

Sitting in my home office in front of my computer, I pieced together some vital clues of the enigma known as Billy Cunningham. What had been only a hunch a couple of days ago was now coalescing into a much clearer picture. I thought I just might know where B.C. had been hiding. I held the phone in my hand, carefully considering my next move. I took a deep breath and began to dial.

## Chapter 19

I returned from Kenya to an empty apartment. It still had all my furniture, but without Mom and Carl it just didn't feel like home anymore. They had moved into Carl's home in the Mission District in late January, soon after they returned from Hawaii. They went to the islands for their honeymoon.

The lease on Haight didn't run out until June. Carl had paid off the last four months, and we agreed I could use the place when it was convenient. Before Africa I'd taken the GMAT, the entrance exam for my master's program in Business, but still hadn't decided on a grad school.

A lot changed during my three and a half weeks in Kenya. The journey to Kenya was gas on a fire for me. If I thought about it, I had to admit I'd just been going through the motions for most of the last semester. I did what was expected of me, got the 4.0 average and high results on the entrance exam. All I had to do was stay on the bus I'd been riding and I would do just fine. I would have the MBA in two more years, and with my GPA I wouldn't need to go looking. The best in the business world would find me. I would have all the security in the world. But there'd been Africa and Sam, and of course Michael King. The thought of slugging it out with my head in books for two more long years wasn't nearly as palatable as it once seemed. I began to wrestle with some of the things that, only a short while ago, I'd taken for granted. I grew increasingly restless as spring faded into summer. A month went by. I gave up the dorm at the University. I still had a couple of weeks to figure out if I wanted to sign another lease on Haight.

Sometimes decisions are made for you, but Sam was no help, playing the diplomat. He said it was my future, and I had to decide what was best for me. Just when I was at my wits' end my cell phone rang. I heard it as I was getting out of the shower. I ran to the breakfast nook and grabbed it off the table.

"Hello?"

"Coco," the voice on the other end was all smiles.

"Michael!" I exclaimed. "It's so nice to hear your voice," I wrapped myself in a plush towel as I spoke. "I've missed you."

"I've missed you too, sweetheart. Where are you?"

"I'm in San Francisco. At least for now I am. The lease on my apartment runs out in two weeks. I'm thinking about grad school."

"I see," I could tell his voice was guarded. Why didn't anyone want to talk me into anything anymore? "Is that what you want to do?"

I sighed into the mouthpiece. "The truth?"

"Isn't that what counts?" he asked the rhetorical question.

"You're no help. I was thinking I need a break from school. If I were to be perfectly honest with myself, I'm probably more tired of it than I've been letting on."

"May I ask you how long you've been thinking about this?" His sincerity elicited feelings I suddenly realized I'd spoken to no one else about – not even Sam.

"I've probably given it serious consideration since January, when my mom got married and moved out."

"Empty nest, huh?"

"Something like that. It gave me time to think. I was staying on campus most of the week, but I'd come back here on the weekends. There's only so much studying a girl can do."

"So you're quitting school?"

"More like thinking about it. Why? You got a better offer, Michael?"

"Coco, I don't want to say anything which might influence a decision that should be yours alone, especially one of this importance."

"Have you been talking to Sam?" I said half jokingly.

"Not since Kenya."

"Give, Michael. I know you're dying to tell me. Did someone see the pictures?" It had to be the reason he was calling. I wasn't so naïve to think it was purely social. I was becoming excited.

"Remember I told you I was sending the elephant shots to some friends of mine?"

"Yeah?"

"Well, don't sign a new lease. You're moving to L.A.. First stop, my place. You can stay with us for as long as you like. We live in a mansion in Beverly Hills," he said matter-of-factly, not at all bragging. It was the comfort level of the rich, I realized. "Sebastian is looking forward to meeting you."

"When?" I said. I heard what Michael was saying, but my mind was still struggling to catch up.

"When can you be here?"

My head was spinning. "Michael, I…I'll need a job. I can't just move in with you guys. What about the rent?"

"Don't be silly, Coco. We're family. I've seen you naked. I have the pictures to prove it."

I laughed into the mouthpiece. My head was still spinning.

"And you *have* a job. I sold your pictures for beaucoup bucks. Sebastian will go over everything with you after you get here. Just call me back and let me know what flight. I'll pick you up myself. You're a model now, Coco. By the way, did I tell you which magazine was the first to put you in print?"

"No, I don't think you mentioned it, Michael."

"You're on the cover of September's *Time*, sweetheart. Congratulations. Sebastian's chomping on his gums. He's really uncomfortable working without a contract, but everything has been happening so fast. I told him not to worry. I told him you were the nicest, kindest, most honest person I've ever met, and that you would sign with him."

"Thank you, Michael. I'll sign with whomever you say. I guess I'll need a lawyer to look over the paperwork."

"If you don't have one, I can suggest one. But we can talk about it later, when you're here. For now, relax, pop open a bottle of the good stuff, and get your sweet little ass out here ASAP."

"I'll call you tomorrow. Thank you, Michael." I felt warm all over.

"Thank you, my dear. See you soon," he hung up.

I screamed in delight then, jumping in the air. My towel fell off. I didn't care. I was happier than a tulip in spring.

Sam was in Vegas when I reached him and told him the news. He was supportive and happy for me, but I didn't hear surprise in his voice. He'd been expecting

Michael to call me; he worked with professionals all the time. Michael had spotted the talent. He wouldn't have wasted our time with those pictures unless he knew I was worth it. Michael King was Michael King for a reason. When he sneezed, the industry caught a cold. I didn't fully understand yet, but something told me I had better get ready for the ride of my life.

I called Mom next. I began with our trip to Kenya, so she'd be prepared for the more exotic news. Mom always knew I was a stunner. She said the rest of the world was going to find out what she'd known all along.

"When are you leaving?"

"Soon. I'll give notice on the apartment and give the manager your address. He can send you the deposit. Watch for it in the mail, Mom," I warned her. A lot of times the landlord would have a convenient lapse of memory about sending out the money owed.

"I will," she heard me.

"I've got some friends from school I'd like to say goodbye to. Then there's the change of address I'll file with the post office. I'll use yours for the time being, if that's all right with you."

"That'll be fine. I'll forward your mail to you when you get settled."

"Thanks. I'm sure I'm forgetting something, but that's about it I suppose." It surprised me how little effort it was taking to completely switch over my life. Like changing channels, I thought. It was vaguely unsettling. I knew people who had died to those around them, plunged into new, complicated lives and connections. A week after they were gone – sometimes less – no one seemed to miss them. Now I was leaving. I doubted anyone would miss me very much, either.

"I have to say goodbye to Jack," I suddenly remembered. I had little doubt I'd see him again, but it might not be for a while. Sam had an office in L.A. and sometimes, more often lately, Jack had been going out there with him.

"Don't forget me and Carl," she kidded me. "How's dinner on Friday sound?"

"That sounds good, Mom. How's lunch on Thursday sound to you, just us girls?"

"Sausalito?"

"It'll be just like old times," I smiled, remembering.

"Only this time better."

"I'll pick you up tomorrow then, around eleven."

"Bye baby, and congratulations."

I thanked her, feeling good for both of us. Our lives in the years right after the death of my father were beginning to seem distant and out of focus, like someone else had been living them. Two people who had been in too much pain to see what they had been doing to each other, both of us had fallen headlong into our own private miseries of self-doubt and pity and guilt. Myself feeling abandoned, Mom no doubt feeling in some way responsible. Both of us had been wrong, and we'd come to understand this in our own time and in our own separate ways.

I made my calls and set my itinerary. I called Michael King back with the details of my flight. He was pleased to learn I'd get into LAX early Monday afternoon. That meant no rush hour traffic into Beverly Hills.

Sam would be in Los Angeles Tuesday night. He said he'd call me on arrival. We'd spend time together until he left again on Thursday or Friday.

The week went by in a blur and suddenly, like all futures become, it was a memory I was looking back on, thinking about how happy Mom and Carl had seemed on Friday night. I was standing outside Arrivals at the airport in L.A., a warm breeze in my face, when Michael pulled up in a Silver Shadow. At first I didn't recognize him. I hadn't pegged him for a Rolls Royce kind of guy.

"It isn't mine," he explained, carefully pulling away from the curbside loading area and into the honking congestion of the surprisingly organized chaos of one of the planet's busiest terminals. "Sebastian bought it before we met, about ten years ago. He called it his penis car."

Nothing changed across the genders. "Why not?" I shrugged. "It works on women and not to mention," I kneaded the soft lamb leather upholstery, "it's just plain old comfortable. You got a nice ride here."

"Seb does," he corrected me. "I drive a Mercedes. You can't beat German engineering."

"Speaking of cars, mine's being delivered next week. I forgot to ask if you had enough space in the driveway?"

Michael smiled. "We don't have a driveway, more like a parking lot. Room's not the problem. We're both glad you're staying for a while, Coco. You've got the guesthouse. It's small, but I think you'll love it. It's comfortable and no one ever uses it. It's yours for as long as you want it."

I leaned over and kissed him on the cheek. He smiled.

"Thanks," I said. "For everything, Michael."

He looked across at me, trying his best to stay in the lane as World Way crossed South Sepulveda and merged with West Century. "You deserve it, Coco. And if the ride gets rough, you've got a friend." His eyes were serious and kind in the same moment. "Oh, and if you need to get around until yours gets here, there's a couple vehicles in the garage you can choose from. The keys are in the desk in the front hallway. Don't worry about it," he saw my dazed expression. "We'll go over everything at the house. Relax. Be comfortable. Consider us your L.A. family."

Michael and Sebastian's guesthouse could have easily passed for any normal person's dream house. Their mansion was situated at the end of a tree-lined road in an exclusive section of the city. The entrance was barred from the street by an eight foot high, spiked wrought iron gate that wrapped itself around both sides of the property. The grounds inside the gate were spacious. The main house, guesthouse, and its attached four car garage sprawled across an area roughly the size of two football fields. As the gate swung inward on silent hinges and we drove in, I spotted a tennis court and an outdoor Olympic sized swimming pool near the back, to the right of the large main house. The back perimeter of the house was lushly vegetated, surrounded by plastered wall which disappeared on both sides into more vegetation. Tall palm trees, neatly cropped at their tops, lined the rich blue and white porcelain tiles which made up the pool deck. I spied a large gazebo and what I thought must be a small club house on the near side of the pool, between it and the tennis court. Michael said he'd give me a tour later. The gazebo contained a bathroom, a sauna and, just in case anyone got bored with swimming or badminton, a small game room with a regulation sized billiards table in the middle of it.

We drove up the long, interlocking brick driveway. We passed the garage and the guesthouse on our left, where I'd be staying. The guesthouse, attached to the garage, was two stories. It looked to be around eight hundred square feet per floor. I couldn't believe what I was seeing. Michael continued up the drive for perhaps another seventy-five feet until it forked into a smooth cul-de-sac curve that met itself at the front door. He stopped the car under the mansion's front portico and we got out. Three large, round columns spaced equidistant from each other held up the twelve foot high, ornately decorated ceiling above us.

"Wow!" was all I could manage.

"Welcome home! I'll show you around," Michael invited me inside. We walked across the drive and he unlocked the oversized front door. The surprises continued as he was suddenly assailed by two beautiful, thick pelted golden labs.

"Hi Freda, hi Tessa." Michael knelt down as the two animals lavished him with affection. They turned on me then, tails wagging a mile a second, mouths open in perpetual grins.

"Hi, Tessa – Freda." They lapped at any exposed skin.

"These are our girls," Michael said proudly. "No matter what kind of day I've had, or how long I've been gone, I can always count on them to greet me with an inexhaustible supply of love and affection. Yes, yes, did you miss me? Huh?" He spoke in a bubbling tone, like he might be talking to a baby human as he scratched both dogs behind the ears. Their tails never stopped wagging. "All right, let's get you a treat. You wanna treat?" The dogs began to get excited as they recognized the word. Tessa barked for the first time, and Freda joined in. Michael laughed and stood up. "I better get them a milk bone before they tear me to pieces."

"Right. I can tell these two are a dangerous pair."

"That's enough now!" Michael scolded the barking dogs. They fell instantly silent, tails swishing to and fro in delighted anticipation of what they knew was literally just around the corner.

We took turns feeding Tessa and Freda their treats. After they'd been satisfied and calmed down, Michael mixed us both a couple of vodka and cranberry cocktails. Then he took me on a tour of their home. To say it was stunningly beautiful could not possibly have even begun to describe where he and his lover lived. It took just under an hour to explore all three floors of the mansion.

"Be it ever so humble, there's no place like home," Michael sighed as he finally flopped down onto a sofa in the main floor living room. The dogs suddenly sat up. They looked expectantly toward the front door. Tessa's head was cocked sideways. She looked back at Michael, and then again at the door.

"Who's there?" Michael whispered, playing with the girls. Then I began to discern the dull throaty exhaust of a European sports car. A Ferrari, I guessed as the sound of its engine grew louder. The car stopped, and was suddenly silent as the driver cut the engine off.

"That would be my better half," Michael glowed. I didn't have to be a brain surgeon to see that after ten years they were still very much in love. The dogs took one last look at Michael on the sofa, ignoring me where I sat on a similar one across from him. At the same moment, as if they'd exchanged a silent signal, they bolted for the door.

The big, solid oak door swung wide open and Sebastian shuffled in, only I couldn't see him. I saw only his legs. The rest of him was shielded by the gift wrapped boxes he was carrying, stacked precariously above his head. He kicked one of his legs backwards in an effort to close the door as both Michael and I rose together to help him with his load of presents. The girls wagged their tails, fascinated by the unexpected apparition before them.

## Chapter 20

Michael grabbed the gifts from the top of the pile, exposing his partner's face. I grabbed two more. We all carried them to the wide, low table between the couches in the living room, in front of the fireplace.

"Thank you both so much," Sebastian pecked Michael quickly on the cheek. Michael rubbed his partner on the shoulder, an affectionate gesture.

"How was your day?" he asked him.

"Okay, albeit predictable. How was yours?" He expelled a breath of air, as if to clear his lungs of the day he'd left behind.

"I got up late for a change. I did some shopping. And," he turned to me, smiling, "As you can see, our house guest has arrived. Coco Stevens, meet my partner Sebastian Vilgrain."

I took his outstretched hand in mine. His grip was firm, his eyes blazing azures set in the center of abnormally white irises. His blonde hair matched Michael's. Although I could tell he was perhaps as much as ten years Michael's senior, in his early fifties. Yet the two could have passed for siblings. Both of them were lean and tanned with physiques they obviously worked at to maintain. Sebastian wore Levi's jeans and a tailored denim shirt that accented his shoulders. He could have easily passed for one of the male stars his agency represented.

He'd walked into the house in sensible but expensive loafers. I was in Southern California now, I realized. The only difference in attire between the two of them was Michael's loose, white cotton shirt, similar to the ones I'd seen him wear in Kenya. We sat down on couches in the vast sitting room, surrounded by dogs and gift wrapped packages.

"Michael has told me all about you, Coco. But he didn't tell me how much more beautiful you are in person than even your pictures would indicate. She is absolutely gorgeous, Michael. You are incredible," he appraised me from top to bottom. "But I'm not at all surprised. Michael has always had an extraordinary eye for beauty," he laughed at himself and Michael and I joined in.

"There is so much we need to discuss. Can I offer anyone a drink?"

Michael refreshed our drinks, and poured a neat rye whiskey for Sebastian. He resumed his seat on the couch beside his partner. I sat on the couch across the large, low coffee table from them. The unexplained presents were piled to the side so we could see one another and talk. It was four o'clock on Monday afternoon, in Beverly Hills, and I was already feeling a buzz. This was turning into some kind of business meeting, I mused happily.

Sebastian Vilgrain had grown his business into one of the premier talent agencies on the West Coast. He mentioned offices in New York, London, and had an affiliate in Hong Kong. It seemed the Eurasians also appreciated the long legged picturesque blondes from California. As with many great achievements, Sebastian's had humble beginnings. His first client had been a boyfriend from San Diego State. They'd both been twenty. Seb had demonstrated an eye for talent and a head for business early in life. Word had gotten around campus that he and his *client* were making enough coin to put them through college without the shackles of a student loan. Soon others stood in line. Sebastian's dormitory grew crowded with the comings and goings of some of the most beautiful people in Southern California. Being gay hadn't hurt. Most of the male models he'd signed to lengthy modeling contracts in that last year of college were similarly inclined. They understandably enjoyed keeping it in the family. The female models also felt more comfortable dealing with Sebastian. They never had to worry about being hit on, or about the come-ons from greasy charlatans who claimed to be legitimate talent scouts but were more interested in the casting couch.

The school administration, together with the student housing authority, asked Sebastian to leave the dormitory halfway through the second semester of his final year. He was being disruptive. Seb understood refusal wasn't an option. Rather than concern himself with the hassle of locating new off campus accommodations, and the accompanying commute logistics, he took the route of least resistance. Seb told San Diego State it had been nice, but didn't stop for his gold watch on the way out the door. The week after he quit school, Sebastian incorporated Creative Arts Management. Six days later he opened his fist office in a plain second floor lease in an older recently renovated building on the edge of Ocean Beach.

Within a year, Seb realized that if he wanted to play with the big boys he'd have to move to L.A.. His heart was in San Diego, and he didn't really want to leave the city. When he did, he had it in his mind that he would return in a couple of years, after he'd cemented the necessary relationships to the north. That, of course, never happened. Sebastian left his boyfriend and moved to Los Angeles, taking his contracts with him. He'd stayed, prospered, and came to enjoy the lifestyle his success afforded, far more than he could have predicted. He met Michael King at an industry social function a little over ten years ago. The rest, as they say, was history.

"Who does your housekeeping? Your home is the size of a small apartment building." I had seen two or three grounds keepers earlier, when Michael showed me the pool and the tennis courts. The home was immaculate; spotless from top to bottom.

"The staff works Tuesday through Saturday. They manage the entire home, starting in the guesthouse and working their way through to the main house. There are six of them: three maids, a cook, a maintenance supervisor, and a mechanic-slash-handyperson," explained Sebastian. It had emerged that he was the more dominant of the two. Michael deferred to his older lover not in an effeminate way; he merely quietly acquiesced to greater experience and, perhaps, the wisdom accrued by an older man. Theirs was a truly integrated relationship that, as I was observing first hand, worked better than most. They truly respected each other for their differences, and enjoyed the things they both had in common.

"Just in case we want to change the color in the bedroom," Michael joked.

"He paints?" I was amazed.

"She," Michael said. "Our mechanic is a woman. Maria Sandoval. She's thirty-five and she's the absolute best at what she does."

"She tunes the Ferrari?" I was impressed.

"The shop does that," Sebastian chimed in. "She could, but it would void the warranty. Maria does the rest of what I call the motor pool, though. She's the only person I'd trust with my Rolls."

"I'd like to meet her." I was thinking of my Mustang. "Maybe I'll talk her into showing me a few things."

"I didn't know you were interested in that side of the hood," said Michael, referring to the mechanical end of the auto maintenance.

"I'd like to learn," I admitted. "There's just never been anyone to teach me."

They both looked at each other, mild concern etched across their faces.

"Did I say something wrong?"

Sebastian spoke. "You're a model now, Coco. Grime under those pretty finger nails of yours won't go over too well in the shoots, I'm afraid."

I nodded, seeing his point. "I'll look, not touch," I assured them. Both of them looked relieved. I'd better get used to it, I reminded myself. I would soon be a paycheck to a lot of people who'd be counting on me, especially these two. And Sebastian wasn't like gentle Michael. Behind those crystalline baby blues was a wolf in sheep's clothing. I was on trial, I realized. Sure, they were nice people. But that only went so far. The welcome, the opportunity, the house, all came with strings. They saw in me a goldmine. I thought that was okay, though. I wasn't about to look the proverbial gift horse in the mouth. I wasn't worried in the least about my end of this deal, so I resolved to keep my fingernails clean. Johnny Cash sung it best: 'All I had to do was act naturally.' Michael and Sebastian would see to the rest.

Our conversation migrated, until eventually we got around to business.

"You're on fire," Sebastian told me. "You're the new face in town. Everyone wants a piece of you. You are creating quite the buzz right now."

"They haven't even met me."

"They don't have to. They've seen the elephant shot. That's literally what they're calling it in the press: 'The Elephant Shot'. It's turned you into a commodity, Coco. You're right, no one's met you, but that's a big part of the buzz. It's ironic, but the less they know about you, the more popular you've become."

"So I'm the new flavor of the month? No thanks. What happens after they do meet me? I'll be yesterday's news by tomorrow."

"Uh, those aren't the only pictures making the rounds," Michael confided. His tone changed as he said it and I could swear his eyes darkened a little as he cast a sideways glance at Sebastian.

"The only other shots we did were the ones beside the…Wait a minute; I was naked as a jay-bird in those pictures. Are you telling me *those* ones are out there? How is that possible, Michael?" I was confused. My third vodka wasn't helping matters any. A hint of discomfort edged its way into the conversation. I had trusted Michael, and still did. So it must not be those pictures. Those pictures were spur-of-the-moment abandonment. They were meant for our eyes only. I'd expected Michael to destroy them.

"Please don't be upset," Michael began, and I knew somehow they hadn't been destroyed. My indignation wasn't over the photos themselves, but his deceit.

"Michael, I trusted you."

Sebastian cleared his throat, drawing my attention as he reached for his whiskey. I watched as he made short work of over two ounces of the liquid courage in the bottom of his glass. It burned his esophagus and he coughed again, longer and more loudly this time. I waited until he regained control.

He took a deep breath, and confessed. "It was me, not Michael. He e-mailed the photos to his file. We have no secrets – we have each other's passwords. We spoke on the phone and he was raving about the most beautiful, alluring girl woman he'd ever seen, going on and on about how he was certain she – you – were the next Marilyn. He never told me not to. I'd never opened his photo files before, so there was no reason for Michael to mention it, but I had to look. I just had to see this new wonder for myself. He was right. I couldn't believe my eyes. They're beautiful, Coco. *You're* beautiful. And I'm an idiot. I am truly sorry. Michael had nothing to do with my stealing his work." I could see he was genuinely remorseful.

"I wouldn't go as far –" Michael began and Sebastian immediately raised his hand to stop him.

"Even if you didn't say anything I know how you felt about it, Michael." He reached for his partner's hand and squeezed it. "It's one of the many reasons why I fell in love with you. You've taught me things about myself I never would have learned without you. You've never judged me, and this is one more example of that. And you've always forgiven me no matter what. Sometimes too quickly, I think." They looked at each other. "I've often thought I didn't deserve you."

"Hey guys, you're going to make me cry already." I couldn't let him continue, now that I knew what had happened. In his zeal he'd made a mistake. There was no sense rubbing it in his face. After all, we were all going to be working with one another. Not to mention living seventy-five feet away from each other. And personally, I didn't really mind whoever had seen the body I'd always been proud of. I was a liberal girl.

"Shit happens. It's not that big of a deal. I forgive you, Sebastian."

I saw tears form in the corners of his eyes. He smiled at me and whispered thank you.

"And I forgive you too, my friend," said Michael softly.

"What would I ever do without you, Michael?" The two men embraced each other on the couch.

"Whew!" said Sebastian as they disengaged. He stroked the corners of his eyes with his fingers, glad it was over. We were stronger now. We'd been honest with ourselves, and with each other. If this was going to work, that's how it had to be. No secrets. From here on in we were partners, that's how I figured it.

I guess Sebastian saw what happened as a perfect segue into the enigma of the five gifts wrapped in assorted colorful paper. They still sat piled on the edge of the table, untouched since we'd put them there. As far as he was concerned, there was probably no better time than now to address the strange packages. He leaned to his right and snatched the top one from the pile.

"In light of what's just transpired," he smiled, handing the package across the low table to me, "I'm sure glad I got these. Surprise! Congratulations, Coco."

"What's this?" I took it from him. "It's not my birthday." I was a little unsure how to react.

"In a way it is," Sebastian disagreed with me. "As America's next supermodel and after such a faux pas, discreet as the showings may have been, consider this a small gesture of conciliation on my part. Originally I meant these gifts to celebrate the signing with you. If you still want me to represent you, that is. But now they've taken on a new meaning."

"Oh, stop it. I got a sneaking suspicion the results were worth the hanging tongues. Am I on the Internet yet?" I half joked.

"As far as I know, you're still under wraps. At least until we say differently," Sebastian said craftily.

"Sebastian, I get the feeling you're going to make us all a really big pile of cash. Now let's see what wonderful baubles you've gotten me," I said with a child's sparkle in my eyes.

## Chapter 21

I faxed my contract to Sam, who ran it by his General Counsel, Nathaniel Katz. It came back two days later with only a few minor changes. Creative Arts Management – CAM – didn't see a problem. They incorporated the changes in a new draft, and I was officially onboard less than a week after I'd moved into the fully furnished guesthouse.

Sebastian asked me if I could live on a ten grand a month cash advance until about Christmas, when he'd have his vendors' contracts in order. Then he'd start cutting me the big checks. The ten grand was clear, but I'd have to pay my own taxes. Of course, Michael just happened to know a good accountant. The magazines would pay all of my travel expenses on any of the remote shoots, which would be just about every one of them. Nothing was going to get shot in Beverly Hills, Seb assured me. Everything was out of town, a long way out of town. My first shoot was in Barbados.

I looked forlornly at one of my suitcases, sitting unpacked near the large opening of the walk-in closet in the guesthouse's master bedroom. I'd just hung up the phone from speaking with Melinda Carlysle, Sebastian's Executive Assistant, or EA, as they called it in the world of dancing, prancing, and high financing. I shook my head, dizzy from the pace. They all seemed to move as if they were running cars at the Darlington Motor Speedway. I realized with a twinge of guilt that I hadn't called Mom since I'd been out here. I reached for my cell phone. It rang just as I was reaching for it. Startled, I let it ring twice before answering.

"How's my supermodel?"

"Frazzled, doing ninety in a thirty. It's nice to hear your voice, Sam. I miss you. Are you in L.A.?" I asked hopefully.

"I'm in New York, baby. Sorry. I can hear it in your voice. You need some TLC, don't you?"

I was disappointed. I'd hoped he was here, but I soldiered on. "Do I sound that bad?"

"You'll be okay, Coco."

I rubbed my eyes. It was only eight o'clock in the evening and I was beat. I'd been up since five, getting ready to leave on Monday. I couldn't believe it was already Wednesday. I'd been here for over a week.

The devil was in the details. I'd actually accomplished a lot in the last nine days. My car had been delivered, and by now I knew all the staff by name. Maria Sandoval in particular was a real fireball. I kept my word and kept my nails from getting dirty, wearing gloves to help Maria tune the Mustang. Sebastian almost fainted when he saw black grease smudged across my face. He looked sternly at the mechanic, who shrugged.

"I tried to tell her, Mr. Vilgrain," her Dominican accent sounded cute in coveralls. "She insisted that she help." I shrugged when Seb looked back at me. I held up my gloved hands to show him I'd at least done that much. Seb shook his head, displeased, and walked back out of the garage saying nothing. Maria and I burst out laughing, instant conspiratorial camaraderie of the highest order. I was certain we'd be good friends for a long time.

It seemed there were a million other details to attend to. I changed the address on my driver's license, redid the paperwork for my car insurance because of my new zip code, studied a local map of where I lived in relation to Seb's office in Bel Air. The list went on. Travel arrangements for the Barbados shoot were in full swing.

"I'm going to Barbados on Monday," I told Sam. "It's my first assignment. I think it's a layout for *Vogue*. We'll be there all week."

"Is Michael going with you?"

"Yes. From what I can tell, he and Sebastian work together often. No one seems to mind."

"Who would?" said Sam. "They're both on the A-list. They work in tandem. Everyone wins."

Call waiting beeped in my ear. I glanced at the number. "Sam, it's Mom on the other line."

"Enough said. I love you, sweetheart. Get some rest. You sound tired. I'll call you later."

"If I don't call you first. Love you, Bye." I switched over, "Mom?"

"Your one and only, baby. I was worried. You haven't called."

"I'm sorry, Mom. Moving. It's a pain in the you-know-what. How's Carl?"

"He's fine, and he says hi. I got a letter from your landlord."

"That was quick. It's probably the check for the damage deposit." I'd signed a sublet agreement with the building's management. That way, if anything came up while I was still there, I wouldn't have to bother Mom or Carl with it. Mom opened the letter while we talked.

"That's it all right," she informed me. "Should I send it to you?"

I suddenly realized I hadn't yet had a chance to even tell her my new address. "Just endorse my name on the back, Mom. It's your deposit."

"Are you sure?"

"I'm sure." Mom was a dear. Even though she must have known my income had spiked, she still worried about me.

"So how are you Coco, really? This is your Mom talking now. How is it out there in La-La Land?"

I sighed. "I've been cramming a lot into a short amount of time. I guess I'm tired, but it's a good tired. Sebastian and Michael have been just great. They even gave me a key to the main house and said I'm welcome to use it any time. I'm still staying in the guesthouse, but it's beautiful here. The place has everything, and it's private."

"Do you feel safe there?"

"Everything's behind these huge iron gates. They've installed a state-of-the-art security system." I didn't mention Freda and Tessa. They probably wouldn't hurt a flea. "Plus, Michael's got a full time staff of six who are here five days of the week, not to mention the pool man. It's a surprisingly busy place most of the time. They told me they entertain two or three times a month, as well. They're a really nice couple, Mom. I couldn't have wished for a better situation. Oh, I won't be around next week. I'll be in Barbados. It's my first professional gig."

"Does that mean you're getting paid?"

I laughed. "That's exactly what it means, Mom. From now on it's cash and carry. They've set me up with an accountant, too. I haven't met him yet, but Sebastian and Michael use him so he's got to be good."

"It sounds like you've hit the lottery, Coco. I'm happy for you."

"Looks like our luck has finally changed," I said. "We deserve it, Mom."

"I keep waiting for the hammer to fall."

"Don't." Always the pessimist, I thought. Why couldn't Mom bury the last of her depression and just accept her good fortune? "Remember what we talked about that time in Sausalito?" I reminded her.

"How could I forget?" Mom said. "You're right again, baby. We deserve the happiness in our lives. I'm sorry if I rained a little on your parade."

"I forgive you, Mom. Go and sin no more," I joked, smiling. Mom was better than I ever remembered her being. I suppose depression was her cross to bear, and she'd learned to live with it in the most manageable way she knew how. I wondered how Carl coped with it, surmising he no doubt handled it with the patience of Job. They were a tailor made couple, a perfect blend of two uniquely separate yet complimentary personalities. One's strengths were the other's weaknesses, and vice versa. They deserved each other.

I told Mom I'd e-mail my address and call her when I got back from the Caribbean. We made mention of tentative plans for a reunion in September, possibly on the long Labor Day weekend. I told her I was happy and that I loved her. She told me the same.

The Barbados shoot went well. Every day I grew more confident under Michael's watchful tutelage. I couldn't believe how beautiful the other models were. They were tall and striking, flawless, and had a lot more experience than me. I thought they might be standoffish, resentful or even envious of the stranger among them, but it was exactly the opposite. The four of them helped me at every turn. Together with Michael, we all grew incredibly close in the five days we spent together romping in the surf. The models made me feel as if I was born to be a model. In the end, we exchanged particulars and each of us said we'd keep in touch. The modeling world was a small one; we would definitely work together again soon.

Michael was particularly proud of me. He'd waited until we were back in Beverly Hills to tell me. Although he was a professional enough photographer that no one would ever dream of calling him on it, he'd showed no favoritism while we'd been on location. I appreciated this, since I wanted no special treatment. Either I'd fit in and make it on my own merits, or I wouldn't. What I demanded from my photographer, and received, was honesty.

"You're a natural." The photographer said as he looked at me and Sebastian. We were sharing drinks on the sofas in the main house. It was Sunday night, two days after we got back from the shoot.

"It was the gloves," I teased Seb. "Not a speck of grease under my fabulous finger nails." I raised my fingers and wiggled them. Even Sebastian couldn't help himself, breaking into a good-natured chuckle.

"Touché," he said. "But I still want you to stay out from underneath those machines." He knew I had a love affair with cars. "That's why we hired Maria," he pleaded.

"I'll take it under serious consideration," I promised, winking at Michael. But we all knew my vow carried no substance. Maria, I already knew, was an excellent teacher. She and I had our lecherous eyes on the Ferrari. Warranty or not, we were circling the Enzo like a pair of hungry Arctic wolves on a spent doe.

"I'm meeting with Time Warner in the morning," Sebastian was suddenly in the mood for business. "We're going to ink the contract for their September cover."

"The Elephant Shot. That was fast," I complimented him.

"They jumped on it. I told them if they dragged their feet I'd put them at the back of the line. They didn't want to risk losing that shot to one of their competitors."

"That shot being your career launcher," Michael reiterated.

"It's all about the money, isn't it?"

"I'm not going to apologize for what I do," Sebastian spoke with measured cadence.

"No, no. I didn't mean…" I fumbled for words, "I just meant…suddenly I'm getting all this money – these accolades – and I'm exactly the same person I was before I went to Africa. Before all this happened. Don't get me wrong, please," I emphasized. "I'm not complaining. I'm very grateful. I guess I find the whole thing – this new life of mine – what's a good word for it? Surrealistic. It's like I'm living someone else's dream. Maybe I'm just not used to it, all this opulence I mean," I waved around the room. "It's just *little ole' me*, playing in the sand like I've always done. Suddenly there's all this hoopla. I got treated like a celebrity in Barbados. Do you know I got asked for my autograph? I couldn't believe it. I was eating dinner and this couple from Miami came over to my table and asked me to sign their freaking menu. They thought I was a celebrity or something."

"You are," Michael tutored me.

"It's going to come up," interjected Sebastian, "Especially when your pictures start appearing in magazines. You're not going to believe what happens when September comes around and *Time* hits the stands."

"I'm not so sure I like the sound of that," I worried.

Sebastian looked at Michael. A silent conversation passed between the two of them.

"Elizah Doolittle," they both grinned.

"Who?"

"My Fair Lady," Michael began to explain. "It's a wonderful story about a girl with a few rough edges."

"Are you implying my edges are rough?" my eyes twinkled.

"Elizah Doolittle," both said again, nodding to each other.

"The main character of the play accepts a challenge to sophisticate poor Elizah. He teaches her to speak proper English."

"Wait a minute. Is this the one about the rain in Spain falls mainly on the plain?"

"You know it, then."

"Vaguely, it's a really old movie, guys." I didn't want to age them. "I think I saw it with my mother once a long time ago. What happens in the end?" I genuinely couldn't remember.

"In the end they fall in love." I looked sideways at Sebastian. We all knew *that* wasn't going to happen.

"She didn't change," said Michael. "Well, maybe a little on the outside. The point is, in here," he tapped his chest, "in her heart she was still the same. Her outside didn't make any difference. That's who the main character fell in love with – The *real* Elizah, not the manufactured one."

"Are we going somewhere with this?"

"We are packaging and marketing the *real* you, unless I miss my guess."

"And he is seldom, if ever, wrong," Michael interrupted Seb.

"Thank you, Michael. Unless I'm wrong about this, and I'm staking my professional reputation that I'm not, the world will fall in love with the real Coco Stevens. It's why they fought over The Elephant Shot. No one else would have reacted the way you did, Coco. That shot was from the heart."

"In that moment you were my snowflake," Michael picked up where his lover left off. "Different from the rest, you were unique among a rolling storm of humanity. Think about it. Those villagers – that logging operation – had enslaved those noble beasts. You responded to what touched you on a level few live to experience. You're one of a kind," he repeated. "The world will bow to that side of you. It's what we all seek to accomplish, but seldom achieve. You felt their pain, Coco. You reached into the heart of God's creation. Your tears will touch us all. They will cause us to search our own souls and maybe, if we're lucky enough, we'll feel what we've forgotten. We'll feel what it's like to be human again."

A solemn silence descended on the room. It had a dampening effect, magnifying the sounds you only hear as dark clouds roll in, their blackness blocking out the sun before electric fury strikes the land. There's a deafening silence as the air stills, readying itself for the onslaught. A clock somewhere ticked heavily. The room waited.

In a hushed voice I said, more to myself than to Michael and Sebastian, "I wonder if they'll be able to separate me from those ideals? I wonder if they'll know the difference, or if I'll just be one more pretty face in a never ending lineup?" I looked at them. "If what you say is true about that photo, then I want them to feel what I felt. Do you think that's possible? Do you think they'll know why I was crying?"

The room waited. *The silence was deafening.*

## Chapter 22

The nude shots of me dancing among the flamingos mysteriously hit the Internet the day after I appeared on the cover of *Time*. The magazine was furious, but what could they do? They threatened to sue, but the threats were empty ones. It became the biggest selling issue ever. Every site the photos were uploaded to smashed records for the number of hits in a day. I became a household name, Coco this, Coco that. When we tried going out to celebrate, the paparazzi hounded us. A crowd of cameras was waiting when we pulled up to Laguna's, a popular restaurant in Bel Air. I was able to squeeze out of the front door of the Rolls past the throng, but Michael barely made it out of the back seat. Sebastian's voice screamed into the melee of cameramen from where he, intelligently, remained behind the steering wheel.

"Get back in, this isn't going to work! There's too many of them!"

I clambered back into the front seat in time to see a shoving match develop between the valet parking attendants and the cameramen. I somehow got the car door closed. Michael made it into the back seat and did the same. Sebastian pulled out of the lot as carefully as he could manage, dividing the frenzied herd with the heavy engine of the Silver Cloud. He punched the accelerator to the floor on the roadway out front and sped into traffic, dodging between cars in the surprisingly nimble Rolls. Waiting until the last possible moment, he cranked the steering wheel hard right. We careened across two lanes of traffic onto the freeway entrance ramp, losing two or three pursuing cars in the lanes to the left of us whose drivers couldn't react fast enough.

None of us spoke. I was scared to death. My heart was racing in my chest. I held my hand against my head, leaning on the car's passenger door. Sebastian checked the rearview mirror.

"I think we lost them," he muttered, not happy at all. "Are you hurt?" he asked, looking over at me.

I forced back tears. "I'm okay, but…they were like a pack of wild animals." I had never experienced anything remotely similar to what I'd just been through. "They went crazy. They could have hurt somebody."

Michael leaned forward from where he sat in the back seat. He put his hand on my shoulder, trying to comfort me. "It was a mistake," he admitted. I turned around to see what he meant. His hair was tousled, his face flushed. He smiled feebly. I managed to climb back into the car right before the shoving started, but he'd waited a few seconds too long and been caught in the initial onslaught. "I guess we underestimated your star power."

Sebastian's complexion had initially been waxen and pale. Color was just now returning to his face. He'd kept his cool and maintained the presence of mind to get us out of there, but clearly he'd been shaken worse than I had.

"That's putting it mildly," he exhaled a deep breath, still nervously checking the rear view mirror every few seconds. "I've never seen anything like it," he admitted, rattled. "I'm sorry, Coco. If I had the slightest inkling of this, I never would have agreed to going out, at least not so soon after the cover spread. I knew you'd be big, but that –"

"That was a tsunami!" Michael finished for him. "What?" From the back seat, he saw Seb shaking his head.

"The billboards, it's too late to cancel the billboards."

"What billboards?" I was perplexed.

"Those billboards," he sighed, pointing ahead of us and groaning, "I told the ad agency next week." He slapped the steering wheel in frustration.

I followed Sebastian's gaze. My breath caught in my throat when I saw what he meant. It was as big as a ten story condominium, by my estimation. The billboard was wedged between two others on the side of one of the highest profile thoroughfares in the world. It towered over everything near it, ten stories of me and the elephant. I had to admit I didn't leave much to the imagination in my thong bikini. I realized then that I hadn't ever seen the photo, I'd only heard it described through the eyes of the photographer. What struck me immediately was the stark contrast between the smooth, bronzed texture of my skin and the dull, rough hide of the elephant. What jumped from the picture more than anything else were my eyes, slightly downcast, exuding pathos. They were dark pools of light that seemed to embody a deep, unbridled sorrow. Angst filled, they reflected a world in free fall; the twisted irony of the conflict of man pitted against his dying environment. Looking at the billboard, even I couldn't help but feel a terrible sadness at what the photo represented. Tears fell from the corners of the picture's eyes, lamenting the unseen yet undeniable carnage of man's desires, and spilled down the ten foot cheeks of my face.

"You said billboards," I gasped, "As in plural. There are others?"

Sebastian nodded. "New York, Miami, Minneapolis, London, Tokyo...oh, and Sydney. There are six more."

"My God," I gasped.

"That explains what happened at Laguna's restaurant," said Michael. The giant billboard rose skyward as we closed in on it. Now I could tell it was somehow fastened to the side of a building with a matching number of floors. It was colossal.

"The shot heard around the world," Sebastian conceded, not believing it himself. He whistled softly. "This will garner a hundred million in advertising, folks, maybe even two. This will make the six o'clock news in every major market in the world, as well as all the newspapers. Every talk show host from Ellen to Letterman will want to have you on." He looked at me. I stared blankly back at him, feeling more and more like a lost little girl in a dark forest with nightfall fast approaching. Only the sudden ringing of my cell phone brought me back from the broken, jagged edges of panic.

"Coco, aren't you going to answer that?" Sebastian asked.

Wordlessly I fumbled to retrieve the phone from inside my purse on the bench seat between us.

"Hello?"

"Coco, it's me. Have you been watching television?"

"Where are you, Sam?" I desperately wanted him near me.

"I'm in New York, but I'll be in L.A. tonight. We need to talk. Don't bother to pick me up, I'll be late. I'll grab a limo from the airport and come right over. Jack will be with me. We should get to your place around midnight. Have you seen the news?" he repeated.

"No...I," I was still absorbing myself in ten stories and in six cities.

"You're it; it's fantastic, you and the elephant. It's unbelievable. Listen, something just came up, I've gotta go. I'll see you tonight. Are you okay? You don't sound your usual self."

I swallowed hard. I could feel myself fighting back. Damn, I'd been sent for a loop. "Yeah, I'm all right," I said. "I'm feeling better now that you called. Will you be hungry? You said Jack was coming with you?"

"Yeah, me and Jack – he's always hungry. Watch the news. I have to go now, baby. I'll see you tonight." He broke the connection.

"Okay. I love you, Sam," I said automatically into a dead phone. I put the phone back in my purse, feeling a bit more like taking on the world again. I looked at Seb. "Next time I want to know *before* something like this happens." It came out with an unexpected, harder edge to it than I'd intended. But I realized in the same instant that I didn't regret my tone. Softening it, I said, "If that's not too much to ask, I mean."

"It was my mistake. I should have informed you, Co-co."

"I don't want you to feel you need to inform me of every detail of your business decisions, but this one blindsided me," I explained. "I wasn't prepared for it."

"It was more like an assassination. I'm sorry. I promise you this will never happen again. If it's any consolation, none of us could have prepared for this. It's never happened before, not like this. This...is *intense.* It scares me, if you want to know the truth. And *nothing* scares me. But we'll live through it. Back at the restaurant was the worst of it. From now on, there will be security in place for any of your public appearances. I'm afraid things have changed for you, sweetheart," admitted Sebastian.

"Changed?"

"It happens to every celebrity. It's the price of fame," Michael spoke from the back seat. "It's called the Elvis syndrome. The man with the original posse couldn't go anywhere by himself. If he went out for a cheeseburger, he was mobbed. To the extreme, fan adoration can prove fatal. Gianni Versace paid the ultimate price for his notoriety in '97. Too late for the Italian clothing designer who walked freely among his subjects to learn celebrity can turn on you without warning. They adore you one minute, the next..." he shrugged, not finishing the sentiment.

"Like the guy who shot Lennon."

"David Chapman, he's another example. And Lennon was nice to him. He obliged David with an autograph just before the asshole shot him five times, pardon my French," Sebastian made his point.

"Bottom line is," said Michael, "from here on we've all got to recognize what happened, and how quickly things are changing. There's no time to play catch up. We've got to be careful now, not tomorrow or next week. I think we should consider a bodyguard, at least some sort of personal security for you, Coco."

I slowly smiled, understanding now why Sam said he wanted to talk with me and why he was bringing Jack out here with him. "I think that's already been taken care of," I said, suddenly feeling more confident I might be able to deal with my new reality.

Sebastian stopped checking the rearview mirror. He took an off ramp and we circled back, heading home. He glanced at me with a worried expression across his face, but said nothing. Neither did Michael. They had heard one side of the phone conversation and both knew who

Sam was. Michael, of course, had met him. Sebastian knew him by reputation.

"We're going to have rewrite your contract," said Sebastian. "I'll set up a meeting with Andy Black if you'd like." Black was one of CAM's accountants. "On Tuesday if that fits." I was leaving for Baja on Wednesday. We were doing a fall line in Loreto, a quaint and beautiful seaside resort town halfway down the Baja peninsula. Michael had chartered a propeller driven Saratoga out of San Diego. I almost talked him into a couple days of rest and relaxation afterwards in Los Cabos. The Capes were further south, a thousand fifty miles below the U.S. border, on the very southern tip of Baja, California. It was truly beautiful down there, a collage of pristine beaches. I couldn't wait to have a cold beer in Sammy Hagar's Cabo Wabo nightclub. The Van Halen front man was known to pop in unexpectedly from time to time and play his own stage. In light of what had just happened, I wasn't going to delude myself. I thought I'd been busy up until now, but I could tell I was about to jump into warp drive.

The content of our conversation evolved as rapidly as the scenery around us. Michael continued, "Your biggest problem will be taxes. Andy can show you how the shelters work to minimize your liability. Real estate is always good, especially in your case, because you're so young."

I was listening carefully, trying to understand what was happening. What I heard was a shift in direction. I wasn't a coddled guest anymore. That had changed quickly. The chemistry between us was different now, or maybe it had always been this way and I just hadn't noticed. Either way, I couldn't escape the shroud of melancholy which had settled like a shadow across my mind. I wondered with a touch of angst in my heart if this was what they meant by innocence lost.

I asked the only question it seemed I hadn't asked. "How much do you think I'm going to earn over the next couple of years, Sebastian?"

"More than anyone who's come before you," he stated with conviction. "It's hard to put an accurate number to it. There are so many different variables to account for. But work hard, keep your nose clean, we'll try the best we can to retain all the publishing and residual rights we can, and I'd say twenty, thirty million. Maybe more if things go right. We've got to really capitalize out of the gates. We've got to use The Elephant Shot to build your momentum. It's a magnificent foundation, and we'll run with it. Build on it. It will be hard work, but it will be more than worth it. You're young. You've got a long and very prosperous career ahead of you. What's wrong, Coco?" Seb finally saw the stunned look on my face.

I hadn't heard most of what he said. All I was thinking about was the numbers. Twenty or thirty million dollars was unimaginable to me. What could one person possibly do with all that money? It was more than enough for five lifetimes. I remembered the time after Dante's when I was seventeen and looked at myself in the bathroom mirror. I had wondered what they saw that they would pay so much for. Now I wondered the same thing. I was so much more than an object of desire, and therein lay the irony. All they wanted was the object. Was I the only one who figured the rest of me was what truly held the value? It was the real treasure, hidden beneath the glitter. It was the submerged, dangerous part of the iceberg that sank Titanic.

## Chapter 23

Billy Cunningham didn't seem much different than the majority of people I had come to know in my life, myself included. We were all creatures of habit. He was going somewhere, all right, but I never believed for one second that a man his age spent as much as three months at a time in the desert. I had no doubt he enjoyed the sojourns with his donkey Pete, and that he possessed all the skills necessary to survive out there for extended periods of time. He must enjoy the challenge, but the man was nearing the end of his trail. I surmised there was something else that kept him away from Brittle for those lengthy absences or, more likely, *someone* else.

If there was someone he was traveling across the desert to see, then my search area would be limited to where he could reasonably trek to and return from, with the supplies he took with him each time he left Brittle. I had a few more talks with the supply store owner, since by now we'd become friends. He was a treasure trove of information. It turned out B.C. was more regular in his habits than people around town knew.

As the seasons came and went, so did Billy, four times a year as a rule, always carrying the same amount of supplies when he set out across the desert for parts unknown. Usually, no one saw him leave. He departed in the predawn hours, leaving public roads soon after. I guessed there was probably only one other person awake at that time to witness Billy's departure. I hit jackpot; the rural postman.

I thought a man with a bushy, snow white beard walking off road with a pack laden donkey would be easily recalled. I was right, and another piece fell into the puzzle. The enigmatic Billy Cunningham left from the same end of town, supplies stowed on the back of his trusty steed Pete, and returned the same way between five and seven weeks later. B.C. spent six months of the year away from home, in the somewhere else he journeyed to. In situations resembling this one, a woman was usually involved somehow, a woman or the memory of one.

B.C. was close to ninety years old, albeit an extremely fit ninety. Recently he'd cut his annual trips down to three, probably due to his age. I was curious why he didn't take his old truck. I had a friend at Motor Vehicles in Vegas discreetly run his name. Nothing came up. Billy had never had a Nevada driver's license. I suspected that alone wasn't the reason no one saw him drive. I suspected a man like Billy had his own set of rules, and not having a driver's license wouldn't matter much to him. He was a throwback from a bygone era. He belonged in the past, when people's word was gold. Everyone knew everyone they lived with back then. Families moved across the continent to settle in a new land they believed offered them opportunities not available in the place they'd left. But once they got there, they stayed. They rolled up their sleeves, worked hard, and planted roots. The place became their home. They stayed for their lifetime, perhaps never traveling more than twenty or thirty miles down the road for the duration of that stay.

So people looked out for one another. The liar in town was the pariah and the stranger tolerated, looked upon with suspicion and, if deemed dishonest, unwelcome.

That B.C. apparently never drove didn't surprise me. He'd probably used the truck at some point, when it ran. But that had been eons ago. Billy hadn't been in a hurry for a long time. In the entire time his family had owned the land, there'd been only one transfer of title. Billy had sold a small piece on the tip of his holdings back to the government in nineteen sixty-three when they'd been thinking about a site for a nuclear power plant. The money, invested in a conservative portfolio, would have more that satisfied Billy's simple needs and kept the tax man at bay. And that wasn't counting the odds and ends, other people's junk for the most part, that B.C. collected and then resold for whatever he could get from whomever would buy it.

At one point, the postman told me, he recalled a huge pile of scrap metal – aluminum mostly – that Billy had collected. Over time, it had grown to the size of a small baseball field. It was so far out of town that no one had ever complained. In fact, they'd even added their own scrap to it. Then, one day, the price of aluminum had shot up higher than the Stratosphere Casino. Trucks had hauled all Billy's scrap metal to a refinery outside of Vegas. No one knew exactly who they were, or what they paid B.C. for it, but it had been a lot. Billy Cunningham, the town then agreed, was nobody's fool.

I agreed. Behind the facade of age, maybe even the facade of a simple minded prospector, a different picture of a man began to emerge as I went over B.C.'s profile. I began to *feel* his character. As I pieced the bits of information together, a personality I liked very much began to coalesce. I began to understand who B.C. was and, more importantly, how he had become that person.

I learned Billy had been married once. She'd been a woman from over the hill. The certificate had been signed in fifty-three, but Dorey Cunningham had died from influenza eight years later, at the age of thirty-three. B.C. himself had been closing in on forty.

What amazed me the most the more I researched him was how the man had lived his life. An anonymous stranger when I began to dig, I had now unearthed a complex man of many faces: a husband, a lover, a contemplative, obviously spiritual man of the land. As far as I could tell, he'd never remarried. That could mean a number of things, but I was betting it simply meant he'd really loved his wife, preferring his memories of her to the prospect of a fresh start with another.

But he must have met somebody; either that or he was at least seeing someone. Why else would he have taken all those trips to wherever it was he went, for as long as people could remember he'd been going? That part of the puzzle remained a mystery, but I wasn't short on ideas. B.C. was coming back, probably in less than two weeks. I was running out of time. If I didn't find him before Sam did, I was sure the crazy plan I'd concocted would fall to pieces.

I looked at the phone on the desk in front of me, thinking hard. Google Maps provided me a thirty-five mile radius around Brittle. An approximation of the area I felt B.C. could safely and predictably cover on foot with Pete and return, given his supplies. The biggest towns on the periphery of the radii were Kingman to the north and Laughlin to the south. Other, smaller hamlets dotted the rest of the map within the yellow highlighted circle, resembling airplanes on a traffic controller's radar scope. But I was hunting for a person, someone who lived in one of these towns. Where did you go? Where are you?

The spread of possibilities on the map made me realize I had less time than I thought.

If B.C. had traveled to one of the farther towns, he'd be leaving sometime next week in order to get back to Brittle per his schedule. My theory that Billy was in one of these towns, possibly staying in the home of someone he knew, was based on the fact that he hadn't been spotted from the air. Both of Sam's twin-engine Cessnas roared off the sandy clay runway every morning in a tenacious, albeit futile effort to locate Billy. From what I could tell they searched most of the day, returning several times for refueling and pilot breaks. The pilots would wolf down some food and quickly return to the air, picking up the search from where they left off. They were determined. Sam, I was sure, was pulling out all the stops. But like I said, you couldn't find someone if you weren't looking for him in the right place.

Suddenly I had an idea. With a few clicks of the mouse, the plat schedules surrounding Brittle and B.C.'s holdings were plainly visible on the screen. They extended from the north edge of town outward, surrounding most of the creek. He owned the land I thought must cover the mother lode, that part was obvious. I looked carefully at the display for the land that bordered his. I discounted the smaller photo to the south, the land that crawled outward from the town's center. It was guesswork, but at this point I had to get lucky in order to win the race against Sam. It made sense to me that whoever I was looking for would be where it had all begun.

It was likely a relative, certainly a person Billy's grandfather had known. Someone present not long after the birth of B.C.'s father. A few more clicks on adjoining parcels and I had a short list of titles going back to just after Billy's grandfather had staked the first claim to begin the town. Now I had something. I clicked again, this time interposing the earlier map of the towns within the thirty-five mile radius onto the titled parcels of land. Off in the corner, split on the screen in miniature, was the land titles list. My luck was holding. My heart picked up its pace as adrenaline began to flow through my veins. My hands felt moist. I wiped my palms on my jeans and leaned into my work. I used the cursor to correlate the three fields of information, integrating three separate banks of data into one. I was looking for someone who had known the Cunninghams the longest, who had settled with them early enough that they knew each other's families, and who owned land adjacent or near enough to the Cunningham plot. A person who shared the same lifestyle. If I could find such a person, they might know more about Billy than anyone else. If I got really lucky, they might even have knowledge regarding his whereabouts. It was a thin straw, but I had no other options that made any sense.

Three names emerged, three whose chains of land titles had remained in their families and went back far enough to match what I was seeking. Nervously I searched the Internet for the most recently listed owners. I was looking for someone older, perhaps approaching Billy's age. Whoever I found would be the last of a line. I hit a home run on the third name. Leslie Hastings was eighty-seven years old. The title listed, among other things, her last known telephone number and address. She lived on a rural route, perhaps ten miles outside Kingman. The town had not made it on the map. It was too small. In fact, it probably held no more than a dozen or so inhabitants. The land she owned had been in her family for one hundred and eight years. A year less than the tract B.C. owned.

Fighting off an urge to jump up and scream, I reached for my cell phone on the desk beside my laptop. My fingers trembled. Somehow I managed to punch the numbered keys. Surely it couldn't be this easy.

The phone on the other end rang seven times before it was answered. "Hello?" The voice sounded old. I could tell by the effort it made to form each syllable, the same kind of sound old people made when they got in and out of chairs. Even speech was a chore.

"Mrs. Hastings? Leslie Hastings?"

There was a clattering sound on the other end, like dice being thrown onto a hardwood floor. Whoever answered had dropped the handset. There was a pause, then, "Hello? Are you still there?" From the same tired voice.

"Yes, I'm here. Are you Leslie Hastings?"

"Leslie?" my heart was in my throat. She knew the name. "She's not here right now. May I take a message?"

"Do you know where I can reach Mrs. Hastings? Will she be there later?" I had no idea where there was.

"Oh, no. She's gone to the city."

"My name is Coco."

"I'm Claire Anderson, Miss Coco. Are you a friend of Leslie's?"

"We've never met," I confessed. "I was hoping I could speak with her about someone who may have been a neighbor of hers. His name is Billy Cunningham."

"Oh, Billy is a very nice man."

"You know Billy Cunningham?" I fought to keep from hyperventilating.

"Oh, yes. He comes here quite often. He drops by on his way to the city, maybe three or four times a year. He lives in Brittle, I think. Yes, Brittle. The strangest thing, though…" she seemed puzzled.

"Yes?"

"Billy travels by donkey, at least to get here he does. Says he prefers it over the Greyhound bus. Says the bus is too noisy, too expensive. Can you imagine? Traveling in the desert with a donkey? Land sakes alive, I can't imagine that. But he says he's fine by it. He says if God had meant us to travel on a Greyhound bus He would have given us wheels. Can you imagine? Oh, lord, he's too old for that desert. I wouldn't tell him that, though. He can be a might bit touchy about that sort of thing. He acts like he isn't a day over eighty. Can you imagine?"

"Mrs. Anderson, how do you know Mrs. Hastings?"

"Why, Leslie is my sister," she replied, as if I should have already known.

"And Billy is a friend of your sister's?" I was amazed.

"Oh, yes. We both are. We've known Billy since before the wedding."

"What wedding is that? May I call you Claire?"

"That would be fine, Miss Coco."

"Just Coco."

"Oh my, that's an unusual name, Juscoco. I've never heard a name like that before."

"No…it's…What wedding?"

"Why, when Billy married our sister Ethyl. Back in nineteen fifty-three. I'll never forget that day. It was such a lovely ceremony," she spoke as if it had happened a month ago.

I smiled, spirits soaring. "Are they still together?" I launched a long shot.

"Ethyl died eight years after they were married." I could hear the sadness in her voice, even after all the intervening years.

"It was just terrible – so unexpected. Ethyl was such a dear. She was so young, and she wasn't ill. She was never sick a day in her life, that's why her passing so surprised us all. In the end, we thought it might have been her age. She may have waited too long."

"Not sick? Well, how did your sister pass?"

"Why, she passed in childbirth, dear. She died while giving life to a precious baby girl."

# Chapter 24

I didn't need coaxing. I grabbed my purse and cell phone and flew out of the garage and into the subdivision. I think the car might have clipped the arm of the wooden barrier at the front security gate as it raised too slowly for my liking. I put the pedal down hard, sending the Corvette into a controlled sideways drift as I roared onto the parkway leading out of Summerlin. I peeled around the perimeter and took the first exit south, doing a hundred twenty as I straightened out along the highway. The radar detector was on. The clock was ticking. Luck be a lady, I thought as I raced down the road, the adrenaline rush feeding the hungry edge in my gut.

Claire Anderson's place wasn't easy to locate. I took a couple of wrong turns, bottomed out a few times on dusty potholed roads of sand and clay. I stopped a couple of times, once to ask a weathered, dark skinned Mexican at a gas station for directions. In broken English and with his toothy but genuine smile he got me closer.

Three hours and twenty minutes after I had left Summerlin I pulled onto a narrow, winding dirt driveway. A surprisingly elegant two story house was situated at the end of the long drive. Eight or ten trees had been strategically sprinkled around the property, barriers to the sometimes violent winds which all too regularly blew across the Nevada plains.

The stucco on the house was painted a dull brownish-orange color, like the western sky looked close to sunset after a rare bout of desert rain. The windows were flanked by pale white, plastic louvered shutters, badly faded from the merciless midday sunshine. All told, the house was in good shape. Obviously someone tended to it.

I pulled up in the front yard and cut the engine. I climbed out of the low slung sports car, wondering if in my haste I'd damaged the undercarriage on a particularly bad bounce in a nasty fight between the frame's metal and the stony gravel on the road beneath it.

It was the nineteenth of August and still hotter than blazes. I glanced across the Corvette's glossy black lacquer paint. The car's surface simmered, vibrating like a mirage where plastic fiberglass met air and heat. I could hear what sounded like a small dog barking from inside the house. It sounded like it might be a Chihuahua.

I climbed the front porch steps up to the veranda, where the gray painted floor wrapped itself around the right side of the house. A bench swing held up on either side by triangles of chain hung motionless in the middle of the veranda, close to the front wall. Three pale green plastic lawn chairs were positioned around it. What looked to be a bird feeder hung from the ceiling of the porch four feet above the banister railing, which circumvented the porch's outside perimeter. The banister and its supporting balustrades, like the window louvers, were painted white. The paint's gloss had long ago succumbed to the relentless pounding of the sun's cruel, ultraviolet light. Here and there, flakes of dull dried white that looked like the edges of painted cardboard peeled away from the primed wood beneath them. I wondered how many times and through how many seasons the railing had been repainted, a redundant, never ending exercise in futility.

I knocked on the front porch's screen door and waited. At first there were no sounds from within. I noticed a slight breeze as the shaded porch area acted as a conduit for the air it cooled and circulated around the front and side of the house. Here was much more tolerable, I noticed, than a mere ten feet away on the other side of the covered porch's protective umbrella. There, the afternoon heat was unbearable.

Just as I was about to knock again, a little more forcefully this time, I heard the sound of a rattle from behind the screen and the inner, solid door. Everything happens in slow time when you're old, I thought to myself. It was one of the paradoxes of life. By the time you kind of had things figured out, it was too late. When you most needed to match the wisdom of an experienced mind with the dexterity and nimbleness of a quick heart and youthful limbs, your body betrayed you. Nothing remained except the frustration and angst of the inevitable. They called them the golden years. As far as I could see, the only thing golden about them was the urine which trickled into the bag between your hip and the side of your wheelchair, which was exactly what Claire Anderson was sitting in when she finally answered the door. She had a look of curious expectation on her face as she peered through the screen at me. Her features were somewhat distorted by the barrier between us, but I could see her face had traveled many miles. She'd forgotten more than I had seen.

"Mrs. Anderson? Claire?" I gently pulled back the screen door.

"Juscoco?" her voice was feeble, yet possessed a certain kindly strength. Her cataract effected eyes, still found a way to resonate light. They sparkled, hanging in there. Though she may have had the money, I guessed she wasn't one for surgery.

I smiled warmly. "That's me."

"Well come in, child," she smiled, revealing a perfect row of ivory dentures, and began to back away to allow me to enter. I moved swiftly, propping the screen door open with my foot to give me enough room to help her.

I rolled Claire into the living room, understanding as I saw her gnarled, arthritic hands why it had taken her so long to answer the door, and why she had dropped the phone when I called earlier. I felt that, if there was somehow a way of managing it, I'd like to give her some of my youthful strength. In some magic way, I wanted to trade a bit of it for her wisdom. Despite whatever medication brought her temporary respite, Claire would endure the pain of arthritis until the end when, mercifully, she will feel it no more. The time would come when I too would face such endurances.

Claire Anderson in the chair, I realized full well, would be me in time. There was no escaping it for any of us. In Claire, though, I noticed immediately a proud dignity. The fact she was here, in this home, alone, meant everything. It spoke volumes to me. Hers, like many of her background, was a character forged of steel and grit. I had no doubt she would be self-sufficient right until the end.

Claire had temporarily locked the dog in a main floor bedroom. It was, in fact, a Chihuahua. Claire ignored the sound of its tiny nails against tile as the dog desperately hoped to dig its way out under the bedroom door and join us.

She told me where I could find some herbal tea and cups. I found a kettle on an old electric stove in the kitchen. I filled it half full with water and set it on top of a live element. I found some honey on the kitchen counter, searched the refrigerator and found some fresh cream. By the time I located some cookies the kettle had started to whistle. I set it on a cool element and turned off the stove top, spotting a tray beside a well-used, antique looking toaster. It was then I remembered seeing some strawberry pop tarts on the middle shelf in the cupboard near the tea, which just happened to be my favorite flavor. I retrieved the box, and inserted two of them in the toaster slots while I fixed the tea. A couple of minutes later, the pop tarts popped. I placed everything on the tray and carried it out to where Claire waited in the living room.

"You're such a dear." I was scoring brownie points big time.

"You have a very nice home," I stated conversationally. I had noticed how clean it was. There was no way Claire could have kept it this way. She was too infirm. "Does someone help you with it, the cleaning and the cooking, I mean?" I noticed the washing machine and clothes dryer on the screened-in back porch off the kitchen.

"Yes. I'm afraid I'm not much of a housekeeper myself these days," she admitted. Claire's face was cracked and worn, her jowls sagging around her chin. She was rail thin, so fragile I feared she might break at any moment. My heart went out to her, but I could see she wasn't losing sleep over her infirmities. She was living life to the last drop. Her eyes shined with alertness inside her bent and ravaged body. They were kind eyes, unmistakably so, but not so much trusting as open. She had been, I realized, reading me from the moment I entered her home. In her younger years she must have been a handful. Now she was tired, and probably on some level looking forward to the long rest, when it finally came.

"We have a neighbor about five miles from here. Bruce Millhausen is a nice young man. He's retired now, and I doubt if he needs the money, but we pay him anyway. He and his wife Sally look after some things for us. They're the nicest people you'd ever want to meet. Sally cleans twice a week, does the laundry, and prepares meals for us. Bruce tidies up around the house. He paints and he's pretty handy with a hammer and nails. They're a blessing. I don't know how we'd manage around here without their help."

"You keep saying we," I noticed. I placed the tea cup on the coffee table in front of Claire's wheelchair. She had positioned herself near one of several comfortable looking sofas that lined the walls of the room. Surprising me, she began to push herself up to a standing position. Awkwardly I leapt to help her, unsure of how I would manage to do so.

"That's all right dear," she waved me off with her words. I stood watching over her literally, her bent posture forced her to stand no more than five feet, as she carefully shuffled to the edge of her sofa, pivoted around in about six short steps to face me, and slowly sat down. "There, that's better. That darned contraption is a life saver, but it can be so uncomfortable on my hips. I can only sit in it for so long, and then I have to rest. I'm lucky, though, because I still *can* sit in it. I suppose one of these days I won't even be able to that much. That will probably mean I'm dead," she spoke candidly.

"Aren't you worried about falling?" I was concerned.

"All the time, but I can't let that stop me. What's the alternative, dear? Lie down and die? They gave me this some years back, when Billy worried about me being alone in the house." She was digging for an object under her sweater. It hung from her neck by a small gold chain.

She held out the rectangular, black plastic box for me to inspect. It looked like a small garage door opener. "A lifeline, I think they call it. I've never had cause to use it, but if I press this red button here," she showed me, "they come running." She chuckled. "The calvary," she shook her head. "I think if that were to ever happen, I'd be gone before they got here. Still, I suppose then what I left behind could be scooped up and dumped out. The place wouldn't smell up like some do when they don't find what's left for a few days, or a week, or more. They say that dead smell never goes away, no matter how hard you clean it."

Claire had strayed considerably from my earlier question. I asked it again. "Do you live here alone?"

This was the first time I saw a flash of concern in her eyes. It wasn't suspicion, but I was reminded she knew very little about me, only what we discussed on the phone when I asked to come out here to see her. I guess it was time to fill her in.

"I don't mean to pry. I guess I'm curious about Billy. I know he leaves Brittle with his donkey three or four times a year and he always heads in the same direction. I guess now I know where he goes, but I still don't know why. I'm assuming he's with your sister, Leslie Hastings."

Claire sipped gingerly at her tea. She had loaded it with cream and honey. She concentrated on holding it steady, setting it back down on the table in front of her. It rattled as it made contact with the wooden table. Tremors had invaded her body. She looked up at me and asked kindly, "Just what is your connection to B.C., Miss Juscoco? You came a long way in such a hurry. Why do you want to find Billy so bad?"

I smiled. "My name is Coco, Claire. Coco Stevens. I'm from Las Vegas. As far as my interest in your brother-in-law..." I shrugged. "Where shall I begin?"

"Why don't you start at the beginning?" she suggested innocently. "It usually makes more sense that way."

"Claire, you could charm the horseshoes off a stallion."

Her eyes twinkled. "Not recently, I'm afraid. But why don't you talk to me? I haven't heard an interesting story in a good long while. I've a hankering to hear one now, and I'm betting you're my ticket, Miss Coco Stevens."

So I told her. Everything about myself, from the time I was a little girl and the problems Mom and I had after my dad was killed, through to when I'd run away in San Francisco and started stripping at Dante's for a man I didn't know who would become my boyfriend, my lover, my confidant. I told her about my college days at Sacramento State. I told her about the elephants I'd seen when I'd gone to Africa for the first time, and about how Michael had snapped that famous shot. I kept talking and Claire Anderson kept listening. She sat quietly, spellbound through the story of my short life.

I told her all about Sam Spielman, and how I'd tripped across the darkest of secrets. I cried then. She leaned over and grasped my hand with her own fragile, vulnerable yet strong hands, consoling me as best she could.

I didn't know the answer why; maybe it was because I knew I wasn't the only one running out of time, but I trusted Claire in those hours more than I'd ever trusted anyone. She asked me for my story with the sole intent of listening to it, the whole time never judging me. At times I felt I was speaking with an angel. In the end, I bet it all and told her about B.C.'s land.

## Chapter 25

"I remember your picture now; you and that magnificent animal. We saw it on the news. Your tears, they touched us. They were real, weren't they?" I nodded. "It made all of us sad but angry," she confessed.

The room had grown dark as we spoke. The sun was dying. The little lamp beside the sofa, the only one in the living room that was lit, spilled a pale orange glow across the room which melted into the sun's own waxing colors near where they poured in through the room's front windows. What was left of the tea was cold. Long ago Claire's little dog had given up. She told me it had curled up in the blanketed basket beside her bed and gone to sleep. I got up and switched on another lamp, which cheered the room somewhat.

"Angry?" I reminded her.

"Yes," I noticed Claire's voice was stronger now. I would have thought she would grow weary as time passed, but the sofa was a kind old friend to her aching, arthritic bones. Its cushions had given in the places most needed, abating her arthritis temporarily. The couch was old, but often times old things were the most comfortable. Especially to the ones most used to them.

"Those animals have been here a lot longer than we have. They deserve our reverence. Land sakes alive, at the very least they deserve to be left alone. Instead, we've made them into our slaves. We grow them and we kill them for our pleasure. It's not right. Billy and Leslie and I talked about it often. It's one of the reasons Billy hasn't driven all these years. I told him it didn't make a lick of difference, but he said what if everybody thought that way? We got real quiet then, I remember, because we all realized that's why the world was going to hell in a hand basket – because no one cared anymore. Many of us leave these wrongs to the next person to fix; we don't have the time to put actions to our concerns. Many of us feel helpless, like we can't make a lick of difference, but Billy didn't. I must confess I never understood why he always traipsed across the desert with that donkey of his."

"Pete."

"Can you imagine? Naming a donkey…I never understood it until we all talked about it."

In my mind, I could picture the three of them sharing their stories, drinking their tea, speaking of better times when the world hadn't seemed so crazy to them. What a round table that must have been.

"Now I understand him a whole lot better. Billy isn't crazy, Coco. He's a kind man with a big heart who doesn't care two twigs for this modern world of ours. He loves the desert, he loves his donkey Pete, and he has no need for what he thinks is a world gone mad with greed and corruption. He once said if Satan came to earth, the Master of all evil would come in the form of Benjamin Franklin. He didn't mean the man, of course. He meant the lust for money. We've all seen the terrible work of the devil's hand. Good grief, what it does to some people," she shook her head with sadness.

"I can't speak for my brother-in-law. Billy's his own man. I reckon he always has been. We used to think he was a might bit odd, but now at least I know better. I think he'll be able to help you, Miss Coco, though I don't know exactly how. We'd be up against some powerful forces, and we're not young. Facing these sorts of challenges isn't the same when you get old. You'll find out. The fight tends to go out of you. You get tired more easily, Coco."

At this, I took the sweet old lady's crooked hands in mine. I stroked the gnarled joints gently. Her knuckles felt like small stones beneath her skin.

"I'm young, Claire. Maybe I've got enough fight in me for all of us. Where is he? I've got a few ideas. If we put our heads together, we can come up with something. It's Billy's land. He owns it, and he gets to do what he wants with it. That option he signed runs out in two months and it's his again. That's the law."

Claire nodded, though I could tell she was not totally convinced.

"He's in Kingman, Miss Coco. They rode up there on Thursday, like they always do."

"Leslie and Billy?"

She nodded. "We have a car, an old Buick, as reliable as Billy's old mule. Leslie drives. She's still got her license, but I worry. My sister's going blind, Miss Coco. She wears glasses thicker than Coca-Cola bottles, but she's more stubborn than Pete. Won't take no for an answer. Both of them are two peas in a pod that way. Neither of them would think to take the Greyhound bus."

The truth, both of us knew, was there was no bus. Not one that stopped out here, anyway. Driving was the only way, aside from asking Bruce or Sally Millhausen, their neighbors, for a ride. And if I knew Billy, he wouldn't put them out. He'd been too independent for too long.

I wondered why B.C. didn't have his daughter pick him up. Obviously she was still alive, though she must be at least fifty now. She had to be the one they were visiting in Kingman. I guessed no one else would warrant the extraordinary effort by the eccentric desert man. I wondered why his daughter hadn't tried to stop him from taking what had become risky trips. Had her job prevented her from assisting her father? Perhaps her immediate family had taken priority.

I asked Claire, "Leslie and Billy are seeing Billy's daughter, aren't they?"

"Yes, that's right. I'm sure he'd like to see her more often, but he's torn. Billy loves the desert – his home. They named the town of Brittle after his father, did you know that?"

"Yes."

"He loves that town and the land around it like two brothers, but he loves his daughter too. In a way Billy lives in three worlds. He spends his time divided equally in those worlds. Billy is a very happy man, Miss Coco. I suspect he feels in his heart that things have worked out pretty much exactly the way God planned them for him."

Outside the front window, the sky was a creamy ooze of reddish purple rimming the horizon. The sun had set, leaving a muted richness of dark pastels, the only remnant of the day's passing. I heard a donkey bray in the distance. The sound it made was lonely and forlorn.

"Was that Pete?"

Claire nodded, smiling. "He's telling us he's back. He wonders off sometimes, but he senses when it's time for Billy to return."

"So Billy and Leslie should be back soon?" I was hopeful.

"They should be back any time in the next day or two. You're welcome to wait for them. We have the room. I think Billy is going to really enjoy meeting you, Coco. I don't think he much cared for that boyfriend of yours so I believe he'll help you with your plan. You have a good heart, Coco. You didn't deserve what happened. Maybe there's a way to right that wrong. Time catches all of us in the end, one way or another. This might be Mr. Spielman's time. Billy will help you," she said again, more convinced now than ever. If anyone knew B.C., his sister-in-law did.

Suddenly the phone on the stand next to Claire began to ring. "That's odd," she said, leaning towards it. "Who could be calling at this hour?" It wasn't late by my standards, perhaps a little after nine, but Claire's world was different. Everyone she knew had probably been in bed for an hour or more. That's how it had been for years. They were early risers though, up long before dawn, sometimes as early as four-thirty but never past six.

"Hello?" she said, finally managing to hold the phone to her ear. After a few seconds, "Yes, I'm Claire Anderson." A pause. "Oh, oh, my God – no. Are you sure? Are you sure you didn't make a mistake?" Another, longer pause. "In the morning. Yes, I'll be here. No, there won't be any need for you to come out here tonight. Thank you. I'm with a friend, we'll manage. Where did you take them? Thank you. We'll come first thing in the morning." The telephone floated down from Claire's ear and rested in her lap. She seemed spacey. Her face had lost all color. She seemed like she was made of wax.

"Claire?" I spoke softly. "What's happened? Are you all right?" I was suddenly gravely concerned. She looked like she was about to have a heart attack. "Claire?"

She startled. I'd called her back from a trance. She looked at me and I saw tears in her eyes. She sniffed.

"That was the Sheriff's Department. There's been an accident." She hesitated, trying to blink away the tears – the sudden realization that her life had taken one more insult to add to her others, maybe the last one this time. "Leslie and Billy…it was a head on collision on the highway outside of Kingman. They're gone, Coco. Just like that, they're gone." She bowed her head into her hands. Her tiny frame moved up and down in small, painful sobs, barely audible. I moved quickly and sat on the couch beside her, softly rubbing her crippled back, feeling helpless. Why her? Why now?

# Chapter 26

I let Angelo, Claire's precious Chihuahua, do his business in the yard that night and again first thing in the morning. Claire took a sedative to help her finally get to sleep. I peeked into her bedroom and she was fast asleep, her breathing easy and regular. She looked peaceful.

Pete stuck around. He came right up to me when I was in the yard with the dog. Angelo was skittish, warily appraising the donkey, but not frightened. No doubt he and Pete had met before. I stroked Pete's long nose, wondering what would become of the animal now that B.C. was gone. I knew they'd miss each other, wherever Billy was now.

By the time I took Angelo back inside the house, Claire was up. It was six, and outside the blackness of night was yielding to a more grayish hue lit by a narrow purple haze across the eastern horizon.

I made tea in the kitchen while Claire sat in the living room in her wheelchair. She had tried to be a convivial hostess but drifted off, staring into the emptiness she now felt at the loss of her family. What would she do now that her sister couldn't help her any longer? Bruce and Sally had their own lives. They couldn't provide Claire with the level of care Leslie had. As good of friends as her neighbors were, they were getting on in age as well. I was sure they'd planned their retirement around spending their twilight years in their own company, not with the unexpected burden of nursing an invalid. As kind as I presumed them to be, I knew this new arrangement would not be fair to them.

Angelo jumped into Claire's lap, disturbing her soulful reverie, as I set a tray bearing tea onto the coffee table in front of the couch. I was certain she'd been thinking similar thoughts to my own. The dog seemed to awaken her from a stupor. Angelo's little tongue licked her hands, his bulbous eyes staring up at her inquisitively when she didn't respond at first. Then she smiled, as if she'd figured out something she'd been thinking on. She stroked Angelo gently and the dog settled into her lap, resting its head on her knee.

"I never thought I'd feel so vulnerable, Coco. So alone," she finally said. "At least I know. I could have been here alone for a long time, without knowing." She looked at me, looking even frailer than yesterday, if that were possible. "The Buick," she pronounced. "It was registered to me. I guess that's how we found out so quickly." She smiled, but nothing was behind it.

"Claire, I haven't known you very long. But I want you to know you have a friend. I'll stay with you for a while. I've got nothing else to do. I came to see Billy, but when I leave I'll know a family. I wish I could have gotten to meet him and your sister."

"I wish so too, sweetheart. And you don't have to stay, I'll manage somehow. I always have."

But this time was different. Claire wouldn't be able to manage. I didn't ask for it, but somehow by being here and injecting myself into this family mix, I'd become a part of their lives. More importantly, I found I desperately wanted to help Claire. I knew her neighbors Bruce and Sally would probably have good intentions, but with my resources I could make certain she'd be looked after properly.

Someone was going to have to sell the house, and Claire couldn't stay here. She'd need a nurse. Angelo would have to be carefully considered, as well. I knew it wouldn't take long for her new home to look for a quick way to shuffle the added responsibility of a dog out of the picture. Most nursing homes didn't allow animals in the first place. And that was where Claire was now headed. Billy had traveled extensively to see his daughter, and for whatever reason she had never reciprocated. I suspected she either couldn't, or wouldn't, want to look after Claire. Besides, she didn't have to. She was Billy's daughter – not Claire's.

Billy's estate was large. Lawyers would descend on his assets. There was no doubt in my mind Sam would immediately commence legal wrangling. The moment he learned of B.C.'s passing, he would wrest whatever control he could over the estate by using his land option. Claire needed help. I didn't think she would survive too much longer without it.

"I want to stay, Claire. You need someone in your corner." I knew I was giving up on my own plans, but I couldn't leave her. "Billy's daughter won't be able to look after you, and his estate is substantial. She and her family will be consumed by it. She just won't have the time. I'll help you, Claire. I'll stay as long as necessary."

"But the oil," she faltered. "You can't give up, Coco. Not after what's happened. Not after what Mr. Spielman has done."

"It's not important," I sighed. "Not anymore." I smiled, feeling good about my decision. I'd come close, but I guessed it just wasn't meant to be. Sam would probably end up with everything now. I was sure he'd find a way to enforce his options, even with his cash crunch. At the very least, it was certain he could extend the options until he could arrange financing, which was more suitable than that offered by his associates back East. I'd lost, but surprisingly, it didn't bother me nearly as much as I thought it might. The bad guy had won. I accepted this and I turned my attention to where it was needed most. I looked at the dear old woman, helpless as a newborn on the sofa across from me. She was alone and scared. It would rain in hell before I left her. I decided then and there I'd stay and help for as long as it took.

"You would give up all that – for me?" she was astonished.

"It was never for the money, Claire."

"For Sam Spielman," she whispered. She believed me.

"Yes. But I guess that's going to have to wait until another lifetime. Maybe that's what I needed to learn. To accept what happened, and to forgive. Not Sam. He was – is – an actor. God pulls the strings of all our lives."

"God's not responsible for what happened, Coco," she said gently but forcefully. "If you think that way you might get angry."

"I used to be," I admitted. Then I smiled. "But I'm not anymore. The best revenge is living well. I can't think of a better way of living than making sure you'll be all right, Claire."

"You are an angel," she said.

"I wouldn't go that far."

"No. You truly are."

I looked at her closely, wondering if the reality of her situation had finally caught up with her and this was her way of coping. Maybe she was having a breakdown. Perhaps the emotional stress of losing her loved ones so suddenly was falling on her head like an anvil dropping out of the sky. Any minute, I expected I'd have to rush Claire to the hospital, or worse.

An odd, unpredictable thing happened then. It was as if ten years were suddenly washed away. Her face loosened as she smiled. The tight wrinkles of despair around her eyes seemed to evaporate before me. The color flooded back into her cheeks, an almost rosy orange hue that I thought for a moment must be the sun coming through the window, but it wasn't. She seemed to straighten. She did straighten her back arching slightly with a vigor she summoned from who-knew-where. The change in her appearance was so stark and it happened so quickly that it startled me. She seemed not so much transformed, though, as resolved.

"I will miss them, Coco," she breathed deeply. "I loved my sister and Billy with all my heart. Now they're gone. I guess that's to be expected, when you get to be our age. We all live on borrowed time. We just don't like to admit it, is all. I'll be leaving soon, too." She held up a thin bony hand to stop my protest. "It's all right. I'm under no illusions. When you get old death can be a friend, but I'm not dead yet. And there are a couple of very important things I must do before I leave. Yes, indeed. And you my dear, Miss Coco Stevens," she smiled broadly, a cat that had finally caught its canary, "can certainly help me."

Soon after, I learned old people don't keep secrets from the ones they love. They don't have the time.

## Chapter 27

It was eleven-thirty when Sam called me from the Los Angeles Airport. He told me he'd see me in less than an hour. Instantly, I felt relieved. We had both been so busy with our respective lives we hadn't seen each other for two weeks. Now I longed to make love with him. I wanted to devour his strength. I wanted to feel safe again.

The incident at Laguna's restaurant had shown me a side of the business of fame I'd certainly known existed, but had never applied it to me. Now it hit home with a punch. I was one of *them* now. I was a celebrity – a supermodel. Life would never be the same. I'd have to watch my step, keep steady on this roller-coaster ride. Privacy was a luxury of the past, like the Elvis syndrome: an appropriate enough description. The restaurant, I feared, was an ominous harbinger of things to come. The bright side was the money was good, but that wouldn't last forever. When the adoring, impulsive, hero-worshipping public finally decided they'd had enough of me, I'd pick up my chips from the table a rich woman, and go home to a well deserved rest. In the meantime, I'd find a way to enjoy things before the fickle masses moved on to the next flavor.

Seb and Michael invited me to spend the night with them in the main house. I politely declined, telling them I needed time to be alone and to think. They respected this, but insisted I take Tessa and Freda for company. "They never talk back, and they always have a smile for you," Seb said.

I was glad I agreed. The girls were good company, both of them lying quietly near where I sat in the main floor of the guesthouse. I'd tried reading to take my mind off things while waiting for Sam and Jack. I switched back and forth from a new bestseller to the TV, unable to concentrate on either. I looked at the dogs. They sensed my restlessness, opening their beautiful eyes and looking expectantly at me.

With Freda and Tessa, I found myself wondering if I was the one who granted them my attention or if they somehow planted thoughts in my mind. Was I a willing actor in a play they had conjured up? There were times when I thought about taking them outside for a walk only to find them in front of me, smiling and wagging their tails in anticipation of the walk they appeared to already know about.

Sam's limousine pulled up outside the gate just before twelve-thirty in the morning. The dogs rushed to the door when they heard the intercom buzz. I let the limousine onto the property by pushing the button to open the gate, and went outside to meet Sam and Jack. To say I was happy to see them would be an understatement. I jumped into Sam's arms the moment he got out. My arms locked around his neck like a vise. I was trembling.

"It's good to see you, too," he said after a long, passionate kiss. "You remember Jack."

I unlocked myself from Sam. Jack was getting out of the driver's side, beaming a toothy grin. "Hi baby girl. Good to see you."

"I missed you guys," I said as I hugged the giant.

He popped the trunk. I pitched in and we all carried their luggage into the guesthouse. I showed Jack to one of the guest bedrooms, which contained its own bath and shower. I kissed him on the cheek goodnight. Next I helped Sam bring his luggage into my bedroom.

"Nice," Sam said as he checked it out. He put his suitcase next to the closet, and removed a black lambskin overnight bag from around his shoulders.

I fell into his willing arms. We kissed each other with passion and hunger, wordlessly. I began to fumble with the buttons of his vest as he slewed out of his jacket and blindly tossed it in the direction of a chair. He missed the mark and the jacket crumpled onto the floor in a disheveled heap. Sam unbuttoned my blouse as I finished with his vest. He stopped, searching my eyes with savage hunger while I peeled the vest off his shoulders. "Did you have to wear so many clothes?" I managed huskily. I started to unbutton his shirt, then smiled into his eyes and switched to the zipper of his pants.

"My shoes," he mumbled. He fumbled them off while I continued.

He finished the job of unbuttoning my shirt. I dropped it to the floor and held him in my hands, his pants still on, rubbing my breasts against him. Sam let out a low groan.

"You like that?" I cooed softly into his ear.

He groaned again. Now he fumbled with the button on my jeans, popped it open, and unzipped my pants. They were tight Calvin Kleins. I stopped stroking him for a moment while I slid my jeans down over my hips. They fell to the floor at my ankles and I kicked them to the side, near where his jacket lay. He fumbled for the last button on his shirt while I undid the metal clasp above his zipper. His pants fell to the floor, like mine had, and I stripped off his underwear.

Sam lifted me up and cradled me in his strong arms. He walked over to the bed and lowered me gently on top, following me. Neither of us thought about turning down the sheets the first time, or turning out the lights.

I moaned softly as Sam slid into me. My fingernails dug into his back, but he remained oblivious to the claws of a starved feline. Ten thousand crystals of light fell behind my closed eyes, exploding in silent thunder. The darkness split into jagged broken filaments of white light. I moaned muddled words into Sam's ear, "Don't stop baby, don't ever." He didn't.

In the morning, I woke to Sam staring at me, propped up on one elbow. His smile was that of a child's, innocent and fresh. I leaned up and gave him a quick peck on the lips.

"Now isn't that better than all the billboards in China," he asked.

"Much more preferable," I smiled, "It was great with you last night, Sam. It was like…" I searched for an adequate metaphor.

"Fire on the water?" he helped me.

I stroked his shoulder. "It was great," I purred. "How do you think Jack slept?" I asked conversationally.

"Lightly, as always, Jack's a soldier. If he's not on high alert, he's close to it."

I silently cursed myself for asking. The question and the answer had brought us back to my new reality. It reminded me of the reason Sam and Jack were here. I looked at Sam again. Fighting the remnants of sweet memory from the previous night, I rolled out of bed and headed for the shower. For as long as I could bear I stood under cold water, a whiplash across my back. By the time I came out of the bathroom I was ready for the day.

Sam, surprisingly, had tidied up the room. I spied his jacket, his vest and our pants neatly folded on top of the armchair near the nightstand. He took his turn in the bathroom while I went out into the kitchen to make some breakfast for all of us. Jack was already up, fully dressed. He sat on a stool at the half table which separated the kitchen from the dining room. He was munching on an apple from the large bowl of fruit I kept on a shelf above the microwave, reading a day old copy of the *Los Angeles Daily News*.

"Hey there," he beamed when he noticed me, setting the paper aside onto the table. I went to him and hugged him, kissing him on the cheek.

"Sebastian and Michael said you guys can stay forever," I informed him.

Jack Holliday chuckled, more of a low rumbling from somewhere deep in his guts than an actual laugh. "I doubt we'll be here that long. Did Sam say anything to you?"

"Last night?" I scrunched my nose at him. "We didn't exactly do a whole lot of talking, Jack."

"I know he misses you when you're not around."

"Does he ever talk about me? When I'm not there, I mean. I know Sam's busy and all…" I trailed off. "Sorry," I apologized.

"He talks about you all the time, little girl."

I looked at him skeptically.

"Truthfully," leveling his gaze to mine. In that moment, his eyes had the innocence of a child. I knew he'd never lie to me.

"I believe you, Jack. It's just that I really miss him when we're apart. I miss both of you. I think about you guys all the time." I moved to the fridge, took out a carton of eggs and a pound of Canadian bacon to make breakfast.

"You're supposed to miss him. You *are* in love with him. It's normal to feel that way. But both of you lead very active lives. I hate to be the bearer of bad news, but I'm afraid you might have to get used to it, especially now." He took his last bite of the apple and glanced around for a place to put the core.

"Compost is under the sink," both my hands were busy laying the strips of bacon into the frying pan.

Jack sat back on the stool. "I saw the famous picture. It's an amazing shot, Coco. Michael really knows what to look for. It's no wonder there's been so much hype."

"Michael would appreciate that," I spoke for him.

"Everything okay with those guys?" His question came across innocently enough, and normally I would have completely missed his probing innuendo, but I wasn't as naïve as when we'd first met.

"They're not the problem," I assured him. "Sebastian's already hard at work renegotiating all the contracts, mine with Creative Arts Management included. Michael's agreed to work with me on all the location shots. The two of them have treated me like their daughter. Their hearts are bigger than Manhattan."

"You're not comfortable with all the sudden attention." It was a statement.

"Comfortable or not, I better get used to it. Either that or get out now while there's still time."

He searched for my eyes as I tried to avoid his. "That's always an option," he pointed out candidly.

The bacon sizzled in the bottom of the pan. My mouth began to water as the aroma of the fried meat permeated the house.

"Morning," Sam appeared from the direction of the bedroom. He was dressed in jeans and a long sleeveless blue colored cotton shirt, but bare footed. He stretched, came across the kitchen floor and kissed me in the middle of cracking some eggs. "Smells delicious," he winked.

"Oh, you mean breakfast," I played with him. He sat down on a stool near Jack. "You guys want to eat here, or in the dining room?" I asked them.

"Here's fine," Sam spoke for Jack, who nodded his agreement. He asked Jack, "What were you guys talking about?"

"Options," Jack replied.

"They always make life richer," Sam offered.

"Jack was being a good listener," and I realized he always had been, ever since the first time we'd met. I took a pitcher of orange juice from inside the fridge and set it down on the narrow table between them. I had squeezed the oranges myself only yesterday. I took down three glasses from the cupboard above the counter and set them beside the OJ. Jack picked up the pitcher and began to pour it while I returned to the stove on the island in the kitchen's center. The eggs looked like they were almost done. *Toast*. I'd forgotten the bread. I stepped to the counter beside the fridge and retrieved a loaf of seeded multi-grain wheat. I popped four slices onto the racks in the toaster oven. All I needed now was the strawberry jam and butter. I found them and set them beside the orange juice.

"Are you okay, after yesterday?" Sam asked for the first time. "I saw it again last night on the news. It was quite a mob scene in Laguna's parking lot. You looked frightened, sweetheart, and it scared the hell out of me. I should have seen it coming," he chastised himself.

"None of us could have seen it coming," I remembered what Sebastian said, agreeing with him. "It's no one's fault. It scared the hell out of me, but I'm fine now," I reassured them. "I was fine as soon as you called me, Sam," I said honestly.

"Grab three of those table mats from the dining table, Jack," I instructed him as I parceled out the eggs onto three plates next to the stove. I added the bacon to the plates from the napkins I put the strips on earlier to soak up the grease.

"Breakfast is served," I sat down on the stool on the kitchen side of the counter. "Any complaints, take it up with the management."

There were no complaints.

## Chapter 28

"Jack's going to stay with you until things settle down a bit," said Sam.

"Come on, girls! Freda. Tessa." The beautiful animals stiffened at the mention of their names. They looked back at me, like two children caught with their hands in the cookie jar. "Come. Leave it alone. That's not for dogs," I admonished them. They had found something, perhaps some squirrel droppings, near the edge of a bit of low slung shrubbery on the far side of the pool. Reluctantly, they trotted past whatever it was and immediately broke into a jousting run, laughing and tussling with each other as they romped in the grass beside the swimming pool apron. Sam and I were taking a stroll around the property. It was like our own private park. Sam, I realized, was inspecting the estate's security.

"Jack will go with you whenever you go out."

I didn't say anything. How could I object? All I had to do was think back to the mob scene at Laguna's. I knew if Jack had been there things would have gone very differently.

I watched a scrub jay as it flew from the lower branches of a giant oak tree and skipped through a row of sixty foot palms. The trimmed clump of fronds at the top of the trees squawked with the sounds of green parrots. All around us there were the sights and sounds of wildlife.

The gardener had planted roses on the sides of the shower house. I spotted a huge bumble bee favoring the yellow ones. I wondered why it seemed to avoid the red roses. This was the first time I'd ever seen a fickle bee, I thought with amusement.

"Sebastian and Michael are hosting an industry party tonight." I said. "They were all going to be there: Models, actors, designers, magazine reps and some big names. Kind of a who's who list of industry heavyweights."

"Might be fun."

"More like work for me."

"Am I invited?"

"Of course," and then I realized Sam was being polite. The joke went: where does a six hundred pound gorilla sit? The answer was anywhere it felt like. It was dangerous not to extend Sam an invitation to go where he wanted to be. Here, he was a guest. He was welcome, so it wasn't an issue. That he'd asked me only showed his class and that he respected my individuality. Sam was telling me that it was my career and that he didn't want to intrude into my affairs. But he was with me now, and I needed him. I wanted him.

"Good thing I brought a black tie," he parted some branches as we moved through the thick undersides of two adjoining trees.

"How long do you think I'll need Jack?" I had started to say bodyguard, but stopped myself. I didn't want to see Jack that way, even if it was true.

Sam shrugged. "I'm not sure, Coco. Long enough to send those creeps with the cameras a message, though. Call it a strong hint. Jack makes an imposing figure. It shouldn't take them too long to figure things out."

"They're paparazzi, Sam. It's their job to take pictures of famous people."

"Maybe so," he continued. "But that doesn't give them the right to endanger the safety of those same people. They can take their pictures, that's fine. I'm not saying there's anything wrong with that. But a line's got to be drawn somewhere. They can't do what they did yesterday. I don't want anything happening to you, sweetheart. Nothing will. Not while I'm around. I'll see to it," he pronounced an edict.

"Well, I can't say I really mind. You make me feel safe when you're around, Sam," I smiled and kissed him on the cheek. I grabbed his hand, wanting to hold onto it as we walked through the taller grass. "My guardian angel," I said, feeling strangely like a butterfly back inside of its cocoon.

"What would you do without me?" Sam smiled back at me.

"Hire Pinkertons, I guess," I teased him.

Holding hands, calling the labs when I had to, we strolled back to the main house where preparations were in full swing for the party tonight. Two caterer's trucks were parked near the side of the house, close to the kitchen entrance. Women clad in white catering uniforms filled the small entrance gate, laden with bundles and trays filled with the evening's meal. Later, the tantalizing food would be laid out with meticulous care onto a long table on the back patio area, near where the five piece band would be playing. I noticed an events truck was parked in front of the caterer's vehicles, its roll-top back door open. I caught a glimpse of two athletic looking guys unloading one of many round tables that would be set up on the patio, where the smorgasbord would be served. The place was abuzz, a small anthill in motion, organized chaos at its finest.

Michael's Ferrari was parked under the porte-cochère, near the mansion's front door. Sebastian's Rolls Royce was nowhere in sight. We entered the house.

I heard Michael before we saw him. His voice was a minutely higher pitch than normal, and contained a barely noticeable touch of strain at its upper end. He was always mildly stressed as the principle organizer of the house's social functions. Sebastian usually disappeared, leaving his partner to deal with the details that were indeed the devil. No matter how many parties he organized, usually with most of the same people, Michael confided in me his near-fanatic desire for perfection. As he strove to attain the penultimate, knowing something always managed to go a little wrong at the most inopportune moment, Michael became anxious. He was a showman about to take the stage in front of the hometown crowd, nervous as a cat on a hot tin roof, but once the curtain went up he'd be fine.

As always, Michael turned the kitchen over to the Sous Chef, Chad Mellon. Most of Michael's handpicked key personnel were gay, and Chef Mellon was no exception. He refused to wear the traditional puffy baker's hat, bald as a billiard cue ball, but absolutely insisted his assistants did. Five of them now worked in precise tandem, each readying his specific area of the now commercial grade kitchen. Michael and Chad spoke together in the middle of the melee, gesticulating with animated fervor as an integral part of their ritualistic communication unfolded. The process never went smoothly, the final product polished like a ten carat diamond from Tiffany's.

Michael spotted myself and Sam just after we decided to leave, not wishing to interfere with an obviously busy man. He ended his conversation with the chef abruptly, no doubt vowing to bust his friend's chops down to the wire, and moved purposefully to where we stood in the middle of the living room.

"Good morning, good morning," he was clear eyed and filled with energy. As much as he railed against the seemingly endless incompetence of some of the help every time he did a party, he truly loved putting these affairs together. He kissed me on both cheeks, European style.

"Samuel," he called Sam by his formal name, grasping his hand warmly in his own. "It's so good to see you again. How is everything? Is there anything you need, anything I can get you?" Michael's eyes were lit like candles.

Sam pumped his hand. "No, we're fine," he glanced at me. "Thank you. By the look of things, we should be offering you our help." Sam nodded to the commotion in the kitchen. Outside in the backyard, through the sliding glass doors beyond the dining room, I could see at least a half dozen of the waitstaff dressed in traditional white shirt, black slacked porter uniforms unfolding chairs around the circular tables being brought around back.

Michael followed Sam's gaze. "Chad is one of the best caterers in all of Beverly Hills, and he has the attitude to prove it," he smiled. "I'd be lost without him. Between you, me, and the lamp post, I think he's still pissed off at me. He and I used to be an item. That was before Sebastian, and definitely before poor Chad lost his hair." He'd lowered his voice in a conspiratorial tone to impart this last tidbit of gossip. I wondered with a small amount of humor which had cost Chad his old flame – the loss of his hair, or the advent of Michael's new lover. Probably a little of both, I decided. Michael enjoyed what he viewed as perfection, and that obviously did not include bald, heavyset, middle-aged men.

Sam said seriously, "You know about my driver, Jack Holliday?"

"Coco told me all about him. Sebastian and I agree with the arrangement one hundred percent. You're welcome to stay here as long as you feel necessary."

"Thank you, Michael. I will view this as a personal favor to me." Sam extended his hand to Michael this time.

"Don't mention it," Michael said. "Anything we can do for you and Jack while you're here, just ask. We all want safe passage for this sweet, valuable cargo of ours," he smiled over at me. "Now I hope you don't mind, but I must ask that you both please excuse me." There was a sudden clattering sound from the kitchen. Someone had bumped into someone else and a container of shrimp had ended up on the ceramic tile floor between them, both blaming the other in what sounded like Italian slurs. Michael shrugged. "A man's work is never done."

"Thank you, Michael," I said.

"We'll talk more later," Sam indicated there would be more to go over. "Tomorrow, when all of this is finished."

"Sebastian and I are looking forward to it," Michael named his partner, whom Sam had not yet met.

"Likewise," Sam said.

"Perhaps we'll have dinner with the two of you and Mr. Holliday. We'll have leftovers tomorrow night."

"Sounds like a plan," I voted for us.

Michael made his departure and Sam and I left to meet with Jack back at the guesthouse. On the way out we noticed the valet attendants had arrived. Four of the valets were dressed in deep maroon short-backed jackets and small, round, tasseled hats. They wore white slacks and white shoes. Someone was rolling a four foot wide red carpet out across the front of the house beyond the portico, the reception line for the guests. Michael and Seb would stand inside the front door, under the magnificent chandelier which hung down from the ceiling two floors up, and greet everyone who entered personally. While their guests shuffled into the house from outside, two models in elegant evening gowns would serve champagne to those moving forward in the line, slaking not only their thirst, but many of their sensitive and oversized egos.

As we walked back to the guesthouse, I noticed Maria with a man I'd never seen before on the other side of the front gate. Both of them appeared to be examining the key punch above the security entrance phone. I waved. She smiled and waved back. Tonight was going to be another busy night, at least in this part of Beverly Hills.

# Chapter 29

Jack and I walked up the driveway toward the main house ahead of Sam. He'd stayed behind to phone someone in Hong Kong, promising to join me in no more than fifteen minutes.

We could hear the band playing around the back of the house. Muted strings floated across the lawn, shadows dancing under the moon. The front of the mansion was brightly lit from the ground up. Embedded among the lush ferns which lined the front flower beds, hidden green and amber spotlights pointed skyward. Their beams highlighted the home's Tyndall stone facade, caressing even the farthest extremities of the uppermost parapet walls. The house resembled more a medieval castle than a modern dwelling. Its presence spoke of power, unbridled and insistent. There was nothing subtle about what we walked toward. The mansion was more Sebastian than Michael, meant to impress. It accomplished that mission.

We stepped aside and I watched in amusement as one of several, large electric golf carts passed us, loaded with two tuxedoed gentlemen and women I assumed were their wives. The carts were driven by the maroon vested valets I'd seen earlier. The carts were for those who didn't want to walk the short distance from where their cars were parked, on the other side of the iron gate, to where the driveway met the public access street. The valets would park the guests' vehicles for them on the street. Michael had bought a permit. He'd also, I'd noticed, hired at least three of Beverly Hills's finest just in case anyone got curious and thought about crashing the exclusive gathering. They kept a watchful eye on things from outside the gate, a cruiser car parked conspicuously beside the entrance. No one uninvited was getting in tonight.

Jack and I stepped to the back of the line of about thirty party goers moving toward the front door. We became a part of a moving serpent as we shuffled along the red carpet. We didn't have to join the line; we could have gone into the house through the kitchen entrance. But, number one: it was fun. It was like being a part one of those long, undulating dragons used to celebrate Chinese New Year. I was handed a glass of champagne. Jack politely declined one. I'd never seen him drink alcohol. Number two: Jack mentioned it wouldn't hurt for him and me to be seen together. Already there were whisperings in the line ahead of us, and stolen glances backwards. Furtive, coded hand gestures were cast in our direction. Jack and I both noticed.

I leaned into him and whispered, "You have to admit, Jack, you're not easy to miss." He was as big as a house when compared with just about everyone else. He'd left for a while earlier in the afternoon, on Sam's instructions, and returned a couple hours later with rented tuxedos. Jack looked smart in his, a standout even in the middle of all this glitz and glamour.

He whispered in my ear, "I don't think it's me, baby girl," implying I was getting the lion's share of the attention.

"The billboard," of course they recognized me. These people lived for publicity. Selling themselves was the very essence of this industry. Even bad publicity, everyone here knew, was far more preferable than none at all. Silence was feared above anything else. When people stopped calling their name, the emptiness became unbearable. When nothing was said, it was the end of everything they held dear. In this business, late finishers and has-beens might as well be dead.

"You're the talk of the town. That's why anybody who's anybody has shown up for this shin-dig. By the looks of things, there must be five or six hundred people here tonight. And that dress you're wearing doesn't hurt you any, either."

"Do you like it, Jack?"

"It makes you look older. More sophisticated."

"It's a Halston. Sebastian got it for me."

I thought about what Jack said. "Sophisticated? Isn't that another word for matronly?"

Jack laughed. He'd gotten better at it. "Not out here in Hollywood. Here it means sexy, as in movie star quality. It's curb appeal plus."

"I'm a model, Jack, not an actress."

"You could be." He noticed my skepticism. "I'm not kidding," he said. "There's something different about you, I've always known it." He grinned. "From the moment I first saw you back in San Francisco, I said to myself, now here comes trouble."

I grinned along with him. "I guess you weren't far off the mark then, were you?"

He rubbed his eyelids with an oversized finger. "I got an eye for trouble. I can see it coming from a mile off."

"And I was trouble?" We were almost at the front door.

Jack looked sideways at me, his lips curled upwards in what others might mistake for a slight sneer. "With a capital T, Miss Stevens."

I looked past Jack toward the driveway, hearing some commotion. A golf cart was pulling up near where the line of people moved forward to greet the hosts, inside the front landing area of the mansion. My breath caught in my throat. Four stunning blonde bombshells rode in the cart. The jewelry around their necks and on their wrists seemed to be on fire as the pieces caught the lights of the front yard, and those under the porte-cochère. They wore sequined, form fitting evening gowns, white in color with revealing slits up the sides that exposed the thin black bands of their Frederick's undergarments, the kind where the least amount of cloth cost the most cash. The payoffs of wearing such undergarments were usually well worth the investment.

The girls could pass for quadruplets. A thinner, older gentleman with wisps of gray hair falling across his face sat in the middle of the girls. The man had to be in his seventies. He looked dapper – sophisticated – in a dark tuxedo with a single red rose attached to his lapel. Someone made a joke and all of them laughed as the cart came to a stop close to the front door. Whoever it was had no intention of waiting in line. I'd been following the cart, so I didn't see the one that pulled up beside Jack and me until I heard the brakes chirp.

"What are you guys doing in line?" Sam said, getting out of it. He handed the driver a five. "C'mon. I want you to meet somebody." With no hesitation he grabbed my hand and plucked me out of the line. Jack followed as we walked up behind the old man surrounded by the four Barbie clones.

"Hef," Sam clamped a hand across his back.

The thin man turned with a stiffness borne of age. His eyes were gems of light. He seemed always to be smiling.

"Sam," he instantly recognized him. "I didn't know you were on the West Coast. Why didn't you call?" They shook hands warmly.

"It was last minute," Sam explained.

"Will you have time to come by the Mansion?" he said it like the name of a town. "I'd love to catch up with you."

"I'll have to take a rain check, but thank you." We were being shuffled inside by one of the security guards Michael had hired. Inside, ten or fifteen people milled about in the front foyer, drinking champagne while they waited for their turn to say a quick hello to a half hidden Sebastian. I couldn't see any sign of Michael.

"Hef, I'd like you to meet the love of my life." I took the original playboy's outstretched hand in mine. "Hugh Hefner, this is Coco Stevens."

He leaned over and kissed the back of my hand. "Hello, Coco. I'm delighted." He looked at me closely, his eyes locking onto mine. He looked quickly back at Sam, and then again at me. "You're the girl on the billboard, aren't you?"

"Guilty as charged, Mr. Hefner."

"Hef, please, that mister stuff makes me feel a lot older than I look. These days that worries me."

Everyone chuckled.

"Miss Stevens, you're a natural beauty. I look forward to seeing a whole lot more of you." There were more chuckles. His eyes twinkled. His grin was infectious. "Girls, I'd like you to meet Coco Stevens." In turn, he introduced the glamorous women he called his girls. "Miss Stevens, meet my posse. This is Bambi, and this is

Barbi. Over here we have Loni, and last but certainly not least, I'd like you to meet Tina." All their smiles seemed genuine, but I noticed something else. Was it wariness? They'd staked their claim. Not so far beneath their civil veneers I could tell there was a ruthless, cut-throat savvy that indicated in no words claim jumpers would be shot on sight. I wanted no part of it. I smiled reassuringly, indicating as much in the appropriate body language only a competing female would understand. Hef was nice, but he wasn't Sam.

Hef turned back to Sam, "Don't be a stranger, Sam. It's good to see you again. Come by if you can."

"I won't – and I will. You look your usual, healthy self. Whatever you're eating, I want some." They both laughed.

"I'll see you inside. Come over and we'll share a drink."

"I'll bring the diet colas." Sam knew that was the strongest thing Hef drank since he'd had his stroke all those years ago. The government had been largely responsible. They'd gone on a witchhunt to nail him on some trumped up drug charges. His secretary had committed suicide and Mr. Hefner's health had suffered for it. I imagined there was no love lost for the g-men. Sam and Hef both had that much in common.

Inside, I turned to Sam. "I didn't know you and Hef were friends." It was a rare treat to meet the legend. In many people's minds, he had single-handedly sparked the sexual revolution back in the sixties. Although some still weren't aware of it, a lot of the supermodels, actresses and dancers who traded their looks for big bucks owed him a debt of gratitude they could never repay.

"We've bumped into each other a few times," he soft pedaled an obviously more-than-casual-relationship.

"We've traveled in some of the same circles. Don't let him fool you, though," Sam warned me. "He's a shrewd businessman. He's seen your pictures. I'm talking about the ones on the Serengeti when you got crazy with the flamingos."

"So this wasn't just a casual happenstance?"

"Hef's a bottom line guy," he explained. "His magazine has already spoken to CAM about you."

"Sebastian never mentioned a thing to me about appearing in Playboy."

"He won't until he's got a number. Besides, he probably thinks you are still shocked about what happened yesterday."

"Why didn't Hef say anything?"

"That isn't how it's done. This is a party. People jockey, deals are made, but no one ever talks openly. It's one of the rules of engagement, the game they all play. The details get worked out behind the scenes, between the managers and among the agents. The principals show up, on parade. The bidding happens afterward."

I leaned closer to Sam. I was halfway through my second glass of champagne. "How do you think my stock is doing?"

Sam looked across the crowded backyard. The musicians, who'd been on a twenty minute break, were up on stage quietly tuning their instruments. They would start back up any minute.

"You're hotter than the core of the sun, Coco. It gets better. Come Monday, they're going to have to pay a lot more cash for you. They can't keep their eyes off you now."

"That's going to worry a bottom line guy," I referred to Hef.

Sam smiled knowingly. "His daughter Chrissie worries about those things now. Hef still approves most of the layouts, but he cares less than he once did. The prerogative of age, I guess. He's just trying to make the most of the time he has left."

"He's doing a good job as far as I can see," I gave credit where it was due.

"Viagra bought him fifteen years. Don't fault me on it," he saw the way I'd looked at him. "Ask him yourself. He's unabashed about it."

"So I'm going to be in Playboy," I mused rhetorically. I fleshed out the idea in my mind.

"Only if you want to be."

"How would you feel about it, Sam?" I asked seriously.

He turned to meet my gaze. "I want what makes you happy. At the end of the day, that's what makes me happy. If you want to do a pictorial for Playboy, I'll support you one hundred percent."

"You won't be jealous of all those men seeing me nude?" I straightened his black tie.

"It wouldn't bother me. I get to take you home at night." Sam kissed me, his tongue inside my mouth. I responded in kind, knowing probably half the guests in the backyard were watching. I rubbed my body against him. Sam responded. If they were going to watch, then why not put on a good show?

# Chapter 30

I rode the wave of celebrity for the next eighteen months before accepting my first acting contract, but not before Sam flew me to Frankfurt for my birthday. We rented a car at the airport and drove the six hours on the Autobahn into Prague, in the Czech Republic. The city was ancient and beautiful. It was the middle of July and the streets were overrun with tourists and vacationing students. It was a good place to lose ourselves, kick back and think about nothing but nothing. We scheduled a ten day hiatus. Both of us needed it. Sam had begun to spend more of his time in, of all places, Nevada. But interestingly enough, he wasn't looking in the city of Las Vegas. Instead, he'd been traveling in the southwest part of the state, in the desert. I didn't pay much attention to where. I never asked him why, either. Lately I'd been too busy myself.

Sebastian and Creative Arts Management were looking to diversify. I was their ticket onto that train. He wanted to move into Hollywood. Seb was looking into representing certain select clients in their acting pursuits and needed bankable star power. He figured I could provide his team with that segue. It wouldn't interfere with the careers of his models; the two avenues were meant to complement each other. I hadn't really discussed any of this with Sam. I wanted us to enjoy the artists' Mecca in front of us.

"Isn't this wonderful?" We were looking out across the water of the swiftly moving Vltava River under Charles Bridge. Musicians and long-haired artists from all corners of Europe and beyond were out in droves. It was noon and eighty-two degrees in the shade. The bridge swarmed with life. Easels were set up everywhere. Painters' brushes stroked their canvasses, drawing from Sistine masterpieces of stone and ancient architecture and the ribbon of the river gently meandering through what many had of late, taken to calling the heart of Europe.

Sam should have been relaxed, but he wasn't. I felt his restlessness and it concerned me. He had a lot on his mind before we left Vegas, but we always managed to find a way to relax on our sojourns together. We had learned to seize the moment. When a small window of time presented itself, we left the world behind and dived into our own private bubble of togetherness. So far it had worked every time. This time, for whatever reason, Sam couldn't seem to find a way to temporarily leave the real world behind. I decided to let it ride. Sam deserved that much. He'd come around after a day or two, I was sure of it.

"This legend on the statue says if you kiss this guy's feet you'll come back here again." I leaned far enough over the stone railing to plant one on the ancient edifice. "Now you," I cajoled him, wanting desperately to see him laugh again.

"Is that healthy?" he lamely protested.

"That's not the point, Sam. Come on. Please," I begged him. "Do it for me."

His effort was half-hearted, but he finally did it anyway.

"There. Now we'll both come back." I grabbed him under his arm and hauled him off. We sidestepped a string quartet on our way through the throng to the other side of the bridge. We stopped for a glass of wine on the Castle side, resting on wooden-backed chairs set out around small, round tables. Sparrows played a game of hopscotch for the reward of discarded bread crumbs and spilled pieces of cheesecake on the cobblestone street in front of us. I watched as a dominant male among them chased another, smaller bird between the legs of the table beside us. Both flew off, chirping defiance, only to land again at the feet of a vacationing couple eating nearby. It was a feast for the birds.

We sat in direct sunlight. The heat was strong, but the caress of those rays on my bare shoulders felt therapeutic. Sam didn't seem to mind, either. He brushed his forehead, removing a fine patina of perspiration. I thought life was good. I didn't know what he was thinking about behind his dark glasses. The glass of sweet white wine on the table in front of him remained full.

"I know the cure."

He shifted his chair.

"Is it that obvious?"

"If I was insecure, or really ugly, or divorced with five kids, I might be worried. But since I'm none of the above, I'm not."

Sam held up both hands in surrender. "It has nothing to do with you, baby," he assured me. He dropped his hands. He took off his sunglasses and wiped his brow again, this time with the sleeve of his red cotton shirt, darkened from the moisture. He reached for his glass of wine, draining half of it. At last he looked at me.

"Lately I've been thinking about my life."

"This is heavy isn't it?" I took off my own sunglasses then. I reached for his hands and held them in mine.

He nodded. I waited. This was the first time in the years Sam and I had been together that he wanted to talk to me about what I referred to as his lifestyle. Thus far, Sam had walked the proverbial tightrope. Somehow he'd gotten away with compartmentalizing who he had to become in order to be successful in the shadowy netherworld at the upper echelons of his organized criminal enterprise. He gave orders and they were carried out without question. He had the muscle to back up his edicts. He used this muscle as a highly skilled surgeon used his scalpel.

On the other hand, he was also extremely successful as a legitimate and respectable businessman in the legal world. He knew politicians and mayors and a handful of governors, along with an assortment of entertainers. Admittedly, they were as careful as he when it came to their public personas. But those who met the legitimate side of Sam usually liked him well enough to include him as their peer. On rare occasions these strategically fueled, mutually beneficial relationships actually evolved into friendships. Over time, word had gotten out. Sam could be trusted, His discretion counted on. He was a man of honor. Favors were traded, influences optioned. When one of the so-called 'straights' crossed the line and needed something which required his unique talents, Sam would of course reluctantly oblige, knowing full well whoever traded their soul was his forever, or at least until their usefulness expired.

Sam was a master of this game, one of the best to ever play it. But for the first time, I saw that he was bothered by this constant wire walking. Something – or someone – had gotten to him.

He looked at me as if he was seeing me for the first time. He smiled. I waited. He finally sighed, "You grew up on me, Coco."

"It had to happen one day, Sam. But don't worry, I won't tell anyone if you don't." I said it with love, and he knew it. There was no joking in a moment like this.

"You know who I am." It wasn't a question.

"I know most of you, Sam." I thought of lyrics written by Billy Joel, "'We all have a face that we hide away forever.' Every one of us has our dark corners." I'd known for a long time that we were as sick as our darkest secrets. I was no fool. I knew the man I loved had more than most. I wondered what might be his darkest.

"'And we take them out and show ourselves when everyone has gone,'" he completed the line from 'The Stranger'.

"I'm here, Sam," I squeezed his hands. "I've never left, and I love you. Do you hear me? I love you," I said softly, but with incredible strength.

"Sometimes I wonder why. Maybe in the beginning, when I first saw you, maybe things were different for both of us back then. I guess that's not important now," he seemed to change his mind about something he was going to say.

"Things *were* different. At least for me they were. You're right, I have grown up. Now I have more mature feelings. They're sharper, stronger, and so are my convictions. I know what I want, Sam. I want you. The past doesn't mean anything anymore." I could see he was wrestling with demons that wouldn't turn him loose.

He smiled then. "I wish it was that easy. To just forget yesterday's sins as if they never happened. But that's not reality. They haunt me, Coco." His smile disappeared. "I've done things. Not so nice things." He was fighting to be honest – to reconcile his worlds. "Bad things," he admitted. Sam's eyes turned darker, as if cruel images were playing across the theater of his mind.

"We've all done bad things, Sam. If you're thinking about getting out, why can't you leave the mob thing out of it? By now, after all these years of piling ill gotten gains into legitimate businesses, I don't see why the illegal stuff is even necessary any longer. Don't you have enough? Couldn't you just tell your partners you're done with it? Even if they demanded restitution, I'm sure you can work out a deal with them. It isn't as if we'd be penniless. We could live like royalty on the money I make alone." I'd thought about it before, but been afraid to talk about it with him. I always thought Sam loved his work, that his addiction to the power that came with it was all that stood in his way. Could it be that I'd been wrong? "Why don't we both just walk away?" I was suddenly emboldened. "We don't need it, Sam. We could cash in our chips. We could open a bed and breakfast somewhere in the South of France, or a neighborhood pub in London. It wouldn't matter to me, as long as we could be together."

"Whoa, I never said anything about leaving Las Vegas. I may be having a slight attack of conscience, but I'm not thinking about quitting. I love what I'm doing."

"Then why the long face?" He was confusing me.

He sighed, "I don't know. Maybe it's the balancing act. I'm being pulled in a lot of different directions right now."

"That's why we came here, isn't it? So we could get away from all the crap for a while. I can help you to relax, Sam," I reminded him.

"That's never been a problem," he admitted.

I leaned back in the chair and raised my face to the sun. It felt warm. A soft breeze rippled through the sidewalk café, catching the edge of my gossamer shirt, playing with it for a moment before moving on. I was frustrated because, for now at least, nothing I was saying was working. Then suddenly, the solution dawned on me. I bolted upright in my chair.

"What?" I'd almost startled Sam.

"Nothing." We'd never talked about it openly before. Things were too good the way they were. There had been no sense fixing something that wasn't broken. "I think I know what might be ailing you."

He looked at me, waiting for me to continue.

"Are you thinking about taking this to another level, Sam? You and me? Is that what this is all about?" I avoided the 'M' word.

"I'd be a liar if I said it hasn't entered my mind," he spoke honestly. "Do I lose sleep over it? No. I think we're way past that, don't you?" He turned the question back around to me.

"I'm fine with what we've got," although lately I'd been feeling perhaps something was missing. I'd just turned twenty-five. I was still young, but we'd gotten along better than most for longer than was necessary, in my opinion, to know if we were a strong enough match. I hadn't pushed Sam to get hitched; most of the time I was too busy to even think about it. I didn't think it would change much about the way we lived. We had separate lives, and when it suited us we met somewhere in the middle, usually on quiet getaways like this one. Why spoil a good thing? The answer, I felt then, was because it was the final thing you did to say I love you. It was the binding commitment before friends and God as witnesses that said you loved and respected each other enough to spend the rest of your lives together, warts and demons and all.

"I just thought that's what might be bothering you," I lied nonchalantly. "But I'm definitely okay with things the way they are, Sam, if you were thinking I wasn't. I mean, we can always talk about a change," I backpedaled. "But I'm in no hurry. It's not like I hear the biological clock ticking. You should hear the thirty some-things at some of the parties I go to. By thirty they're panicking if they haven't got someone on the line. If they hit thirty-five and they're still single they can be downright suicidal."

Sam was shaking his head. "Women."

"It's everyone: men, women, straight, gay. They're jockeying for position around that age. Whoever coined the phrase 'meat market' wasn't kidding. From the women's perspective, it's how much can I get from this guy if he walks on me in five or ten years. Think about it for a minute, Sam. They're already thinking about the divorce even before they've said, 'I do'. And the men, don't get me started. I can write you a book. Do you know it's a feather in the cap if they can pay for a boob job? I ran across a guy at one of Sebastian's parties who'd paid for eleven breast augmentations. He was someone's agent, I think. He'd accepted that was the going rate for three months of half-decent sex. Worse, the women who had theirs done all accepted his terms."

"Where'd this come from?" Now it was Sam's turn to wonder about me.

"I'm just saying," having finished my tirade, I began more slowly, "that we aren't like most other people out there."

"You and I could never be like that," he agreed. "We wear coats of a different color."

"Precisely, and that's exactly my point. We don't need to be married. There's no pressure on either one of us. I'm not in it for the money and you don't need to buy sex, at least not yet," I needled him, unable to resist a good jab.

"I am a few years older than you," he reminded me, playing along.

"Exactly how I like my men: seasoned, cultured, experienced. I don't like boys, Sam. I never have."

"I, for one, am real happy about that. I guess that means you're going to hang on to me for a little while longer." He was perfectly secure in his man-suit. It was only one of the many endearing qualities in Sam which had allowed me to overlook the other side, the shadows cast by the man, but rarely if ever seen in anything other than their dark silhouettes. He hid that side of himself from me more than from anyone else. If I had any concerns about Sam and me at all, that was the only one worth mentioning. Still, I figured that wasn't such a bad deal. I was betting that, sooner or later, Sam would be funneled into a choice between the job he claimed he loved so much – the lifestyle – and me. I trusted he would make the right decision.

# Chapter 31

"So what's this I hear about a movie contract?" Sam was out of the doldrums. We held hands as we strolled up a winding cobblestone street with the rest of the shuffling tourists. Half of the people seemed to be moving in the same direction as we were. The other half, a colorful mix of sightseers, were headed the other way, back down from what awaited us at the top of our climb – the Hradny Castle – the crown jewel of Prague.

The wine we drank at the café had caused my cheeks to flush the color of pink roses. I felt at peace as we walked along the streets of what was termed the City of a Thousand Spires. I looked across the sea of red roofs which, until now, had seemed more a part of Germanic architecture than the Czech Republic's. The roofs of the homes cascaded down the rolling, hilly topography like a bleeding waterfall. We continued our ascension to the highest point in the city, where in ancient times the richest and most powerful men positioned their castles.

"Sebastian thinks it will be good for my career."

"Not to mention his bank account," Sam pointed out.

"I don't begrudge him his check." Seb had ended up with nineteen percent of everything I brought in. A manager usually got twenty-five percent, a good agent fifteen. Since Sebastian was navigating uncharted waters with me as the ship's prow, and acting in both capacities, Nathaniel Katz had negotiated for middle ground. I would do my own accounting. This would run me an additional one to one and a half percent of my gross. It was a sweet deal. I didn't think Seb would have normally agreed to it, but Nate *was* Sam Spielman's lawyer. I guess it had just been easier for CAM to go along. Of course The Elephant Shot hadn't hurt my bargaining position either. "He earns every penny of it."

"I wasn't saying he doesn't," Sam agreed with me. "Are you nervous?" We hopped off the street and onto the wide sidewalk to step around a small group of visitors who had stopped to snap some pictures of a restaurant.

"About making a film? No way. I've got nothing to lose. It's free publicity for my modeling work, and as far as I can tell there's really no downside. I'm relaxed, tanned, and ready to have some fun."

"How big is the part?"

"I'm not a lead, but it's a pretty good supporting role."

"Do they have the final script yet?" Sam obviously knew more about film making than he'd let on.

"The writer's been asked to make some revisions based on the part I read for last month. The producer was in the theater for the test. He demanded I get more lines," I said proudly.

"Imagine that," Sam said, almost to himself. I looked at him but he was looking straight ahead. He could be avoiding meeting my eyes, or he could be examining the turn in the street. I couldn't be sure which. I'd realized long ago Sam was capable of just about anything, but if he helped me get that part by using his peculiar kind of influence, I didn't want to know. Somehow, I knew that would take the fun out of it. I never asked him.

"The director was impressed. He's confident in me. Otherwise, I don't think he would have agreed to expand my character's part."

"He would have overruled the producer?"

"I'm just happy they agreed. I didn't want to be in the middle of that kind of spat before we even began to make the film. I don't think that would have endeared me to anyone connected with this project. My first movie probably would have been my last. No matter what happened, in the end you can bet they would have blamed me." I could see Sam was skeptical.

"I'm learning on the fly, Sam. Hollywood isn't a part of our solar system. They don't think like us mere mortals."

Sam agreed with me, "They're ruthless all right, but they're going to make you a star, sweetheart. Bank on it."

"How can you be so sure?" Now I was skeptical.

"Because you have what they need. Those studio executives are parasites and you're the new blood. Plus, someone else has already spent a billion dollars putting your likeness on the cover of every twenty-fifth magazine sold in the world last year. As the saying goes, they may be crazy but they're not stupid. It works both ways, though."

"What do you mean?"

"They'll use you, but you can use them right back."

"I'm not like them, Sam. I'm not a parasite."

"That's why you've got Sebastian Vilgrain. Remember, in this game you're out front. Let his team take care of the rest. Sebastian may be one of the best, he is, but you…" Sam's eyes were piercing black, aimed. The sun was brilliant, there wasn't a cloud on top of us, but no light escaped from those pitch dark barrels. As if aware of this, he fished out his sunglasses and put them on. He looked back at me and resumed, "There are over six billion people on this planet. There are plenty of Sebastian types, but there's only one Coco Stevens."

He walked in silence for a while after that, accompanied by the sounds of languages from all around the world as we passed by people coming and going. One last turn and the Hradny Castle exploded into the sky in front of us.

"Oh, Sam!" I gasped. "It's absolutely beautiful." In the same moment, I noticed some tourists beginning to take photographs. Not of the Castle, though. They were suddenly taking my picture as we stood in front of a three foot high stone wall which marked the castle's outer front perimeter.

At first there was a trickle, but quickly they turned into a flood as more of them, curious about the first few, wandered over to where Sam and I stood and recognized me. In no time there were about thirty people crowded around us. Their cameras clicked away, a forest of cicadas during mating season. They weren't pushing and shoving like their paparazzi counterparts. They were smiling and polite. Many asked first, and I willingly obliged them.

The so-called professionals, the ones who photographed celebrities for money, were different. These quiet, modest tourists from as far away as Japan, who wanted something to talk about with their relatives back home, weren't nearly as aggressive. I would be one of their many souvenirs from their trip to Prague, probably destined to a place on the mantle next to the family picture of the trip to Cape Canaveral. Dusty and forgotten, my picture would quickly become a quiet anecdote in their precious, individual histories. In time, sooner than one might expect, they would forget my name. Later, they might wonder who I was. After that the photo would be deleted, or lost. Printed copies would be sold at garage sales, or more likely discarded, destined for the nearest landfill. Somehow, the thought of this fame fading gave me comfort. The world, I realized, was still filled with very ordinary people living very ordinary lives. They lived and died, every one of them, but like me they had opportunities to laugh and cry and live and love.

The tourists finished taking their pictures a few minutes after they'd begun. They were appreciative, offering thanks in several languages. Some nodded, some bowed, others approached and shook our hands.

I smiled at Sam, "Now why can't they all be as nice as these people were?" I said.

The sound was like a circus ringmaster's whip used by the ringmaster to forcefully coax animals around a ring on the outside of a circle in which clowns and acrobats staged their shows. The sound split the still air open with a *shak*, a farmer's scythe cutting grass. A flock of sparrows hidden among the front parapets of the entrance to the Castle took flight as one. Sam moved instinctively. He was still in motion when the second whip cracked, a sound identical to the first, and I felt a sharp sting across my shoulder. It felt like when I was a small child and I happened across a wasp's nest. One of the nasty winged devils had let its temper get the better of it and stung me.

Sam flung himself across me. His momentum carried him on top of me and I wondered why he was tackling me as we both fell sideways and hard onto the cobblestone path under us. Then I saw the cold blue steel in Sam's hand and somehow I knew I'd just been shot.

# Chapter 32

"I always thought I would be the one who went first, that Leslie and B.C. would outlive me. Who would have guessed I would be going to their funerals instead of the other way around?"

I marveled at Claire Anderson's resilience. She had been deeply touched by the unexpected deaths of her sister and her brother-in-law, but had recovered quickly. Death for Claire was a far more significant part of life than for those her junior. It was her constant companion. If there was any doubt of this, she had only to glance at her reflection to be reminded it would soon be calling on her.

I guessed such acceptance came easier with age. When young people passed, especially children, the transition was tragic. These were the innocents robbed early of their birthright to life. On some level, we feel we deserve at least the number of years that others we deem less worthy than ourselves have lived. We envied the elderly even as we loathe the infirmities of old age. We want the years without the price of growing old.

Claire had bounced back from the brink. It was her attitude which had kept her alive while her sister had lived with her, while B.C. had made his quarterly sojourns across the desert. It was her attitude that kept her alive now.

I tried to say something I felt would help. Not having very much experience with dying, I was careful with what I said. Not meaning to sound trite, I observed, "You never know your last hour."

"From the mouths of babes," said Claire. "It's true. I'll tell you what my granddaddy told me a long time ago: 'Live each day as if it were your last. It just might be.'" As if to assuage any second thoughts to the contrary, she added, "I know Leslie and Billy did."

"Don't take this the wrong way," I began as delicately as I knew how, "But are you and B.C.'s daughter's family estranged?" I figured they at least could have called. As well, I noticed Claire had made no effort to reach out to her niece. She hadn't even mentioned her name since learning of the accident.

"Oh, in heavens name no, child," Claire immediately protested. "I'm sorry, I should have told you. I suppose I assumed you already knew, but how could you?"

"Told me?"

"B.C.'s daughter was never married. She couldn't possibly. Linda has been institutionalized since she was a little baby. Lord knows, Billy couldn't raise her. It tore him apart to give her up, but there was just no other way. He cried for a whole month the first time."

"What's wrong with her?" I was stunned.

"She's got what they call Down syndrome these days. She can't fend for herself. She's as helpless as a four year old child."

"She's in a hospital?" I almost couldn't believe it.

"No, she's not that bad. She's in a private home. They take care of her real nice there. She lives with six other women at a very pleasant residence known as All God's Children Home. It's run by a family. It's always been that way. Leslie helped Billy find the home after

Ethyl passed away giving birth to Linda. I always said they were heaven sent, the family who runs the place, I mean."

"That's why Billy made his trips here through the desert."

"He said it always calmed him. I don't think he wanted us to see him crying, if you ask me. He wanted to get it all out before he saw Linda. So she wouldn't be upset if she saw her daddy with tears in his eyes. I didn't think Billy had any reason for crying. That child is a miracle, born to bring out the best in whoever she touches. She's God's reminder to us all that we are only as strong as how we treat the weakest among us. I believe she is the test we all must pass, Miss Coco. And may God bless Billy, he got himself a perfect score every time he crossed that desert. Can you imagine? Every year, for all these years. And now…and now what?" It was as if Claire suddenly understood that he was gone, and that Linda would never see her daddy again. To confirm this, she lamented, "God in heaven, who will tell the child?" She rested her head into her hands, sitting on the old sofa in her old living room, wracked with tiny, soundless sobs.

I comforted her as I had before, until she regained control of herself. It didn't take nearly as long this time. It was a small consolation.

I rented a Chevy Suburban in Kingman. I left my Corvette parked at the rental office and said I'd pick it up later, probably a few days after the funeral. They were sympathetic; the terrible tragedy was front page news. I could leave my vehicle on their lot free of charge, for as long as I had the Suburban. I would need the larger vehicle to ferry Claire and her wheelchair around town in the days to come.

I inherited the funeral arrangements. Claire and I went to a local attorney in Kingman. Since Claire was the descendants' closest relative, they became her legal responsibility. She willingly allowed me to manage the closing affairs. Her lawyer certified the transfer as legal. I dropped Claire off back at the house and then returned to town, somewhat surprised at how simple it was to arrange a funeral.

Claire had arranged for her relatives' remains to be cremated. A signature on a contract with Shaded Acres Funeral Home was all that was required for them to handle the details. In the proprietor's office I selected two simple, yet elegant urns that would become Leslie and Billy's way stations to forever. Shaded Acres also sold floral arrangements and provided space for a service, along with a priest or preacher depending upon faith and, if desired, a choir of three with a solo of Amazing Grace. I politely declined all of the above. Claire felt a small, private service at the house with the preacher from her own rural church would suffice. I called the preacher. He'd heard the news of Leslie and B.C.'s accident and yes, of course he would be honored to say a few prayers in the backyard of Claire's home. He'd known both of them; they had been friends. And no, there would be no charge. If someone wished to make a donation to the church, he would of course accept this kind and generous gratuity. We agreed on a time for the service to begin and he promised to be fifteen minutes early. Oh, how many people was I expecting? I didn't know. Ten? Eight? There wouldn't be many. They had been old, seen friends and family pass, but they wouldn't be forgotten. Not while I was still alive.

I dropped by the coroner's office and signed a few more papers after producing the papers from Claire's lawyer. The bodies could now be released to the funeral home. The details were almost complete. Was there anything I'd forgotten? I left my card behind in case they thought of anything else after I left.

After tucking my MasterCard back into my purse, I remembered the papers. No one had written an obituary. In her grief, Claire had forgotten.

I asked a secretary for directions to the largest newspaper in town and found myself at their front desk a few minutes later. I took the pen from the stand on the counter in front of me, wondering what to write about two people I'd never met. After a few minutes hesitation I began, writing Billy Cunningham's first. It became easier as I wrote. I'd gotten to know the desert man, even if I'd never had the pleasure of his acquaintance. Leslie's obituary was more difficult. I thought about calling Claire, but didn't. She told me enough about her sister in the time we spent together that I felt I could say what needed to be said. At the end of both obituaries, I invited whomever wanted to come to the backyard memorial, which would be held in four days. I smiled at the receptionist, handing her both scripts. Yes they took MasterCard, and yes they sold papers in both Brittle and Laughlin. Those who read the newspaper would now know where to pay their last respects.

Feeling better, I headed back to Claire's place. I knew I'd probably forgotten something, but I wasn't too worried about it. The service would be held on a Saturday, at one o'clock in the afternoon.

I pulled back into Claire's driveway just after six o'clock in the evening. I was tired from all the running around, but felt good about what I'd accomplished that day. I pulled in beside a 1998 F-150 pickup truck that had seen better days. Its brown-and-tan body was scraped and bruised, the beginning of rust baring its teeth in one of the back wheel wells. The truck had worked hard in its day.

I'd noticed a lot of the trucks looked like this around here. Their bodies didn't necessarily speak for their engines, though. In most cases the older trucks' engines were clean and strong, what their drivers knew was important. The owners didn't really care how they looked, just as long as they were reliable and the rust damage hadn't spread dangerously.

I stepped across the porch and entered the house without knocking. I heard a man's voice, and followed it into the living room.

"Oh, speak of the devil," Claire smiled warmly up at me, perched in her usual spot on the sofa. I went to her and kissed her on the cheek.

"How was your day?" I asked, for the moment ignoring her company. An elderly man and a woman sat on the couch opposite Claire. A spread of tea had been set on the tray in the middle of the coffee table. The cups were empty.

"Fine dear, but you look tired."

"I've been busy, but I'm fine." I turned to meet her company. "I'm Coco Stevens," I held out my hand to the woman first.

"Sally Millhausen, and this gentleman is my husband Bruce."

"I'm sorry for your loss," I said. I shook both their hands. Bruce's hand was big and rough as sandpaper. He was silver haired, maybe ten pounds overweight. It was obvious he stayed active. I could see firsthand why Claire's home had looked as good as it did, but Bruce was aging. There would be no young blood to replace the old, and Claire's home would deteriorate rapidly now that Leslie was gone. Bruce and Sally would not be able to keep it up and care for Claire, who was quickly becoming an invalid. The Millhausens knew as much as I did that the house would have to be sold, and soon. Claire would have to be relocated into an assisted living environment.

Before leaving, the Millhausens thanked me for my kindness and help. We would see them again on Saturday, at the service. From the porch we watched them leave, a whirling cloud of dust by the time they reached the road at the end of the driveway, the Ford's red taillights the only sign of the truck as it slowed to turn right and head northward.

Another vehicle suddenly came into view from the south. I watched as the late model Cadillac slowed to almost a stop, and turned right into Claire's long driveway.

"That will be Brian DeSilva," Claire recognized the car. "He did our wills," she explained. "I called him while you were out." There was a resigned, yet determined look in her eyes. "It's one of those last details I mentioned earlier, one of those things we have to do before it's too late. I need your help now, Coco. I need you to be strong. Most importantly, I need you to say yes."

I looked from Claire to the spot where the Cadillac had just pulled up and stopped on the hard packed clay next to the rented Suburban. Another lawyer, I thought. They were everywhere, inextricably woven into every fiber of people's lives.

We talked on the porch, since the desert had cooled. Fresh air shifted through the breezeway. I could almost smell the cacti.

Brian DeSilva was in his forties, and stood about six feet in height. He was lean and fit, a testimonial to regular work-outs at the local health club down the street from where his law practice was located in Kingman. His office was a fixed up house in the oldest part of town. He looked at me with clear eyes, all business. His dusty shock of full reddish-brown hair matched the color of the dirt I remembered taking from the dry creek bed in Brittle.

Claire listened carefully, shifting slightly in her wheelchair. We talked back and forth for over an hour as the sun sank lower in the west. Bright and angry reds and oranges began to muscle their way into the calmer blue haze that had dominated the afternoon. Hints of turquoise and purple, which moved into the final frames just before sunset, began to appear near the horizon.

"Mr. Cunningham's estate is fairly straight forward, all things considered. There are…" DeSilva shuffled the deck of paperwork on his lap, setting a sheath of paper onto the table I retrieved for us from inside the house just before we'd begun our meeting. "No liens, no encumbrances whatsoever; he owned all of his land outright. There was, however, an option to purchase. It was sold to a numbered corporation sequestered in…Delaware. That's not surprising; this is often done for tax reasons. The option expires at the end of December, the thirty-first to be precise. I see it is renewable contingent upon renegotiation and acceptance by owner." His eyebrows arched upwards across his forehead when he saw the price. "I see the corporation paid a handsome amount for the option. Very fair," he muttered, almost to himself, "Considering the land in question is essentially barren desert." His tone indicated he felt there had possibly been a mistake. He seemed to recheck the figures. He smelled another fee, "I can renegotiate this option for you if you'd like, Ms. Anderson." He'd pretty much ignored me up to this point.

"No thank you, Mr. DeSilva. We don't intend to renew the option. The land won't be for sale."

"It's your call, Mrs. Anderson. But it seems to me you'd want to capitalize on this. It's a good chunk of change on land that is, for all intents and purposes, without significant value."

I finally spoke up, "If the land has little value, then why are you so confident the numbered corporation will want to renew an option?" I could tell he was immediately annoyed.

"I didn't say they would renew, I simply offered to renegotiate. It will benefit the estate. I can set up a trust; we can defer taxes until –"

"Until I'm dead, Mr. DeSilva?" Claire cut him off. A coyote howled in the distance, a lonely and desperate sound. "The only thing that will get me is a fancier solid oak coffin."

DeSilva didn't like the way things had turned. He'd come out to Claire's thinking he'd fallen into a goldmine. Several years back, on one of B.C.'s trips to see his daughter, Claire had accompanied him and Leslie into Kingman to draw up their wills. Each had left their part of the material world to the other in a simple, legal, three page last will and testimony. Claire now owned everything. Leslie's will was the simplest: by elimination, and because Leslie had never married and had never had any children, Claire was her sole beneficiary. B.C. had wanted the same, in the event his death preceded those of his two sisters-in-law. He'd known 'the girls' for close to sixty years, built trust during that time. B. C. had wanted to be certain Linda would be taken care of for as long as she lived. Of the three of them, they had all believed that Leslie would live the longest. B.C. had trusted she would have the time to appoint her successor.

They'd spoken at length of this probability, Leslie suggesting a few individuals she felt could be relied upon in the event of her own death to carry that mantle forward. Their prime mandate had been to look after Linda, to make certain she had a life of dignity. This still remained the only thing that mattered, a fact that seemed to escape Brian DeSilva.

All he was beginning to see was the evaporation of years of siphoning off the hefty fees associated not only with the administration of Claire's estate while she was still alive, but the subsequent fees associated with the maintenance of a fifty-year old woman who apparently couldn't count to ten. His first order of business would have been to sell the land outright to the numbered Delaware Corporation for whatever he could get for it from them. Then he'd trim the rest of the expenses to justify his percentages as he eventually bled the estate dry. He'd planned on moving Linda to far less expensive digs, perhaps even a State home, the moment the old lady kicked it. He hadn't counted on this. He could see what was coming and he didn't like it one bit. Who the hell was the babe, anyway? Who was she to Anderson? It didn't matter, he decided, realizing in the same instant it really *did* matter because – damn it – he wasn't the executor of the will. That job had gone to the woman in Kingman who'd styled the ladies' hair for the last twenty years. Shit! What did she know? It was one old bitty looking after the affairs of other old bitties. The world was going to hell in their hand baskets. What if everyone decided they didn't need lawyers?

"I'm not dead yet, Mr. DeSilva. And while I'm alive and still kicking," she smiled slyly at me, "I'm going to make some changes. Number one, I am giving Coco Stevens power of attorney over everything."

"Coco Stevens?" He stared blankly at Claire, then back at me, not sure what to make of things. "Power of attorney? Over your entire estate?" His fees weren't just evaporating, they were on a one way space mission to Saturn.

"The whole enchilada, Mr. DeSilva," Claire set her plan in motion.

He stared at us with an even blanker expression across his face than when Claire first made her pronouncement. "Well, I'll be hogs waggled," he suddenly recognized me.

"You're that model, the one with the elephant."

"Mr. DeSilva, why don't we stick with the business at hand?" I wasn't prepared to tolerate gratuitous hero-worshipping, particularly since I knew full well what he would have done with Claire and her estate.

He recovered quickly, realizing he'd come a hair's breath from leaving Claire's home tonight with a whole lot less than he'd come out here with. "Of course, I apologize. It's a genuine pleasure meeting you, Miss Stevens." He moved on quickly, "However, there may be a complication."

"What might that be?" I hammered him. There was no forgiveness in my eyes. I was close to firing him, and I knew it wouldn't matter an ounce to Claire.

"It's Mr. Cunningham's daughter, Linda. Technically she's the next of kin. She could contest the will."

"She won't," I shut him down.

The lawyer stared at me, and then at Claire, who stared back at him. "Okay, in that case there shouldn't be a problem. But I would recommend an adoption, just to fortify the net. That would prevent, say, the State from jumping into the fray to protect the interests of the, uh, daughter," he almost said 'child'.

"I thought the wills you drew up were air-tight," said Claire.

"They are. I'm not saying anything like this will happen. It rarely ever does. But we want to eliminate any possibility that something might go wrong."

"I'll adopt Linda," I declared.

"Oh, Coco, I can't ask you to do that." Claire instantly protested.

"I'll do it," I said with finality in my voice. "It would be an honor."

Tears welled up in Claire's eyes. "I *knew* it," she smiled, worry absent from her face. "You *are* an angel. How can I ever repay you?"

I winked at her "You already have, Claire. It's me who has to worry about repaying you," I was thinking of Sam and the expression on his face when he found out who controlled the oil field.

We spent another hour speaking with Brian DeSilva. He accepted the fact he had never really been that close to all those fees. He'd filled his head with illusions of grandeur but came around quickly. At the end of the meeting, after the sun was down, I was reasonably confident we could work together.

We discussed a blind trust, since I didn't want my identity known. It would surface eventually; I knew this was inevitable. Sam would have his lawyers sue the estate for some reason or another, just to flush me out, but by then it would be too late. The wills would be probated, the trust strengthened, and I'd be Linda's adoptive parent. Full trustee of the entire estate would be firmly vested in me.

I helped Claire into the house.

"Tea?" I suggested.

"It's late." Then she shrugged. Out of character, she said, "What the heck? Let's live dangerously. I'll have a half cup. That should stop a flood. I wouldn't want to wear a diaper to bed."

"You can call me if you need my help. I'm a light sleeper," I gave her an out. "I'll leave my bedroom door ajar."

"In that case I'll risk a full cup," she chuckled mirthfully.

I had the tea ready in ten minutes.

"Are you okay with all of this?" I asked, blowing across my tea to cool it. "I mean maybe we should give it some time. You really haven't had a lot of time to get to know me," I cautioned her.

"Are you having second thoughts about the adoption?"

I shook my head forcefully. "No, absolutely not. I'm resolute. It wasn't as spur of the moment as it seemed."

"You thought about it?"

"As soon as you told me about Linda," I looked at Claire with clear eyes.

"Your kind of integrity doesn't grow on trees. You had me when you were willing to give up when you thought that Linda maybe had a family, and that they would deal directly with Mr. Spielman at my expense. No one had to ask you. You wouldn't – couldn't – leave someone like me who you'd known only a few hours. You were prepared to walk away from what was probably the most important fight of your life – for a little old lady you barely even knew. And the only reason was because you cared. No one does that. And now you want to adopt dear, sweet Linda."

"Maybe I'm not so altruistic. Maybe I'm agreeing to all this to get my hands on the money, or maybe I just need a way to even the scales with Sam. Perhaps I'm the most selfish person alive, and I've fooled you. Don't forget I'm an actor, Claire."

"I've seen one of your movies, Coco. Leslie rented it one time by mistake. We didn't usually watch R-rated movies, not that they weren't any good, mind you," she didn't want to insult me. "It's just that we preferred the more family oriented ones. Our favorite TV show was the one about the angels. What was it called?" She looked off into space.

"Touched by an Angel, with Roma Downey?"

"Yes! That's the one. It was a wonderful program. We never missed it," Claire sighed. She knew she'd never see another episode with her sister. "Anyway, we rented the film you did where you played an actress. *That* was acting. The real you could never act like the person you played in the film, Coco."

"I don't understand." I was fascinated. I'd spent a small fortune to learn how to act from the best. My reviews had always been more good than bad. I thought I knew what I was doing. "What do you mean?"

"I mean I can always tell when someone's pulling my leg. It comes with age and, I'd like to think, an honest heart. I could always recognize one of my own, Coco."

"One of your own?" she was confusing me.

"A kindred spirit. You weren't acting when you said you wouldn't leave me. I could see that someone left you once, Coco. You know how that feels. To you, that was more important than everything material this world has to offer."

"My Dad," I whispered, tears rimming my eyes as my soul filled with angst.

"You won, child. In that moment, when you decided to stay with me, your heart was healed. But that doesn't mean we can't still teach Sam a lesson. This is one time when we can have our cake and eat it too. I wasn't at all surprised when you volunteered to adopt Linda. It's in your nature. You can't help it Coco, you're an angel. It's the truth. Old folks don't lie to their friends. They don't have the time."

# Chapter 33

Pete the mule was first to arrive at the memorial service. He wandered in from the desert looking for his old friend, Billy. The mule had no reason to believe B.C. would not meet him, as had been the case every time before. If the animal could feel what humans felt, it would have been aware of a building anxiety in the pit of its stomach. But people maintained, as a rule, that animals couldn't feel such things. I only knew the donkey moved with a certain hesitation. He seemed confused. He came when I called probably because he saw the long orange carrots in the plastic bag I carried. Until then he had paced restlessly, moving to one end of the yard, stopping, traipsing to the other end. He would stop at the hitching post occasionally and sniff it, almost as if he missed being tied to it. Claire told me Billy always stripped Pete bare when he left to visit his daughter in Kingman. It was as if he were making sure Pete could leave if the time ever came when, for whatever reason, his friend and travel companion never returned.

Pete gratefully accepted the carrot, which was no doubt a delicacy to him. He took it from my hand gingerly, careful not to mistake my fingers for the vegetable. I stroked his long snout, smoothing his coarse hairs in the direction of his big ears.

"I wish you could understand me, Pete," I spoke softly to the animal. His ears twitched at invisible flies, then perked up. He was listening to me. He nudged me for another carrot.

"You're on your own now, pal. No more high times with your friend. There won't be anymore desert hikes. Billy is gone, but he's waiting for you. The two of you will have quite a reunion up there. You'll have lots of time to walk new deserts together, and you'll never be thirsty. Sorry, Pete," the donkey nudged me again. "No more carrots, I'm afraid." I held my hands open to show him. I think he understood, because he lowered his head and turned, ambling once again in the direction of the hitching post. A man cleared his throat behind me.

"Hello."

"Hello, Father. Sorry I didn't hear you. Is it time?"

He walked closer to me, extending his hand. "Soon," he said. "We've a few minutes. No one else is here yet."

"There won't be many," I said.

His smile was wise. "The ones who come are enough. You must be Coco Stevens."

"I am. Father Bertrand?"

"Yes. Good to meet you." He gazed over my shoulders at Pete. "They'll miss each other."

I turned to look at the donkey. His head was slightly lowered. He stood a foot from the railing, as if tethered to it by an invisible rope.

"They loved each other."

"I've always found that sad, but not surprising."

"What's that, Father?" I asked.

"Sometimes we show – and receive – more love to our animal friends than we do to our fellow humans."

"Sometimes they're worth more to us, Father. Our pets love us unconditionally. That's something most humans never seem to master."

The priest kicked at a stone on the clay in front of him. "That's what's so sad. We can't seem to just love one another. Is it so difficult? We are made in His image, closer to God than the angels, and yet at times, we seem farther away from Him in spirit than that mule over there."

"And they say *he's* the stubborn one." We both laughed, I think happy to feel this way before the memorial got started. "I'm glad you could come on such short notice, Father Bertrand."

"Thank you, Miss Stevens."

"Coco, please."

"Coco, Claire told me what you're going to do for her."

"With her, Father," I corrected him. "She needs to know – we all do – that everything will be all right after she's gone. If I don't step in that might not happen."

The priest's eyes never strayed from me. "Normally, I might be concerned. You've known each other for less than a week."

"But?"

"But, I know Claire. I've lived a long sixty-seven years, and in all that time I don't think I've ever run across anyone like Claire Anderson. If I believed in certain things, I might even suggest she's clairvoyant. I don't believe in that, but I do believe in God, and I've always known of His strange ways. Ours is not to question Him, and I know Claire never does. Neither did her sister. They were a paradox, you know."

"How was that?" I wondered.

"Leslie was as strong as an ox. She was over six feet tall, a giant for her time. You know how Claire is. But

Claire was by far stronger in the mind, as if what the good Lord took from her body he gave back to her in will. She was the reason they hung onto this place for so long – not Leslie. In many ways, it was Claire who looked after her sister."

"I didn't know that," I was surprised.

"People make assumptions," granted the priest, "that are not always correct."

"Are you going somewhere with this, Father?"

He sighed. "I try not to judge people, Coco. But none of us is without sin. Maybe that's why I became a priest all those years ago; perhaps I knew of my own hypocrisy and wanted to atone for it. I'm confessing to you, Coco. I've seen one of your films. I know who you are – strike that," he corrected himself, "I know who I *thought* you were. I saw the film; saw your image in all those magazines. I judged you in the image of Hollywood, even though I knew nothing of you. I want to ask for your forgiveness. I have already asked The Lord."

"You don't need my forgiveness, Father. This isn't about me. You know more than most about sin. I forgive others because I know more than most about judgment. That's my department, Father. I hold a Ph.D. in it. Maybe it's because I'm always being judged. You judged me, and I bet you spend a fraction of the time most people do watching movies or reading magazines. I'm a celebrity, under the microscope. Whatever I say or do becomes public fodder. It's how I have earned my living. If I believed one percent of what people write about me I'd go crazy, so I've learned to forgive them instead. It works better that way."

"You are wise beyond your years. Now I know what Claire saw in you. Thank you, Coco."

"Thank me for what, Father?" I was puzzled.

"For teaching a stubborn old man a few new tricks, and for your forgiveness," he smiled at me, comfortable now in his own mind Claire had been right.

"Thank you, Father. For the vote of confidence, I mean." I took a deep breath and let it out in a whoosh to clear my lungs. I looked over to where Pete meandered near the hitching post. "I just hope I'm up to it all. I keep thinking that, sooner or later, I'm due for a fall."

"Don't worry," said the priest knowingly, still smiling. "He'll catch you."

I pushed Claire in her wheelchair into the backyard, trying my best to avoid the rougher areas of uneven ground where a slight dip might send a sharp pain shooting into her arthritic joints. Bruce Millhausen had helped me lower the chair down the six inch drop from the back deck onto the ground. If Claire felt any discomfort at all, she didn't show it. She remained stoic until I finally parked her beneath the shade of one of the large trees beside where Father Bertrand would say a few words about Leslie and Billy. The urns filled with their ashes were on top of a small table Sally provided. A total of fifteen people were in attendance. I was the only one under sixty years old. We'd thought about bringing Linda out from All God's Children Home, but decided against it. Claire told me she wouldn't understand what was happening, and if she did it would just upset her. I'd see Linda afterwards. I found myself desperately wanting to know B.C.'s daughter.

Minny Javenchuck and her husband were at the funeral. She'd been Leslie's hairdresser, and volunteered to trim Claire's hair at the house before the ceremony. She'd done just that while Father Bertrand and I spoke.

Of course, Sally and Bruce Millhausen were there, God bless them. As if by magic, Bruce had produced a dozen folding chairs from his home and set up three rows in front of the small dais Father Bertrand brought with him. With Claire's chairs added, everyone had a place to sit for the ceremony. Pete stood, and Angelo the Chihuahua sat in Claire's lap.

There were a pool of seven people, two married couples and three widows, all at least in their seventies. I couldn't remember their names, but Claire knew them well. They'd been friends of Leslie's and had all known Billy Cunningham, the man who religiously crossed the desert to see his daughter. Some dabbed their eyes with handkerchiefs while Father Bertrand reminded us all of the precious little time we have, and, as evidenced by the terrible tragedy on the State highway outside of Kingman, no one knew when it would be their time.

He said some beautiful things about the deceased, but made it short because even in the shade of the big tree it was still hot, and the old feel it worse than the young.

The last part of the service was the spreading of their ashes. All three, including Claire, had stipulated to this in their last will and testaments. I pushed Claire in her wheelchair to where the backyard ended and the desert took over. Everyone shuffled in around us. There was a hushed, warm breeze blowing from the west. One urn at a time, I helped Claire empty the respective ashes on the desert floor, side by side, as per the wishes of Leslie and Billy. Stronger winds would spread what the breeze could not.

We all walked quietly back to the house, lost in the private, lonely thoughts that seem to surface among the living only at funerals. The pallor of mortality hung in the air, a sheet hung on the clothesline on a day turned drizzly. Most knew the wait would not be long before they too passed into oblivion.

People stayed long enough to consume the requisite tea and a piece of the crumb cake I'd bought along with the carrots for Pete. Father Bertrand was the last to leave reminding me and Claire on the way out that he was only a phone call away should we find the need to talk.

Melancholy is the retrograde cousin to depression. Claire and I felt it then. The house seemed uncommonly empty and silent. Claire was tired, so I helped her to bed for a much deserved midday siesta. Even Angelo seemed subdued. Without encouragement, he curled up in his basket beside Claire's bed. He rested his head between his paws and stared up at me with those bulging eyes.

"Go to sleep," I whispered to him. Claire had nodded off the moment her head had hit the pillow. Angelo continued to stare at me, but didn't move. I eased the bedroom door closed behind me and tiptoed out to the front porch.

I sat on the swing and stared out across the desert in front of the house. I felt sad at the death of B.C. and Leslie. I felt, in some small way, that I had known Billy and Leslie, or at least in the past few days I'd gotten to know the essence of their spirits. They had both been good, decent human beings. The world would be less for their loss. As I ruminated on how their lives had gone, I couldn't help but think about the strangeness of my own. My life could not be called ordinary, by any stretch of the imagination. I knew I was different, but wasn't everybody? I thought about Sam and our life together. Damn him for what he'd done. He'd ruined it all. And now I had the means to exact revenge. I was sure they'd save a special place in hell for me before I was done.

When I thought about it that way I felt empty inside, like a used can of paint. It was true that a part of me hated him with every ounce of my being, but another part loved him. This was my cross to bear. For the ten thousandth time since I'd learned what happened, I cursed God. He was a cruel trickster. I knew right from wrong, but why did Sam make it so hard to choose between the two? I could never forgive the man I'd loved for what he'd done. I remembered entire nights staying awake until morning, unable to sleep, watching the dawn's light finally, mercifully, invade the bedroom and dissipate my horrible thoughts. Hate could make you think of things you never dreamed possible. Vengeance was its ugly daughter.

I fought every day to forgive Sam, but I couldn't. And now I had been given the means to right the wrong. Sitting on the swing, staring into the heat, I became more resolved than I had ever been. Sam would pay for what he'd done. I would see to it that he did. Damn the consequences, anyway.

# Chapter 34

Claire was awake an hour later. We had a small bite to eat before I finally helped her up into the rented SUV. We headed for Kingman, and All God's Children assisted living home.

The home was situated on a tree-lined street in the oldest part of town. Twenty-five years ago, when there had been a more tolerant building and zoning department that allowed for residential expansion, the owners of a small bungalow had knocked out two of its outer walls. The couple, Mr. and Mrs. Benedict, then added two satellite sections of equal size, each with three self-contained living quarters.

Originally, B.C.'s daughter was the only client of the husband-and-wife business. Linda had stayed in the home's only spare bedroom before the property was renovated. It had been more of an adoption than a business relationship. Sometime later the Benedicts' only son, Todd, had been enterprising enough to see the potential for expansion. He applied for the permits under a grandfathering clause, and no one in the neighborhood objected.

Todd Benedict built the wings himself, adding a second floor to original house in the process. Mr. Benedict lived on the second floor with his wife of thirty-two years, Mary. They had no children, a large part of the reason they genuinely cared for the six disabled persons now in their charge. Mr. Benedict used the main floor of the original house as a reception area. His office was now in the back room where Linda had first stayed.

To the left of the administration desk was the home's former living room. It had been turned into a comfortable lounge with a twenty-six inch Zenith color television, a microwave oven, and a coffee maker on a table under the room's only window.

I rolled Claire up the wheelchair ramp at the side of the front stairs and we entered the office. A clean-shaven man with silver flecked hair looked at us over the top of his reading glasses. He wore a cheery smile.

"Afternoon, Claire," he recognized her immediately. Todd Benedict came around from behind the counter. "Why don't we talk in the den?" he suggested, knowing why we'd come. Claire had filled him in on everything that happened after the accident. He already knew about the adoption, and had been anticipating our arrival.

Todd was a gregarious, outgoing man in his early fifties. I liked him instantly. He was an inch or two taller than me, and about twice as heavy. I'd shut my phone off for a couple of days to get through helping Claire with the funeral, forwarding all my messages to my email. I asked Todd if he had a computer I could use. He happily obliged, showing me to his office at the back of the main floor. His computer was already on. I told him I'd join him and Claire in fifteen minutes. Todd told me to take all the time I needed, there was no hurry. He was a gracious host, complimenting me on a movie he'd seen me in before excusing himself.

Sebastian had called five times. There were others, less important. Sam had tried to reach me three times in the last two days, but wasn't worried that I hadn't returned his calls. He knew I sometimes got so busy I couldn't. But he was wondering where I was.

I turned on my cell phone. My voicemail was full. I called Seb and reached his secretary. She begged me to hang on.

"Coco, I'm glad you called back. Where are you, sweetheart?" He didn't sound pissed, which was a good thing.

"I'm handling some personal business. I should be finished in less than a week."

"Is it your mother?" He was suddenly concerned.

"No, Mom's fine. So is Carl."

"You know we've got that gig in London in ten days. Donatella wanted the models there this Friday to do the fittings. She'll throw a hissy fit if you stand her up. You know how she can be."

I sighed. "I can't make it by Friday, Sebastian. There's no way."

"Whatever it is must be important. Need help?" After years of working with me, he knew better than to argue.

"I'll be fine, Sebastian. Thank you."

"Are you okay? Michael is worried. It's not like you to disappear like this. You've been incommunicado going on a week now. We're worried about you. Sam's been calling here. When he can't reach you, it would lead us to believe something is wrong. You're talking to your friend now, Coco. Not your manager."

"Hmm," I said thoughtfully. "And all these years I thought the two of you were the same person," I teased him.

"You know what I mean."

"I'm just teasing you. I'm fine, I promise you. I'll fly to London on Sunday. I'll be strutting my stuff down the runway on Tuesday, right on time, just like always. Tell Donatella not to get her panties in a knot. She can use one of the other girls with my size to do her fittings. Tell her I will be there. I'll see her on Monday, but don't pencil me in for anymore fall shows. I'll be taking some time off," I announced to him.

"That will disappoint a bunch of people."

"Not me. Take care of yourself, Mr. Manager."

"When will I see you?" I heard the edge of panic in his voice, but I knew from experience that he'd weather the impending hurricane of pissed off clients. Every year it was the same. Magazines and fashion houses took for granted that I'd usually accept the kind of money they threw on the table. This year, I was alerting Sebastian, things would be different. He was my friend. He wasn't going to ask me about it now, over the telephone. He knew me well enough to know I'd tell him in my own time, when I was ready. Sebastian had always respected my privacy, which was one more reason why things worked so well between us. I didn't want to even hint that it was all coming to an end. In all likelihood, the Versace show would be my last. I'd fulfill my contractual obligation, but that would be it. There would be no new contracts.

"I'll call you from the airport on Sunday, before the flight leaves. Take care, Seb. Tell Michael I'll see him in London."

I would read my emails later, when I had the time. I'd call Sam tonight, from Claire's house. Right now, more than anything, I wanted to meet Linda.

I found Claire and Todd where I left them, in the lounge. Claire had wheeled herself over to the window where the three o'clock sun spilled into the room, washing over the potted four foot high ferns and into her lap.

Inevitably she found the air conditioning too cold, another peculiarity inherent to the aging process. She would never request for it to be turned down, since others might find it too warm. It was a constant seesaw battle for Claire to balance herself in the narrow confines between tolerance and kindness. This parameter grew narrower as she aged. As a consequence, Claire never went anywhere without one of her many wool quilts.

I sat in a wooden rocking chair opposite them, and joined their conversation.

"Do you have any experience with people with Down's syndrome?" Todd asked after some pleasantries.

I shook my head. "None, I don't mind telling you how scared I am. What if Linda doesn't like me?"

"I don't think you need to worry about that, Coco. Linda has always craved company. She's a sweet, loving, adorable human being. I will warn you, however, that Linda can be very demonstrative at times. She's very touchy-feely. She doesn't see it as an invasion of someone's space, to her she's just showing love."

"I think I can handle that," I smiled. I knew a little about being demonstrative.

"She functions on par with someone about eight years old." It sounded better than I'd been led to believe. "You may see a fully grown, fifty-one year old woman, but she thinks and acts like a child. Linda sees the world through innocent eyes."

"Does she know about what happened to her father?" I looked from him to Claire.

"No," Todd said. "We haven't told her yet. I decided to hold off until after she met you. In Linda's mind, she lives in an extremely ordered and predictable world. Everything is slotted into its own special place. She has a routine and lives by it. Billy and Leslie were naturally a part of that. Her father showed up four times a year, regular as clockwork – three times lately."

"Did she miss him when he came here only three times? Has she missed him when he didn't show up again this time?"

"We found that curious. If she noticed, she didn't seem to be aware of it. Linda lives in the moment much of the time. As for now," he slowly shook his head, pondering my question. "It's really too early to tell how she's going to react."

"Did she know B.C. was her father?" I asked.

"She called him daddy, and that had a special meaning for her. She's aware, on her own unique level, that Billy Cunningham was her father. Again, Linda sees the world differently than you and I, and I know what you're thinking," his kindness put me at ease. Todd Benedict cared about the people who lived in his home. He thought of them as his family.

"Will she miss him now that he's gone?"

He sighed. "I think she probably will. She remembers people, so I'd like to think she'll miss her dad. Will she cry and fall into a black hole of depression? Probably not, again, she lives much more in the moment than you and I. My guess would be she'll hear us when we tell her that her daddy's gone to heaven, and that he'll wait for her there until she joins him, but her concept of death is very limited. Six months from now she might ask us where he is, but she won't pine for him. I'm sure of this. God has blessed us all with a short memory. It allows us to forgive and to move on. In Linda's case, her attention span is shorter than most. She'll be fine," he assured us. "She's surrounded by an abundance of love."

"I can see that. I feel somewhat guilty this adoption is a legal maneuver," I confessed.

He held up his hand. "Don't. Claire has explained everything to me, and I agree with it. It must be done this way. It's best for everyone. You have to understand, Coco…we're different than folks in the big city. Out here, we've had to look out for one another. There was a time when our lives depended on it. We learned we could count on each other. Now, I know you're one of them –"

"Todd –" Claire started to interrupt him.

"It's all right, Claire," he stopped her, smiling. "There's no need to defend Miss Stevens. I wasn't going to criticize her career. I saw that picture a few years back, the one that pops up here and there every once in a while. I may even have a copy put up somewhere so Mary can't find it."

"The Elephant Shot."

"You have to admit, that bathing suit you were wearing didn't leave a whole lot to the imagination. My point being, I read the stories afterward, and now I've met you for myself. Those were real tears, weren't they?" There was an abnormal clarity in his eyes as I stared into them. I nodded.

"Yes, they were real."

"That's good enough for me. You know no one's ever said a bad thing about you? Not that I've ever run across it. When Claire explained your story to me, I knew right away I wanted to help. My wife Mary feels the same way. A lot of good can come from the world you're a part of. You just happen to be right smack dab in the middle of it all. I say fight fire with fire. You're a city girl Coco, born and bred. You know people like Sam better than you realize. You know how they think, and you can out-guess the best of them. If you have to become Linda's legal guardian in order to do it, then so much the better.

We'll help you any way we can. All of us have decided to trust you, Coco, Linda included."

I was touched. Tears welled up in the corners of my eyes. Claire was smiling, nodding in agreement.

"Thank you both." I fought back tears, but lost. They dropped onto Claire's blouse as I leaned forward and hugged her. I looked at Todd, sniffling, slightly self-conscious of my emotional state. "I'll try my best not to disappoint any of you."

"You won't," replied Claire, her eyes twinkling.

"I'd like to meet Linda now, if it's all right," I said to Todd.

"I think she'd like that," Todd said, smiling warmly. "Her room is this way."

## Chapter 35

Sam was on top of me screaming in my ear. "Are you hit? Are you hit?"

"My shoulder!" I screamed in pain.

"We have to move, Coco! Can you do it?"

Another crack split the air. In the same instant a piece of the cobblestone street next to my head separated in a flash from the stone under it. The shot ricocheted into space.

I pushed myself up from the stones in answer, at the same time feeling Sam wrench on my arm.

"Over the wall!" he shouted, pulling me with him. He half-yanked, half-shoved me across the twelve-inch wide top of the three-foot stone wall separating the Castle's front approach from another building's grounds on the other side. My shoulder burned as I fell roughly to the ground. Another bullet ricocheted off the top of the stone fence as Sam dropped to the stones beside me. I looked at him. His eyes were wide and focused, dark and menacing. A gun was cradled between his knees. Keeping his head down below the level of the wall, he examined my shoulder. Crimson red spread across the cotton of my shirt. It looked obscene in the brilliant sunshine. Sam found a tear in the cloth about three inches down from the top of my shoulder. He touched my arm and I felt like he'd hit me with a branding iron.

He looked at me, concern flooding his face, but also relief. "The bullet grazed your arm. It didn't go in."

"Thank God," I muttered. "Who –"

"It could be anyone. I've got a number of enemies."

"I wish Jack were here."

"So do I." Sam took out his handkerchief and folded it into a neat square. Careful to keep his head down, he shifted closer to me. "Can you sit up?"

With some effort and Sam's help, I managed to maneuver into a sitting position with my back against the wall. Sam ripped my shirt along the tear the bullet made. When it was wide enough, he inserted his handkerchief. "This is going to hurt," he warned me. He pressed the white cloth against the wound. It hurt, but the pain wasn't as bad as I expected. My shoulder was throbbing now, pounding with every beat of my heart. "Are you okay?"

"I'll live," I squinted.

"Can you hold this pressed against your arm?"

"I think so."

"It will stop the bleeding. It isn't bad."

"As far as bullet wounds go?" I forced a smile.

"I'm glad to see you've still got your sense of humor."

"Who in Prague is trying to kill us?" I repeated my earlier question.

Sam slumped beside me, his back against the wall next to mine.

"I don't know, Coco. I'll find out, though," he promised, menace returning to his eyes.

"It's awfully quiet out there," I noticed.

There had been screams right after the first couple of shots, when the tourists realized the tranquil square in front of the Castle had turned into a shooting gallery. They'd scattered in all directions. The world was a dangerous place, and getting worse by the hour. Even tourists knew this. They didn't mind watching the six o'clock news, but they certainly didn't want to *be* the news. In the distance I heard the first bray of police sirens. Thank God for cell phones, I thought.

"What now?" I asked the obvious.

"Whoever the shooter was is probably gone," Sam was assessing the situation. "We'll wait here until the police arrive, just to be on the safe side. Then I'll get you to a hospital. We'll leave that way," he pointed to where a stone walkway butted up against the side of the buildings in front of us, away from the Castle. "That way we can avoid the police."

I knew enough not to question his decision. The police couldn't help us now, anyway. They'd only get in Sam's way.

"It was meant for you, wasn't it?"

Sam looked at me. "The bleeding's stopped," he avoided answering my question. "We were lucky."

"Sam?"

He stared into my eyes. "Probably, you were in the way."

"I could have been killed," the realization was donning on me, hitting me full on, an ice cold bucket full of water.

Sam just looked at me, and then looked back at the walkway near the buildings we would leave by. The sirens were getting louder, racing up the winding streets toward the Castle. They were almost here.

"Can you walk?"

"I think so."

The first police car rounded the last turn and careened into the square in front of the Castle.

"Walk like we're tourists. Don't hurry until we're behind that first building, out of their line of sight. Ready?" A second police car arrived behind us, on the other side of the three foot wall.

I nodded. Sam helped me up, and we walked purposefully in the direction of the path that led away from where the assassin's bullets originated. Sam walked a little behind and to the side of me, hiding the bright red stain of blood splayed out across the left side of my blouse from the inquisitive, prying eyes of the police, who now swarmed like ants on a stepped on hill behind us.

We hailed a cab as soon as we'd cleared the police cordon and made it to a hospital without incident. A hundred dollars U.S., courtesy of Ben Franklin, insured the cabby's silence.

The bullet had grazed my arm near my shoulder, taking a quarter inch of skin with it at the deepest part of the trough. I was surprised at how much it hurt for so little damage. I knew I'd been extremely lucky. Seven stitches, some strong painkillers and two hours later we hopped in another cab in front of the hospital and headed for the hotel.

"I called Jack while you were getting sewn up. He's getting our people together. We're leaving Prague in an hour." Sam's pronouncements were final.

"It might have been someone crazy," I ventured. "One of those random shootings you always read about in the newspaper."

Sam looked at me long and hard, but said nothing.

"Okay, so it wasn't a random shooting. Do you really think it's necessary to head home? I mean, do you think whoever it was will try something again here? The police know something happened. They'll be watching, won't they?" I sounded stupid to myself.

"He was a professional," Sam explained patiently.

"Or she."

"I doubt it, but maybe. Next time whoever it was won't miss. If we give them a second chance, that's it. It isn't safe here, Coco. They're still out there. I blinked, should have seen this coming. It's all right if I get nailed, but I'm sick to my stomach right now that you were caught in the crossfire."

"Why'd you have a gun, Sam?"

"I always bring a weapon."

"Not on a site seeing trip to Europe, you don't. You always leave it in the hotel safe, Sam. You've always done that."

Sam stared out the window of the cab. We were five minutes from the hotel.

"You're in some kind of danger, aren't you, Sam? That's why you've been acting weird ever since we landed in Frankfurt, constantly looking over your shoulder around the next turn. You knew about this, didn't you?" I was angry.

"I never would have brought you here if I thought there was any danger in it."

"You mean you never thought they would follow us all the way to the Czech Republic." I accused him. The pieces were falling into place. It was obvious there was trouble back at home. Sam had underestimated its consequences. It was a high level beef, too, probably sanctioned by the upper echelons of the mob – his peers. No lone wolf with a private grudge would have tried to hit Sam on his own. Even I knew enough about how things worked in Sam's other life to know this. Lone wolves were ruthless, but they weren't suicidal. It was apparent Sam's two worlds had just collided, and he had no idea how to deal with it. Sam hadn't exactly lied to me, but he hadn't told me the truth, either. I couldn't help thinking that if he'd been straight with me, if I'd known about the potential danger to us both, then we wouldn't have come here. It wouldn't have been a big deal to postpone the trip until Sam cleared up what I thought must be some sort of misunderstanding. As it was, because of his refusal to admit the problem was worse than he thought, I had almost taken a bullet.

"Why didn't you tell me?" He reached for me. For the first time in our lives, I pulled away from him. My shoulder hurt like it had been hit with a hammer. I had a headache and my period nearing, and I felt Sam had somehow lied to me. I wasn't in any kind of mood to be trifled with. I thought I deserved some answers. This wasn't a tiff about some grocery list, this was serious.

"Why didn't you warn me?"

"It wasn't your business."

"Not my business?" I was beside myself. "Whose business is it when I get shot, Sam?" I was becoming livid.

Sam was trying his best to calm me down. "I'm sorry. I didn't think this would happen."

"Well, it did happen. It probably wouldn't have happened if we had talked about it. I want to be included if it affects me, Sam. If someone is coming after you, I want to know."

The cab pulled off the street and came to a stop under the Four Season's front portico. I got out, using my good arm to open the door. Sam paid the driver and ran after me.

In the suite we packed in silence. Sam's cell phone rang a couple of times. I went into the bathroom and closed the door on both occasions. After the second call, I stripped and took a shower. I turned the water on as hot as I could stand it and stood there, thinking about nothing. The water pressure acted as a massage. I felt some of the steam go out of me. I stayed under the water for a full fifteen minutes.

By the time I had dressed, applied my makeup and left the bathroom, it was forty-five minutes later. I wasn't in the pissy mood I'd been in an hour ago. My wound hadn't reopened; I'd kept it away from the shower blast as best as I could. In the mirror above the vanity, before I redressed it, the gash hadn't looked too bad. Sam had his back to me when I finally came out of the bathroom. He was speaking softly on his cell phone. Things were busy back in the States. He saw me and clicked off quickly.

"Jack says hi." He didn't know whether to smile or frown. He was trying to read me, without much luck. I saw he'd set our suitcases beside the door. My purse was on the desk beside the computer. I started for it, and changed direction mid-stride. I walked over to Sam instead, wrapping my arms around him, burying my head in his chest. He stroked the back of my hair.

"I'm sorry, sweetheart. You were right. I should have warned you."

"I was scared, Sam." I broke our embrace and searched his eyes, moving from one to the other. They were calm, in control now. For the moment, he was back in my world. "I didn't mean those things I said. I was angry. I'm sorry. I hate it when we argue."

"That makes two of us." He pressed my head back against his chest.

"It isn't about wrong or who's right," I spoke softly. "I don't care about being shot, either. What worries me the most is you. That bullet was meant for you, Sam. If you had told me, I could have helped you."

He said nothing.

"Remember that the next time, okay?"
"I'll remember. I love you."
I mumbled into his shirt, "I love you, too."

## Chapter 36

We left the rental car in Prague and caught an afternoon flight to Frankfurt. By the time we got back to Las Vegas twenty-two hours later, we were on the same page. Sam was resolved to keep me abreast of any part of his other-world life that might affect me, as it had in Prague. He wouldn't just assume the parts I needed to know. We would talk about them and make decisions together. We both knew I'd get filtered explanations of more sensitive endeavors. That way, if anyone ever started throwing around subpoenas and tried to get at him through me, I couldn't tell them enough. There was another way, of course. We both knew a wife could never be compelled to testify against her husband. That, we agreed, was unnecessary under the circumstances. For me, it wasn't an option. If Sam and I were ever going to walk down the aisle, this wouldn't be the reason. That was non-negotiable.

Sam wanted me to spend a few days in the penthouse atop his casino. I needed the space. Six months ago I'd bought a home in a gated subdivision in Summerlin, west of downtown, out near Red Rock Canyon. I'd spent a grand total of six weeks there since I'd bought it, if I was lucky. Now I missed that home. Sam insisted I take Jack, and I refused. Whoever was gunning for him wouldn't involve me. I was certain of it. I was extremely high profile and, more importantly, even though I was with Sam it was common knowledge that I wasn't a part of his business enterprise. I was innocent. I would be left alone unless, like in Prague, I happened to be there when the shit hit the fan. Upon arriving home and ensuring all the doors and windows were locked, I called Sebastian from the landline.

"I've been trying to reach you for the past six hours. Are you all right?" For the first time since I had known him he sounded frantic.

"I've had my phone off," I fumbled for it in my purse to turn it back on. "Why wouldn't I be?"

"I thought so," Seb had been riding an emotional roller coaster. Now he sounded relieved, "I got a call from a friend of a friend in London at four in the morning. The idiot woke me up to ask me about you being shot. He was from some rag or other, one of those tabloids. Where do they get this stuff from? How do they make this shit up? Sorry. So you're okay? You haven't been shot? Obviously you weren't, because I'm talking to you," he answered his own question.

"Sebastian, there was an incident while Sam and I were in Prague. I don't know how anyone could have possibly found out about it." And then I thought of the hospital. They asked for my identification in order to treat me. "The hospital," I said. "Shit."

"Are you saying you *were* shot?" his voice rose a full octave.

"I'm all right, Sebastian. Really I am. The bullet grazed my left shoulder. I got seven stitches, it's nothing. Relax. Please. Otherwise we'll have to take you to the hospital for a heart attack."

"Someone tried to kill you," he waded in.

"Sam was with me."

"Sam was the target?" I could hear him thinking. Seb had a keen mind. When it got back on track, and his panic subsided, I knew he'd put two and two together. If anyone was listening in on the call, I'd said nothing more than the fact that Sam and I had been together. I hadn't said when or where.

"I don't think it's such a great idea to discuss this over the phone."

"You're right," he agreed instantly. "I understand. We'll talk about this later, when we see each other. Right now we've got to circle the wagons. Don't answer your phone unless you recognize the number." Damage control was commencing. "Don't speak to anyone without a lawyer, and absolutely no comments to the media. They already know, Coco. They'll be coming at you with knives between their teeth. Where are you right now?"

"I'm in Vegas."

"At the casino?"

"No, I bought a house in Summerlin. There's a guard at the gate."

"They'll find you." Controlled panic was rising in his voice again.

"No they won't. I bought it under a numbered corporation. You referred me to a great accountant, Sebastian. Remember? He doesn't miss a trick. They'll never find me here. The first place they'll look will be the casino. If that reporter called you at four this morning, they probably already have it staked out." I was glad I'd made the decision to pass on Sam's invitation and come straight home. No one but the front gate knew I was here, and I'd plug that hole as soon as I got off the phone with Seb.

"I suggest we cancel all of your public appearances for at least two weeks. I'll book you on Letterman for an explanation. That'll give us plenty of time to float a cover story. We'll bring in a damned writer if need be. We'll control the story, and we'll set the pace.

"We'll sell it as an accident. It *was* an accident." It seemed to occur to Seb that he could have asked, but that it would not have been safe. "Don't answer that," he quickly covered himself. "Of course it was. We just need to flush out the details. Stay put, Coco. I want to make some calls, and then I'll call you. Have you even been to sleep?"

"I got some on the way over. We took Sam's jet."

"Thank God for small favors. It would have been a disaster had you flown commercial. The paparazzi would have swarmed you on arrival, trust me. You threaded the needle, sweetheart. An hour later and they would have met you on the tarmac outside General Aviation."

"I hope our luck holds," I mentioned.

"Don't worry, we're in control now. Just keep out of sight until I call you. It might be a while."

"What if I need something? Like food, for instance."

"You're an actress. Wear a good disguise."

I was already thinking of a grocery store chain that had brought back the old fashioned delivery service.

"I'll manage," I assured him. "How long do you think I'll be on the lam?"

"You'll stay put long enough for us to leak *our* story, which will then become the official story."

"A self-fulfilling prophecy," I noted.

"They always believe who's first," Seb spoke from experience.

"What about the film?" I finally asked him.

"If memory serves – and I'll check to verify it – you weren't supposed to be on the set for another, what, ten, twelve days? Nothing's changed. Until this story prints, the studio will be thinking you're still in Europe. As a matter of fact," Seb was thinking at light speed now, "there's nothing wrong if they keep thinking that. That way no one will be looking for you here. It's perfect," he sounded proud of himself. "We can probably buy two or three days with it, but don't get sloppy," he cautioned me.

"Yes, boss."

"I'm serious, Coco. If this thing's handled the wrong way it can really hurt us."

"Ah, but it won't be, Sebastian. If I know you, you'll pull your usual diamond from the ashes. You'll probably find a way to parlay the extra publicity into a fat bonus on the movie."

"That's not a bad idea," he was already considering it. "We'll definitely turn this to our advantage."

"That's why they pay you the big bucks. If anyone could turn a disaster into a paycheck, it's you."

"On a serious note: be careful, Coco. I need your cooperation in order to do my job, which is ultimately looking after you. By the way, I was working on a better cash split for this film but I'm going to have to agree to drop your guarantee."

"By how much?" I was interested. Suddenly Prague seemed like a long time ago. After only a few days, I missed the action. I realized how excited I was to be on this film project. It was my first one. I wanted to do it right. The idea of acting professionally fascinated me. I thought I'd taken enough lessons to compliment my talent to the degree that I could be a good actress. I had no illusions however, the studio had hired me for my brand.

I didn't need the money. I wanted to be a serious actress. Both Sebastian and I read the script, and, for good measure, Michael did as well. We all agreed it was well written. The director was top notch, and the project was fully financed. My role was supporting, but it was a strong part. I might even steal a scene or two. Maybe I had my head in the clouds, but I didn't care. I wanted the spotlight in the worst way. This was my shot, and I wasn't about to screw it up.

"You're getting one point five million. They said they'll throw in one percent of the gross to drop it by fifty percent."

I did the math. "Doesn't sound good, it'll have to gross seventy-five million for me to recoup the loss on the guarantee. That's a lot of gate, or am I wrong?"

"No, you're not wrong. I told them the same thing."

"Are they short of cash?"

"Their financing is solid, but the less they pay out up front the more they can put into something else. The old grapevine is a-buzzing. Apparently, they're working on a deal with DreamWorks. It's big, another animation job. But making those films is expensive. Voiceovers by Tom Hanks, Penelope Cruz, Ashton Kutcher, they don't come cheap. The studio's got deep pockets, but they're not deeper than forever."

"What if we dropped it all together?"

"The guarantee?"

"Yeah, the whole wad. I don't need it and neither do you. What kind of points would they give us then?"

Sebastian paused on the other end. I could hear him breathing as his pencil no doubt raced across the note pad in front of him.

"Here's what I have. They don't know what's about to happen, so we've got to move fast. If I don't get it done today, before the news breaks, it probably won't happen. They'll flip out when they hear you've been shot, but they won't if I tell them first. Then they'll do what they always do. They won't panic, they'll think about it the same way we are. It's free publicity. When I explain to them how we're going to spin it, they'll come around. Bottom line: from what I know, they'll bite for three and a half points on the gross. We'll ask for five," he quickly added.

"So what does the film need at the box office to equal what I'm giving up?"

"The film has to do forty-three million. It's a gamble, since it could easily bomb. There's the brand recognition factor due to your supermodel status, but this…this is different, Coco."

"How do you feel about it, Sebastian?"

The phone was silent while he considered our options. "I'm game if you are. The waters are uncharted. I'll do my damndest to make it work, but," he chuckled, "obviously there won't be any guarantees."

I laughed with him. "It'll make us all try harder."

"We could end up working for nothing. Well, we'll end up with at least something."

"See what you can do, Sebastian. Our fate in Hollywood is now officially in your hands. If this works out, maybe next time we'll try walking on water." We both laughed.

"Do you need anything?"

"My arm is a little sore, but no thanks Sebastian. In a few days I should be well at least physically. Psychologically I may become the poster girl for the bullet ridden babes club before this is over," I kidded him.

"I'll call you tomorrow. If you need anything…" he left it hanging. I heard his other phone ringing in the background.

"Thank you Seb, you're a real trooper. Now go." I let him deal with his trappings.

I paused, collected my thoughts for a moment, and then called Sam.

He picked up on the first ring. "I was just getting ready to call you. How are you?"

"All things considered, I'm surprising myself. My arm hurts. How about you?" I knew he couldn't say much.

"Getting a handle on things," he was speaking too calmly. "Are you going to be at home tonight?"

"Sebastian has forbidden me to go anywhere, at least until he can manipulate the press. I'm a prisoner in my own home, probably for a week or more. Are you aware they know about this?"

"I'm aware there's some chatter about the accident," Sam was talking in code. "Right now everyone is just fishing. They know something happened, but no one really knows what. There are a lot of rumors on the mill. For now it's the media's turn."

"It came from the hospital," I said.

"We should have seen that one coming. But it's happened. What else did Sebastian say?"

"He thinks he can spin this into three and a half points on my movie," I summed up our entire conversation.

"Good, that's really good news. The police might call."

"I know, I've thought about that."

"I'll see you tonight." Now I knew at least one of the items on the agenda this evening.

"We'll talk more. Does anyone else know you're back other than Sebastian?"

"No, he said it was better if they thought I was still in Europe. Sam?"

"Yeah, I'm here."

"Is…are you going to be all right?"

"We'll talk more tonight. Jack will call you later to let you know when." It was a cryptic message. He hung up without waiting for my reply, knowing I'd recognize Jack's number when he called again.

# Chapter 37

The Internet was a window on an ever shrinking world that now included me. I never would have dreamed that I'd be shot in front of the Hradny Castle in Prague on Tuesday, only to be all over cyberspace by Thursday night. It was worse by the weekend. On Saturday, some sites had me dead. Sebastian put out the fires. I didn't bother him, even though he had his hands full and then some.

Jack called me at eight o'clock Wednesday night, on Sam's behalf. They were on their way over. Everything seemed so cloak and dagger. I wasn't used to it, and I wasn't sure I liked it, but I didn't see that I had much choice. Sam and I weren't married, but we might as well have been. I'd signed on, for better or worse. I didn't appreciate almost being killed, but how must Sam feel? He'd been the target. I had just gotten in the way. I was collateral damage. I knew Sam, and expected he'd be more pissed off than he was letting on. And when he got pissed, people got hurt. People disappeared. That was the part I didn't want to know about. There was no stopping what was coming, so I played ostrich.

The limousine pulled up to the curb in front of my house about a half hour after Sam had called. Another dark, late model Ford Lincoln pulled in behind it as I watched through the bedroom window. The doors of both vehicles opened in unison. Jack got out of the limo's front passenger door. Someone else was driving. Jack held the back door open as Sam emerged, then four large men got out of the Lincoln. They looked around the cul-de-sac as if they were searching for something, while at the same time trying not to look too obvious about it. They stuck out like an oil spill on a snow bank. The whole scene looked ominous.

I didn't go out. I waited while Jack and Sam came up the crosswalk. I buzzed them through the side gate, and was waiting for them at the open side door. I fell into Sam's arms, surprised to find I was trembling.

"Hi Jack," I smiled weakly at the giant when I finally untangled myself from Sam.

"Hi baby girl." He accepted my hug. "Long time no see." It had been about a month, but we talked on the phone at least once a week. He noticed me favoring my shoulder. "How is it?"

"Better. I've taken some pain pills and it's down to a dull throb. Come on in," I led them both into the living room. Buddy Guy rifted some soft blues from a music station on the television. I grabbed the remote and turned down the volume so we could talk. I'd already made coffee. I brought it out from the kitchen and poured each of us a steaming mug. I sat down next to Sam, across from Jack. Jack stirred some honey into his coffee in silence, and added some cream as we watched. The tension in the air around us was a werewolf in San Francisco fog.

"I guess I don't have to ask who those guys outside are." I finally broke the ice. "It isn't just a minor misunderstanding, is it?"

Jack looked at Sam.

"I told you, no more half-truths." Sam set his mug on the table. He shifted on the leather sofa so he could look directly at me. "No, it isn't a minor misunderstanding. Someone has been killed. It happened in New York, but it affected everybody. The actual details aren't important."

"Who was killed?" I almost couldn't believe I was having this conversation. We were discussing a hit on a New York crime boss as casually as if we were talking about a storm coming in. I hadn't read the papers or watched the news, so I was in the dark.

"It doesn't matter. It was someone important. We're finding out who ordered it. No one wants a war. Everyone is in agreement on that."

"They came after you, Sam." I was scared. "Why, you had nothing to do with it." I phrased it as a statement. I didn't want to even entertain the thought that Sam was in some way responsible.

"We don't know who did it," he repeated. An involuntary shiver coursed through me. I noticed he hadn't denied his involvement, electing to skirt the question instead. It didn't prove anything one way or the other. His answer was innocent enough. It was probably my own paranoia working overtime, seeing shadows again. Still, even though I wasn't about to call him on it – especially in front of Jack – I wondered.

"Can you fix it? Can this be cleared up? I'm scared, Sam. Will whoever it is keep coming?"

Sam reached for my hands. He held them in his. "Some contracts have gone out," he admitted. "One of them has my name on it."

It was like he was telling me he had a terminal form of cancer and the doctor had just given him three months to get his affairs in order. I felt lost. My head began to feel light. It felt like I was swimming in tar. I fought the rising nausea in my stomach back down my throat.

"It's serious," he spoke softly, almost hypnotically, revealing what I'd demanded to know back in the hotel room in the Czech Republic. Now I was almost sorry I'd set those conditions. A trite phrase came into my mind: Be careful what you wish for because, you just might not like the answers. I *hated* these answers.

"How is this going to affect us?" I asked, unsure of what to ask.

Sam's voice sounded as if he was speaking to me from a long way off, from the other end of a cold, empty corridor. "It's best if we don't see each other for a while. Until I get a chance to clear things up. I may have to go to New York."

"Sam, no," I was shaking my head. I fought back tears. All I could think about was him never coming back. Visions of old gangster movies invaded my mind, convincing me that Sam's trip would be one-way. But this wasn't the movies. I fought a losing battle inside, trying desperately to convince myself that this was real life, that this wasn't Hollywood with Al Pacino playing Don Corleone. Everything would be just fine. Contracts on people's lives weren't reality. No one did that anymore.

"It's a precaution. I want you to pretend we never met. You have to do this, Coco."

"How long is this going to take, Sam?" I felt the first flames of anger lick my face. Who were these people to threaten us like this? How dare they step out of the shadows and disrupt our happiness?

"I don't know." I could tell he was being honest.

I looked from Sam to Jack. He couldn't meet my gaze. He looked down at the floor. I looked back at Sam.

"What if I say no?"

"Coco," he spoke to me softly, like he was putting a child to sleep. His eyes bore into mine. His worlds were colliding and he was making his choices, fighting to keep them separate.

"What if I told you no?" I whispered this time.

He moved closer to me, and I fell into his embrace. I could hear Jack ease up from where he sat on the couch opposite us and move toward the side door. I heard it open. The latch clicked as he closed the door behind him.

Sam pulled back from me. He softly stroked the blonde locks of my hair, and moved an errant strand from where it had fallen across my face.

"It's only for a while, sweetheart. I'll get it cleared up. I promise. Two men will stay behind to see that nothing happens to you. You won't even see them. It isn't even necessary, but it will give me peace of mind. I can't be worried about you while this is happening. I can't be distracted. They'll watch your place twenty-four hours a day until this goes away."

"Why can't I call you?" Tears spilled down my cheeks. "Why can't we talk?"

"Maybe we can, I'm not ruling that out. But for now, we can't, baby." He slowly shook his head from side to side. "Someone wants to hurt me. Sometimes they get the idea to hurt the people close to me to get at me."

I nodded, sniffling. I understood, but hated it. I looked down. Sam put his fingers under my chin and lifted my head. "I won't let that happen. I won't let anyone hurt you. I won't be gone long."

He smiled into my eyes.

"You promise?" We were lost in each other.

He crossed his chest, "Cross my heart."

"Can you stay another night before you leave?"

Sam whispered, "I can't. I'm sorry." We embraced again. I hoped he wouldn't see me crying this time.

## Chapter 38

I was pleased the movie was being filmed on a closed set. The location shots would of course be different. But for now, no one without a pass was allowed through security. The old maxim of 'hurry up and wait' was borne out in fact. I'd been sitting around for three days, it was closing in on lunch and I was bored silly. I'd struck up a friendship with one of the grips.

Danny O'Brian was my age and he was a lot of fun. His quirky Irish sense of humor made the time go quicker. Danny had taken to dropping by my trailer on his breaks. He proved welcome company.

At eleven-thirty in the morning I was alone, hoping he'd arrive soon so we could have lunch together. At least I was doing something constructive, I thought, even if it was painting my nails. My cell phone came to life just as I was putting the last strokes on my small toe. It was Sebastian.

I answered the phone and said, "I was going to call you this afternoon. I'm going crazy doing nothing."

He laughed, "Look at the bright side; at least you're being paid for it."

"Ten weeks of this and I'll need a real job."

"You'll be busy soon enough," he tried to console me. "How are the other actors?"

"So-so. The A-listers pretty much stick to themselves. I've been to Brad's trailer once. He's cool, very much in love with his partner. He misses her. I miss Sam."

Sebastian sighed. "Life can be a real bitch sometimes, Coco. Have you heard anything at all?"

"Nothing, it's like he's dropped off the face of the earth."

Sebastian was silent.

"He's fine," I knew what Seb must be thinking. "I do know that much."

"From Jack?"

"Yeah. We talk every couple of days. Poor Jack's between a rock and a hard place."

"So are you."

I knew what Sebastian meant. I didn't want to squeeze my friend for information, but I was dying to know how Sam was doing. I knew Jack wanted nothing more than to tell me, but he couldn't. At least for now, those were the rules. I'd call Jack to ask him how things were going. He'd tell me as well as could be expected, negotiations were still in progress. I didn't exactly know what that meant, but at least I knew Sam was okay. We wouldn't talk long. It wasn't much, but it kept me going.

"I wish I were busier, Seb. At least then I wouldn't have time to think about it so much. I'm going nuts on this set. When I get back to the guesthouse I'm exhausted, and I haven't even done anything."

"It'll get better; you're just a little depressed. Try getting a little exercise."

"Sounds good, but it's still no substitute for some good loving, Sebastian."

"You're preaching to the choir on that one," he conceded. "Michael called me from Paris just before I called you. He's stuck out there with *Match Magazine*. They've asked him to stay another five days. The weather's been horrible and it's put the shoot back."

"He should have turned them down."

"Michael? No way, you know him. They were in a bind and sweet talked him. He asked me if I minded."

"And you said no."

Sebastian sighed. "I'm a pushover," he claimed leniency. What he really meant was it was Michael's call. He would never pressure his lover. They had a standing rule: one would not decide for the other. Each was his own person. Their relationship thrived on trust and respect. Michael would no doubt miss Sebastian as much as Seb missed him. The *Match* shoot had been important enough that Michael had stayed.

"Five more days isn't so long. Just think about the good times you'll have when he gets back."

"Believe me, it helps. How does the set feel?" he suddenly changed the subject.

"You're asking an amateur? I don't know the first thing about making a film."

"That doesn't matter, you're smart. I'm not asking you to snoop around or anything like that, but start talking to people. Ask them some questions. Try to get a feel for the morale. If the actors are relaxed, it will show. Same thing if they're tense, that might spell trouble. Don't spy, just…talk to people. A happy set might indicate how the film's going to turn out. Watch how the director deals with the cast. Does he respect them? Does he get impatient? Is he angry? Again, all this might give us some clues as to how this film is really doing. Chemistry on the set is extremely important."

"Brad seems happy, but then again he's in love. I've been having lunch with one of the grips," I remembered

Danny O'Brian. "He seems nice enough. I'd say from what I've seen, aside from the usual chaos I've heard I should expect things are humming along. I haven't seen anything out of the ordinary. Not even any booze, aside from the occasional trailer parties after the day's shooting. But that's to be expected. I haven't seen any drugs, which kind of surprises me. I heard some of these sets were bad with that kind of thing."

"Maybe in the day," said Sebastian, "but not anymore. That quickly becomes a liability. Those folks are uninsurable. That can shut down a film more quickly than just about anything. Even Robert Downey Jr. left it for his slumming. He never got high while working on a film. People would have known. It's what saved his career. Believe it or not, not only is Robert an incredibly gifted actor with talent coming out of his ears, he's also incredibly reliable."

There was a knock on my trailer door. I opened it and waved Danny O'Brian inside.

"My lunch date just arrived," I told Sebastian.

"In that case I'll let you go. Remember –"

"I'll keep my eyes open. I'll look after us for you. If I have anything to do with it, this will be a great movie."

"You do and it will. See you tonight, Coco. Come up to the house around eight. Angel's making lamb chops."

"Count me in, I'll see you tonight."

Danny had already taken a seat on the bench beside the fridge. I smiled at him.

"Beer?" I offered.

"I don't drink on the job," he smiled back at me.

"They're light," I opened the fridge and retrieved two Amstels.

I popped them open and handed him one. "They're not exactly real beers and I promise I won't tell anyone."

"Twist my arm." He took the bottle from me.

"That might be fun," I teased him, knowing he was newly married. I sat across from him, the foldout mahogany table between us.

"How's work?" I began with small talk.

He sipped on the beer. Danny was twenty-four. He wore a full beard and had a round, tanned face, which made him look older. His blue eyes twinkled with mischief and kindness. He was far more mature than his years would indicate. His full head of hair was thick and dirty blonde. He looked like he lifted weights.

"I can't complain. I get to drink beer with famous models."

I laughed. "I'm trying to be an actor," I pointed out.

"You seem to do a lot of sitting around for an actor," his acerbic wit was endearing.

"Isn't that the way it goes? The less you do the more you get paid." I gave it right back to him.

"And vice versa," he examined the calloused palm of his free hand. His other hand cradled the beer.

"Have you ever thought about acting?"

"It's crossed my mind. It's a real long shot though, especially for someone like me."

"What do you mean?"

"I'm from Vegas. I grew up there. We're addicts, not actors. Maybe if I'd grown up here, things might be different."

"I didn't know you were from Vegas."

"I was born there. My father moved there from New York."

"What did he do?"

Danny picked at the label on the Amstel, "A little of this, a little of that. He was a hustler from what I understand."

"You guys aren't close?"

"He calls me about once a month. Usually he wants to brag to me about some big deal he's working on. It's like he's still trying to prove to me he's a *somebody*. I listen and I try not to judge him. I guess he's still trying to make it up to me."

"What's that?" I was curious, but didn't want to pry. Danny seemed willing enough to talk, and I was interested enough to encourage him.

"He left us when I was about five years old. He came in one night all sweaty and agitated. I guess he was strung out. He had a pretty bad dope problem back then. I remember he and my mother woke me up with their screaming. That was the worst argument I ever heard them have, and believe me, there were some real doozies. I opened my bedroom door a crack to see them. My father's eyes were like big round holes. I could see he was really scared of something. He smacked my mom in the head and then he left. He never came back. Over twelve years later he showed up at my high school graduation, of all places. There he was, sitting in the back row, big as life. I don't think he believed I would recognize him. I don't know what he was thinking, to tell you the truth. He walked up to me and asked me if I knew who he was." Danny shook his head, a gesture of resignation halfway between disappointment and sadness, with a subtle undercurrent of disgust. He'd forgiven, but could never forget. He tipped his beer before he continued.

"I remember asking him why he'd come. You know what he told me?"

I shook my head.

"He said to me nonchalantly, 'I'm your father'. As if being my father gave him every right to waltz back into my life after all those years; like he had never even left in the first place."

"What about your mother, was she there?"

"She died from cancer two years earlier. They found me a nice foster home."

"I'm sorry, Danny."

He shook his head, "My foster parents are really cool. We're tight. They're still in Las Vegas and I see them whenever I can. We talk on the phone about once a week."

"Did your father ever say why he left?"

"I never asked him and he never told me. I figured it was just as well, he probably would have lied. At the very least he would have made up some lame excuse. By the time he came back into my life I wasn't really interested, anyway. I'd given up on him a long time before. Even now, I hardly ever see him. I never know where he is. To tell you the truth, it's sad, but I don't much care. If we ever even had anything, it's been gone a long time. I sure as hell don't call him Dad. His name is Quinn."

"I'm sorry, Danny. I guess when some things break there's no fixing them."

"I guess," he agreed. "I would have liked it to have been different."

"And all those years, your mother never said anything about why he left like that?"

"She never talked about it. He either never told her, or she couldn't. Or maybe she figured whatever trouble it was left with him. Like I said, it doesn't matter. He left us for his own selfish reasons. Case closed."

"Were you close to your mother?"

"Yes we were. When I found out she was dying, it felt like the bottom of my world dropped out from under me. But I've got to admit, afterwards I did get lucky. My foster parents were understanding, compassionate folks. They helped me get through some very rough spots, you know, the usual stupid stuff. I got into some drugs and started running with the wrong crowd, but for some reason my parents hung in there. Their love turned me around. I got out of the nastiness just as fast as I got into it, before it was too late. I worked hard, pulled my grades up, graduated third in my class. Then I came out here. I had it in my mind to work a while, save a little cash, maybe go to college. A little while turned into," he did the math in his head, "I can't believe I've been doing this for five years," Danny sounded surprised.

I took another sip of my beer. It was almost empty. "You must enjoy it, another one?"

"I can't. He set his back on the table between us. I noticed it was still half full. "I actually need to get going," rising from the bench seat, he glanced at his watch. "The set manager said he'd pay us through lunch if I made it short. We've got some carpentry work to get out by tomorrow afternoon. I think it involves you," Danny winked.

"Are you any good at that kind of work?" I was getting an idea.

He thought about it before saying, "Yeah, actually I am. I enjoy working with my hands. I like building stuff."

"Hmm," I said.

"Hmm, what?"

"My agent was thinking of doing a little remodeling around his place. He wants to start right after Christmas."

"That would be in three or four months." Danny shrugged. "I'm free on weekends."

I looked at him. "Could you round up a few guys? It's probably a little more work than weekends."

He thought about it some more. That was one thing I noticed early in him: Danny was deliberate. He would never bullshit. "If I'm thinking what you're thinking, the answer is yes. I'm not married to this job, Coco. They're paying me eighteen bucks an hour with a ceiling so low I can't stand up. Five years have slipped by in five weeks. Yeah, I'm ready for a move. And yeah, I know a lot of top notch tradesmen. The guys working on the sets are very talented. They know what they're doing and they like me. If I had something substantial for them to go to, some higher end custom work, they would run with me."

I smiled, nodding. "I'll talk to my agent about it, then."

"Is this for sure?" I could tell he was containing excitement.

"Can you build a house?"

"I'm willing and able, just give me the time to get ready. Building houses is a dream of mine."

"Then it's for sure, Danny. When my agent gets the plans back from the architect I'll set up a meeting."

Danny shook his head in disbelief. "Wow, I can't believe this might actually happen."

I smiled. "You know the old saying. It's who you know."

"I'll never be able to pay you back."

I got up and emptied what was left of our beers into the sink. "You don't owe me a thing, Danny. Just do your usual, superlative job. There's a bunch more waiting in the wings."

"Believe me," he said enthusiastically. "I'm fully aware of what this means. I won't screw it up. Gloria is pregnant, Coco." I noticed tears in his eyes, tiny sparks of light. "We couldn't really afford it on my wage, but we wanted a baby more than anything in the world."

"Well, if you ask me, Gloria is going to sleep a little easier from here on in, Danny"

"Can…can I hug you?" he asked awkwardly.

"As long as you don't break me," we laughed together.

## Chapter 39

I stayed with Michael and Sebastian while I worked on the film. We were eight weeks in when their architect produced the first set of drawings for the renovations to the main house. The plans for the guesthouse would come a week afterwards. The budget was three and a half million. Danny flipped when he first looked at them. He had no idea what he'd agreed to. But to his credit, as good as his word, he rolled up his sleeves and began to spend every spare moment poring over the documents. I gave him a key to my trailer. The place was big and luxurious, and I probably never used more than half of it. I hadn't touched the back bedroom. It didn't take long before the trailer took on the appearance of a construction trailer office.

Plumbers and electricians began to show up to meet with Danny during lunch breaks. Painters and drywall tapers picked up plans and then dropped them off later in the day. In the evening they would gather around and talk about construction scheduling, and what they called the 'critical path'.

The amazing thing about Danny's burgeoning construction enterprise was that no one, aside from the construction people, seemed to know it existed. In fact, the men worked harder than ever to build the sets. Construction was always finished ahead of schedule. The director and the other actors were oblivious to the increased work ethic. That was probably the best compliment the trades would ever be paid, aside from their weekly paychecks. In construction, it was rare not to hear a complaint. Usually there was some sort of discord, somebody was always bitching or complaining about something. But on the set of 'The Exalted' there wasn't a word of discontent. Amidst the constant, controlled explosions of compressed air nail guns, the steady hum of the spray paint compressors and the occasional laugh, complaints were scarce.

"It's remarkable," I said to Danny over coffee one morning. Some rewrites had added two weeks to the shooting schedule, and no one had griped. The director had gathered the entire cast and crew together to express his appreciation at how wonderfully accommodating everyone from the actors' agents to the trades' unions had been. He was genuinely overcome by the cooperation he was receiving. He stated unequivocally that it was the best set he'd ever had the privilege to work on.

Danny sipped his coffee. "I'm nervous," he stated candidly.

"About the film?"

"No, that's not it. You heard the director yesterday; even the actors are happy. That's unheard of. There are a lot of prima donnas in this business, but it's like we've all become a family here. I get the impression no one wants to see it end. The camaraderie and the cooperation is great, everyone is pulling together, everyone cares. It's as rare as snow in June. This is how I heard it used to be back in the old days when people made films and built sets because they *wanted* to. Our job is just about finished; you guys are going on location soon. Brad's already left."

"Then what's the problem?" I was curious.

"The problem is I've made some representations to my crew. I didn't lie to them, but I haven't corrected their assumptions either. They think I've got a contract, Coco," he confessed. "You and I are the only ones who know I don't. And in this game, nothing's for sure until the check clears. I should have said something. I was going to and then things started to snowball. Before I knew it, it was too late. I know of six guys who've given their notice. They're taking off December to be with their families, and then they're set on coming to work with me. I haven't even met your agent and your photographer. I'm sure their intentions are honorable, but I've got to tell you, I haven't been sleeping too well lately. I don't want to let anyone down by making any promises I can't keep. What if your friends change their mind? What if something bad happens? What if their financing falls through?" He finally stopped, staring at me. He'd put a lot of work into his dream, on good faith alone. He trusted me, and I suddenly realized he'd wanted to prove it. He'd suffered in silence, not wanting to question my word that Seb would eventually sign a contract with him. It had finally boiled over, not on his account, but because Danny didn't want to disappoint those he was about to lead.

"Funny thing you should mention all this, because it's exactly what Sebastian was bitching to me about earlier this week. I'm afraid it's my fault, Danny. You know they wrote me more lines." He nodded. I'd told him this a week ago. My new lines were one of the reasons they had extended the shoot.

"I apologize. I should have addressed this weeks ago. It's how people like Seb and Michael work." I hesitated to say people with money, because some people with more cash than they knew what to do with – than they could possibly spend in ten lifetimes – often delighted in screwing over the less fortunate. They weren't honorable, and could never be counted on to conduct their affairs with a sense of integrity. I knew Seb and Michael were honest, but Danny couldn't know that. He'd never met them. He trusted *me*, believed in me and wished for his dream to be true so badly that he'd assumed the risks that went with such blind trust.

Without hesitation, I picked up my cell phone and called Seb's private number. He answered on the second ring.

"I was just thinking about you," I could tell he was smiling.

"That makes two of us," I said. I had always believed in some form of spirituality, a kind of psychic connection between people who loved each other. I'd lost count of the number of times when I'd been thinking of someone close only to have the telephone suddenly ring, and it was that person on the other end of the line. The reverse seemed to happen just as often, like now.

"I don't have a lot of time," he warned me upfront.

"This won't take much. Danny O'Brian, your builder, needs a contract. So do you." I looked at Danny, measuring him. "He needs seven percent upfront for mobilization." Danny's mouth dropped open.

"Tell him three."

"He's done a lot already, Sebastian. Six of his subs have already given their notice to the studio. They are a dedicated, hands on, hard working crew. They're looking forward to this project. Not to mention what's been happening on this movie set. Danny's the one who's responsible for it, Seb. They believe in him, they've put it out there, and we're the ones who are benefiting. They haven't left a lot on the playing field on this set. We stand to gain a lot from this film because of his efforts. The buzz is it's shaping up to be a big fat surprise, as in box office receipts surprise."

"You had me after the part where the subs quit their studio gig. That means they're serious. If they're as good as you say they are –"

"They're better," I winked at Danny.

"On your word we can do seven, Coco. That's a big load on the front end, before a board's been nailed. Anymore and the architect will quit on me. He'll be screaming as it is when he finds out about this."

"Don't let the tail wag the dog, Sebastian," I jerked his chain a little. "I'll tell Danny the good news."

"Ask him over tonight. It's about time we met. We'll pop some corks and go over some of the details. Tell him he'll have the deposit check by the end of the week. He's incorporated?"

I smiled at Danny, thinking of his pregnant wife. "He will by the end of the week," I assured Seb.

"Excellent."

"I've got to go now, sweetheart," he was in a hurry.

"Thanks a million, we'll see you tonight. I'll let him know. You're the sweetheart, Sebastian."

"Don't ruin my reputation," he scolded me right before he hung up.

Danny was as pale as a wet sheet. His mouth hung open like a broken gate. If I didn't think he was about to have a heart attack, I would have started to laugh.

# Chapter 40

Making 'The Exalted' not only helped Danny get his new home building business started, but I was so busy I didn't miss Sam as much. I still called Jack, and still pined for my lover's company, but my focus was on the movie. It occurred to me after the eleventh week of intense filming that it would all soon be over. That's when it first hit me how long Sam and I had spent apart. That's also when I hatched a plan to change this unacceptable circumstance just as soon as we wrapped the last day of shooting. That was less than a week from now. In fact, the wrap party was scheduled for the last Saturday night in November, one week from today.

I'd gotten very busy after sitting around in my trailer those first three days. Since then I'd been up at four-thirty every morning, reporting for makeup at quarter to seven. Makeup took ninety minutes, then came costuming, memorizing lines, sitting and waiting, and then take after take until the director was satisfied. By the end of each day I was dizzy with exhaustion. Finally I'd be driven back across the city to the guesthouse, where I would collapse in bed after a quick late night dinner with Michael and or Sebastian when our paths crossed. The driver was always waiting to take me back to the set at five the next morning. I had never worked harder at anything in my entire life.

Most of the time, I saw Danny only in passing, one of us rushing out of the trailer while the other rushed in. Danny seemed a man bent on a mission after Seb cut him the deposit check. I felt guilty. I knew his anxious obsessing was because of me. He was bound not to disappoint me under any circumstances. After what had seemed like an eternity one minute, and simply a week of days melted into one another the next, we finally finished shooting.

The wrap party on Saturday night was held at Chilar's, an exclusive downtown restaurant the director rented for the evening. It was a very nice evening, alternately celebratory and subdued.

Everyone felt production had gone extremely well. We'd come in on budget. The bean counters were all smiles. The PR teams were working overtime; the buzz we were already receiving on the Internet and in the tabloids was pure platinum. Stories about the Prague shooting had melted into folklore. It was almost yesterday's news. Even Mom had gotten over it. After all, it had been over three months since those first stories had broken.

I remembered calling Mom from Sam's jet on the way back across the Atlantic. She had been understandably upset. We spoke for an hour before I felt comfortable enough to say goodbye. She invited me to ride out the storm with her and Carl in San Francisco. I thanked her, but declined. I'd gone overboard warning her about what was to come, the media reports, the innuendos and the outright lies. I had made it sound worse than I felt it was probably going to be. This had been for her benefit. If I soft pedaled it, tried to lessen the impact of the impending media frenzy, it would have started a whole new bout of concern. Mom would have been desperate to know if I was okay. The only thing I didn't foresee were the rumors concerning my death, but I'd prepared her for just about anything else. So when the first death rumor slipped out, Mom was angrier with the tabloids than worried about me.

Danny O'Brian sidled up to me. He was smiling at first, but then I saw his concern for me wash across his face. "Nice party," he mentioned. He was chewing on a piece of crab. He washed it down with a swig of Amstel Light.

"It turned out all right," I surveyed the restaurant around us. Conversation filled the room like the sound of a startled flock of sea gulls, one sentence indistinguishable from another as voices mixed together in a cacophony of noise. Canned music ebbed and flowed between bouts of laughter and mindless bantering. In the end, it was just another Hollywood party. The aroma of sweet and sour shrimp assailed my senses as we stepped aside for a white clothed server. Another trailed behind him. I watched as they set their silver loads down on a white linen covered table where the smorgasbord was being assembled. Tonight, dinner would be self-serve. The servers immediately retreated back to the kitchen for more of the sumptuous platters.

"You seem a little off. Can I help?"

"Thank you, Danny," no one else had noticed as I'd tried my best to rid myself of the melancholy descending over my psyche like a gathering storm. Idle hands were indeed the devil's workshop. In my case, he was working overtime. I felt weak now that my grueling work schedule had come to an end. All I could think of was that I hadn't heard from Sam in over three months.

Paranoia was beginning to set in. In the absence of any information to the contrary, I was beginning to think crazy thoughts, thoughts that struck fear into my heart. I fought my baser instincts as best I could, but with each passing day I began to fear the worst: that for some reason known only to him, Sam had left for good.

Calling Jack always lifted my spirits, this was undeniable. But these calls were also maddening. It was always the same, like a recording. I couldn't blame Jack, obviously people's lives hung in the balance, Sam's among them. There was no way Jack could speak freely. He couldn't tell me what I needed to know. I knew this, but it didn't help. At times I felt I was being selfish, but didn't I have that right? Sam and I did love each other…or was I the only one who felt it?

There were times over those three long months when I imagined the way I felt wasn't too different from someone who was in prison, coming up to a parole hearing. Not knowing what the outcome would be and having to grin and bear it, to suffer the uncertainty of the unknown, must be horrible. I felt my life was on hold.

I sighed deeply, leaned over and kissed Danny on the cheek. "You're a sweetheart, Danny," I smiled. He had cheered me up just by being my friend and caring enough to ask.

"How is Gloria?"

His smile returned, like the sun peeking out from a bank of clouds. "Two months to go," he said proudly. "She's as big as a house."

"She *is* pregnant." I rolled my eyes.

"She's sleeping a lot, which is good. I told you about the ultrasound. My son is healthy, Coco. Having a pregnant wife is strange. I'm having all these different feelings. It actually makes me cry sometimes, for no reason."

I laughed. "I've heard it does that to you sometimes, Danny. But it usually happens to the woman."

"I know," he admitted. "But I'm so emotional over this whole thing. Sometimes the thought of having a baby overwhelms me. I guess at heart I'm really the one who's a baby."

"But you're a very nice baby. I noticed you moved a trailer onto the property," I changed the subject.

"Yeah. I gave the production assistant my notice. Or rather, she gave me the notice when I told her I couldn't make the next movie in January. She was disappointed, but she understood when I told her where I was going. She said anytime I wanted to come back, I was welcome. But I don't think I'll be taking her up on the offer anytime soon," he spoke with blossoming confidence.

"So I figured I'd get the jump on things. That trailer at the side of the pool will be the general construction office. I was going to put it out front, near the gate, to double as security."

"Let me guess, Maria had a better idea."

"She's quite a lady."

"That she is," I agreed.

"I didn't know she handled security. The first time I saw her she was all greased up under the hood of Michael's Rolls Royce."

I laughed, remembering the time the two of us had confounded Sebastian's best intentions. "She's a woman of many talents."

"That has become apparent," said Danny.

There was a noticeable commotion near the entrance vestibule of the restaurant as a party of large, dark suited men moved into my vision. Danny and I were standing about thirty feet away from where two restaurant security personnel had greeted everyone earlier, checking their names on a list provided to them by the Director's assistant. Now, as I watched, they seemed confused. It was obvious that the three men who'd entered the restaurant were not among the invited guests. A fourth, huge bald black man filled the entrance doorway and my breath caught in my throat. It was Jack Holliday. Sam was right behind him.

# Chapter 41

I must have knocked over at least three people as I frantically pushed my way through the crowd to get to Sam. Jack spied me coming, and a moment later so did Sam. In the same instant, it seemed everyone at the door realized what was happening, and who Sam Spielman was. The security first, followed by everyone else, parted like the Red Sea and Sam was suddenly in my arms. I was crying and blubbering and hanging onto him like I'd never let him go. I was almost hysterical. I finally calmed down enough to look into Sam's eyes.

"I missed you more than you'll ever know," I whispered. I knew everyone was watching. I didn't care.

"Me too, baby."

"Is it over?" I searched his eyes.

He nodded, smiling. "Yeah, it's over. I'll tell you about it later."

"I'd like that, Sam."

We stared at each other, losing ourselves in the moment. Sam's eyes were dark and sparkling and wonderful. At that moment, I felt I could dive into them and come out on the other side of forever.

"Please don't ever leave me again," I pleaded with him.

"I promise," he shook his head. "It will never happen again."

We kissed, long and passionately. A roar erupted as people in the room around us broke into a spontaneous cheer. They applauded loudly, as if the midnight hour had arrived at a New Year's Eve gala event. There was no other way of putting it for me. I felt like Sam and I had finally found us again. After a long and arduous journey across a barren wasteland I never wanted to venture into ever again, we'd finally come home.

I looked across Sam's shoulder and saw a tear in Jack's eyes. "Are you crying, Jack?" I smiled, half laughing, half crying.

He looked around, a deer in headlights. Then he relaxed, shrugged and smiled. "It's good to see you again, baby girl."

I let go of Sam long enough to wrap my arms around his thick neck. I stood on my toes as usual, and planted a big kiss on his cheek.

"For some reason I never get tired of that," he said.

I turned back to Sam, taking his hands in mine. He brought me closer and put his arm around my waist. I draped my arms onto his chest. Suddenly I was in the mood to party.

"Do you want to leave?" I deferred to him.

He looked around the room. People had gone back to what they'd been doing before the interruption. Sam looked back at me. "It looks like a hell of a good party." Someone turned up the music. The song was Randy Bachman's famous speech impediment rock anthem, 'You Ain't Seen Nothin' Yet'.

"It would be a shame to waste it. This is the first time the boys have been out in months," Sam nodded over his shoulder to his soldiers. He winked at me. "Why don't we tease each other for a while?"

I beamed, leading him to where someone had cleared some tables to make way for an impromptu dance floor.

Sam and I fell in love all over again, at least that's the way it felt to me. I'd never taken Sam for granted, but I had to concede that I appreciated him more than ever. We kissed, we danced, we drank lots of champagne, and we both relaxed in a way we hadn't been able to since before our ill-fated trip to Prague.

At the end of the night, back at Seb and Michael's guesthouse, we tore each other's clothes off and fucked, more like animals than humans. Then, after a short rest, we made love. We caressed each other tenderly, allowing our emotions to melt into one another, to wash across our bodies like warm tropical waves. There was only Sam and I then, no one else in the universe. We stayed together until, finally spent and thoroughly exhausted, we fell asleep in each other's arms as I watched the finger of the dim predawn light slowly stroke Sam's beautiful face.

I got up just before lunch, feeling invigorated. Life had begun again. I showered and dressed in shorts and running shoes. Hollywood weather in late November was perfect for jogging, and I took advantage of it often. While working on the movie, I rarely went out for my long runs. I had been far too exhausted for exercise by the time I got home from the set. I glanced at Sam just before I left. He was sleeping, purple down filled comforter strewn about him. I closed the bedroom door quietly behind me, and headed out for a much needed three-mile run. I noticed on my way out that Jack's bedroom door was ajar. I heard the regular rhythm of his soft snoring. Even the gentle giant needed some occasional rest, I mused. I didn't doubt it was well deserved and long overdue.

I unlocked the pedestrian gate beside the driveway gate. I noticed the dark sedan immediately, then recognized the man behind the wheel as one of the guys who'd arrived at Chilar's ahead of Sam. He nodded his acknowledgment of my wave. I stretched for a couple of minutes and took off down the tree lined cul-de-sac. It didn't disturb me, but I was somewhat surprised when I saw the sedan following at a discreet distance. Sam had told me last night that it was over. I began to wonder just what he'd meant. It may be over, but things had certainly changed. What had Sam meant last night? I glanced back at the soundless, dark sedan as it followed discreetly, a hundred yards behind me. It cruised like a great white shark in still gray waters.

# Chapter 42

Todd Benedict wheeled Claire Anderson down the linoleum tiled hallway on the other side of the lounge. I followed closely behind them. We passed a large, solid oak entry door to our left. A few more feet and we turned right through an identical door and entered a dimly lit, comfortably accessorized suite. A lone figure sat hunched over a plain rectangular table butted up against the far wall. The plane of the table was six inches below the bottom of a large curtained window. Afternoon light fought to enter through the red and beige cloth, but the material's thickness prevented most of it from intruding into the subtle, diffused peacefulness. Instead of natural light, a single lamp burned on the table to the right of the woman who worked there.

"Linda?" Todd called softly to her.

Linda either didn't hear him, or was too involved in what she was doing.

"We've got some company, sweetie," Todd moved to where he could reach the draw strings of the curtain. "Mind if I let some light into your room?"

"No," Linda spoke to the desk in front of her.

Todd drew back the curtains. The suite was suddenly flooded with the brilliant afternoon sunlight. It spilled across the large double bed against the side wall of the room. The bed was covered with a thick yellow quilt with white panda bears in various poses printed on it. To the right of the bed was a smaller, closed door. I assumed it led to an attached bathroom. There were other pieces of furniture: an armchair with a towel draped across the back of it, an armoire opposite the bed, and a second desk to the left of it. Everything was neatly in its place. The white towel, in fact, was the only article not tucked neatly into a drawer of the chest of drawers on the wall near the bed. I noticed there was ample room where Linda lived and slept. Nothing was crowded. The walls were painted a cheerful lavender, the ceiling a flat white. The ten inch wallpaper border that separated the two matched her bedspread; white panda bears frolicking just below the room's ceiling. I felt relaxed. A peaceful vibration seemed to emanate from somewhere inside the room.

My focus returned to Linda Cunningham. At first glance, she indeed appeared to be a woman in her fifties. She wore comfortable beige slacks with an elastic waistband, and her hair was turning gray.

Her living quarters, except for the white tiled bathroom floor, were carpeted with a medium pile floor covering, a light violet color which blended in with the painted walls. It was soft beneath my shoes. Linda wore pink socks. Her blouse was white cotton, and if you looked twice maybe a size too big, which would only serve to make her feel more comfortable. Her hair was neatly combed and fell just below her blouse's décolleté. Its brown base was so liberally flecked with silver she could be mistaken, from behind, as being much older than she really was. But when she turned to look at Todd Benedict, and revealed her profile to the sunlight, I smiled. Her features were soft and smooth, the almost pudgy face of a girl, not a woman. Somehow, it was as if God's hand had gently brush-stroked the customary lines of age away from where they should have appeared by now. Though she was oblivious to the fact, Linda was now the wealthiest woman in the entire State of Nevada.

"I'd like you to meet our guests, Linda. Do you remember Auntie Claire?" Todd talked softly, as if speaking to a child. His words were almost musical.

"Hi sweetie." Claire moved closer to Linda and reached her arms out to hug her, to which Linda reciprocated, visibly brightening.

"Hi, Auntie Claire. I've been drawing a picture. It's color."

"Yes, it is. I can see you've done a nice job of it. Is that the TV in the lounge?"

"Yes." Linda had not looked up at anyone. Her eyes focused back downward, on something only she could see.

"And what is that beside the TV?"

"It's a plant," she emphasized the last word.

"And that's Avery beside the plant?"

"Yes. Avery," she drew out the name, pronouncing it more deliberately, as if Claire had not heard it correctly the first time and she was clearing up this minor indiscretion.

"The house cat," Todd smiled, clearing up any confusion. I looked over Linda at the drawing. In my mind I thought it was a pretty good rendition of the home's mascot. Her drawing could have fit right in with the best of any of the first grade sketches I'd seen.

"That's a pretty picture," I complimented her. Claire smiled at me and moved backwards, allowing me to enter Linda's field of vision. I knelt down beside where she sat in the chair in front of her drawing. "Did you draw that today?"

"Yes." She continued to stare at the picture.

"My name is Coco, Linda."

"I know." Linda began to rock back and forth a little, like a swing does in a slight breeze. I looked up at Todd, who was still standing near the curtains. He looked halfway between surprised and puzzled. I took it Linda didn't get many visitors, so it was probably unusual for him to see her interact this way with a stranger. But there had been no hesitation in her discourse with me. I took her last comment as a simple acknowledgment to me that I was there. But what happened next floored all of us.

Linda suddenly looked up at me, focusing clearly on my eyes.

"You're my new mommy." Then her eyes seemed to lose that brief clarity, and whatever had come to the surface was again submerged. Her gaze fell once more onto the paper in front of her. Still barely rocking, she picked up a blue crayon and began to purposefully fill in the window above the plant, as if night had fallen in her picture of the lounge. The cat on the floor in the picture seemed to be watching.

She didn't say much more after that. She answered like she'd done in the beginning, mostly with single words. I'd never met her before, so I couldn't know that in the whole time Todd had known her he couldn't remember ever having heard her volunteer a sentence of more than a few words. What she'd said to me was completely off the radar.

We said goodbye to Linda soon afterward and quietly left her room. Todd closed the door behind us, ensuring our privacy and Linda's. We reassembled in the lounge.

"I can't explain it," his expression was blank.

"You must have said something when you weren't aware she was listening. Perhaps your wife and you were talking and Linda overheard the conversation," I suggested.

He was shaking his head. He was adamant. "I've known Linda for…" he threw up his hands, "must be twenty-five years or more," he guessed. "First off, she *never* talks to strangers. I've never seen it. Let's say, for argument's sake, Linda did overhear Mary and I. She would not have understood what we were saying. Simple things sure, but I doubt it. To put a conversation she *might* have heard together with you, and to grasp the complicated part of it – that you're her new mother? That just isn't possible. There's no way Linda would grasp the connection. She isn't capable."

"Land sakes alive, Todd. None of us are deaf, we all heard her," Claire injected her thoughts into the conversation. "The fact is Linda said what she said. And we were witnesses." Claire looked at me again then, this time shaking her head with a reinforced conviction. "It's God's plan. You'd have to be blind not to see it. I've been telling you: He's sent an angel."

I stared at her. A chill ran up my spine. This time I couldn't disagree with her. I remained silent, Linda's words rolling around in my head like a child's toy train, around and around on a circular track. Neither Todd nor Claire had seen the clarity in Linda's eyes when she looked into my soul.

## Chapter 43

I didn't want to do Versace's runway gig in London. There were far more important matters at hand, but I didn't want Sam to think anything was out of the ordinary. It was Donatella's Spring line. If I cancelled at this late date, they would make a stink about it in the papers. They would call me an unreliable prima donna – a bitch. I might even get sued, but that was unlikely. For certain Donatella would blacklist me, at least for a while, until she felt I'd suffered enough. If I apologized we'd hug and kiss and things would be lovey-dovey-back-to-normal. That's how it worked in the industry. In the end it would spell a lot more press, which would translate into bigger numbers at the cash register. That's why models did it. Everyone benefited.

Everyone but me, because Sam would get wind of it and start to wonder why I hadn't gone to Europe to model the collection. And I knew Sam better than anybody. I knew he'd be suspicious. That would not be good, since I would need every advantage I could use in order to pull off my plan off.

Sam wouldn't go down easy. There was a very good chance my mad scheme would still blow up in my face, but surprise was on my side. Surprise was a clever ally when pitted against a worthy opponent. I was still worried, though. The outcome was unpredictable. More importantly, when Sam learned of what I'd done, he'd be unpredictable. I would become his enemy, and I knew how he dealt with his enemies. If I didn't build up my failsafe, if I missed inserting just one of the fragile links in the delicate chain I designed, Sam might have no choice. He just might have to kill me.

So I went about my business as if nothing out of the ordinary was happening. I almost believed that Sam thought I had all but given up on the action in Brittle. The truly diabolical aspect of the end run I was planning was that it was so huge. It was so damned arrogant that Sam would never in a million years suspect it. His was a man's world. A woman just wouldn't have the balls for it. The sheer audacity of my plan would prohibit the notion form ever entering his mind.

The runway show in London went off without a hitch. I was on the phone constantly with the lawyers in Kingman. They were shoving through my adoption of Linda at supersonic speed. My legal team was calling in favors from judges they knew, filing the necessary paperwork, expediting procedures, and generally breaking all the established legal records while somehow managing to stay within the law. It turned out that Brian DeSilva was quite a gifted attorney. Somewhere along the line he must have realized that if he just rolled up his sleeves and did an amazing job, he probably would end up with that pot of gold he'd originally had his eyes on. He'd gotten with the plan and was doing just that.

I'd need a good lead attorney, especially after B.C.'s land was legally turned over to the control of Linda and Claire's trustee. DeSilva would be a natural choice, because in the front end process he would have the inside track. I was more and more impressed with his new attitude and his willingness to help, and I told him so. I admitted to him that, initially, I hadn't cared for him. I told him my reasons. He forgave me, admitting unabashedly he was a greedy man and that sometimes got the better of him. In turn, I had accepted his apology and we had started over with fervor. In a sense, he was giving me his resume. He told me he expected nothing but top dollar for his services and he hoped I would see the value he offered and, in the event of our success, ask him on full time. I told him things looked pretty good. DeSilva had some rough edges, but he was still a diamond.

The march toward control of B.C.'s valuable holdings moved toward its inexorable conclusion. On my authority, Brian hired more attorneys to assist him with the trusteeship. I think it benefited us that he was working out of Kingman. If it had been the Las Vegas legal community, what we were up to would have probably somehow leaked out by now. Each day that passed without anyone finding out that I was wrestling control of Billy's estate from Sam's corporate tentacles was one more day Sam would have to catch up. Now I was in sight of the finish line. Soon it would be too late, and as per Claire Anderson's wishes, I would be the sole trustee of what was now becoming Linda Cunningham's estate.

On Claire's insistence, in the event of Linda's death, I would continue to administer the estate according to the caveats and interests laid out in the trust agreement. My identity would be shielded under the numbered offshore trusts Brian DeSilva was now preparing. Any and all questions would need to be filed through Georgetown, Grand Cayman, and the legal firm hosting the trust account. A battle royale over venue and jurisdiction in the event of litigation by Sam, or anyone else for that matter, would end up drowning in a sea of legal morass. Extrication from the resulting legal and political quagmire would take years, if not decades. The only way anyone would ever find out who really controlled the oil enriched land beneath the Nevada desert would be if I, or someone inside my network of lawyers and accountants, told them. I was under no illusions. It wouldn't be a matter of if this would happen, but when. It didn't matter. Most of the scheme was meant to buy the precious time we needed to steer the proceeds away from Sam and others like him. Claire and I were adamant, and in stolid agreement, as to where to put the money. It was her wish as it was mine. We both knew Linda, the owner, would approve.

By the time I got back from Europe, there wasn't much for me to do but wait. I kept my eye on the ball and my ear to the ground. Brian reported the team's progress to me at least twice daily. A month in, and the bill topped a million dollars. I wired the funds to the Kingman team immediately. I didn't want anything to slow down the billion dollar machine. I'd made him a believer. Brian promised to redouble his efforts, and that the end was in sight. We'd have our land. Sam would never be granted a renewal on his option, and he still had no idea of what was going on.

I was driving down the Strip the morning of the last Saturday in November when my cell phone rang from where it lay on the passenger seat. I grabbed it, prepared to speak with Brian DeSilva. I'd been expecting his latest update. Odd, I thought, not recognizing the number.

"Hello?"

"Coco, it's Danny." his voice was frantic. "Danny O'Brian."

My brow wrinkled. Danny and I hadn't spoken in a few weeks. The bottom fell out my stomach and I felt a cold wash of adrenaline flush through my veins.

"Danny, what's wrong?"

"It's Quinn, it's my father. They have him, Coco. He's been kidnapped. They're going to kill him. They *know*," he almost screamed the word into the phone. "They said back off or they'll mail him back to me in pieces."

"Who?" I shouted at him, trying to make him hear me. "Who's got him, Danny?"

Danny was crying now, he was almost hysterical. "Sam! Somehow he found him," he moaned, as if to say if anyone knew how, I would. "They're going to kill him. They're going to dice him up into little pieces, make him last forever they said. You've got to help him Coco, you have to do something, he's my father!" Danny was scared half out of his wits, and so was I. I knew if Sam had Quinn, it wouldn't be long before he put two and two together. Danny's father had valuable information, and right now it was all he had to trade for his life.

# Chapter 44

Halfway through the second week of December, the O'Brian Construction Company pulled its first building permit, and Danny proudly taped his Notice to Commence onto one of the glass panels on the mansion's big front door. Sebastian and Michael's three and a half million dollar makeover had officially begun. It would take a little over a year and a half to complete everything.

Danny was smart. With an eye to the future, he'd begun to study for his California General Contractor's license not long after landing the studio job. He had written and passed it a year before we met. There was nothing like being ready when the opportunity you were looking for finally came along. Most people never bothered to prepare for this eventuality, particularly in the trades. It was a whole lot easier swilling Budweiser in front of Jerry Springer. As a result, most people in the construction industry were little more than paid slaves, servants to the brighter stars among their ranks who could see what was coming. Danny had seen it earlier than most. When he'd gotten his Builder's license at age twenty-three he'd been among the youngest. That license was the manifestation of his underlying personality. He possessed all the necessary attributes to make himself into a very successful contractor, should the circumstances of his life meet the opportunity. He was honest, patient, a stickler for details. He was also a natural born leader.

Danny truly seized upon his opportunity. I'm sure thinking of Gloria and his unborn son didn't hurt him any, either. If ever a young man had an abundance of incentive, it was Danny.

In his personality there was also an element of self-effacing fair play. It came with his integrity. It was the cement which held the other qualities together. As a result, Danny's worst nightmare on this, his first project, was that he'd somehow screw things up and then disappoint me. He worried constantly. He couldn't help himself. It was his nature, yet it ensured his success.

By the end of February the mansion was a hive of activity. Sebastian decided to change the roof line at the back of the house to accommodate an addition which would become an in-home theater that sat thirty. The cribbing subcontractor brought in a small hydraulic crane to facilitate the placing of the trusses. A roofing crew had stripped back the red standing seam aluminum, and now the cribbers were doing whatever was necessary to ready things for the placement. Inside, the finish carpenters busied themselves with the onsite construction of new cabinets and other built-ins. Marble craftsmen were fighting with a countertop that wouldn't fit. The high pitched whine of an impact drill screamed as someone, somewhere, drilled holes into concrete. In the middle of the seeming bedlam, Danny remained surprisingly cool and collected. He knew a lot of his subs from working with them, and it was obvious they respected his work ethic. I noticed early on that he favored the proposition of leading by example. Most days during construction he was the first one to arrive, and the last to leave. He usually disappeared for two or three hours from late morning to mid-afternoon. Sometimes he'd do some banking, other days he'd meet with the architect or race away to an engineering firm to verify some calculations. He was busy, but very well organized. Sometimes I thought there must be two of him. He seemed to be in several places at the same time. So when Danny left late one morning and didn't return until late the next, I noticed.

I'd been in the guesthouse, between a couple of local shoots, gearing up for what was likely to become a second film. I'd gotten interested in the renovation since Danny tried to explain some of the plans to me. He'd been patient, but as I tried to follow his finger across the blueprints I realized Danny was in a league by himself. It didn't stop me from watching the tradesmen, though.

By now, all of Danny's crew knew me. I think they enjoyed the idea that I was interested in what they did for a living. I knew I was eye candy at first, but in no time they began to accept me as a woman who wasn't just another of those Hollywood types. By February, some of the guys had taken to inviting me to their lunch breaks. When I had the time, I joined them.

"Where's Danny?"

"Coming this way," one of the carpenters nodded his head in the direction of the back of the house. The clock above the stove read eleven. I followed the crews' eyes as they gazed through the sliding glass windows that led out to the backyard patio, which had been halfway demolished to make room for the theatre. I spotted Danny walking toward the mobile hydraulic crane. Instantly I noticed the worried expression across his face.

I excused myself from lunch and hurried outside. I wanted to intercept Danny to find out what was wrong. I climbed through the wooden foundations the deck demolition had exposed and across the grass toward where

Danny was speaking with the crane operator. As soon as he saw me, he excused himself and met me out of the operator's earshot.

He smiled wanly. He could see the concern in my eyes.

"Does it show?" he pre-empted my question.

"You look like you need some company. When I see someone with an expression like yours it usually spells w-o-m-a-n."

"Were it that simple." Danny looked around self-consciously, waving back at one of the electricians, a friend he'd brought with him when a bunch of his men had quit the union to work on his first project.

"You got a few minutes?"

"For you? Yeah, of course. This sounds serious. Let's take a walk outside the gate."

The high pitched whine of a buzz saw pierced the backyard's still air. The pow-pow of a nail gun punctuated the background. A compressor kicked in as we skirted the swimming pool, now drained in preparation for who-knew-what. As we strolled up the long driveway towards the guesthouse and the cul-de-sac, I began.

"You were conspicuous in your absence."

"You noticed that as well?" he was surprised.

"Everyone noticed. They weren't worried, didn't break stride. They've got good momentum, and they know the plans backwards."

"Maybe I should stay home," he joked, only he didn't chuckle.

"You're still the boss," I pointed out the obvious. "The ship needs a rudder. Without you, sooner than later it would drift off course."

"You're preaching to the choir on that one. Don't worry," he added, "it would never even come close to that."

We walked the rest of the way to the wrought iron pedestrian gate. I used my key to exit the property, and we stepped onto the wide end of the cul-de-sac. I could still hear the saws and nail guns. An engine turned over and roared to life – the crane.

"So what's up?"

He looked at me, and then back along the road in front of us. We walked slowly and deliberately under the branches of the tall palm trees that skirted the edge of the circular private road. Danny's lips were pursed, framed by his bushy beard.

"My father popped in to see me for lunch yesterday. He was waiting for me in the apartment building parking lot when I swung by to check on Gloria."

"Quinn?" I remembered his name.

He nodded. "The *mighty* Quinn," he said quietly, his expression devoid of humor.

"I see," was all I could think to say.

Danny bent down, picking up a ripened grapefruit that had fallen into the roadway a few feet from the curb. He tossed it back onto the grass. It rolled close to the base of the parent that had produced it before finally coming to rest against the hard brown trunk of the tree. A gray squirrel, watching the fruit from where it hung upside down, scurried four feet up the trunk and suddenly darted sideways. The animal produced a scratching, skittering sound and disappeared from view, now cleverly hidden around the backside of the tree trunk. Danny stopped and turned to me. Confusion was written across his face.

"I thought he would change, Coco. I thought somehow that would be possible. When I was a kid I prayed for my father all the time. I convinced myself that he hadn't abandoned my mother and me. I didn't want to believe that. Instead, I made up stories about him. To the other kids in school, I mean. For a while I told them he was an ambassador, always out of the country on national security business. I lied because to face the truth would have killed me inside. One day, I think I must have been in tenth grade, I finally accepted he'd left us for no good reason. I could have probably convinced myself otherwise, but I could never rid my mind of seeing him striking my mother the night he left. Nothing could ever explain away the pain and anguish I'd seen in her eyes – the fear.

"I accepted that my father was a deadbeat, which made things a lot easier. I started making friends. My grades climbed, my self-esteem improved. By the time Quinn finally showed up a couple years later, I didn't need him to love me anymore. At least, I thought so at the time." He sighed, "I guess no matter how much dirt you shovel into a hole, it's always going to be a hole."

"It fills up after a while," I consoled him.

"Not if it's bottomless." We began to walk again. "I tried to get to know him. God knows, I made the effort. But he would always leave again before I could get close enough. I think I've finally figured it out. He's afraid of me. Maybe he sees in me what he could have been and never was – can never be," Danny shrugged. "I don't know because he's never told me. And Mom never told me what happened to make him cut out in the first place. I've got a hole in my heart. Guess I better accept it's always going to be there. He's broken, and there's no fixing my old man. Sometimes I feel like Charlie Brown running for the football. He never wanted to do it. He knew Lucy was going to pull the ball out from under him, that he was going for a ride and would end up flat on his back staring up at those little birds. I keep making the same emotional investments in my father. Just when I think maybe he's going to be the dad I never had, I end up lying flat out on my back, just like Charlie Brown. Why do I keep beating myself up over him? Why am I such a sucker?"

It got quiet then, the rhythm of our footsteps keeping time with our thoughts. Birds chattered in the treetops. It should have been a beautiful day, but for Danny it was one of his worst.

"Because you love him Danny. That makes you a better man than he is. You're the improved version. Your son won't have to go through what you did. There's a lesson in all this. Maybe that's it."

We kept walking. He was so quiet I wondered if he'd heard me.

"After all the things he's devised that have fallen through, his schemes to get rich quick, scams that were all sure things, he asked me about you. None of his easy ways out ever work for him, and he's always the last one to admit it. Then he asks about that actress I knew. I was almost surprised at first. Quinn is always fishing for an angle. I didn't say much. The last thing I wanted was to encourage him, Coco."

Images of Charlie Brown doing upside down cartwheels in the air above a football came into my mind.

"I knew he was probing for an angle, and I wasn't going to give him an inch. He was up to something, I could feel it. There was nothing in the world my father could say or do to get me to go there." Watching Danny's face as he explained his complex relationship with his father was like watching a tarantula shed its skin. It was a painful process, leaving the new creature underneath exposed and vulnerable.

"He told me he wanted to talk to you and I refused. I don't want him to soil our relationship. I owe you debts I can never repay. Quinn is poison. I told him I was going to make certain he never got within ten miles of you. Whatever he was cooking up, you were off limits. He argued with me and got angry. I said some things, but I don't regret saying them. They were the truth. I may have been angry, but I'm trying to make a life for myself. People enjoy my company, and I've got friends who care about me. I work hard, and I'm determined to make this business a success. Quinn is a threat to everything I've overcome to get to where I am. I wasn't prepared to let him in, Coco. In the end, I told him to get out of my life. I told my own father I never wanted to see him again."

"I'm not here to tell you what to do, or if the decision you made was right or wrong, but if you want my opinion he didn't leave you with any other choice. Quinn backed you into a corner. He did this to himself. From what you told me, it wasn't just one time. This has been a pattern of his throughout your entire relationship. It may not be my place to say this, Danny, but as hard as it is for you right now I think you're better off this way. Anyone can father a child, can keep it alive and safe, but not everyone can be a dad. It seems to me that you never had a dad. That's tough to come to terms with, but in your case I think it was necessary. I'd start thinking more about the son you'll have and less about what you might be leaving behind. Bury the ghosts of the past; otherwise they're liable to haunt you. Your baby's going to need you. Gloria is going to need you. You're going to be someone's dad soon."

Danny swallowed hard. His upper lip quivered. I'd spoken the truth as I saw it, without sugar coating it. I figured Danny was ready for it. If he wasn't, then he wasn't the man I'd judged him to be.

Danny nodded, forcing a weak smile. He stopped again, and turned to face me. "You're the best friend I've ever had, Coco. Thanks for everything you've done for me." He took a deep breath, searching my eyes.

"There's more?"

He nodded. I could tell a war was waging inside him. "I thought about not telling you, but I have to. If I didn't he'd find another way."

"Quinn?" I was puzzled. What was he talking about? "He'd find another way for what?"

"He didn't take no for an answer. He demanded I tell you."

"Tell me what?"

"It didn't make sense. You never lived in Vegas, not when we were there. Not when I was five, when Quinn left us."

I realized I'd never told Danny about the first six years of my life – my childhood. The time we had lived in Las Vegas, and then after Dad was killed how Mom and I had left to start over in San Francisco. A wave of grief suddenly washed over me. I realized Danny actually knew nothing about my younger years.

"We *did* live in Vegas, Danny. I spent the first six years of my life there. My mother and I left when," I hesitated, "when I was six years old, when you would have been five. Why, what's this about?" A rising sense of dread invaded my being. It was like I was halfway through a long tunnel and could hear a train sounding its horn from the other end.

Danny's cheeks lost their color. He stared at me as if he was going to be sick.

"You said you and your mother left. What about your father, Coco? Where was he? Why didn't he go with you?" He was oblivious to his own shouting now. It was like he was short circuiting. He was refusing to believe what I had said.

"My father died in Las Vegas when I was six. He was shot and killed one night in a break-in. I was there when it happened. I saw the murder." My own voice was a raspy, hoarse croaking sound in my ears.

"Quinn says he knows who did it, Coco. He told me he knows who murdered your father. I thought he was crazy, thought he had you mixed up with someone else. If I knew, I never would have…" He trailed off, lips quivering, eyes burning with the pain he could see in my own.

# Chapter 45

If Quinn had wanted to get my attention, he had succeeded in spades. Nothing else could have worked better. Even if his information was bogus and he figured he could sell it to me, I had to know. I demanded to know. Scam or not, I was determined to get to the truth. Somehow, Danny's father not only knew that I had lived in Vegas as a six year old, but that my father had been murdered there as well. That lent no small amount of credibility to his claim.

Danny followed me back to the guesthouse, visibly reluctant. No doubt he felt responsible for opening a wound so old and so deeply buried he hadn't even known it existed. Until his miserable excuse for a father devised a way to capitalize on it.

Quinn was tempting me with information he'd known would not only seize my attention, but compel me to rush headlong into a twilight zone of memories which had long lain dormant. My father's murder rushed to the surface of my mind like a flow of molten lava from a seething volcano.

"Call him," I demanded of Danny. We stood in the living room of the guesthouse. I held out my cell phone. Dead fingers plucked it from my hand. In a dreadful trance, dutifully, like Judas taking his bag of silver, Danny took the phone and punched the numbers that would connect me with Quinn. He handed my phone back to me, uttering a barely audible instruction to hit the green connect button.

"Yes," the voice answered almost eagerly.

"This is Coco Stevens. Is Quinn there?"

"I'm Quinn. I've been expecting your call, Miss Stevens. Or may I call you Coco?" he feigned civility.

"I'm here with Danny, Quinn. He's told me some disturbing news. I think I'd like to speak with you."

"About what happened in Henderson," he stated, identifying the city southeast of downtown Las Vegas where I'd lived. I tried to keep my hand steady as I held the phone. Inside I was shaking like a leaf on a tree.

"Yes."

"Put my son on the phone, I'll give him the instructions. Come alone, Miss Stevens, Coco. Tell no one. I'm risking my life talking to you, yours as well. If the wrong people find out about this, we are both dead. If I find out you've talked, I disappear. Then nobody wins."

"What do you want from me?" I was suddenly angry. "How do I know you're not lying? Maybe I should go to the authorities."

"If I find out you've spoken to anyone – anyone at all – you'll never know what happened. Your father's killer will go to the grave with me, and you will regret it for the rest of your natural life." He knew he had me. "Do I make myself clear?"

"Yeah," I said, hating him.

"Put my *son* on the line," he growled. "It's been nice making your acquaintance, Coco. I look forward to meeting you in person. We have a lot to talk about." His feigned civility returned.

Without replying, I handed the cell phone to Danny. I fought the urge to vomit, trying to remember every word he'd said. None of it made sense to me. My sharper instincts told me to go straight to the police, and if not to the police, then Sam. Surely he would know what to do. But I couldn't banish Quinn's threat from my mind. For the time being, I had to play his game. I'd get on the ride and see where it took me, and then decide who to go to with the information, the police or Sam.

Danny hung up without speaking to Quinn. He had a glazed, disbelieving look in his eyes. "He said we'd talk later. I am so sorry, Coco. I don't know where any of this has come from. I had no idea your dad was killed, or that it happened in Las Vegas."

I nodded. Danny wasn't connected to any of his father's infamy. Quinn had deserted his family when he was five years old. Danny knew less than me about his father's involvement in my father's death. I knew any attempts to absolve him of guilt would be useless.

"It isn't your fault, Danny. You didn't choose your father."

"How can I help?" he offered lamely.

"Keep the site running. These men need your leadership, and Michael and Sebastian come first. Don't worry about me; take care of yourself. You're going to be a father soon and your family will be counting on you. Let me know when Quinn wants to meet me. I'm assuming he won't want to hear from me until he's ready to deal, and he probably uses different cell phones for different people. The line we just talked on will be useless by this afternoon."

I had to assume Quinn was being careful. If nothing else, he was a survivor. He'd been at these kinds of sordid games for a long time. If he knew anything about my father's murder, he'd tread lightly from here on in. He wanted something and I had no doubt it involved money, but Quinn was playing with fire. If he kept the company of murderers, he knew the stakes were high. I believed his warning that our lives would be in danger if I spoke out of turn.

"Go back to work, Danny."

He nodded, anguish flooding his eyes.

"Do you know where he is?"

"No. He usually lets me know, but this time it's different."

"This time he's holding a fatal needle to someone's arm. If that someone is still around and they find out, Quinn's in big trouble. If they find him, they'll kill him. He'll call you when he's ready to meet with me, Danny. When that will be is anyone's guess, but he's made his first move. It will be soon. Until then, we'll just have to wait."

"Like waiting for a call from a kidnapper," said Danny.

"I suppose so. There may not be a live person for ransom on the other end, but there is someone, maybe still out there, who murdered my father. I have to know what happened. I have to know why, Danny."

I needed closure, filling for the hole in my heart. Then Mom and I would sit down and have a long talk about it. Maybe I'd take her back to Sausalito and tell her. She needed the healing, too. I'd always known there was a good reason for the depression she struggled with. Maybe this knowledge would finally free her from those shackles.

Danny dove into his work with a zeal borne of his desire to lose himself in it. Work was cathartic for him, a strange form of meditation that took his mind away from the trouble he felt responsible for. I did the same.

I had Sebastian book me some regional shoots for a few southwestern accounts. I didn't want to be more than a few hours away when Quinn called. The shoot was on the Pacific Coast, near Carmel by the Sea, a quaint, upscale town west of the Pacific Coast Highway

The town was once governed by Clint Eastwood. The actor and producer needed a variance from the local building department for his "Hog's Breath Saloon". The town's former mayor opposed the plan so Eastwood ran for mayor and won in a landslide vote, replacing the snot-nosed egomaniac standing in his way. Clint got his variance, and the publicity was good for the town. He did not seek re-election.

If Michael noticed my pensive anxiety, he was kind enough not to say anything. As usual, he made me look good. I wanted to talk to him more than once. Michael was a confidant and a friend; I could trust him with just about anything, but this was different. I bit my lip and said nothing. Somehow I got through the shoot and found myself back at the guesthouse in Hollywood.

I was eating lunch on February thirteenth, the day before Valentine's. We'd gotten back from Carmel the previous night. Michael rented a car and drove south along the beautiful Pacific Coast Highway; we shared a joint on the way back, then another. It was relaxing not saying much, just cruising down the coast listening to some excellent used CDs that Michael had picked up at an eclectic record store in Carmel.

I was wondering why Sam hadn't called when the doorbell chimed the first few bars of Beethoven's Ninth. I let Danny in. I could tell by the look in his eyes he'd heard from Quinn. This wasn't going to be a repeat of the last time, though. A month ago he had taken me by surprise, but now I was ready for him. Although visibly possessed by anxious guilt, a result of convincing himself he was to blame, I noticed Danny was more composed.

There was a resolve in his eyes that said he was here to help me, no matter what. I felt relieved. It felt good not to be alone.

"Coffee, or something stronger?" he managed a wan smile accepting my offer.

"Quinn called me last night."

"I could see it in your eyes."

"Am I always so obvious?"

"Let's put it this way Danny; don't ever take up Texas hold 'em." I set a steaming mug of hot coffee in front of him, then went back to the fridge and returned with a decanter of half-and-half.

"Thanks for the java and the advice, even though I've never been a gambler."

"Don't you have any vices?" I was beginning to wonder about him. He wasn't your typical, rough and tumble construction company owner. He was far too cerebral. But then again, times were different. These days, I knew from conversations I'd had with Danny, the construction industry had become an applied science, run more by computer software and math than beefy rednecks. It was still a very physical endeavor, but with the advent of new technologies brought about by 'going green', tradesmen were smarter now than they'd ever been. Building green meant everyone associated with the construction had to be familiar with more modern, innovative products and techniques designed to lessen the endeavor's carbon footprint.

"Oddly enough, I never had *that* problem." He sat on a high stool and fidgeted with the handle of his coffee mug. Both of us enjoyed the reprieve of small talk, but there was no escaping why Danny had come.

"What did Quinn say?"

# Chapter 46

When I ruled out everything else, I came to believe I had missed the obvious. Once more proving the old saying that you never had to worry about the big things; the devil was always in the details.

I had forgotten about the newspapers. Kingman was a small town and Brittle even smaller. Two beloved local citizens perishing in a tragic automobile accident was headline news in both communities. It wasn't a stretch that Sam would have assigned at least one person to cruise the geography in the areas B.C. might be expected to turn up. They were looking for him high and low. The Cessnas were still running grid searches from early morning to late in the evening, scouring the desert from the air. Nothing had changed. I should have used more common sense. I should have guessed someone would have seen the article.

I had to assume Sam was now aware of B.C.'s passing. I had to think like he would in order to leapfrog ahead of his next move. Sam must have gone like a torpedo to the probate court in the county where B.C. had lived. He knew that would be where any claims against the estate would be presented, and any last will would be presented to the probate judge. Additionally, he would soon be aware that Claire Anderson was the beneficiary. After that, thanks to Brian DeSilva, things would quickly become murky. Linda was sufficiently protected, hidden under layers of a thick corporate veil. For the time being, that hole had been successfully plugged.

I asked myself, if I were Sam, where would I go next? Sam would quickly deduce that someone, or more than one person, was moving in on the estate. Logically, he would go to the lawyers – to Brian's office. He'd apply what pressure he could. DeSilva was a tough, ornery old school type. No way would he cave in to the likes of Sam's thugs' pressure. He'd call the authorities the moment he sniffed trouble. That's probably why I'd heard nothing from him. His character alone would have been enough to intimidate Sam into calling his dogs off. Sam would know that he'd need to finesse this one all the way to the Land Titles Office. He wasn't dealing with the underworld, so his underworld tactics would fail miserably. He might consider corrupting DeSilva, but he'd rule that out quickly. There wasn't enough time. The irony in Sam's life was his biggest score had to be one hundred percent legal. Goon tactics, normally a staple in his enterprise, wouldn't work under these circumstances. I smiled in spite of myself. The frustration must be driving him out of his mind.

This new wrinkle couldn't have come at a worse time for me. DeSilva had assured me that we were in the home stretch. The adoption was almost complete. Since the probate judge hadn't received either any claims against the estate or contradictory wills, she had bent to Brian's cajoling legal pressure. Officially, the judge would have to follow the time guidelines required by statute before the will's final adjudication. The only encumbrance registered on the land so far had, of course, been Sam's option to purchase the land from Billy in the event the prospector decided to sell it to him. The judge was a long standing member of the Kingman Community. She knew all the players, except for Sam. DeSilva had assured her, under sworn statement, that the land would not be for sale. The judge had accepted this assurance as adequate since the option, which Claire kept in a safe deposit box in the Bank of America in Kingman, had been produced. It was notarized, simple, and legal. Leslie, B.C., and Claire had all kept keys. Claire's had been the only one left to open the deposit box.

I would be Linda's legal guardian in less than two weeks. I would also become the legal trustee of her estate. Two short weeks had suddenly become an eternity. The hitherto unthinkable now crossed my mind. How much was Quinn's life worth? How much for a worthless, selfish, misguided con artist's life? No doubt Quinn had led a life of crime. Scam was his middle name. He had authored his own destiny. That he found himself in his current predicament was surprising to no one.

There were two big problems, though. The first was that Quinn and Danny shared blood. Try as he might, Danny didn't have it in him to write his father off, to sign his death warrant by doing nothing. No one would kill Quinn before Sam gave the order. I assured Danny that wouldn't happen.

The second problem wasn't as obvious, but it was just as salient. It was me. I wasn't a murderer. I couldn't let Quinn die, not when I held the check to buy his life. Danny knew nothing of B.C.'s land. He was completely ignorant of my battle with Sam over what was likely some of the most valuable real estate in the country. I remembered the hand written note on the prospectus in Sam's office. I bet whoever wrote it rued the day they learned how to spell. The small liner note, innocuous to all but me, had been the undoing of a brilliant plan to wrest a king's fortune from a desert bumpkin. If I hadn't happened across it, Sam very well might be the one who now controlled the fortune, and not I. In a Machiavellian twist of fate, things had turned in my favor. Revenge was mine. I had stumbled onto the only way to make Sam pay for what the only other man who had been there – Quinn – could prove. That Sam murdered my father.

# Chapter 47

Danny sipped his coffee, setting it back on the kitchen counter before replying. "He wants to meet with you alone, Coco. I told him absolutely not," Danny surprised me. "Quinn started to object, but I shut him down. I told him he was a miserable, conniving son-of-a-bitch and that he hadn't lifted a finger to help his family, or anyone else for that matter, in his entire life. I threatened to go to the authorities if he didn't shut his trap and listen to our demands." He was breathing hard. He'd conjured up deep seated feelings. The issues he had with his father were as potent and unresolved as ever. Danny's collective 'our' hadn't been lost on me, either. He was thinking the same as I. We were a team.

"Go on." I gave Danny my tacit approval regarding his temerity.

"I told him hell would freeze over before I allowed any friend of mine to walk through his demented minefield. I didn't hold back, Coco. I told my father some things I'd never said before. It kind of threw him a little, I guess. He actually listened to me."

"That must have surprised you."

"Yeah," he nodded, thinking about it. It was as if it was just occurring to him, the chink in Quinn's armor of emotional blackmail to a kid who only wanted his father to love him, but would never receive it.

"I have to admit it did. But I was angry, Coco. I was angrier than I can ever remember. My father is an asshole, through and through. He exists with no redeemable purpose in life but to manufacture misery, in this case mine and yours, and my mother's while she was still alive. It hurt her the most, Coco. I'd see it in her eyes every day. She died a broken woman. I'll never forgive him for what he did to us."

"You have to, Danny. For yourself and your family, you have to." I stared straight into his unflinching eyes.

He looked down after a few seconds. "I know," he said softly. "I don't want to pass this curse on to my son. God knows I don't." He wiped away a tear before it had time to drop.

I gave him time to collect himself. After a minute, he took a deep breath and looked up at me. "I let him know you'd only agree to meet with him if I went with you. It's the only way you'd be safe," he noticed the flash of objection in my eyes.

"He won't hurt me, Danny. I'm the goose that's laying his golden eggs."

"He can't be trusted. I'm the middle man. He can't see you unless I'm there." He stared at me. "I won't let you go alone, Coco. It's too dangerous. My father…he's not normal."

"How could he be? I guess I have no choice. You're the only one who knows where he wants to meet."

Danny stared at me. I'd stated what he hadn't wanted to.

"Where and when?" I capitulated, much to Danny's relief.

Quinn was cagey and hard to pin down, but I had something he coveted: money. He had information to sell, and for a transaction to be consummated, we would have to meet. That moment had arrived. I made the call.

Quinn arranged the meeting for that same day, a Sunday, at one o'clock in the afternoon. We were to meet in his hotel suite at the Holiday Inn near Sunset Boulevard. I picked Danny up in the Corvette. Traffic was light. We pulled into the hotel parking lot ten minutes early.

I swung the car into a visitor's parking stall and cut the engine. I was nervous, maybe even a little scared, but I wasn't going to let it show. The biggest part of me was perplexed, though. How could Quinn Garret possibly have information about my dad's murder, much less proof to validate it? The whole thing, I realized, could be some kind of a shakedown because Quinn had learned of his son's connection to me. He was an opportunist. From what I'd learned about him from his son, Quinn wouldn't have a problem stealing a blind man's cane. In another time and another place he'd be robbing graves for a profession, selling the unearthed goods and bodies for whatever profit he could get.

Were it not for Danny's warnings I'd have given no credence to Quinn's bold proclamation, but now I couldn't simply write him off as a gold digging quack. He knew about us living in Henderson all those years ago. I hadn't told anyone about that. It was a chapter of my life I always omitted, thought better forgotten or at least suppressed. Quinn knew something, and we were minutes from finding out what.

We crossed the parking lot in tandem, heading for the hotel's front doors. The weather was sunny, patches of billowy cumulus overhead, a perfect seventy degrees. One of the reasons everyone seemed to want to live in California. We nodded to a bellhop, ignored the front desk and headed for the elevator on the other side of the mezzanine. We rode up in silence, getting off on the sixth floor. We took a right, following room numbers black lettered on gold plates towards Quinn's suite.

The noiseless carpet muffled our steps. We stopped in front of Quinn's door. Danny cast a last look at me. I stepped up before he could, knocking loudly on the door. Thirty seconds later it swung open, exposing the man himself.

Quinn was shorter than I expected him to be, probably no more than two or three inches taller than me. He was stocky, like his son. He was clean shaven, but hard living lines in his face ran much deeper than they should for a man his age. His hair was thick and brown, matching Danny's. They had the same eyes, but there was something else in Quinn's that would be forever absent from his son's.

Quinn looked at me with a cross of suspicion and fear. His were tired, hungry eyes, borne of too many miles of staying one step ahead of whoever happened to be chasing him, and of always sizing up his next mark. It was a hell of a way to waste a life – running, hiding, hustling. He was dressed in blue jeans, a white V-neck pullover, and a pair of polished black shoes. I noticed one of his hands was hidden behind the door. He tried to make his pose look innocuous, as if he were holding open the door. Quinn glanced at the hallway behind us then stepped aside, motioning with a quick jerk of his head for us to enter. He took another quick, nervous look up and down the hallway before closing and dead-bolting the door.

The suite was a standard, cookie cutter Holiday Inn room, neat and very functional. One of the beds had been hastily made. Two empty cans of diet soda had been left out on the table, and half the ashtray was filled with the butts of a nervous chain smoker. Quinn had left the slider open a few inches to air out the room even though the AC compressor was running on high.

"Go ahead, have a seat," Quinn gestured to the chairs. It was his best attempt at civility all day. He tried to hide it, but I noticed the quick flash of chrome as he tucked the gun he held into a duffle bag next to the television. Quinn wasn't taking any chances. He was one paranoid motherfucker.

"How about a drink?" he asked both of us. "Beer? Whiskey?"

Danny was shaking his head. "We didn't come here to socialize." He stared at his father. I said nothing. I pretended to be relaxed as I stared down Quinn. I was wondering if I'd made a mistake coming here. The man gave me the creeps. I could almost bet the lapses of time between visits in Danny's youth were spent behind bars.

"All right," he said, coughing. The reflex reminded him of his habit. "Mind if I smoke?" he reached for a pack of Marlboros on the nightstand between the beds.

I said to his back, "I'd prefer if you didn't."

Quinn turned back and looked at me, pack of cigarettes hanging limply from his fingers. He saw I was serious. He shrugged and tossed it back onto the table. He walked over to the sliding glass doors and pulled the open one shut. He locked it, tested it with a solid tug on the handle, and tucked the dark, floor-to-ceiling curtain that covered the windows around the edge of the locked one. All outside light was now completely blocked from entering the room. Quinn walked back over to the middle of the room between the beds and sat down on the edge of the one farthest from us. He looked from his son to me.

"You're a very beautiful woman. I've admired your pictures," he leered at me. It felt like he was looking at me through my clothes. I was suddenly glad Danny had insisted on being here. I continued to stare at him. I was sure if I looked up the word smarmy, it would say Quinn. Very few people I'd met had truly repulsed me.

"Okay," he said, clasping his hands together and giving up on the pretense of cordiality. "Why don't we get down to business, then?"

"That's why we're here," I said without emotion. "You said you had information regarding my father's death."

"Murder," he corrected me, oblivious to the pain caused by his callousness. I fought the urge to leave.

"Quinn," Danny chastised him with the tone of his voice.

"Sorry," Quinn held up a hand. "In defense, I'm afraid I got into the habit early on of calling a spade a spade. I promised Danny boy here I'd be civil. And I always keep my promises," his smile was sinister. Then, in an instant, it was gone.

"Let's turn the old clock back a few years, when we all drove older cars, shall we? I'll tell you a story about a couple of young gangsters. Then we'll get down to the business of what comes next."

Looking at him, I couldn't fathom Danny coming from the same gene pool as Quinn's. They were as different in personality as two people could possibly be. Were it not for the obvious physical similarities, no one could have possibly guessed they were father and son. I wondered about his wife – Danny's mother. What had she been like? What could have possibly attracted her to this man? As far as I could tell, he had no redeeming qualities. I was amazed Danny had turned out as he had, a man of principle and conviction. I'd never tell him what I thought, but I believed Danny was probably the luckiest kid alive that his old man had left them when he had. If he had been tutored by Quinn, there was no doubt Danny's life would have turned out very differently.

"I was a young kid, filled to the brim with testosterone. You couldn't tell me a damn thing because I already knew it all," Quinn began. "I wasn't much older than you, Danny, and I was definitely running with the wrong crowd."

"Doesn't sound like a whole lot's changed over the last twenty years," Danny said scornfully.

His father cast him a sidelong glance, thought about saying something, but for some reason decided against it. He chose to ignore his son's bitterness, and continued with his story.

"It was late in the afternoon, hotter than a bitch," Quinn began. "I'd known this kid Sam Spielman for maybe a couple of months."

He saw my eyes go wide.

"Yeah, that's right kid – your boyfriend. At least, that's what I've been reading in the papers. The same guy who owns half the Strip," he exaggerated. "But it wasn't always that way. In the beginning, he was just a punk kid like everybody else. He was another wannabe gangster with a chip the size of Detroit on his shoulder. He was running numbers for the Outfit back then. He was Sicilian, I think, so they kind of favored him over a lot of other guys, me included. He was one of them. Those fucking Italians stick together like flies on shit. And if anyone thinks the mob wasn't in Vegas back then, they've got fucking spaghetti for brains. They're *still* in Vegas, in case you want to know. They've never left. And Spielman's the guiltiest motherfucker of them all. I need a drink," he suddenly said. It was like he was disgusted, certainly resentful, that he and Sam had apparently started out together and he'd been the one left behind. It was becoming obvious he blamed Sam for his own deplorable life.

I was still stunned that Quinn Garret had even known Sam Spielman. But when I thought about it, why not? Sam was a mobster who'd cut his teeth on the streets of the New York. He'd moved out to Vegas at a relatively young age. All the mob families knew each other. That he'd been paired up with the likes of Quinn, at least for a while in the beginning wasn't really surprising. It was a small zoo. Only Quinn had obviously been frozen out of any upward mobility because he wasn't a pure bred Sicilian, like Sam. Quinn wasn't even Irish. Danny had taken the surname of his adoptive parents, Glen and Lynn O'Brian. That had probably pissed off Quinn, too.

Quinn walked back from the fridge with a Mickey of Seagram's whiskey, a glass, and another diet cola. He mixed a stiff one, no ice, and swallowed half of it in one draught. He wiped a dribble of it off his chin and said, "That'll put hair on your chest if nothing else will. Where was I? Oh yeah, I was getting to the part about the desert. Hotter than fuck it was. We'd gone out south of Henderson, on the way to Lake Mead, to talk about a job they wanted us to do. We took our guns along to do some target shooting. I remember it like yesterday. Sam had this dull steel Smith and Wesson .44 Magnum. It was the old Dirty Harry gun. We'd gone out Lake Mead Boulevard – that's right – I remember it now. It wasn't toward Lake Mead, it was toward Lake Las Vegas. Back then there wasn't anything out there but desert. We'd set some bottles down in a ravine and got back about thirty yards or so. I remember telling Spielman, 'You can't hit jack with that gun. It's built for close in, just like in the movie.'

"Sam looked at me with those black beady eyes of his, no smile, nothin' on his face. 'I wouldn't bet on it,' he said. He held it out in front of him and squeezed off a round. The thing sounded like a fucking cannon going off. But there wasn't anyone around for miles to hear it. Thirty yards away, the Budweiser bottle disintegrated in a shower of brown glass, red and white label exploding into nothingness."

# Chapter 48

"Bull's-eye," said Quinn. "Nice shot buddy."

Sam didn't acknowledge the compliment. He moved the big gun slightly to the side and squeezed off another round. Ka-Boom! The cannon sound ricocheted off the rocks around them. Another bottle was blown to smithereens. This time Quinn said nothing. Again, Sam moved slightly sideways to line up with a third bottle. He fired. The same result.

"Wow," said Quinn in his best deadpan voice, trying to downplay the fact he was impressed. "Three for a quarter, huh, Sam?"

Sam was checking his gun. He popped it open and began to reload it.

"You ought to try mine," Quinn offered, holding it up for inspection. It was old. Sam glanced at it, noticing something that interested him. He looked more closely.

"That's right," Quinn almost sang. "You don't see these babies around every street corner." He held it up like a trophy. The scorching Nevada sun played off its dark, sleek lines. "It's a Colt .45 baby, manufactured in nineteen hundred and thirty-two. It's one of a kind, Sammy."

Sam had told him about calling him that name. He leveled a serious gaze at Quinn, hefting the .44 in his right hand, as if checking its weight. The nuance wasn't wasted on Quinn. He was dumb, but he wasn't stupid.

"Sam," he quickly corrected himself.

"It's a nice weapon," Sam agreed. "But they made a lot of these. There's nothing unique about this gun."

"Au contraire, my friend," Quinn begged to differ. "You know who owned this gun? The original guy, I mean?"

Sam wondered how long he would have to put up with this guy. The two were an unholy partnership. Sam had been paired with Quinn by higher-ups to learn a few things, they'd said. Sam was smart enough to know what that meant. Quinn didn't know it, but the bosses had something in mind for him alright. They were probably planning something and they needed a patsy. They'd needed someone to stay close to Quinn – watch him – until they were ready to use him. Quinn would be really lucky if he didn't end up dead. He was just too stupid to see it coming.

Sam didn't answer. He stared at Quinn, cursing the sun. Sweat poured down the back of his neck and dampened his light green shirt. He squinted at Quinn, whose face made it seem like the man was about to go into cardiac arrest. It was beet red; rivulets of sweat were dripping down his temples and forehead. Beads were dropping off the edge of his bushy brown eyebrows. These, coupled with his imitation Elvis sideburns, made him look like Lon Chaney in an old Werewolf film.

Thinking he hadn't been able to pull so much as a guess out of Sam, Quinn proudly pronounced, "Clyde Barrow." He was beaming like the Cheshire cat.

Sam didn't react.

"Clyde Barrow, of Bonnie and Clyde. The gangsters."

"No shit?"

"No shit, man."

"How do you know that?" Sam's suspicion tempered his curiosity.

"I nabbed it from some rich guy's house we broke into in the Valley. The guy was a gun collector. He had other ones, but we were looking for cash and jewelry. It's not like we brought a fucking five ton truck with us," Quinn laughed at the thought. "But I recognized the name on this one. Clyde Barrow. Everyone knows him. I still got the case and everything. The fucking gun was hermetically sealed. Can you believe that? Vacuum fucking packed, just like a pound of fucking bacon. It came with some kind of authentication number from some big auction house. This fucking gun's worth a fortune. Here," he proffered it to Sam. "Why don't you give it a try? It's a real beauty. I wonder how many guys Clyde killed with it? I bet plenty."

"Hold this for a second." Sam traded Quinn his .44 Magnum for Barrow's Colt .45.

Sam liked the way it felt lying across his palm. Virtually the same caliber as his own weapon, it seemed lighter, less bulky.

"Go ahead Sam, shoot something with it."

Sam pointed the gun at Quinn's forehead. Quinn's eyes bulged out like a koi goldfish. He just about shit himself.

Sam laughed, drawing it back. How it would look if word got out he'd shot Quinn with Clyde's gun?

"I was just screwing with you, Quinn. Put your eyes back into your head, man."

"I knew it, I knew it," Quinn stuttered the phrase. Fucking grease ball Italians, crazy motherfuckers. He could kill this son-of-a-bitch, but if they ever caught him the crazy fuckers would torture him for a month before they ever killed him. He shivered in the sun, happy he was still breathing.

There were three Bud bottles still nestled into the clay beside where the first three used to be, eighty or ninety feet down the slight grade they were standing on. Sam leveled the .45 at the first one and slowly squeezed the trigger. The ground exploded about three inches to the right of the bottle he'd been aiming for. He made a slight correction in his aim and squeezed off another round. This time the dirt behind it kicked up an inch to the left. The brown bottle ignited on the third shot. Sam wiped his forehead. Sweat was dripping in his eyes like a fountain, wrecking his vision. The grip of the gun was wet. He wiped the handle on his shirt, gripped it once more, aimed and fired. The second bottle exploded. He got the final one on his second shot.

"Not bad," he had to admit, looking down the barrel. He considered something for a moment.

"How about a trade, Quinn? The Magnum for this piece of shit."

"An even trade?" Quinn's jaw dropped. "It's Clyde Barrow's gun, Sam. It's gotta' be worth a lot more than a new Smith and Wesson, even if that is Dirty Harry's gun."

"It didn't cost you anything," Sam reminded him. Then he added, "I'll tell you what. I'm having a good day, Quinn. I'm feeling generous. I'll throw in an extra five hundred and we'll call it even." It was Sam's final offer. Negotiations were over even before they had begun.

Quinn carefully considered his response. His survival instincts were kicking in. An idea came to him. "Tell you what, Sam. I wanted to wear it one more time, but what the hell? It's yours. Forget the five hundred. We'll just call it an even trade, my .45 for your .44."

"Are you sure?" Sam thought he'd given in a little too easily. "You sure I can't give you a little something on top for it?"

"Nah…hey, maybe there is something."

Sam raised his eyebrows.

"I've got to see someone tonight. He's a dealer over in Henderson, owes me a little money. Nothing serious, three grand for some coke I dropped off the other night. I'm not expecting any trouble. He's a good customer, but it never hurts to have a little backup, you know?"

"How long have you known this guy?" Sam wasn't opposed to it. After all, it was Clyde Barrow's gun.

"It's been at least a couple of years. I never had a problem with him. He's moving more than his usual, though. I just want him to know we're serious is all."

"Has he done anything to make you think otherwise?"

Quinn shook his head. "No. No, he's a good guy. I just want him to understand whom he's dealing with, that's all. That way, we nip it in the bud. Later on down the line, if he even thinks about doing something stupid, he won't."

Sam thought about it. "Yeah, why not? I'll go along for the ride. I can't see it hurting anything," Sam was admiring his new gun. "What time were you supposed to drop by this guy's place?"

"I told him around ten o'clock. Is that all right with you?"

"Where'd you say he lived?"

"He's in Henderson. I'll pick you up later tonight and we'll go right over. The whole thing will take maybe an hour. It's a nice gun, isn't it?"

"It's all right, Quinn." Sam agreed, thinking maybe Quinn wasn't such a bad guy after all. Too bad about what was probably going to happen to him. Sam pulled up short of thanking him, though.

"Fuck is it ever hot out here," said Quinn. "You feel like a cold beer?"

"Yeah. We're out of empties, so I'm done. Let's get the hell out of here." It was so hot Sam's shirt was sticking to his body. "You got the case for this thing?"

"I'll bring it with me tonight," promised Quinn.

# Chapter 49

Quinn noticed right away Sam was acting funny. He was waiting outside for him as he pulled up in his late model Chevy Astro van. Sam jumped in the passenger side. He seemed nervous, agitated for some reason.

Quinn gunned it down the ramp onto 95 from Anne Road. It was already ten-thirty. If he hauled ass they would still be at least an hour late. Maybe that was what Sam was pissed about, he thought. That heat and those afternoon beers had knocked the hell out of him. So what if he'd taken a nap and slept in a little? No reason to get your balls tied in a knot.

He noticed Sam dig into his front shirt pocket under his dark shirt. He pulled out what looked like a half-ounce, dark glass bottle with a black plastic lid. Quinn watched from the corner of his eye as Sam unscrewed the top and flipped open the tiny black spoon on its hinged side. He dipped it into the dark bottle and came out with a mound of white powder large enough to fill a nostril. He sniffed hard at it, and then repeated the procedure for the other nostril. That explained a few things, thought Quinn. He figured he could ride out the late part. At least now he could probably get some conversation out of Sam.

"You okay?" he asked in the darkened confines of the van.

"I'm fine." Sam's eyes were dark wheels. No light reflected from them. Quinn thought he didn't look himself.

"Just don't speed," Sam warned him.

"No chance," Quinn assured him. "I wouldn't want to get popped for some inconsequential on the way to collect." Quinn liked using a big word from time to time, even if he didn't use it quite correctly. It made him feel smarter than he was.

"That would be dumb."

Quinn didn't like the way Sam sounded, kind of metallic, like that machine Schwarzenegger played in that 'Terminator' movie. Hah, he smiled to himself, remembering the wrestler Jesse Ventura was in that movie, too. Or was that one called 'Predator'? Fuck it; he couldn't think straight right now. Not with this crazy Italian doing coke in the seat next to him. Maybe he shouldn't have asked him to come. Maybe the kid was a screw-up after all. Oh well, too late now. They were coming up on their exit just a few more miles down the highway. He breathed deeply, trying to calm the edginess he'd caught like an instant cold from Sam.

The dealer lived ten minutes drive from the exit off 215.

"Pull up over there, away from that streetlight, under that Chinaberry tree," Sam ordered.

Quinn did as he was told, pulling the blue Astro to a silent stop two houses down from the dealer's home. Sam grabbed his arm. "Wait a second." He snorted another couple of spoonfuls while Quinn watched. His eyes got bigger and rounder, like something had moved inside him and was taking over. Sam motioned the vial and spoon to Quinn.

"Never touch the stuff," Quinn lied. It was bad enough one of them was high.

Sam shrugged, "Suit yourself." He screwed the lid on and slipped the vial into his pocket. Next he reached below it, and seemed to unfasten something. He withdrew the Colt .45, Barrow's gun.

"Hey, Sam," suddenly Quinn became alarmed. "I told you, this guy's cool. He's a family man, got a kid and everything."

"I won't be using it on him, dickhead," Sam spat. He slid the dark gun back under his sweater. The fucker must have a shoulder holster, Quinn thought.

"Yeah, well you know, it's not necessary with this guy. I know him, man. Maybe you should wait in the van while I go talk to him."

Sam threw Quinn a look that gave him the shivers.

"I was screwing with you, is all. Let's go see him." Man, thought Quinn, I'm walking in here with a fucking time bomb.

The house was located in a standard, middle class subdivision. It was a bungalow, a three bedroom cookie cutter model. The builders had probably worked from eight or ten basic floor plans. The whole neighborhood repeated itself. Most of the numbers on the fronts of the houses were harder to find than pennies in a gutter, but apart from the street names they were the only way to know where you actually were.

There was one light on over the front door. Quinn rang the doorbell and they waited, Sam more hyped than he'd been on the way over. The coke was kicking him like a mule. Quinn wondered how long the kid had been into the shit.

Quinn was about to punch the bell a second time when he heard someone on the other side of the door rattling the lock. It opened and a man appeared in the doorway. He was young, twenty-something. He wore blue jeans and a plain white Fruit of the Loom t-shirt. Sam thought he looked like one of those daytime soap stars, the one who always had two foxes playing against one another, vying for his attention.

"Hey, Quinn. How you doing?" he smiled. "Sorry I was late getting to the door. My little girl was having a nightmare. I just got her back into bed. Come in," he beckoned, eyeing Sam a little nervously.

Quinn noticed. "He's cool, man. You got nothing to worry about."

"Any friend of yours is all right by me."

Sam shuffled in through the front door after Quinn. They waited as the dealer bolted the latch. Sam's eyes got a little bigger. He didn't like his back to a locked door. His instincts were firing on all cylinders. He became even more anxious than he already was, but he let it ride.

"C'mon into the living room," the man spoke quietly.

"Why are you whispering?" Sam's paranoia was ramping up as the cocaine crossed the blood-brain barrier of Sam's physiology.

"I told you, my kid had a nightmare. I just got her back into bed. My wife isn't here. It's ladies night at Mulligan's Saloon, so she's gone to unwind."

"Oh," Sam raised his head, acknowledging maybe that was the reason this guy was so quiet, and maybe it wasn't.

"Over here," the dealer walked away, going around the partition in the short hallway that divided the front door landing area from the living room.

This was the third time, in Sam's mind, that this guy was trying to maneuver them away from the hall and into the front living area. Sam didn't like it one bit.

"I'll wait for you guys here. I'm kind of in a hurry. No time for chit chat." His forced smile made him look like a wax mannequin as the living room's pale lamplight searched his dark features. Sam smelled a setup. He *knew* this guy was up to something.

"I thought we could do a couple of lines together."

"Nah," Sam wouldn't meet the young man's gaze. His own eyes darted about the confines of the house. He felt claustrophobic. The walls were sinking inwards. "Maybe another time."

The dealer seemed puzzled. "All right." He shrugged. "If you change your mind…"

"Yeah, sure. Thanks." Sam thought he heard something from down the hallway on the other side of Quinn. Ten feet away from where they were standing, the small front foyer hall took a ninety degree turn, down to where the bedrooms must be, and he couldn't see around that corner. But he sure as hell had heard something.

"What was that?"

"What was what?"

"That sound."

"What sound?"

"A shuffle."

"Hmm," the dealer shrugged again. "I didn't hear anything." He smiled, and Sam *really* didn't like that.

"It must've been the cat."

The dealer was about six feet from the front door, facing Sam. In the living room to the right, Quinn sat on the sofa waiting, eyeing Sam with concealed concern. The hallway behind the dealer turned a corner, leading to the back part of the house and the bedrooms.

The next sequence of events was so bizarre that in hindsight, they took on a fuzzy, surreal quality, as if Sam were watching for creatures in the dark through night vision goggles. Everything happened so quickly that no one had time to think before they acted.

Sam and the dealer each heard a second shuffling sound come from the hallway. The dealer began to look over his shoulder the same instant Sam went for Clyde Barrow's gun.

The hallway light was off. The corridor was bathed in the penumbra of the single lamp switched on in the living room. This and the faint, undulating glow from the images playing on the living room's muted television, a Zenith bought used the Christmas before, were the only sources of light that reached around the corner of the hallway and into the darkness beyond.

Sam saw the gun first. Whoever was beyond the corner eased it across the plane of the landing wall, ten feet from where he stood at the home's front entrance. It was waist high, and he could just make out its shape in the dim light. If his senses hadn't been heightened by the cocaine he probably would have missed it, along with the sound that betrayed it.

The Colt .45 came out of the shoulder holster hidden beneath his sweater in a single, paranoid motion. Sam swung the barrel in a sideways arc, leveling it in the direction of the gun, figuring he'd go for it first, aiming higher after the first shot, when whoever was the target came into view from around the corner. His action was totally reflexive, no planning or forethought. The same would apply to the drug dealer.

The man screamed something that sounded like the word 'coke' or 'cocoa', flinging himself at Sam, moving directly into the path of the bullets.

Sam got off three shots in quick succession. It was like lightning struck right beside him three times, ripping open something that could never be sealed. The pungent smell of gunpowder filled the hallway instantly. The inside of Sam's nose burned.

Out of the ringing in his ears he heard the first faint, high-pitched sounds of a little girl's screams. She was standing where she'd entered the hallway from her bedroom. The small blonde girl was terrified and screaming at the top of her lungs.

Sam kept the gun leveled at the little girl's head; at the height he thought he'd seen the gun. His eyes swam. His mind was numb. What had he done?

Mercifully, the little girl stopped screaming just as the ringing in Sam's ears began to recede. She was dressed in a flannel nightgown that seemed to swallow her from the neck all the way down to the floor. It looked like she was hovering there, with no feet. Only a moment ago the nightgown had been light blue, with what looked like little Casper the Ghosts floating all over it. Now it was streaked with the crimson of her father's life.

She ran to him, sobbing hysterically, falling across him.

"Daddy, Daddy, get up! Daddy?" she wailed, burying her face in his shredded body.

Quinn appeared. He'd seen everything from his vantage point inside the living room. Wild eyed, he stepped around the body. He had the presence of mind to avoid the widening pool of blood. He grabbed the Colt from Sam's frozen hand, pushing him toward the front door. He fumbled at the latch and somehow, he got the door to open. Quinn produced a handkerchief. He wiped the lock on the inside of the door and pushed Sam outside. He wiped the door handle on both sides and started to push Sam down the front walkway. He stopped, remembering the doorbell. He went back and quickly polished his prints from it.

Sam was moving now, too, wondering what the fuck just happened.

## Chapter 50

"We didn't run, but we sure didn't waste any time," said Quinn. "I have to tell you, I was scared shitless. I had never seen anyone shot like that before. We got into the van and got the hell out of there as fast as we could." He paused long enough to finish the last of the Seagram's. He almost put the empty glass on the nightstand between the double beds, but thought better of it in the last second. I watched him in silent, horrible fascination as he mixed himself another drink.

I felt like throwing up. The room seemed to spin around me as if I was in the middle of some weird, giant top from which there was no escape. Sam killed my father! The thought hammered my brain. It wouldn't stop. I couldn't stop it. He was the man I saw, standing with his back to the front door at the end of our hallway twenty years ago. The empty hole in his hand had been the gun barrel pointing at me. I remembered misty gray smoke coming off it, trailing in the air like an obscene whip. My mind grappled to assimilate Quinn's account. I felt violated. No betrayal had ever been more diabolical. Nothing could have prepared me for these revelations. Then came the coup de grâce.

"I kept the gun. I saved it. I told him I would get rid of it where even God would never find it. I think I said later that I dissolved it in a bucket of acid. He believed me. Why wouldn't he?" Quinn actually laughed. "We were brothers in arms. But I didn't get rid of it; I'm not that stupid. That gun, with Sam's prints and DNA all over it, is what's kept me alive all these years. I put it back in that hermetically sealed case and then took it down to a bank and locked it away in a safe deposit box. If anything ever happens to me, out it comes, and it goes straight to the police with the same story I just told you. Clyde Barrow's .45 has been my twenty year insurance policy."

"And now?" Danny asked his father.

"And now, boy, it's time to cash in my chips. It's time to call my marker. I figure in light of what Spielman's been able to accomplish in the last twenty years while I've been eating nothing but table scraps, I'm owed. The way I see it, that gun has appreciated to where it's now worth pretty much whatever I decide. Yeah, it's been a great investment," he seemed proud of himself.

For my part, all I could think about was the fact that the man I'd given all of me to was the same man who'd murdered my father. It was as if an immovable object had met an irresistible force and the two were waging war inside my soul. I thought about confronting Sam with the truth, but he'd probably just deny it. And then he'd go into damage control. No. That wasn't the way.

Suddenly I wanted to hurt Sam in the worst way imaginable. A hate I never knew existed welled up inside me. It replaced the anger, which had replaced the indescribable pain that tore my heart open when Quinn finished his account of my father's murder. If the list of suspects had included everyone in the world, the last man I would have guessed responsible was Sam.

"How did you keep your fingerprints off the gun?" Danny's question was so obvious I'd overlooked it myself.

"I used the handkerchief. The same one I used to wipe the doorknob with. Sam was in such a panicky mind fuck he never even noticed I had it in my hand when I grabbed the Colt from him. I stuck it in my waistband right before I wiped the place clean.

"Hmm," said Danny.

"Sam Spielman murdered your father, Coco," Quinn's statement had the finality of a dropped guillotine. "And I've got the proof. I need you to negotiate a deal with your boyfriend to get it back. Otherwise my little Colt is going straight to the Feds, and Sam goes down for murder-one."

## Chapter 51

When you travel down the road of vengeance, you better dig two graves. Knowing this and then being able to accept it were two separate things.

I wanted to hurt Sam for what he'd done. Sending him to prison for the rest of his life would be a hollow victory. What Sam had done to my family had been up close and personal. I wanted to repay him in kind.

I knew I could use Quinn's greed against him. Convincing him to hold tight so I could reconnoiter Sam for a bigger score than imaginable wasn't a hard sell. Buying time from Quinn had been easy; he'd already waited twenty years.

He'd put on a blustery show that he wanted money now, and he'd even tried to shake *me* down for a good faith deposit as he called it. But I didn't buy into it. Without me and my close proximity to Sam, Quinn didn't have much in the way of options. His bargaining position was revealed to be more tenuous that he'd first led himself to believe. Sure, he could nail Sam and no doubt put him away for a very long time. But then he wouldn't have a cent to show for it. Plus, he'd end up running and hiding for the rest of his natural life. And if they ever caught him, his demise would be a grizzly one.

So Quinn was forced to wait. In a sudden reversal of fortune, I was now running the show. In return for not barking and waiting until I came up with the right moment for retribution, Quinn would receive his thirty pieces of silver. He didn't much like it, but I didn't much care.

So I made another movie, and I watched the first one get released to some surprisingly good reviews. The three and a half points on the gross eventually tripled the producer's original guaranteed offer. Sebastian was ecstatic. The studio was hedging to mitigate negotiations on subsequent dealings with me, but the general consensus for the reason behind the film's success was that I'd been the actress mostly responsible. They still talked about the shooting in Prague. The stir it caused had created a lot of curiosity, but that in and of itself hadn't been enough to boost the film's revenue at the box office. Much to my satisfaction, the word spread that I could act. A third film was in the works; Sebastian was getting several excellent scripts a week. And all I could think about was how I could even the score with Sam.

It was especially difficult for me because, in many ways, I was now leading a double life. I wasn't faking it, and that made it ten times harder. If all of me hated him, it would have been easy. But a part of me really cared for Sam. We were in love. And love wasn't some kind of a switch on a wall I could turn off and on at my convenience.

I'd watched a lot of Hollywood bimbos change partners more frequently than their underwear. Somehow they could do it, although true happiness always seemed to remain just beyond their reach. Perhaps they weren't capable of ever attaining it. Perhaps they'd never know what love truly was. I knew that the brook in a lot of people's backyards ran only so deep. For me it was different.

Even as I plotted my vengeance against the man I loved, I never stopped hurting. In this way, although I wasn't pretending when Sam and I made love, I did feel like I was perpetrating a fraud. I felt like a hypocrite. For the first time in my life I knew what it must feel like to be an undercover operative. But I rationalized what I was doing by slaking my thirst at the fountain of hate. Every time I felt guilty for deceiving Sam, all I had to do was remember him standing in our hallway, gun smoking, while my father lay dying in a widening pool of blood on the floor in front of me. That image was always more than enough to rekindle the flames of enmity.

Where I never had before, I now eavesdropped on any of Sam's conversations within earshot. I noted the comings and goings of his friends and business associates. I asked seemingly innocuous questions of Jack, which he believed to be no more than idle conversations, all the while digging for information I might use to exact retribution from Sam. When I could, I looked at any of his unopened mail, examining addresses for a clue that might lead me in a direction Sam could not foresee. I was looking for something with which to hurt him.

Finally, there came that day in his office when he left me alone with his mistake; the prospectus report out on the table in his casino office. Called away in a hurry, he'd either forgotten to lock it securely in his safe where no prying eyes could peruse it, or thought he'd be absent a short enough time not to worry. Whichever it had been, Sam's slip was the break I had patiently hoped for. I knew he was looking at something big in the desert. I knew about Brittle. But I couldn't have dreamed Sam had stumbled across a vast underground reservoir of black gold.

The cryptic, hand-written notation in the margins of the report's last page led me into the Mojave Desert. My quest took me, finally, to a dimly lit room in the All God's Children's Home and the darling, innocent daughter of the enigmatic desert rover, Billy Cunningham. Becoming Linda's adoptive parent was what Claire Anderson wanted. She knew her days were numbered, looked into my heart and saw an angel. I didn't see what she saw, but I knew that I'd carry through with the plan she and I envisioned. Claire read my intent correctly. I was honest. When she wasn't around anymore, she could count on me. She had nothing to worry about.

But now, Sam had Quinn. Soon he'd have me as well, because I knew if I didn't come forward in the very near future, they wouldn't hesitate to follow through with their threats. Quinn would end up coming home to Danny through the U.S. mail.

For the first time in years I had time to think, just when I needed it most. As per my instructions, Sebastian hadn't penciled me in for any obligations past the Versace runway gig in London. A part of me felt free. Were it not for the impeding calamity I faced, I might have been able to relax.

Someone once said there's no rest for the wicked. What had I done that had been so bad, I thought to myself as I sat at my office desk in my home in Summerlin. No matter which permutation of the outcomes I experimented with in my mind, I always ended up back at the same place: I would have to call Sam and tell him everything I knew. Then I'd negotiate with him. In the end, he'd get what he wanted. It was the same as it always was. The bad guys won.

Quinn Garret was going to cost a fortune. What had the idiot done to get himself picked up by Sam's people?

The only thing that made sense was that Quinn had gotten frustrated waiting for his money. He had probably tried an end run. I bet he'd tried to blackmail Sam on his own. That would have been just like the arrogant fool. They'd gotten him, probably banged him around just enough to get him to talk. Maybe they had even taken a stout pair of electrician's pliers and cut off a finger or two to show him they were serious. Sam's freedom was at stake.

Quinn was still alive. He had to be. He was smart enough to have left himself a failsafe. He'd have arranged things so that, if was caught, they could only retrieve the firearm if he was alive. Now that I had time to think things through, I realized Sam must already know about Quinn approaching me to broker his blackmail. That would mean Sam also knew Danny O'Brian was Quinn Garret's son. Would they pick Danny up? I doubted it. Danny couldn't hurt them, nor could he be of any help either. He was of no possible use, so chances were good they'd leave him alone. But I was different. Sam would wonder why I hadn't come forward with what I knew. Had Quinn told him it was my father he shot to death in Henderson? I had to assume yes, since Quinn would sing in a heartbeat if he felt it would save his own skin. And Sam would definitely want to know what motivated my silence. As soon as he learned it was my father he'd murdered that night twenty years ago, the pieces would fall together quickly for him.

It was unlikely Sam had connected all this with the Brittle oil field. I doubted that anyone's logic could stretch that far. There had been nothing so far that would connect me with either the lawyers out of Kingman or with Claire Anderson, even if Sam found Claire and questioned her. I could only imagine how she would respond to threats and intimidation. She'd probably smile at them from her wheelchair and come up with something witty like, 'What can you fellows do to me that time hasn't already?' They might threaten her little dog Angelo, but in the end Claire would hold fast. They wouldn't get a damn thing out of her. And they wouldn't hurt her, either. It wasn't Sam's style. I was convinced their efforts on that front had been stymied.

No matter what, Danny loved his father. Quinn's blood ran through his veins. Danny had forgiven his father for what he'd done. Forgiveness was in Danny's nature, even if he wasn't fully cognizant of it. He knew, on some level, it was necessary for his well-being. He'd be fine, but recovery would take longer if things went south. I didn't want that, and neither did he.

Reluctantly, inevitably, I concluded I must call Sam. When I thought about it, I realized now we hadn't spoken in over a week. Was it coincidence? I doubted it. Sam knew something, what and how much was still up for debate.

Searching for a way out, I glanced at my cell phone, on my desk. There wasn't one. I plucked it from the charger and punched Sam's number.

# Chapter 52

"Look out your window, in the street." He didn't even say hello.

A long limousine sat idling thirty feet from the edge of my driveway, a sleek, black shark floating menacingly in the current.

"What's going on, Sam?" I asked guardedly.

"You tell me." In his voice I thought I heard his own, particular hint of menace. Or was I seeing ghosts in the shadows?

"What's the ride for? Is it Jack?"

"Jack's busy. The ride is for you."

"Why all the cloak and dagger, Sam? If you wanted to see me, why not just call like always?"

"This isn't like always, Coco. But you already know that, don't you? Get in the car. I'll see you when you get here."

"Where's here?" I asked

"Just get in the car, damn it," he barely controlled his anger.

"What if I decide not to?"

"Would it help if I asked you nicely? We need to talk. I'd rather do it this way."

I breathed into the mouthpiece. "I need ten minutes to get ready," I said at last.

"I'll tell the driver to expect you." He hung up without saying good bye.

I didn't know what to expect on the other end of the drive. The driver didn't say a word as he held the rear door open for me. I wore dark glasses, so did he. I didn't want anyone to see I was scared. I got in, and he closed the door behind me. Fifteen minutes later, we were bombing down Sahara headed in the direction of downtown. I guessed correctly, I was being taken to Sam's casino.

We pulled under the casino's main entrance's portico. This was a good sign. There were cameras everywhere. I would be seen entering the hotel. I knew there were alternate places I could have been taken, where no eyes would see me. We pulled into the area in front of the main doors typically reserved for the whales – gamblers with no limit. It had been cordoned off. The pylons and red velvet were quickly removed to allow us to park. We'd been expected.

I got out, and the driver handed me off to three plainclothes security men I didn't recognize. The first one stepped up. He was polite and professional.

"Good morning", he glanced at his watch, "I'm sorry – afternoon – Miss Stevens. My name is Isaac Turner. Mr. Spielman has asked me to escort you upstairs." I followed him into the hotel. The other two suited knuckle draggers followed me. I wondered for a brief moment what would happen if I suddenly changed my mind and wanted to leave. Would they stop me? It didn't matter, I decided in the same instant. I'd only be stalling the inevitable.

They led me through the private corridors behind the cages where the tellers sat. I'd been here many times before, with Sam. Inside the inner walls, the glitzy casino took on a more professional air cleverly hidden from the public facade outside. There were no lights or bells or whistles. Just corridors painted in soft pastel colors leading to rooms within rooms in which accountants and lawyers and PR people worked. It was cubicle world. There was nothing glamorous about it. The commodity they dealt in was other people's money. Their mandate remained as it had always been; to take it from them any way they could. Everything in the hotel was for sale. Anything could be had for a price. Sam was simply a purveyor of vice, a carnival barker dressed in a three thousand dollar Armani suit. Like everything else in a casino, he looked like something other than he was. In the world of glitz and glamour, appearance meant everything. Beggars got pocket change for their scams; casino owners made billions and looked good doing it.

Our final destination was Sam's penthouse office, the same office I'd been in when I saw the prospectus report. We rode upstairs in a private elevator.

Sam was on the phone when I was finally ushered inside his office. Only then did Isaac Turner leave, closing the big oak door behind himself on his way out. His was a job normally reserved for Sam's Vegas assistant, but I'd noticed on the way in she was nowhere to be seen. It was obvious Sam wanted no civilian witnesses. The only one I was surprised I hadn't seen was Jack. Maybe Sam figured we'd gotten too close and that Jack wouldn't have the stomach for the fate that lay in wait for me. I sat down in one of the comfortable leather armchairs on the other side of his large desk and waited for Sam to finish his call.

## Chapter 53

Sam hung up after a minute. He stared at me with no expression. I stared back at him. Saying nothing, he rose from his chair and walked over to the credenza beside a large potted fern, which stood beside the panoramic window behind him. He rolled open a bottom drawer and plucked what appeared to be a wooden box from inside it. The box was about the size and configuration of a standard businessman's attaché case. He placed it in the middle of his desk and opened it for me to see inside. It was an authenticated handgun, a Colt .45, although that was admittedly a guess on my part. I didn't have to ask if Clyde Barrow once owned it. Sam sat back down and continued to stare at me. His hands were folded across his face, framing his mouth as if he was thinking about praying.

"Why didn't you come to me?" he finally asked.

"I took a bullet for you, Sam," I said coldly.

"Yes, you did," he nodded. Then he said something I could have never seen coming. "Do you know how much I love you?" He continued before I could answer, "I'm talking about how much I *really* love you. Not just words. Not actions. I'm talking from here," he tapped his heart. "I can understand your being angry."

"Angry? Try hurt, Sam. The most horrible pain anyone could ever experience if they lived for a hundred lifetimes. You killed him, Sam," I was fighting back tears. "You murdered my father," I accused him.

"And you think this gun proves it. You think that the word of a low life, three-time loser like Quinn Garret counts for something? You really believe his word would be better than the word of the man who loves you more than life itself?"

For the first time since that my meeting with Quinn, I felt a faint flutter of doubt deep down where it counted the most.

"My fingerprints and DNA are all over this gun," I couldn't believe he was admitting his crime. "But the only thing I shot with it were some empty bottles in the desert. I didn't shoot your father, Coco. I never saw him. I wasn't there. Quinn made up everything that he told you regarding the two of us going to your house in Henderson. Have you ever, in all the years we've known each other, seen me use cocaine?"

I stared at him, doubt invading my soul. What he said was true. Sam had never done coke. He hated the whole idea of it. I remembered him warning me against it when I first started modeling. But that didn't prove he hadn't done it back then. Twenty years was a long time. People changed. I clung to Quinn's explanation, but my fingers were slipping.

"Never, it was Quinn, Coco. He was setting me up."

"But the gun," I said weakly. "Your DNA – your fingerprints – they're all over it. You said so yourself."

"I was with Quinn in the desert that day, just like he said. We were target shooting at some empty bottles. He had the gun that he'd stolen with him, in his truck. It was in the case. I was young, twenty-one, I think. I was green. I didn't think the way I do now.

"I came out in my own car. He was waiting for me in the desert near Lake Las Vegas. We'd done some shooting out there before, so I knew exactly where to find him. He offered to let me try the gun. I was curious about it. He had another one he was shooting with. He told me to get the .45 from the seat in the truck. I took it out of the case. I put it back when I was finished with it. When I thought about it afterwards, I realized he had never touched it the whole time we were there. He went to your house alone that night, Coco. He had the coke problem. It happened just like he told you, but he was the guy you saw standing there with the gun in his hand. Only you couldn't see the glove he was wearing. Or maybe he used the same handkerchief he used to wipe off his own fingerprints afterward. I don't know. But I suspected after the story broke that he'd used the weapon I'd handled in the desert to frame me. I took it up the ladder and they put out a contract on him. He wasn't one of us. He must have found out because he vanished, gun and all. I figured he must have died or someone else had killed him. I'd forgotten about Quinn Garret until he made contact with me a few months ago. I guess he decided not to wait for you," Sam knew every detail. "When I heard from him, I knew exactly what he wanted, and what he had to back it up with. He never stood a chance. It was like he was reading my mind. We grabbed him when he tried to collect the money."

"Is he…?"

"No. Quinn's very much alive. There was no reason to kill him. I have the gun."

"Then it was Quinn who killed my father," I was accepting what I was quickly coming to understand was the truth. It all fit. I knew Sam. I'd seen enough of Quinn to know better than to trust him. I'd been conned with the evidence of the gun. It wouldn't be the first time an innocent man had been hung.

My judgment had been clouded by my strong emotions. I felt foolish and weak. In a Shakespearian twist of irony, it was I who'd betrayed Sam.

He came around to my side of the desk and lifted me out of the chair. He wrapped his arms around me and hugged me while I broke down, sobbing uncontrollably.

When I finally stopped bawling, I said to Sam, "I'm sorry. I'm so sorry. I never should have believed him. I should have come to you, Sam. I should have believed in you."

"That's all right, baby. You do now. I forgive you," he stroked my hair, holding me. I was completely spent, drained of all emotion.

"What happens to Quinn now?" Danny was still worried out of his mind.

Sam gently pushed us apart. He held on to each of my shoulders. His eyes locked onto mine. "He killed your father, Coco. You get to decide what happens now."

He leaned over his desk then and punched a button near the intercom. Thirty seconds later, there was a knock on the office door and it opened.

Other than a black swollen eye and cut lips, Quinn didn't look in too bad of shape. From across the room I saw the fear in his eyes, though. In a different place, he'd have been a dead man walking. Gone was the arrogant swagger I'd seen so many months ago in his suite at the Holiday Inn. He seemed like a scared child now. His clothes were rumpled, like he'd been sleeping in them on a hard floor for a week, which probably wasn't so far from the truth. He was dirty and disheveled. Stubble had given way to a bedraggled beard. I almost felt sorry for him.

Behind him, larger than life, Jack prodded him along. The man who had introduced himself to me downstairs as Isaac Turner set a chair in the middle of the room. Jack forced Quinn into it. Quinn looked around the room. He was terrified. He spotted me and a low, pitiful moan escaped his discolored lips. I was relieved Danny wasn't here to see this. Quinn had been worked over pretty good.

I looked in Sam's eyes. A silent exchange took place between us, and I felt the strength flood back into my veins. I took a deep breath, walked over and stood in front of Quinn. Jack towered above him.

"Quinn," I acknowledged him.

He looked nervously from Jack to Isaac, and then focused in on me.

I must have gone over in my mind a million times what I'd do to the man I'd seen murder my father if I ever found him. After all that and twenty years, here he was, sitting right in front of me.

I realized as I looked at him that I no longer hated him. Instead, I pitied him for the misery he'd caused himself and so many others. It was easy to feel anger toward the Quinns of the world. It was natural to seek justice. I'd always thought there was a fine line between that and vengeance, but people could live with themselves easier when they used the former word to invoke the latter behavior. It allowed them to believe they were the good guys. If it was retribution they were after, then how different were they from Quinn?

A teardrop meandered down across Quinn's cheek. He sniffled. All his bluster was gone. He'd been reduced to the bare essence of a man. He was no different than any of us now. Did he feel sorry for murdering my father? Did he feel bad about it at all? Who could say?

As I stared at the pitiful human being in front of me, I realized I wanted Quinn to feel remorse. I demanded it. But I also realized the arrogance of my demands. Who was I to dictate the terms of Quinn's capitulation? I could no more force Quinn to feel guilt and compassion – a basic empathy for his fellow man – than I could exact those same emotions from the chair he now sat in. No matter how much we all wanted to deny it, there was a little bit of Quinn inside each and every one of us. Ultimately, the strength we so arrogantly subscribed to the heroes among us had to be measured, at least in part, by how they treated the weakest among us.

"I forgive you, Quinn," I said. Tears now streamed freely from Quinn's eyes.

"I'm sorry for what I've done," he blubbered. He sniffed and wiped his nose with the dirty sleeve of his soiled sports jacket.

"Your son Danny has saved you, Quinn. He's the biggest part of the reason you're still alive. He begged for your life. Only God knows why, after what you put him and his mother through. As for your being sorry for taking my father from us…I no longer care." I saw the surprise in his eyes. "This isn't about you anymore, Quinn. It's about me and my mother. It's about what we need to do to finally feel whole again. Now I see more clearly than I ever have. I see why we've felt the pain, why we could never let go of the hate and the anger and the pain. My mother has never forgiven herself for not being there that night. But I think you probably would have killed her too, if she had been. You didn't kill me, Quinn. I think a part of you wanted to. Maybe you thought you didn't have too, that I would be too young to remember you. Maybe you just didn't have the stomach for it. Only you know for certain why you didn't pull the trigger one more time. I believe it was because there was still a small whisper of good in you that hadn't been snuffed out yet by all the cocaine and bravado and selfishness that became your god. And maybe now, a little piece of that good is still inside you. I don't know. It's not for me to say. I just know I forgive you, and I know if my mom were here, she'd forgive you too.

"I'm free now, Quinn. I can't say the same for you, but I'm letting you go. I don't know what's going to happen to you now." I glanced up at Jack. I couldn't easily read his expression, but it seemed he was listening very closely to what I'd been saying. Everyone in the room was. We all wrestled with our demons. We all had our crosses to bear. In the end, we were alone in our decisions, God or Satan our only counsel, our conscience our guide and judge. These men, and Sam, would have to decide for themselves what was best for them.

## Chapter 54

Brian DeSilva called me a week later to tell me the adoption papers had gone through. I was now officially Linda's legal guardian. This cleared the way for the trusteeship over Billy's estate, and the reserves of oil that came with it. Although it could be said the will and the trusteeship were independent, they had also always been decidedly and inextricably intertwined. All this, of course, no longer mattered.

I called Todd Benedict in Kingman when I got the news from DeSilva. I told him he had a blank check for anything Linda needed. He congratulated me, adding Linda was fine. She had what she needed, but he appreciated the added security of knowing she always would, even though I got the distinct impression that he and his wife Mary had never fully counted on me for support. Linda would always be as much their daughter as she'd been B.C.'s.

Sam bought Quinn a one-way ticket to Brazil, where if he was smart, he'd live out the rest of his life searching for the peace that had eluded him here. Danny could see him if he wanted to, but it would have to be down there. Quinn wouldn't be returning any time soon. Those were the rules.

I flew out to San Francisco to see Mom. What I had to say to her wasn't something that played well over the phone. She cried a lot when I told her about what had happened. We talked a long time. I spent three days with her. I knew my mom, and in the end she accepted things. I think she forgave Quinn. It would still take some time for her to forgive herself now that she knew what had happened. It probably wouldn't have ended well if she had been there. We still had each other, and when I wasn't around, she had a good husband who loved every bone in her body.

The sunrises in Kenya were every bit as gorgeous as I remembered. Later, Sam and I came back to free the elephants. It was part of the deal I made with him, part of what Claire and I agreed we should do with some of the oil money. We bought the necessary land, and set up a preserve. We also bought the Kenyan logging company. They'd never have to work again. The trees would be safe for a while as well, until someone else came along in the name of progress. But no one would destroy the habitat on the land we had bought, and the elephants would never toil for humans again.

"Look at them, Sam," I pointed at where two of them stood beneath some trees across the savannah. We watched them from the open jeep. "Aren't they majestic creatures? They're free now, like they were meant to be. Like us, Sam." I looked into his dark eyes. He was smiling.

"What?" I said.

"I was just thinking…I'm sure glad you're on my side now."

"I always was. You know that."

"You can be a tough negotiator. I thought I'd lost it all – the land, the oil."

"Instead you gained everything, Sam."

"You taught me what's important, sweetheart. I'll never stop loving you for that."

"Only for that?" I teased him.

We kissed long and passionately, the rising sun washing across our faces, warming our skin.

"What would you have done if Quinn hadn't surfaced? I mean, you never would have guessed who owned the Brittle oil," I pointed out.

"The more important question is what would you have done, Coco?" Sam sighed. "I'd like to believe it would have worked out anyway. I think Quinn Garret just sped things along."

I thought about it. "Yeah, you're probably right."

I'd told Sam everything after I forgave Quinn. I told him what Claire and I envisioned, how I gave her my word that, as long as I lived, I'd carry out our plan. It turned out Sam had only wanted one thing above everything else – me. The rest had been window dressing.

Sam agreed with the terms of a conservatorship on B.C.'s land. We'd milk the funds in perpetuity. The proceeds from the vast oil reserves would never be used to destroy the environment. Some good could come from the sea of fuel. I was never naïve enough to believe the deposits could lie dormant. Sooner or later, someone would pump them to the surface of the desert. At least we could do some good with the proceeds.

But the first order of business was the elephants.

I'd never stopped thinking about the poor creatures. It broke my heart when Michael first captured that moment. The memory stayed close. When B.C. had died and Claire and I had talked and she'd gotten to know me, there had been only one thing to do. Save them. It was what I felt anyone with good inside them would do. I was in a position to do it, whether by providence or design it didn't matter.

"What are you thinking?" Sam asked, interrupting my reverie.

I looked at him. A warm and soothing breeze tugged at my hair. "I was thinking that it's right to die free, even for elephants."

Sam nodded. He leaned over and started the jeep's engine.

"Let's get back to the hotel, Mrs. Spielman," he smiled. "After all, this is our honeymoon."